A VERY NEARLY PERFECT DETECTIVE STORY

Sir Edmund Godfrey was a strait-laced London magistrate in the loose-laced days of King Charles II. One stormy night he disappeared. Five days later they found him dead in a ditch. Somebody had abducted him, starved him, roughed him up, strangled him with his own neck-cloth, run him through with his own sword, and broken his neck. He was very dead.

The unruly London mob began to seethe. Godfrey, they cried, has been murdered by the Papists! The Papists are plotting to murder us all in our beds! Something like McCarthyism ensued, though much more savage and brutal. When at last the trials were over, the frenzy had died down, and the Popish Plot was history, the historians began to perceive that in all the furore, the truth had never come to light. Who murdered Sir Edmund Godfrey?

When John Dickson Carr tackled that question, historians and mystery fanciers had been making their surmises without certainty for two and a half centuries. Carr said at the start, "The murder of Sir Edmund Godfrey is a very nearly perfect detective story." He has written the perfect book about it.

It has everything: fascinating characters, from debonair King Charles with his Nell on down; a glittering panorama of the picturesque, brawling London of 1678; a mystery unsolved for centuries; a fast-moving narrative; and a compelling solution. And it is all twice as fascinating, because it is all true.

—LILLIAN DE LA TORRE
April 1989

Lillian de la Torre, author of the Dr. Sam: Johnson, Detector *series, is one of the creators of the historical detective story. John Dickson Carr is the other.*

[handwritten: to my dearest niece Ava]

[handwritten signature: Lillian de la Torre]

JOHN DICKSON CARR
Available in Library of Crime Classics® editions.

Dr. Gideon Fell Novels:

BELOW SUSPICION

HAG'S NOOK

HE WHO WHISPERS

THE HOUSE AT SATAN'S ELBOW

THE PROBLEM OF THE GREEN CAPSULE

THE SLEEPING SPHINX

THE THREE COFFINS

TILL DEATH DO US PART

Non-series:

THE BURNING COURT

THE MURDER OF SIR EDMUND GODFREY

WRITING AS CARTER DICKSON
Sir Henry Merrivale Novels:

THE GILDED MAN

HE WOULDN'T KILL PATIENCE

THE JUDAS WINDOW

NINE–AND DEATH MAKES TEN

THE PEACOCK FEATHER MURDERS

THE PUNCH AND JUDY MURDERS

THE RED WIDOW MURDERS

THE UNICORN MURDERS

Douglas G. Greene, series consultant

THE MURDER OF
SIR EDMUND
GODFREY

JOHN DICKSON CARR

INTERNATIONAL POLYGONICS, LTD.
NEW YORK CITY

THE MURDER OF SIR EDMUND GODFREY

Cover, introduction, afterword, and additional material: Copyright
© International Polygonics, Ltd. 1989
Library of Congress Card Catalog No. 89-80438
ISBN 1-55882-014-0

Printed and manufactured in the United States of America.
First IPL printing July 1989.
10 9 8 7 6 5 4 3 2 1

FOREWORD

by Douglas G. Greene

Unsolved murders have a peculiar fascination. Will the shadowy face of
Jack the Ripper at long last be identified? Why did Lizzie Borden take
an axe and give her parents forty whacks, if (that is) she was really guilty?
What happened to the Princes in the Tower after they were imprisoned
at the orders of their uncle, King Richard III?

For many specialists in classic crimes, the greatest riddle of all may
be the mysterious death of Sir Edmund Bury Godfrey in the bustling,
brawling, bawdy London of 1678. With some exceptions – most notably
the 1914 assassination at Sarajevo – few murders have had such
wide-ranging effects, for the discovery of the Protestant magistrate's body
at Primrose Hill led to a political crisis which shook and almost toppled
a throne. How Charles II, the Merry Monarch in a not-so-merry period
of his reign, defeated his opponents makes an exciting story in itself, but
for murder fans the key question remains: who killed Sir Edmund
Godfrey? And that question cannot be answered until other mysteries are
solved. Why did Godfrey act as though he were in mortal danger shortly
before he disappeared? Who made the threat? What was in the mysterious
letter that Godfrey destroyed? Where was he during those five October
days between the time that he left his house and the time that his body
was discovered? What is the meaning of the splotches of wax on his
clothing? How could some people have known of the manner of his death
before his body was discovered? Why was he strangled and, apparently
later, stabbed with his own sword? Was the motive for the murder
personal or political or, in some odd way, a combination of the two? All
of these questions, and the other mysteries surrounding Godfrey's fate,
seem answerable. A wealth of evidence has been recorded, both
eyewitness accounts of the magistrate's last days and descriptions of the
physical evidence of how he met his death.

Yet the murder remains unsolved to this day.

Perhaps I should modify that statement. Although at the conclusion
of this book, John Dickson Carr admits that "we do not know and we shall
never know," many "connoisseurs in murder" (to use Carr's phrase) are
certain that his answer to the Godfrey riddle is the correct one.

In 1678, hatred of Roman Catholics and "Popery" had been a
characteristic of the English for more than a century. In some ways,
anti-Catholicism was a natural response to a long history of Popish
opposition to the Protestant establishment in England. Preachers and
pamphleteers did not let the nation forget that Queen Mary I had gained
the sobriquet "Bloody Mary" by having Protestant leaders executed in
the Smithfield Fires of the 1550's. Just as potent an image was the

Catholic conspiracy centered around Guy Fawkes's attempt to blow up Parliament in 1606. Sometimes, however, fantasies dominated attitudes toward Rome. Catholics were used as scapegoats for all real or imagined troubles that the nation experienced. Many Englishmen blamed the Catholics for the English Civil War of the 1640's which resulted in the execution of King Charles I in 1649 and, during the next decade, the institution of a Commonwealth under Oliver Cromwell. Israel Tonge, who introduced the perjurer Titus Oates to Sir Edmund Godfrey and thus helped to set off the events in this book, actually believed that Puritan Parliamentary leaders during the Civil War were controlled by Jesuits. After the restoration of the monarchy under King Charles II in 1660, fear of Catholics did not diminish. It was, for example, an article of faith with most Protestants that Papists had started the 1666 fire of London, and until the nineteenth century the inscription on the Fire Monument attributed the destruction to the Catholics.

People have sometimes relieved fundamental tensions by looking on their enemies, or those whom they perceive to be enemies, as less than human. Minorities, including Jews and blacks in our century, have been accused of practicing ritual murder or of being dominated by bestial desires. Protestant depictions of the Pope as being advised by demons and having such animal characteristics as scales and a tail are part of this desire to dehumanize one's enemies. During the seventeenth century, Protestants believed that there was no crime that a Papist would hesitate to commit. A pamphlet written in 1679, at the height of the frenzy following Godfrey's death, bid its readers to "imagine you see the whole town in a flame, occasioned this second time by the same Popish malice which set it on fire before. At the same instant, fancy that amongst the distracted crowd you behold troops of Papists ravishing your wives and daughters, dashing your little children's brains out against the walls, plundering your houses and cutting your own throats." A poem from the same period addressed the Catholic Church:

Though many bless and thee the beast adore,
Thou'rt dyed with blood and art the Scarlet Whore.
. . . .
For this damned hag longs still for human food,
Ne'er satisfied till she is gorged with blood.

It is shocking to realize that such lines referred to a small minority: perhaps sixty thousand, or between one and two percent of the population, were Catholics, and few of them had any desire to engage in treasonous activities. Nonetheless, fear of Catholics would become the most important political issue of Charles II's reign, and it forms the backdrop to the strange death of Justice Godfrey.

Historians have long been fascinated with the personality of Charles II, whose brilliant, restless mind could express itself in cynical observations about life, in an amateur preoccupation with science, in a toleration of various religious viewpoints, and above all in a desire not to go on his "travels" again—that is, not to go into exile as he had done during the dominance of Cromwell. For many years, historical judgments of Charles and his reign were dominated by the so-called "Whig Historians," especially Thomas Babington Macaulay, who, as a good nineteenth-century liberal, believed that the most important development in English history was the rise of the House of Commons. Charles's determination to preserve royal prerogatives against Parliament's encroachment meant that the later Whig historians would not treat him favorably. Historians who wrote between the First and Second World Wars, however, evaluated Charles by different standards. They were preoccupied by problems of their own time, especially balance of power and nationalism. These "Stuart Apologists" praised Charles for developing the British navy and for keeping Louis XIV of France at bay despite the problems Charles faced from his penny-pinching Parliament. In his best-selling biography, *King Charles II*, published in 1931, Sir Arthur Bryant summed up the attitude of the Stuart Apologists when he entitled one of his chapters "The Patriot King." In short, both the Whigs and the Stuart Apologists judged the king by the standards of their ages, not his. Recent biographies by Maurice Ashley (*Charles II: Man and Statesman*, 1971) and by Antonia Fraser (*Royal Charles: Charles II and the Restoration*, 1979) have tried to understand the king by the values of the seventeenth century, and the reader is directed to those books for a balanced account of Charles's reign.

John Dickson Carr was not quite thirty years old when he wrote *The Murder of Sir Edmund Godfrey*. He had been born in Uniontown, Pennsylvania, but after his marriage to an Englishwoman in 1932 he had moved to England where, he believed, the true tradition of the detective novel could be found. He was recognized as the master of fairplay clueing cloaked with spooky atmosphere. Dorothy L. Sayers remarked that "Mr. Carr can lead us away from the small, artificial, brightly-lit stage of the ordinary detective plot into the menace of outer darkness." Or, as Carr wrote in *Edmund Godfrey*, "let there be a spice of terror, of dark skies and evil things."

Carr was unabashedly of the Stuart Apologist school. His love of romance, adventure and lost causes made him a romantic royalist. As a teenager he had written a story in which the protagonist tries to rescue Charles I from Puritan captivity, and in 1928 he wrote a manuscript for a novel set in the seventeenth century and full of "gadzookses and sword-play." He destroyed it when he realized that he could not treat the Puritans even-handedly. It is possible that some elements of this lost novel survive in *Devil Kinsmere*, a work that Carr published in 1934 under the pseudonym of Roger Fairbairn. *Devil Kinsmere* is a historical novel of mystery and intrigue with Charles II as a major character. (*Most Secret*, published in 1964 under Carr's name, is a rewritten version of *Devil Kinsmere*.) In *Devil Kinsmere*, Charles is depicted as a puppet-master; in *The Murder of Sir Edmund Godfrey* the king seems about to lose control of the strings. But in spite of that difference, both books are consistently pro-Stuart. As Carr remarked in a letter, *Edmund Godfrey* "contains a few statements contrary to the Whig school-books." Thus to Carr, the followers of the Earl of Shaftesbury, leader of the opposition to the king, were similar to "certain other gangsters we have heard of in our own time" (p. 173). They were "much the more crooked" than the king's men, and their interest in Parliamentary rights Carr found akin to prying (p. 20). Shaftesbury himself is described in ways that Carrian experts will recognize as typical of Carr's villains—"he never took a bottle too many, or made a fool of himself over a woman," and he married for money (p. 26). Charles on the other hand "understood foreign affairs better than all his counsellors put together" (p. 19).

Carr's interest in the Godfrey case seems to have begun when he read J. G. Muddiman's article "The Mystery of Sir E. B. Godfrey" (*The National Review*, September 1924). Muddiman identified a previously unsuspected figure as the true murderer, but his account is only seven pages long. Examining the seventeenth-century sources, Carr found more and more material to confirm Muddiman's conclusion—so much, in fact, that the resulting book contains more than 350 pages.

But enough of bibliographical matters and schools of historical thought. We are dealing with a real murder and a real mystery, one that John Dickson Carr believed could be told—and solved—in the form of a detective story. I will rejoin you at the end of the book to discuss Carr's solution and recent developments in the Godfrey riddle.

*In addition to being the authorized biographer of John Dickson Carr, Douglas G. Greene is a historian specializing in 17th Century England. He has edited **Diaries of a Popish Plot**, a collection of political documents relating to the death of Sir Edmund Godfrey.*

To

MY WIFE

ACKNOWLEDGMENTS

To Mr. C. L. Douthwaite, Librarian of the Guildhall Library, for permission to reproduce the Godfrey playing-cards; to the Guildhall Library for an engraving of Sir Edmund Godfrey and for much valuable assistance; to Mr. Charles W. F. Goss, Librarian of the London and Middlesex Archaeological Society, for a print of old Somerset House and for several helpful suggestions; to Messrs. William George's Sons, for assisting me in obtaining much contemporary material dealing with the Popish plot; to the work of those modern writers mentioned in the text – notably Mr. Arthur Bryant, who has done so much to dispel the myths that have grown up round Charles II – my thanks are gratefully due.

J. D. C.

CONTENTS

CHAPTER   PAGE

A PREFACE FOR CONNOISSEURS IN MURDER -   11

I   'LO, A DAMNED CREW' -   -   -   -   -   31

II   'DIED ABNER AS A FOOL DIETH?' -   -   -   61

III   'THE ENGLISH NATION ARE A SOBER PEOPLE' -   91

IV   'WITH A DARK LANTHORN —' -   -   -   -   118

AN INTERLUDE FOR CONNOISSEURS IN MURDER   149

V   'THEY EAT THEIR GOD, THEY KILL THEIR KING, AND SAINT THE MURDERER' -   -   175

VI   'YOU HAD BETTER CONFESS THAN BE HANGED'   212

VII   'WELL, WOMAN, WHAT SAY YOU?'   -   -   241

VIII   'UNDER THEIR OWN VINE AND FIG-TREE'   -   278

AN ENDING FOR CONNOISSEURS IN MURDER -   313

BIBLIOGRAPHY AND NOTES -   -   -   -   349

A PREFACE FOR CONNOISSEURS IN MURDER

The Argument

'... the difficult jobs, in this age call'd Dirty Work. ...'
ROGER NORTH, *Examen.*

I

'PEOPLE begin to see,' says De Quincey affably, 'that something more goes to the composition of a fine murder than two blockheads to kill and be killed – a knife – a purse – and a dark lane.   Design, gentlemen, grouping, light and shade, poetry, sentiment are now deemed indispensable to attempts of this nature. . . . The finest work of the seventeenth century is, unquestionably, the murder of Sir Edmund Berry Godfrey, which has my entire approbation.   In the grand feature of *mystery*, which in some shape or other ought to colour every judicious attempt at murder, it is excellent; for the mystery is not yet dispersed.'

And the murder of Sir Edmund Godfrey is, lastly, a very nearly perfect detective story.

This is so strong a statement that, for the moment at least, I do not expect anybody to believe it.   It will meet with the just derision of those who have so frequently been lured into reading by the promise that such-and-such a crime from real life is More Baffling and Fascinating than Any Detective Story.   We have heard that sort of thing too often; we have grown cynical.   By some strange paralysis of the critical faculty, there has become established in the world of letters an axiom that any book which deals with crimes from real life, however unexhilarating it may be, must automatically be ticketed as More Fascinating than Any Detective Story.   Perhaps the book must be called good, as the

11

fashion is, merely because it cannot be called improbable. But this blind worship of facts can sometimes still deceive us. We hopefully read the book which is described as More Baffling than Any Detective Story, and we find quite simply that it isn't. With so many admirable writers, it may be a brilliant study in throat-cutting; but it is not a detective story at all.

The fact remains that only in very rare cases can real life be fashioned into the tidy, clipped maze of fiction. There can be no good detective fiction which is not bound by the rule of fair play with regard to presenting the evidence; and real life is bound by no rule of fair play with regard to anything. Fiction must not propound a riddle and leave half of it unanswered, but real life is under no such obligation, even to the Ultimate riddle. Again, the detective in real life may blunder through to a successful capture of the murderer by luck, perseverance, or information received. But we are not fond of such methods in fiction: we do not want Sherlock Holmes suddenly changed into Doctor Watson. Above all, in crimes from real life there is seldom any element of surprise.

For fiction must confine itself within certain artistic rules. In the last chapter its detective must not reveal as the murderer some person who has been the chief suspect throughout the entire course of the story; nor, conversely, must he whisk out of a cupboard somebody of whom the reader has never previously heard. But, with a few noble exceptions, this is precisely the solemn, knavish swindle with which real life is always serving us. And this is the reason why fiction will always be more popular than truth. Fiction dares many hazards, fiction wears a fool's cap and dares to play the fool before high heaven; but it never dares to be artistically wrong.

Nevertheless, there are exceptions: and therefore a few of us have wondered why some writer does not treat them exactly in the fashion of fiction. That is to say, present his evidence, scatter his clues, parade his suspects, and try to keep the identity of the murderer a secret until the end. Of course, in many great cases the secret is already so well known that, to have any hope of puzzling your reader, you must suppose him to be in the radiantly innocent state of the man who sat up reading until 3 a.m. in order to find out what happened to King Charles the First. Again, the serious writer might have grave objections to this form of sensationalism, on the grounds that it is mere sleight-of-hand. The serious writer might point out that he is writing a psychological analysis, not a thriller. He might say that in the detective story we only wish to know the ending; but, in the rather more fascinating study from life, we know the ending and still wish to know the story.

This is true, but still it is not what we want; *c'est magnifique, mais ce n'est pas le roman policier*; and it hardly holds good in cases where the real truth has never been discovered. Instead let the story be arranged like this:

Let the evidence not all be thrown at us in a lump, with comments beforehand; but let it grow up as the story unfolds, so that each new turn is a surprise to us as it was to those who saw it happen. Let the real murderer walk and talk unsuspected throughout the story; let there be no nods or elbow-joggings from the author, no hints to watch his gait, no speculations as to what went on in his mind. 'But let the clues to his identity be scattered shrewdly, for the reader to find if he cares to do so. Let there be half a dozen persons who might have committed the murder, each suspected in turn, and each in turn proved innocent. Let there be a spice of terror, of dark skies and evil things – a pond by a blasted tree, and horsemen galloping by night. Let there be drums behind a great stage – of a nation caught with panic, of kings playing at chess, of fiddles in the drawing-room, and of ladies more fair than any this side the grave. And at intervals, over our pipes and glasses, let us discuss the evidence in a certain long library where we shall sit as the Society of Connoisseurs in Murder. Does it seem much to ask of careless-fingered Mansoul? Yet once or twice the miracle occurs; the scissors snip a rounded pattern; and, with all its orchestra a-blare, life fashions a mightier melodrama than any we have dreamed of. Such was the melodrama which was played out two hundred and fifty-eight years ago, when Charles the Second was king. Such was the murder of Sir Edmund Berry Godfrey.

On Saturday, October 12th, 1678, Sir Edmund Godfrey walked out of his house in Hartshorn Lane, and disappeared. On Thursday, October 17th, he was found murdered. The truth of what happened during those five dark days no man except the murderer has ever known, and the murderer has been unrepentant dust for more than nine generations. Therefore we are on clean, jovial ground for a murder mystery; therefore, with regard to the solution which is outlined in this book, I must add a word of explanation, even of apology.

Since the days when opposing theories were held by Roger L'Estrange and Roger North, since Burnet went a-bustling and Reresby went a-brawling without committing themselves, nearly every conceivable solution of the problem has been suggested. Ranke states the fact neutrally; Hume calls a stalemate; Lingard disagrees with Macaulay. Two biographers of the same man, Christie and Traill, disagree. Within the last forty years much brilliant work has been devoted to it by Sir George Sitwell, Andrew Lang, Mr. John Pollock, Mr. Alfred Marks, Father Gerard, Sir John Hall, Mr. J. G. Muddiman, Mr. David Ogg, and Mr. Arthur Bryant. Legal suggestions have been made by Sir James Stephen, Sir Edward Parry, and Lord Birkenhead. Officially, the door remains locked. The evidence is vast, though it is very far from wearisome. And, in reading through this evidence with the suspicious eye of the detective-story writer, it is even possible to make out a case against several people whom their contemporaries never seem to have suspected at all.

The solution here outlined is not the first, or even second or third or fourth, most obvious one. But it has been suggested by two distinguished historians, and therefore carries a weight without which I, as a novice, might not venture to write of the case at all. I have discovered no new facts (not, for instance, that lost packet of letters mentioned by Andrew Lang); I have only tried to draw a few new deductions from the evidence, and construct a theory which shall explain *all* the contradictory facts. This solution tries to demonstrate that Sir Edmund Godfrey was not murdered by a Gang, with three or four people to do pieces of the same killing. It indicates that he was murdered by one person, and only one; that this person appeared in the story with at least tolerable prominence; and that, so far as we know, he never officially came under suspicion. Thus life has not disappointed us even at the unmasking. That this is the true solution, of course, nobody would be presumptuous enough to declare. It is merely the solution which, while trying to meet with the full requirements of the historian, shall also meet with the requirements of the Society of Connoisseurs in Murder.

And so we come to the crux of the matter. This record does not presume to be history, except insofar as it tries to be true. To write good history is the noblest work of man, and cannot be managed here: the intent is only to amuse with a detective story built on facts. But this is the age of which we have dreamed dreams, when King Charles the Second really did succeed in making the debates in the House of Lords as good as a play; and therefore some effort must be made to tell once more, in however imperfect a fashion, the story of the 'Popish plot'. If overmuch attention is paid to material details – faces, voices, the air of a courtroom, a hillside at dusk – these are the necessities of the detective story. If we idle at Nelly's supper-table, or reel home from a tavern with the Lord Chief Justice, these are the necessities of thundering melodrama. The old mirrors of Whitehall must be repolished, the old candles draw back their ghostly light: we enter not as doctors, but as visitors and even as revellers: in short, as those who are fond of the time, and would linger there when all its arches are dust.

Granted, there are many dark places. There are things which stir hatred to a cry for justice, as in the persecution of the completely innocent Catholics by Shaftesbury's terror-mongers. No four-and-twenty fiddlers, all in a row, can altogether hide the grime and the pain. For it is an ironical fact that the Merry Monarch, of all English kings except only his own father, had the least to make him merry. Yet because he was the cleverest politician of his age, that urbane figure has come sauntering down the years as Old Rowley, and left to lesser men the stilts of more pompous names. It would be a bold writer who could think affectionately of Queen Elizabeth as Our Liz, or metamorphose William of Orange into Old Bill. Yet such has become the legend of Old Rowley. We are almost tricked by a glow of merry-eyed ladies and nimble swords; the light of youth is upon it, and he seems to walk for ever in a world of cloud-cuckoo-land where the parks are for ever green, the jillflirts for ever yield. Perhaps we shall understand him better, presently.

To anyone who would write of this great age in dramatic form, as though it were fiction and not fact, all the elements have been supplied. The task is of cutting, of editing and arranging, of supplying quotation-marks and stage-directions. These materials help to overcome the greatest difficulty of anyone who would deal with past ages: that of making these people walk and talk like recognisable human beings.

It is not only a difficulty: in most cases it is a dangerous trap. Suppose (for example) a writer wishes to reproduce the Middle Ages in all their Gothic richness. Unfortunately, the poets have so tricked and befooled us that to quicken those dead limbs is very nearly impossible. Despite the great medieval humour, the great medieval drinking-songs, the great medieval humanity which rings in the name of Chaucer, there persists a feeling that these characters are as stiff and wizened as figures in their own tapestries. At best those forests seem too dark and windy. At best it seems all declaiming and skull-breaking in a fog, and the considerations of ordinary life come with an incredible jar if they are dropped into it.

A mild instance of this will be remembered by anyone who read *Ivanhoe* in his youth. We were not surprised when Front-de-Bœuf threatened to pull Isaac of York's teeth, or roasted him on a griddle: this seemed very proper.

But we were considerably surprised to find that the grave Bois-Guilbert had carnal notions, and was pursuing Rebecca with a somewhat un-Templaresque purpose. We felt obscurely that instead of fooling about in this fashion he ought to have been out attending to the proper medieval business, storming castles – or pulling teeth. Thus even to-day it is felt that tales of the Middle Ages may properly be concerned with pale sorrows in a turret, like a poem, or with a tumult of arrows in battle, like a boys' book; but that neither has any connection with wheeling the baby or paying the rent. It is untrue, but there it is. For this is the rub: we refuse to accept these characters either way: we refuse to believe in them either as demigods or as ordinary men. When Sir Luke of the Faithful-Heart speaks in blank verse he is dubious, but when he is made to speak like an ordinary human being he becomes completely incredible. Weird is the accent of the medievals when even the shrewdest hand attempts to freshen them up with modern-sounding dialogue, although it may be exactly what they did say. Sir Luke of the Faithful-Heart may be permitted to exclaim, 'Get thee gone from my presence,' but he must not utter the drastic monosyllable, 'Scram.' A great modern play has been written about Joan of Arc, containing poetic passages as fine as any in that sixteenth-century master with whom the author of the play has had so notorious a feud; but sometimes we mutter meekly when a captain-at-arms in 1429 is made to say, 'Gosh!' or when Joan of Arc addresses the Dauphin as 'Charley'. We feel that they had better be careful, or they will bring in Charley's Aunt.

Now with regard to the age of Charles the Second, no such difficulty exists. It is not recorded that this monarch was ever addressed as Charley, but people have now come closer out of the mists. No longer do they all talk like Shakespeare. They begin to speak a dialect we can understand, and have homely motives; they begin, with recognisable humanity, to swear or spit on the floor. It surprises nobody to hear that Charles the Second had carnal notions: indeed, the difficulty is to persuade readers that he ever had any other kind. These wide-eyed men and women of the seventeenth

B

century – with their childlike curiosity, their hilarity, their *naïveté*, their fondness for toys or gauds, their plump oaths and plump women – they are alive, like rowdy adolescents, and preoccupied with much the same sort of thoughts.

Into the midst of such people, then, is dropped a murder mystery, together with such terror as the nation has never before known. How do they act? There is no police-system to set its nets for the assassin; but no matter; we are on familiar ground; the place swarms with amateur detectives, and their methods are amazingly like those in current fiction. And just here is the enormous difficulty of treating this case. It is not, as in the old maxim, that no fiction-writer would dare to be as fantastic as real life; many of us would dare that and not care a button; but no fiction-writer would dare to be as complicated.

The scene is too crowded with characters, all treading on each other's heels and confusing each other's trails. Alleys cross and interweave for the express purpose of going no-where. To set his mind at work on a problem, the reader must have every character vivid and distinct in his mind; he must be able to watch the turn of their eyes and hands; he must be close enough, in short, to see blood on their cuffs. Hence we must concentrate attention on a leading group of characters, and leave others as names or voices in the shadow. Again, this killing on Primrose Hill (this mere murder) is so much a part and texture of the whole age, so entwined in its political history, that we must glance first at a different sort of Dirty Work which was leading up to it in the year 1678. Does history seem too important a business to devote to the end of one small broken body in a ditch? Is the devil evoked in all his majesty merely to preside over the theft of twopence? Yet it is possible to argue that this death in a teacup helped most of all to bring about the huge political quarrels of the latter seventeenth century, the sharp lines of Whig and Tory, the battle that almost swept away James the Second before he had even ascended the throne. For the mountain has laboured, and brought forth – a thriller.

II

In the summer of the year 1678, when Charles the Second had been for eighteen years on the throne, he had outgrown most of his hot humours. The wax-lighted court of the Restoration, the court of De Grammont, the court of the wits, the court of the cuckolds, had grown a trifle sobered. Hoyden sirens – with their large eyes, their black patches and wired ringlets – still crowded the Mail in 'sky, and pink, and flame-coloured taffetas'. But there were worn places on the faces and the fiddles.

King Charles himself, grown gaunt and long in the tooth, urbane as ever despite the fact that the years had left him little hair under his great black periwig, had settled down to a sort of domesticity among his mistresses. His deliberate pose as 'unthinking Charles' did not now deceive those about him. Sir Francis North was aware that he understood foreign affairs better than all his counsellors put together; and Barrillon, the French ambassador, sadly told King Louis the Fourteenth: 'The king of England has a manner so well-concealed and so difficult to penetrate that the shrewdest are deceived by it.' In time of trouble Charles flung out the truth of his policy with something like a snarl, 'God's fish, they have put a set of men about me, but they shall know nothing! – but this keep to yourself.' That ageing saunterer, striding through the galleries at his 'wonted large pace' with which few could keep up, kept his own secrets: which was why they complained that, though he seemed to approve the counsel you gave him, he always listened to other counsels at the back door. He had reason to do so.[1]

When they heard of the Restoration of 1660, it was said that a mathematician died of joy and a translator of Rabelais died laughing.[2] The conduct of both was subsequently

[1] Roger North, *Life of Lord Guilford* (1816 ed.) ii, 181; Barrillon to Louis, Sept. 9/19, 1680; Thomas Bruce, Earl of Ailesbury, *Memoirs*, i, 35; Henry Teonge, *Diary*, 232; Sir John Reresby, *Memoirs*, 199.

[2] Peter Cunningham, *Nell Gwyn* (ed. H. B. Wheatley) 72; V. De Sola Pinto, *Sir Charles Sedley*, 51.

justified. For eighteen years, under three ministries, Charles had been involved in a battle with his parliament over a matter of money and a matter of the rights belonging to the Crown. It was the old question of how far the parliament could curb the king's prerogatives, pass laws he detested, appoint his ministers, and pry into his accounts, by virtue of parliament's power or grant or withhold him money. It was the old contest between the supporters of the king (shortly now to be called *Tories*), and the landed gentlemen of parliament (shortly now to be called *Whigs*) – even to the verge of Civil War, exactly as it had been under King Charles the First nearly forty years before. The rights and wrongs of the wrangle must not be debated here. Modern opinion seems to have determined that the Whigs were right: and it cannot be doubted, as will presently be seen, that they were much the more crooked.

In the summer of the year 1678 the opponents of the court were beginning to believe themselves strong enough to upset the monarchial principle by altering the legitimate line of succession, and substituting either a republic or a republican form of government under a dummy king whom they could altogether control. And their principal means of gaining this end was to play on the mob's fear and hatred of the Catholic Church.[1]

Through the bogy-ridden seventeenth century ran a horror of 'Popery' which could start out at a touch.[2] No scare was so ripe with promise to a politician beating an alarm-bell and screaming, 'Boo!' behind a jack-o'-lantern ghost. It did not matter – on the contrary, for the purposes of embryo Whigs it was very good – that the most loyal supporters of the crown were Catholics. Of all the officers killed on Charles the First's side during the Civil Wars, over a third had been avowed Catholics; Cromwell had called it

[1] 'The House of Commons taking into serious consideration the dangers arising to this kingdom from the restless endeavours of priests and Jesuits, and other Popish recusants, to subvert the true religion planted amongst us, and reduce us again under the bondage of Roman superstition and idolatry ... do therefore think it requisite to apply some remedy to this growing evil.' – Resolution of the House of Commons, April 29th, 1678.

[2] 'How he still cries, "Gad!" and talks of Popery coming in, as all the Fanatics do!' – Pepys, Nov. 24th, '62.

a Papist army.   Their money had been squandered for him.
They had sheltered Charles the Second when he was a fugi-
tive in his own country, and a Catholic priest had saved his
life.   It did not matter.   The 'Jesuit in disguise', with his
knife in his sleeve, was to England more than an assassin and
a lighter of bonfires; he was the devil whistling for unwary
souls.

Against the Church of Rome there were now in force
twelve tolerably inclusive penal laws.   They had been accu-
mulated with zeal ever since the reign of Elizabeth; and, if
it had been possible strictly to enforce all of them, every
Catholic in Great Britain must have been either penniless,
or in jail, or hanged.   To convert anyone to the Church of
Rome was high treason.   No Catholic could come to court,
or to London, or (unless a tradesman) within ten miles of
London.   No Catholic could practise law or medicine, or
hold any government office.   No Catholic could act as execu-
tive, administrator, or guardian.   Any Catholic might be
required by justices of the peace to take the oath of allegiance to the Anglican Church; if he refused, the penalty
was imprisonment until the path should be taken.[1]

Charles himself was known to be Popishly affected.   His
private views were hazy: 'God,' says Charles comfortably,
'will not damn a man for taking a little irregular pleasure
by the way.'   Doctor Burnet observed that few things
touched him to the heart, and it was true of the matter of
religion: he did not care how his subjects worshipped, provided they were able to live at ease, under their own vine
and fig-tree.   Until he lay dying, that dry, restless, satiric
brain found no refuge in any church.   The Anglican divine
provoked his mirth, the Puritan his hatred.   'We have the
same disease of sermons,' he wrote to his sister in France,
'that you complain of there; but I hope you have the same
convenience that the rest of the family has of sleeping out
most of the time.'   He preferred the Catholics because they
had always been his friends: because, moreover, they were
suited to a monarchy and were not inclined to clamour

[1] Penal Laws in force against Roman Catholics; John Pollock, *The Popish
Plot*, appendix E, 400.

unduly in parliament.   But for some years there had been
rumours (not ill-founded) of Popish alliances with France.
And now there was very much worse.[1]

In May 1662, Charles had been married to young
Catherine of Braganza, Infanta of Portugal.   It was sixteen
years since the war-fleet had convoyed her to England, bump-
ing in a gold-and-velvet cabin, together with 'six frights,
calling themselves maids of honour, and a duenna, another
monster, who took the title of governess to these extraordinary beauties', as well as six chaplains, four bakers, a Jew
perfumer, and a barber.   The little Portugee was not ill-
looking, though her teeth wronged her mouth by sticking
out a little – 'but nothing,' as Charles carefully pointed out,
'that in the least degree can shock one.'   He was delighted
with her agreeable voice jabbering Spanish, and her fine
eyes, no less than with a maidenly modesty which must
have shamed a gooseberry-bush; he remained faithful to
her for six weeks, and never ceased to be fond of her.   In
her turn she never ceased to love him, though the first English words she appears to have learned were, 'You lie!'   She
was a Catholic.   But, once the nation had grown used to
the troop of monks which followed her, she achieved something like a dry and furtive popularity.   The whole difficulty lay in a fact which presently became clear, after many
aches and miscarriages: that she would never have any
children.[2]

She would never have any children.   Therefore (unless
Charles could be persuaded to divorce her, which he angrily
refused to do) therefore Charles's brother – James, Duke of

[1] Gilbert Burnet, *History of My Own Time* (1833 ed., with Swift's hilar-
ious comments) ii, 23; Ailesbury i, 24, cf. Burnet i, 169; Edward Hyde,
Earl of Clarendon, *Life*, i, 354-355; letter to Madame, 'last of February, 1664',
Letters, Speeches, and Declarations of Charles II (ed. Arthur Bryant,) 152.
See also *Letters*, 109.

[2] Agnes Strickland, *Lives of the Queens of England*, iv, 372; John Evelyn,
Diary, May 30th, 1662; Charles to Clarendon, May 21, '62, *Letters*, 126,
cf. to Clarendon, August, 129; Samuel Pepys, *Diary*, Sept. 7, '62.   For
conflicting views of those who saw her, there is Burnet's, 'A woman of mean
appearance and of no agreeable temper'; Reresby's, 'Nothing visible about
her capable to make the king forget his inclination to the Countess of
Castlemaine'; Pepys's, 'Not very charming, yet she hath a good, modest,
innocent look, which is pleasing'; Charles's own view (May 25, 1662), 'I
cannot easily tell you how happy I think myself', *Letters*, 128.

York – must come to the throne. And since the spring of
1671 the Duke of York had been a member of the Catholic
Church.[1]

No Popery! No Popery! No Popery! That was the cry
which had now risen to a frenzy. We have heard much of
James, Duke of York, later to become James the Second.
A sharp picture has been given to us: the austere height,
the stiff back and folded arms, the long nose and sharpened
features, the once-handsome face pitted to redness with
smallpox, the blue eye rolling sideways in suspicion. There
he stands in dark clothes and brown periwig, as the painters
have frozen him, with an acre of polished floor around.
There is James Stuart in his later years, in his official posture: the Oppressor of England, the Bogy of Scotland, the
Patron of the Bloody Assize. In his youth, until his first
marriage lessened him, 'he clouded the king, and passed for
the superior genius'. This high posturing collapses somewhat when we see him clattering eagerly after Lady Chester-
field, or imbibing a 'spiritous drink' with Mr. Evelyn, or
chatting with Mr. Pepys in his night-shirt – 'and in his night-
habitt he is a very plain man'. Against the frolicking court
of the Restoration, this Bogy has somewhat the air of a lost
dog. His trouble was that there was no laughter in him,
and it made him half his enemies.[2]

He distrusted wit in men; he was heavy of brain; 'he
would see things if he could,' as Buckingham observed, but
he seems always to move to a noise of breaking china. A
worse politician has never been born. Dissemble his religious views? 'Once for all, never say anything to me again
of turning Protestant! I never shall, and, if occasion were,
I hope I should have God's grace to die for it.' He never
deserted a friend, and a child could trick him. When he

---

[1] The exact date of the conversion is unknown. His official biographer,
J. S. Clarke, says that he was meditating it in January 1669, *Life of King
James the Second*, i, 440-442; Ranke states that he was not converted until
spring 1672, *History of England*, iii, 560-561; Mr. Belloc's surmise is between 1671 and 1672, *James the Second*, 124-126. It is given here as 1671
because it seems likely that he was influenced by the death of his first wife
in that faith, March 1671.

[2] Burnet, 1, 304; Anthony Hamilton, *Memoirs of Count Grammont*, 175-
180; Evelyn, January 16, '62; Pepys, January 20, '63, April 20, '61.

grew older, now the best-hated man in England, his favourite play became 'The Plain Dealer': for in the brusque and forthright hero Manly, hated by the backbiters of a hypocritical world, he liked to see himself. He would be James Stuart, the Plain Dealer.[1]

As a youth he had served hard apprenticeship as a soldier with the French and Spanish, where his stolid bravery won Turenne's praise. But he belonged among ships and the fights of ships. There, with the weather-gauge of a 'fine chasing gale', with the gun-matches lighted and the great Dutch two-deckers butting close-hauled on the port tack, he thawed to a sort of diligent exuberance; he kept his ships in straight lines, as he kept the ruled figures in his ledgers. Thus he writes of the great fight off Lowestoft – where he took or sank eighteen warships along with seven thousand men, and blew up Opdam with his own flagship – as though he were describing the weather for a picnic: 'Never was seen a more proper day to dispute the mastery of the sea.'[2] At the Admiralty his dogged conscientiousness was invaluable at handling the routine work he loved; his stiff wits created the modern naval code and made possible the modern navy. But Charles thought that he must for ever be playing the fool, over a woman or over a matter of religion, and not even parliament itself caused so many headaches to his nimble brother.

Yet it appeared that Charles himself was encouraging Popery and alliances with hated France. His queen was a Catholic. His most formidable mistress, the Duchess of Portsmouth – 'Fubbs', with her copious tears, her dog Snapshort, and her Turkish stoutness – was a Frenchwoman and a Catholic. Finally, in 1673 he had prompted James's second marriage, to the Catholic Mary Beatrice of Modena. It was true that his chief minister, the Earl of Danby (the lean, sickly Lord Treasurer, a financial genius and a master of bribery) hated France and Popery. But men saw a court

[1] Burnet, i, 304-307, ii, 24; Macaulay on the comic dramatists of the Restoration, *Essays* (1885 ed.) 582, cf. W. C. Ward's footnotes in the introduction to *William Wycherley*, Mermaid series.

[2] Clarke, *Life of King James the Second*, collected out of memoirs written by his own hand, i, 410.

thick with Jesuit webs. 'What the consequence of this will
be,' said Mr. Evelyn, when James failed to take the Church-
of-England sacrament, 'God knows, and wise men dread.'
For the first time the Pope was burnt in effigy; a stuffed
figure of a Frenchman was hung up for the crowd to shoot
at; and the opposition to the court crystallised at last.

The badge of opposition was a Green Ribbon, and the
flaming leader of the opposition was 'the little man with
three names', Anthony Ashley Cooper, Earl of Shaftesbury.
My Lord Shaftesbury presents a curious figure. Call him
an apostle of liberty, as it is conceivable that he was. Grow
excited and call him, 'chief favourite of the devil, the father
of liars', as the Earl of Peterborough did; or, like an Oxford
don, call him simply, 'the old knave'. It is certain that he
had a character droll and laughing and slippery. For thirty-
five years he had trimmed in public life, and never failed
to desert the losing side at just the right moment. 'My
Lord Shiftsbury,' some called him; and Captain Cocke once
declared (unjustly) that he would rob the devil and the altar,
but he would get money if it were to be got. Thirty-five
years before – at the beginning of the Civil Wars – he had
served Charles the First as sheriff and president of the king's
council-for-war in Dorsetshire. Five months before the
downfall of the Royalist cause at Naseby, he suddenly
deserted to the Roundheads, became Dorsetshire com-
mander-in-chief for them, and at Abbotsbury wanted to
burn alive a Royalist garrison in a captured house. During
the years of the Commonwealth he became a zealous Presbyterian. But at the Restoration, hey-presto! there he was,
safe neck and crop, smiling among the commissioners who
invited Charles the Second to return from exile. He even
officiated at the trial of the regicides for their treason against
the Crown.[1]

It was some time before he deserted again; his fortunes
grew high, and he sat as Lord Chancellor in an ash-coloured
gown and silver-laced pantaloons. He was now a little

[1] Strickland, 545; Arthur Bryant, *King Charles II*, 320; Roger North,
Examen, 42: 'His changes were, as Caesar's, only *mutando rationem belli*',
Pepys, Sept. 9, '65; W. D. Christie, *Life of Shaftesbury*, i, 47-53, 62-63,
221-222, 243-244.

nimble old man, shrivelled by an abscess in his side, with a long, pale, merry face and pointed chin; and his heavy-lidded eyes moved shrewdly under the shadow of a great flaxen periwig. His tongue was as well-hung as ever, his hands as suave-moving. He perceived that he could not afford to risk associating himself in Charles's secret negotiations with France, and his hatred of Popery was quite genuine. In 1673, plump in the middle of a debate on a Test Act to exclude Catholics from public office, he suddenly deserted to the Opposition and became the Duke of York's most fervid foe. 'What is the reason,' Charles once asked Betterton the actor, 'that we never see a rogue in a play but, God's fish! they always clap a black periwig on him, when it is well known one of the greatest rogues in England always wears a fair one?'[1]

He was not precisely a rogue, for his principles were very high. 'Madam, wise men are of but one religion.' And that? 'Madam,' says my Lord Shaftesbury, 'wise men never tell.' Wise Men Never Tell was a motto which served him well. He was of liberal views and great virtue: he never took a bottle too many, or made a fool of himself over a woman: and, though he sometimes had a trick of calling ladies Bitches to their faces, even what Charles called 'that little fantastical gentleman, Cupid' was hitched to his wagon. He was married three times, a richer and more powerful alliance on each occasion; and he never talked screaming hysteria except when (which was almost unknown) his plans received a check. But he deserted the court, he founded the Green Ribbon Club, he became the first great party-leader, he transformed the 'mobile party' into the dread word *mob*, and in half a dozen years he had got himself into a position to pull down the throne.[2]

No Popery!   No Popery!   No Popery! By 1678 it was

[1] North, 33-61, cf. Christie; Burnet, i, 174-177; Cunningham, 179.

[2] Onslow's note in Burnet, i, 175, and Dartmouth, 'I was told by one that was very conversant with him that he had a constant maxim never to fall out with anybody... and the reason he gave for it was that he did not know how soon it might be necessary to have them again for his best friends', 176. cf. Christie's defence; Mrs. Mary Gibbon's statement in Sir Roger L'Estrange's *A Brief History of the Times*, III, 101. For his genius as a politician along modern lines see H. D. Traill's *Shaftesbury*.

like the pound of a drum. At the King's Head Tavern in Fleet Street (from whose balcony they watched the burning of the Pope with perukes laid aside, pipes in their mouths and 'diluted throats') was the Green Ribbon Club, nest of the Opposition's brisk boys. Here was the first campaign-oratory. Here was the origin of the whispering campaign. Here were the paid pamphleteers, the heads of the spy-system spread through every coffee-house, the riders to Scotland, the lobbyists for the House of Commons, every agent who groaned in cupboards to affright the mob. Shaftes-bury's great ally was the stout and eager Duke of Bucking-ham, who had turned his slippery talents from women and painting and rhyming and fiddling to politics, having gone over to the Green Ribbon after having called the king and the Duke of York lobsters. Their purpose was to exclude James from the throne when Charles should die, and sub-stitute a figurehead for their management in the person of Charles's favourite illegitimate son – the handsome, figure-headed young Duke of Monmouth – who might be made legitimate if Charles would swear to it. Their appeal was, they said, with the holiest of patriotic motives always. Their cry was Protestantism for ever, and down with the damned king of France.[1]

That was the comedy. For King Louis the Fourteenth was secretly bribing Shaftesbury's chief lieutenants to cry it.

In the past Charles had taken Louis's money with alacrity, and was always ready to get it. But Louis had begun to perceive that in Charles he was dealing with a supple oppo-nent who meant to advance the interest of England rather than the interest of France; and, after the break-up of the Secret Treaty of Dover, Charles had made move and counter-move of such ingenuity that Louis was afraid of his inten-tions. It might mean war with England and Holland

---

[1] North's vivid account, *Examen*, 570-576; MSS. memorandum of Guil-ford, in Dalrymple, ii, 322-323: 'In 24 hours they could entirely possess the city with what reports they pleased, and in less than a week spread it all over the kingdom. They could give out that any men who was averse to them was a Papist; and, when the king did anything pleasing to the people they would discredit it before it could be known.' Mr. Muddiman has demonstrated, however, in *The King's Journalist*, that the 'Protestant flail' was not invented until 1681.

together, at a critical time when Louis was attempting to establish an empire in the Spanish Netherlands. Therefore Louis, to check Charles's power, had begun generously to bribe the Green Ribbon Opposition against him. These patriots were to cry out bloodily for war with France, to sustain their role: but in parliament they were to prevent any supplies being raised for it, compel the disbanding of the British army, keep the navy powerless, brew rebellion against Charles in Scotland and Ireland, and kindle such a No-Popery scare that Charles would be helpless. Shaftesbury's chief lieutenants had their price at five hundred guineas a head,[1] and dealt with the French ambassador. The smaller members were paid by Barrillon's agent, a certain Mr. Edward Coleman – a Catholic intriguer, secretary to the Duchess of York – whose name it will be well to remember. It was a dexterous move, but it might have cost the Green Ribbon men their heads if it had become known that those pensions to cry, 'No Popery, and down with the French king' were being paid by the French king himself.[2]

Thus we have such a spectacle of universal Dirty Work, such an ingenuity of twisting and bribing, as must have drawn a curse of admiration from a Covent Garden bully-rock or the richest jewel in the ear of Tyburn. The late Archbishop Ussher was supposed to have looked into the future and swooned at what he saw. Since 1675 everybody had been bribing everybody else – the French ambassador, the Dutch ambassador, the Spanish ambassador poured gold into the pockets of the House of Commons to such an extent that there was one session when swords were drawn and members spat across the floor at each other – and by

[1] Except the Duke of Buckingham, who got a thousand.

[2] Ranke, iv, 45-49, 104-105; letters of Barrillon to Louis, in Dalrymple, ii, 129-141 (later, 255-264, 280-290); Barrillon's full accounting of money paid, at the height of the plot-frenzy, 314-319; Pollock, 31-32. The list of bribe-takers contains almost all of those who were most active in the House of Commons, crying out against Popery, notably Harbord, Titus, Sacheverell, Armstrong, Littleton, and Powle. Charles, who missed little, had suspected this, and told Barrillon: 'I think they must have lost their senses and they must have had money from you to make such extravagant demands.'

1678 the Dirty Work had become so complicated that some of it remains indecipherable yet.

This, then, is a very small hint as to their propensities in August of the year '78. On one side stood King Charles and Lord Treasurer Danby, supporting the Duke of York. On the other side stood Shaftesbury and Buckingham, with their lieutenants, supporting the Duke of Monmouth. Both sides were alternately taking the bribes of France. It was a hot summer of omens and portents, with thunder a-stir. There were three eclipses of the sun and two of the moon, and the devil piped at a convocation of witches in Scotland, just before the bursting of the great plot and the great murder mystery. I hear also the words which young Matthew Prior was to write not many years later:

'Great claims are made there, and great secrets are known;
And the king, and the law, and the thief has his own:
But my hearers cry out, "What a deuce dost thou ail?
Cut off thy reflections, and give us thy tale".'

THE MURDER OF SIR EDMUND GODFREY

I

'LO, A DAMNED CREW'

The Plot

'The Lord open the eyes of the blind, and be merciful to the souls of those that all this while have swallowed all these shams for gospel!'

SIR ROGER L'ESTRANGE, *A Brief History of the Times, Part III.*

I

EARLY on the morning of Tuesday, August 13th, Mr. Christopher Kirkby stood by the stone sundial in the private garden at Whitehall Palace. Three hundred feet square was that garden, laid out in a chessboard of grass-plots with marble or bronze statues. Towards the south it was closed in by a line of poplars; towards the west ran the high iron railings which shut it off from the public roadway through to Westminster; and on the other two sides it was closed in by the old, smoky huddle of red-brick buildings which lay for half a mile along the waterside. Mr. Kirkby looked oftenest towards a door under the cloisters to the east. By that door the king would presently descend.

The king, he knew, would stroll through the garden, and stop to set his watch at the sundial. Then he would go on for his morning walk in St. James's Park. Beyond the roadway to the west were the Treasury Buildings: against a hot clear sky you might see the red roof of the 'Cockpit', where my Lord Treasurer Danby lived. And, still further beyond that, lay the vast greenery of St. James's Park. It was a brilliant enough morning almost to cleanse the sky of smoke, to set gleaming the weathercocks over the red, blue, and

31

yellow bricks of the Holbein Gate, to make a whole herald's-college of colour.   But Mr. Christopher Kirkby remained sombre, and his conscience was heavy.   He had failed to catch the king's eye yesterday.   He must do it to-day, or (thought his muddled wits) God's mercy might no longer prevail.

He stood by the sundial, holding to one of its corners. Mr. Kirkby, short and square of figure, wore a grey habit with something of the slovenly cleric about it, and he wore no sword.   His fair, woolly periwig shadowed a thin face, a fanatic's face or a dupe's face.   He was a chemist, and held a minor post in the king's laboratory under Dr. Williams. But his mind did not now run on roots and herbs, except insofar as they could be turned into poison.   For this he had been told, and this he believed: that the king's life was in danger, and that his Majesty must be warned.

Now he heard again the familiar stir and yapping of spaniels, and the stir of voices coming out under the cloister. Out into the garden, striding at his wonted large pace so that those about him had to trot to keep up with it, came the familiar tall figure.   There walked the king's majesty, with the expression of countenance somewhat fierce, the long, leathery, supple face, the affable red-brown eyes that were his one fine feature, and the great voice.   There he walked among his spaniels, unconscious of death skulking in the bushes with screw-pistols and champed bullets.   Mr. Kirkby observed that he wore his hat set far back on the great black periwig, and carried a bag of corn to feed his ducks.   In great nervousness Mr. Kirkby took out of his pocket the note he had carefully prepared, asking for a short audience on a matter of the deepest importance.   But to-day the company was too large round the king, and he could not get closer without violating the Rules of Civility.   In an even greater sweat he trotted after them all when they went to St. James's Park.   To-morrow the king would go to Windsor, and this was his last chance.   By the canal in the Park, taking his courage in both hands, Mr. Kirkby hurried forward and thrust the note into the other's hand.   Then he became aware that the king was beckoning to him.

'Your servant, Mr. Kirkby,' said the familiar deep voice, so civilly as to embolden a man, and Christopher Kirkby began to blurt out his hint.

'Sire,' he said, 'I am come to warn you that your enemies have a design against your life. For God's sake keep within the company! You may be in danger in this very walk.'

Charles looked at him. 'In danger? How may that be?'

'By being shot at,' says the other, as fast as he could. 'By being shot at with a silver bullet. If your Majesty will give me leave to come to you in some private place, and tell you more of what I know. . . .'

A minute more, and he was alone in the sanded path while the company moved on. The king had bidden him go and wait in the Great Bedchamber until his own morning stroll was finished. The king (Mr. Kirkby reflected) had seemed not at all frightened; he had even taken out his watch and looked at it, a sure sign that his patience began to wear thin; but he had spoken civilly, and promised to listen again. Mr. Kirkby, his forehead damp and prickly under the hot periwig, went back to the palace. When the king knew the end of their designs, he would not be so cool. There was no limit to Jesuitical cunning: if the murderers failed with their screw-pistols, a higher Papist was empowered to use poison.

Mr. Kirkby, as a chemist, knew that this was the ripe age of the poisoner's art. The worst poisoner since Locusta of Rome, small fair-haired Madame de Brinvilliers, was dead only two years – beheaded and burnt after the water-torture. Let the Burning Court at Paris break a dozen men on the wheel, or send them to the stake alive: still it would not meddle with Jesuit designs, and the craft would flourish. There was François Belot, who (by crushing an arsenic-filled toad in a goblet) brewed a poison so strong that if fifty people drank from the goblet afterwards, even though it had been washed and rinsed, they would all die. There was Blessis, who possessed the secret of manipulating mirrors in such a fashion that whoever looked into them should die. There had been Sainte-Croix, the lover of Madame de Brinvilliers, who sought for a poison that should be breathed in the air as a vapour: and who, when the glass mask slipped from his face in the laboratory, was found dead with his head in his own crucible.

Mr. Kirkby went back through the galleries to the vast, dusky Stone Gallery upstairs, which was nearly as long as the garden itself.   Here was the centre of all gossip.   Here hung the great paintings of Rubens, Correggio, and Van Dyck; here were the doors, curtained in black velvet, opening on the state apartments; here stood the halberdiers in antique ruffs and short scarlet coats; here the matting underfoot was worn black by the tread of the hopeful or the broken.   It was the hour of the levees, so that the gallery was tolerably well-filled.   He saw the two Secretaries of State, Mr. Henry Coventry and Sir Joseph Williamson, going past to the council office, although the council would not meet until eleven.   He saw the new French ambassador, fat M. Barrillon, paring his nails outside the apartments of Louise de Kéroualle, Duchess of Portsmouth, waiting to be let in by Mrs. Nelly Wall.   But none of the king's gentlemen seemed in attendance.   Mr. Kirkby went through even the Withdrawing Room without challenge; he was about to touch the curtain of the Great Bedchamber when the curtain was drawn aside.

'Come, now,' says another familiar voice, and a heavy finger poked him in the chest: 'sure you forget your manners, sir?'

He was looking up at a hook-nosed Hercules in a brown periwig, the eyes puffed, smiling, and streaked with small veins.   For this was Mr. William Chiffinch, Page of the Backstairs and private agent of the king: Mr. William Chiffinch, gentleman, pimp, drunkard, spy, and faithful friend.   Mr. Chiffinch was master of every kind of backstairs intrigue, the go-between with little informers and projectors before the king spoke to them, the fetcher of females, the ear of Whitehall.   He was an impetuous drinker, partly because it came naturally to him and partly because it was his business to fish out men's secrets while drinking with them. Mr. Chiffinch let no man part with him sober, if it were possible to get him drunk.   His stratagem was to urge the visitor to drink down goblet after goblet in haste: 'Drink quickly!' says he, 'for the king is coming.' If this did not produce a reeling head (his own head was like a tun), he might slip into the glass certain salutiferous drops – like Goddard's drops, and brewed in the laboratory – which made men babble. Kirkby knew those drops. So there stood Mr. Chiffinch, large, civil, blinking and smiling a little, his red fists on his hips, and almost sober.

'Let me pass!' says Mr. Kirkby urgently. 'I am on business of great moment. I have leave: his Majesty himself sent me here. You know me, Mr. Chiffinch; sure you know me?'

'I know your face pretty well, Mr. Kirkby,' says Chiffinch with great pleasantness, 'but I do not know your business. I must not let you pass, as you should know well. It will be no great hardship to wait in the gallery.'

'Your servant, Mr. Chiffinch!' roared a voice like the bellow of the Roman war-horn, from over Kirkby's shoulder. A hat was flourished. Christopher Kirkby became aware of stamping and heavy breathing, and of presences like a great wind out of a wine-vault. The two gentlemen who entered were both pretty fresh in liquor. There were candles burning in the Withdrawing Room, which had no outer windows, and the light brought out their faces with the colours of a Dutch painting.

The leader's age was (say) fifty-five. His broad face, framed in a sandy peruke, had begun to sag about the jowl from its old handsomeness. It was roughening, brickish, and large of pore; there were little blue veins trailing out from the root of the nose, and under his staring blue eyes. But he exuded amiability from every pore, as well as from a large mouth puffed with much oratory. His body was ponderous, which gave him the air of a slow man-o'-war when he turned from side to side. He moved with a limp, partly from gout and partly from an old bullet-wound in the wars; and he wore a scarlet surcoat with gold buttons, somewhat bedraggled. When he spoke, he carried himself slightly bent forward, as though he were leaning over the judicial bench. For this man was The Law. He came shouldering forward, wiping his nose with his sleeve,

chuckling, and limping to the clink of his sword-belt. Mal-
contents said that he was the son of a one-eyed butcher at
Smithfield, but this was a lie. He was a man of much learning, great eloquence, and even some sense. His tipple was
claret, and his only curse for the ladies was that they drank
so much of it. He was Sir William Scroggs, Lord Chief
Justice of the King's Bench.

The other man, who stood as though in his shadow, looked
with deference out of heavy-lidded eyes. He was small and
slight. And, though he was scarcely thirty, his look had
begun to take on the same bleariness as that of Scroggs and
Chiffinch. His hand was as delicate as a woman's; yet in
those Welsh good looks, the long nose and short upper lip,
there was a violence slippery and fluent. Mr. Kirkby, who
had seen him at the Duchess of Portsmouth's, knew that this
neat prigster in plum-coloured velvet was Sir George
Jeffreys.

If ever judgment were to be done on traitors, this man
would be briefed for the Crown just as Scroggs would sit on
the bench. Sir George Jeffrey's talents were notorious.
Before thirty he had got himself knighted. He was Common
Serjeant of the City of London, Solicitor-General to the
Duke of York, and soon (this summer, they said) he would
become Recorder of the City of London. At nineteen he
had married a penniless girl, who had respectably died after
presenting him with six children, and in May of this year
he had married the daughter of Alderman Sir Thomas
Bludworth – 'a dame of most slippery courses,' already with
child either by Jeffreys or by Squinting Jack Trevor. Sir
George was high in favour with the City Aldermen. They
were tickled by his Welsh humours; they did not stick
at his officiousness at the council-table, when he could be
such obsequious good company in private over a cold
partridge and a pipe of tobacco. But his great advancement now came from the court. He stood high in favour
with the Duchess of Portsmouth, and in more intimate
favour with the Duchess of Portsmouth's woman, Mrs. Nelly
Wall.

'Is his Majesty gone out, heaven bless him?' cries out

Scroggs, making a broad gesture with his hat. 'Ay; well, then, we go to pay court to the Duchess of Portsmouth, the fairest, the divinest, the most glorious of all her sex, God damn me! Is it not so: eh, Mr. Recorder?'

'You do well to come here, my lord,' muttered Kirkby, his eyes on the floor. 'There will be work for you presently.'

It was Sir George Jeffreys who answered him, with an expression suddenly grown so round-eyed and terrifying that Kirkby fell back.

'Now, God damn me, but here's a pretty fellow!' bawled out Mr. Recorder, staring at him. It was not possible to imagine where he drew up that power of voice. 'Here's a fellow I'd lay by the heels! Who are you, fellow? How dare you, fellow?'

Scroggs, who was wiping his nose with his hand, turned fretful. 'A pox on you and your swearing, Sir George!' he complained. 'Can't you take a large cup overnight without coming out cursing and raving like Orange Moll mumped of sixpence? It's beneath the dignity of the bar, rot me if it's not. Take your morning draught in chocolate, and settle your stomach.' In a change of mood he chuckled, swaying, and folded his hands over his red-coated paunch. 'I appeal to you, Mr. Chiffinch. *We* know what his Majesty himself said of Sir George Jeffreys, even if Sir George Jeffreys don't. His Majesty was graciously pleased to say, "That man has no sense, no learning, no manners, and more impudence than ten carted whores." '

Jeffreys faced him with poised suavity. 'Take care, my lord; you are spitting,' says he. 'Truly, my lord, I have heard the knavish libel. I wish I could find the filthy, lousy, knitty rascal who published it; I'd lay him by the heels; I'd give him a lick with the rough side of my tongue, I warrant you! Why, God damn me, my lord, his Majesty said nothing of that, nor thought it. If you mean the business of the King's Psalter, he was graciously pleased to call me a bold fellow, and seemed not ill-pleased. What is more,' pursued Jeffreys, with a subtle grin like Nick Machiaeval, 'I am not, I agree, in your lordship's exalted position at the King's

Bench. But I was never taken into custody for assault and battery, like a common bully-rock in a Covent-Garden ordinary.'

'Well, faith, *I* was,' admitted Scroggs composedly, and scratched his thigh. 'I half killed the fellow, now you mention it. It was for a good cause: I forget what. But what then?'

'I have recently purchased, my lord,' says the other, 'a house at Bulstrode, in Bucks. His Majesty has done me the honour to visit me there this month, when he is at Windsor. Does this seem as though I am out of favour? I'll tell you something more, my lord, and do you be advised by my example. As long as Mrs. Nelly Wall is my mistress, and the Duchess of Portsmouth is her mistress and the king's mistress – why, I can take my ease at court. What do you think of that?'

'I think, Sir George, that you are indiscreet,' says Chiffinch calmly, 'and I advise you to cool your head. We do not speak of court ladies as common blowens.'

'Ay: he is still boozy. *Catilinae erat satis eloquentiae, sapienitae parum*,' intoned Scroggs, with an air of sonorous piety. Then he flew into a temper, and roared. But the two presently forgot their quarrel, and Scroggs went out with Jeffreys swearing to make up all differences over a claret-cup. Mr. Kirkby, who saw nothing but fear in the spectacle, crept out after them. These men would have a short way with traitors.

But it was several hours before he was summoned to the Great Bedchamber to tell his story. He waited in the Stone Gallery, under one of the great paintings, and did not even heed the gossip. Once the Duke of York came striding through the crowd, his ruddy and pock-marked face as stern as ever when it towered over them. Mr. Kirkby, reflecting on how far another eminent Papist might be concerned in this devilishness, went down to look into the apartments of that French Jael, the Duchess of Portsmouth.

In the farther room where she held her levee, all things were massy silver: vases, tables, chimney-furniture and candle-sconces, so that the sunlight through little-paned

windows made a blaze upon it. Louise of Portsmouth –
'Madame Carwell' in the lampoons – sat among the company in a loose morning-robe trimmed with fur. She looked
less stout after her visit to the baths of Bourbon. She
bloomed under the rouge-pots, and her close dark-yellow
curls were frizzed to a nicety round a head like a beautiful
sofa-cushion. Her manner was one of high and shivering
graciousness; she spoke after the tall-buskined fashion of
Olivia in the play: 'O filthy! Hideous! Peace, or your
discourse will be my aversion!' Mr. Kirkby would not make
up his mind about her. He was somewhat surprised to see,
among the company attending her, the large and addle-
brained presence of her brother-in-law – Philip Herbert,
Earl of Pembroke. My lord of Pembroke, awesome as his
name might be, was of such unpredictable temper that
when he was in liquor prudent men refused to sit with him
in a tavern. It had not been many months since his right
to the pardon known as Benefit of Clergy had pulled him
through a bad brawl in the Haymarket, and he was strange
company to find at the presence of virtuous Madame Carwell. Also, he had once flared out at her, threatening to
stand her on her head at Charing Cross and show the nation
its grievance; but Mr. Kirkby had reason to wonder how
far he was in the right of it. She was thought to be a French
spy. It was possible that she might be concerned in this
design against the king: all things were possible, and evil:
so that Mr. Kirkby had got himself into another sweat when
Chiffinch found him in the Gallery, and told him that he
might see the king now.

When Chiffinch held aside the curtain of the Great Bedchamber, the chemist was relieved to find him alone, at one
window, humming a tune between his teeth and looking
out idly at the wherries on the river. But he came to business without preamble: 'You spoke of a plot against my life.
Who plots against me?'

'The Papists, sire,' says the other, calm enough now. 'I
tell you, you are in danger at this moment. I have seen
the articles. Two men – one Pickering and one "Honest
William", I think they call him – have been given money to

shoot you. If they should fail, you are to be poisoned. Sir
George Wakeman will put the drug into your posset.'

Now Mr. Kirkby was thoroughly alarmed at the way in
which Charles looked at him. 'Do you mean,' says he, 'Sir
George Wakeman, the queen's physician? Take care! Sir
George Wakeman, the *queen's* physician?'

'Sire, as heaven is my judge and witness, if you kill me for
it, Sir George Wakeman has money of the Jesuits to poison
you! I dare not tell you more now. But I was yesterday
acquainted of this by a friend, who has a more full account
in writing. Sire, that friend is near at hand, and ready to
appear when commanded. I tried to make this known to
you yesterday, but I could not get any opportunity of seeing
you, except in the company of the Duke of York. . . .'

Now Mr. Kirkby, terrified, knew he had gone too far.
He heard the spaniels snuffing about the room, snuffing at
his legs.

'Well, well, Mr. Kirkby,' he heard Charles saying, and
took heart, 'let us look to it, in any event. Come back to
Whitehall this night, and bring your friend with you. Come
to the Red Room at eight o'clock, and I will see you.'

'Godblessyourmajesty,' said Kirkby in one breath, and
went down on his knees as though he had been shot. When
Chiffinch led him out, the king was still standing motion-
less by the window, snapping his fingers slowly and
absently, as though to summon his dogs.

II

In the Red Room at Whitehall, the gilt pendulum-clock
had rapped out eight strokes when Chiffinch drew the curtain at the door. Charles wore a new laced suit that night;
he was supping with Nelly and Lady Harvey, and he was
impatient. Now Christopher Kirkby entered timorously –
and after him came sweeping the most curious little goblin
who ever mopped and mowed in the candlelight, or ran
across to kneel at the king's feet.

The goblin was a little, dirty, hairy man in a black skull-
cap. He wore a clergyman's black gown and white linen

bands. Clasping against his chest a packet of papers, sealed up, he peered from right to left as though to make certain the room was empty. He had sly little dreaming eyes, reddish at the lids, and an air of staring at mysterious things: so that the whites of his eyes, the only part of him he seemed unable to get dirty, gleamed with startling purity as they rolled. He was, in truth, as hairy an oldish fellow as Charles had seen, for the black fuzz seemed to crop out of his stringy face like moss in the cracks of rock. His voice was hoarse, sonorous, and somewhat crazed.

Scrambling up from his knees, the newcomer raised his hand.

'Now His ways be praised!' says he. 'As hell and Rome improved their skill and force to manage this hideous Plot, and bring it to perfection, so Almighty God (notwithstanding the provocations of our manifold sins), hath been graciously pleased to appear for our deliverance, by blasting their long-studied endeavours and designs, even as they were ready for birth. Now He hath been pleased to take the crafty in their own net –'

He was waving one skinny spider-haired arm, his face rapt, a queer enough figure in the red and black room. When the king cut him short with a question as to his name and quality, he stopped, sagged a little, thrust his hands into the arms of his gown, and spoke with sagging humility.

'May it please your Majesty,' says he, 'my name is Israel Tonge. I am a poor worker for Christ and the blessed Church of England, being the rector of St. Michael's, Wood Street. I rejoice in my poverty, since indeed my living brings me a bare £20 a year –'

Charles reflected. 'Dr. Tonge? Dr. Tonge? There is a familiar sound in that name,' and Tonge snapped at it eagerly.

'It pleases your Majesty to say so. Maybe you have read one of my poor works? I have writ much against the bloody designs of Popery. May it please your Majesty: I translated, from the French, the third part of *The Mystery of Jesuitism*. The second part of it was translated by Mr. John Evelyn himself; and I have heard you thanked him for it, and encouraged him, and carried the book for two days in your pocket. More recently I translated *The Jesuits' Morals,* unmasking their horrid practices and thereby incurring the wrath of the Scarlet Women (though I do not fear them, no, not the paring of a fingernail!); forasmuch as one was told off to poison me, and got £50 for it, but that it pleased heaven to spare me for the vineyard and reveal to me –'

He was gabbling on, wringing his hands in a very agony of earnestness, and looking round mysteriously as he did so. Charles's attention wandered into impatience. He remembered the man now, for Dr. Tonge was a buzzy fanatic, never without a plot in his head or a pen in his hand. Israel Tonge, Doctor of Divinity of Oxford, dabbled as well with botany, with anagrams, with alchemy, with anything in which he might feed his soul on mystery. But these many years he had been writing furiously against the Church of Rome without attracting notice. If there were any riddle in all this moonshine, it was why this fellow now sought to stir up active harm.

'– revealed to me,' said Tonge, out of breath, 'this.' He held up the sealed packet, and looked over his shoulder at Kirkby. 'But I beseech you, sire, that you let it be known only to the most private cabinet! If this secret is discovered too soon, our lives – Mr. Kirkby's and mine – will be put in hazard. If we may come to you in the guise of chemical students, until you seize their letters, and prove their guilt –?'

'How did these papers come to you?'

Dr. Tonge's expression assumed a dreaming relish, as though he had been waiting for this. Even the tone of his voice changed.

'May it please you, sire: mark this! It was at my good patron's house, Sir Richard Barker's, at Fox-Hall,' says he. 'And there was I, busy at my writing by candlelight – for you must know that I am engaged in another work, *The Jesuits Unmasked,* if it pleaseth heaven to turn their daggers from me – there was I, I say, busy at my writing, when I heard steps in the passage outside my door. These steps passed on; but I was much surprised to hear a rustling noise, and see certain papers thrust under the door. I went to the door, taking up my candle, and looked into the passage, but saw nobody. Whereat (if your Majesty will indulge me) I much wondered, until I went on to examine these papers; and when I had read them, I knew not whether to cry aloud with horror at what was therein, or forthwith fall on my knees to pray for this nation's deliverance from the snares of Babylon. Nay: I wept; I am not ashamed to own it. For –'

'Stay a moment, doctor,' says the king indulgently but very wearily, for he had heard this kind of tale often before. 'Do you know the name of the author of these papers?'

Tonge looked cunning. 'I do not know his name for certain, sire. I think he is the same man who hath been at the house twice or thrice in my absence. . . .'

'Or his condition?'

'I believe he is much among the Jesuits; but whether or not he is a Jesuit I do not know.'

'Well, well, man: but this plot you talk of? Mr. Kirkby spoke of a design against my life –?'

The doctor crept closer, as though secrecy made him writhe. 'Sire,' says he, 'that is not all they meditate, though God knows it would be a sore enough calamity. Sire, the Papists mean to rise in one night and cut a hundred thousand Protestant throats. They call you the Black Bastard. If you will deign to read the first article, you will see that Father Le Shee, the French king's confessor, has placed ten thousand pounds at a London goldsmith's for killing you. Sire, I cannot tell you one tenth of it; 'tis not all writ yet –' He stopped.

'And who is at the head of the business?'

'I will whisper that too,' agreed Dr. Tonge, after peering over his shoulder again. 'The chief conspirator who designs this (mark me) is the present Pope, Innocent the Eleventh, who in the Congregation, *de propaganda fide* – held as I believe about December of last year – declared all your Majesty's dominions to be a part of St. Peter's patrimony, as forfeited to the Holy See, and to be disposed of as he should think fit. The cursed Jesuits are to have control of this realm, once a French and Irish army hath come to cut our throats in the night. Once your Majesty's throat is cut – and I may tell you that one Conyers, a Jesuit, carries a consecrated knife a foot long, "to stick the heretic pig withal," says he (which is you, sire), and he bought the knife for ten shillings, and "not dear," says he, "for the work it has to do" – once your Majesty's throat is cut, I say, then the Duke of York is to reign if he will fall in with their horrid designs. . . .'

Dr. Tonge, very nearly strangling with the rapidity of his own utterance, and breathing himself like a stuck pig, was cut off when Charles rose to his feet. The king had been lounging in a chair of stamped leather, contemplating the lace on his sleeve and letting it slide one way or another over his wrist; but at the mention of James's name he got up with great briskness.

'Well, doctor, we will discuss the matter over a cup of ale at another time,' says he heartily. 'To-morrow morning I go to Windsor. Meanwhile, I will deposit the papers in the hands of one I can instrust. You are acquainted with my Lord Treasurer, the Earl of Danby? – ay, well: in his hands I can answer for their safety. See that you wait upon him to-morrow morning, and he will deal with it. And now good night. God bless you, God bless you! Hum! – Mr. Chiffinch!'

He was absently waving his hand, and snorting with amiable heartiness in his nose, when Tonge again went down on one knee.

'Sire, do you doubt that your brother is surrounded with evil counsellors? One moment more! I will name one of them. *His name is Edward Coleman, and he is the Duchess of York's secretary.* . . .'

'God bless you, God bless you,' says the king. 'Mr. Chiffinch!'

The hook-nosed Hercules in the brown periwig came shouldering in, to take in charge the dazed and sweating Dr. Tonge. Mr. Kirkby, who had been making a leg clock-work fashion whenever the king's eye lighted on him, was shepherded out with the doctor. Then Chiffinch stood holding together the curtains of the doorway behind him, and looking across at the king, who smothered a great yawn as he contemplated his image in a mirror.

'We shall be well out of this to-morrow, Will,' says he. 'Did I tell you, I sup to-night with Nelly and Lady Harvey? Do you remember Lady Harvey, Will?'

'Your Majesty,' says Chiffinch, 'may I have a word?'

'Ten thousand, Will,' says King Charles.   Out of the mirror his sardonic eye caught Chiffinch's dogged one.

'Was the fellow a rogue or a fool?' asked Chiffinch bluntly.

'Do *you* scent plots, Will?'

'Not I, on my life!' says Chiffinch rather snappishly, and sober enough to be irritable. 'I have no wish to meddle in other people's plots; my time is too much taken up with managing your own. All the same, I do not like it. As for their moonshine plots – why, they are always finding cellars full of Papist knives and black bills, and kegs of powder under Westminster Hall; such talk is not worth a lead hog. But here's this Dr. Tonge, who for years has been employing his mouth to no purpose, crying, Popery, Popery! – and now he comes out flat with "So much to be paid, such-and-such a man to do the business", and he seems in earnest. You may depend on it, your Majesty: Tonge and Kirkby are not alone in this.   It lies deeper.   There is someone behind them, prompting their tongues –'

'A master liar?'

Chiffinch nodded violently. 'And what will you do, then?'

'Do?' says King Charles, with great energy, and turned round from the mirror.   Mr. Chiffinch saw that again old Leather-Face was snarling urbanely. 'You know the old saying, the more a T—— is stirred, the more it stinks. I will not have this one stirred, or it will stink like Snow Hill in August. Do? Let it sleep, man! It will die off presently. That,' he pointed to the sealed packet on the table, 'will go to my Lord Treasurer. He will sift the business, and know how to keep silent while we find out if there be anything in it.'

'If there be anything in it,' murmured Chiffinch. 'All

the same, I do not like that mention of Mr. Edward Coleman. How did they get wind of *that*, do you think? I have warned your Majesty before: Mr. Coleman is dangerous. He is too busy, and he has too many uses. He corresponds with Father La Chaise, the French king's confessor – that will be Dr. Tonge's "Father Le Shee" – and he is for ever running about Jesuit business, and pushing forward the Duke of York. I know your Majesty does not wish me to meddle with any but backstairs business; yet I cannot help owning a pair of ears. Damn me, I would even venture that this Mr. Coleman goes further. I apprehend that he was the man chosen by the French ambassador to bribe members of the Country Party against you.[1] Money went through his hands, and it went into the pockets of my Lord Shaftesbury's lieutenants.'

'So I have been told,' says King Charles, and thought of Coleman's shrunken face in its dead-black periwig. 'Well, I desire nothing better than to see it proved.' He fell to chuckling. 'Hey, God's fish, if it could be demonstrated before parliament that my Lord Shaftesbury and his holy patriots have been taking bribes of Popish King Louis – at Mr. Coleman's hands, or another's, as may be – why, we should see whose behind would be sorest then, I promise you!'

Chiffinch struck his hands together gloomily. 'Your Majesty is pleased to say so,' he grumbled, 'but you will never prove it. Shall I tell you how far this Coleman's nets go, and how deep he meddles with everything? Does your Majesty know that one of his closest friends is the staunchest and most upright Protestant magistrate in London? – do you recall Sir Edmund Berry Godfrey?'

'Godfrey? I know the name.'

'Ay; and the man too, if I may say so,' returned Chiffinch

---

[1] There is no reason to believe that Chiffinch thought this, or that he suspected any intrigue between Coleman and Godfrey. This is the one conversation in the book which is unwarranted or for which there is no authority. But, as it does not bear on the evidence one way or the other, I have ventured to include it in order to make clear the danger of the situation. We know at least that Charles suspected Barrillon of bribing the Opposition.

dryly. 'Your Majesty had him knighted, and afterwards, on one occasion, clapped into jail.'

Charles considered. For him, who knew every member of parliament by face and name, it was not difficult to bring to mind this famous magistrate, who had the reputation of being the best justice of the peace in England. Sir Edmund Godfrey was notorious for being an honest, a dangerously honest, man. He combined the extremes of an absent-minded melancholy in himself; and, when roused out of it by public business, of being a martinet – punctual, fussy, rather vain, sometimes meddling and sometimes kindly, with a worried conscience. He had a habit of wandering through the town at all hours and in all weathers: disliking to take a servant with him on these lumbering walks, for he said it was a clog to a man. Everybody round Westminster knew his tall, lean, stoop-shouldered figure; his black camlet coat and broad-brimmed hat with the gold band; his eyes fixed on the ground, his cane dangling before him as though to pick the way. This habitual abstraction was attributed by some to his deafness, and by others to hereditary madness, for his father had died suicidally mad.

Not a rich man, Sir Edmund, though he came of a well-to-do Kentish family. He had been educated at Westminster and Christ Church, Oxford; and he had been trained for the law at Gray's Inn; but his growing deafness made him give up the law. In addition to his duties as justice of the peace, he had set up in business as a wood-and-coal merchant in Hartshorn Lane, near Charing Cross. A bachelor, getting on towards sixty, he lived there with his house-keeper, Mrs. Judith Pamphlin; his clerk, old Mr. Henry Moor; and a maid-servant, Elizabeth Curtis, who came in by day to do char-work. Although he had two brothers who were merchants in the City, he was never so intimate with them as with his cousin, Mrs. Mary Gibbon – a comfortable old lady in spectacles, who made him jellies. Each morning early, Justice Godfrey was at his papers in the little front parlour of the house in Hartshorn Lane, and on the mantel-piece was the silver tankard (inscribed with his name, and a eulogy) which the king had given him for his conduct during the Great Plague. In those black plague days a grave-robbing thief, who had a warrant sworn out for his arrest, jeeringly took refuge in a pest-house among the stricken. When nobody else dared follow him there, Godfrey lumbered into the pest-house and took the man single-handed. For that he had got his silver tankard and his knighthood. But this conscience-stung zeal for justice cut both ways; he could defy organised authority, even the king, just as well.

There had been a bad squabble three years after the plague. Dr. Alexander Frazier, the king's physician, owed Godfrey £30 for firewood; and, when he did not pay up, Godfrey issued a writ against him. Charles remembered having flown into one of his rare rages; he had Godfrey's bailiffs flogged, very nearly had Godfrey himself flogged, and committed both magistrates and bailiffs to the Gate-house jail at Whitehall. Godfrey justified his action. He refused all food, until the hook-nosed countenance looked more haggard than ever; and finally, with the support of the Lord Chief Justice, obtained his release. Even at the beginning of this present year, he had not hesitated to act as the foreman of a Grand Jury which had indicted a powerful young nobleman who in a fit of drunken mania had kicked poor Nat Cony to death in a Haymarket tavern. He risked personal violence there, so much so that he had taken a holiday out of England for a few months; but he had returned now, as grave as ever.

The only laws which he did not strictly enforce were the laws against religious dissenters. Both Catholics and Presbyterians were his friends, especially the Catholics. He never tried to seek out priests or mass-houses, and no man lived on better terms with Catholics than he. It was not surprising to find Catholics among his friends, Charles acknowledged, though it was odd to find that busy fanatic, Mr. Edward Coleman, as an intimate.

'Strange birds,' he told Chiffinch. 'But what then?'

'I do not draw inferences,' said Chiffinch doggedly. 'I only tell your Majesty that Mr. Coleman's nets run far.'

'Well, God's fish, what would you have me do?' says

Charles, rather testily. 'I have warned my brother to get rid of the man. Come, Will: you are too easily upset. If Coleman gives trouble, we shall hear it in time. Go take a bottle, and then deliver these papers to the Earl of Danby. Here's the whole of England in a great stir and fret over something: three eclipses of the sun and two of the moon; astrologers prophesying frenzies, inflammations, and new infirmities proceeding from choleric humours; and the devil himself, I hear, piping at a convocation of witches in Scotland this very month – out upon it, Will! As for me, I sup and I wench and I sleep tight; and I do not tremble before thunder until I hear it.'

He uttered his own deep and noiseless chuckle; he clapped Chiffinch on the shoulder, whistled to one of his spaniels that was asthmatically dozing in a corner, and sauntered out into the passage. 'It is hot to-night,' says Chiffinch, 'notwithstanding.' The little gilt pendulum-clock rapped out nine.

Six weeks later, the thunder broke.

III

In the August haze at Windsor, the flat green lands beyond the river – stretching away into the sixty thousand acres of the royal forest – drummed under horses' hoofs when the field galloped down-wind in the old cries of hawking. On King Charles's wrist perched the royal gerfalcon, on his followers' wrists the lesser peregrine: the fast, long-winged, blue-black hawks waiting for the leather hood to be slipped when a heron should be sighted high up, making his passage home from the river. *'Slip the hood!'* Up flashes the hawk; the heron taking to the higher air, climbing in narrow circles; the hawk flying in broader rings to get above her quarry. *'He's ringing, he's ringing!'* *'She's flying at check – no, she's making her pitch!'* 'BOUND!' High against the pale sky, where the Round Tower of Windsor Castle stands up grey above the trees, the grey and black dots meet and mingle and tumble before they drop. . . .

D

A little hawking, a little fishing, a little sauntering with Louise in the cool galleries where the Holbein portraits hung: thus Charles idled away from London. The Plot, he hoped, was scotched for good. It had come to ridicule at birth, like a calf with six legs. My Lord Treasurer Danby (possibly scenting political capital in the business) had for weeks been running in circles, attempting to prove or disprove the information of Tonge and Kirkby. Although Dr. Tonge assured the Lord Treasurer that the two assassins, Pickering and 'Honest William' Grove, might be found prowling with their screw-pistols in the Park, they never appeared when the doctor said they would. Dr. Tonge found various reasons for this. Pickering, he said, had already attempted to shoot the king on three occasions, but each time he failed. Once the flint of his pistol was loose, so that he could not fire; once he forgot to put any powder in the firing-pan; on the third occasion he remembered the powder but forgot to put in a bullet. Whereupon he and Honest William Grove had decided to go down to Windsor and do the business there; but Grove had a sore throat, and dared not go by water. There were even more dangers of assassination than these. Mr. Edward Coleman, said Tonge, had hired four Irish killers to go down to Windsor and 'observe the king's postures'. Their leader, Conyers – he who had a consecrated knife a foot long – would have killed the king, but that his horse fell lame, and he got sciatica. King Charles, in great amusement, refused to let Lord Treasurer Danby make any formal inquiry.

'You will only alarm all England,' says he, 'and put thoughts of killing me into the minds of people who had no such notions before.'

It then appeared that Dr. Tonge (or whoever stood behind him) grew desperate. On Friday, August 30th, Tonge came flying to Danby with the news that certain letters, containing treasonable designs, had been written by several Jesuits and sent to Father Bedingfield, the Duke of York's confessor, at Windsor. They might be intercepted at Windsor post-office. Danby, hurrying down to Windsor in a fast coach to intercept them, found the king already

examining the letters. Father Bedingfield had that morning received a packet of five letters which puzzled him considerably. Four of them purported to come from Jesuits
whom he knew, but they were not in these men's handwriting, and were full of wild, babbling phrases which
sounded the more sinister for making no sense. Father
Bedingfield took them to the Duke of York, and James
showed them to the king. Danby, arriving flushed with the
report of treason, found the king studying letters which
were manifest forgeries.[1]

And then the Duke of York demanded an investigation.

If James had been content to keep silent, and let the plot
tumble to pieces of its own flimsiness, England would have
slept snug with no bones broken. But James, who had in
all conscience some reason to be angered, had never yet
grown accustomed to suffer knaves gladly. Each new knave
came to him as a new surprise, and a new cause for fury.
Under his pressure, and that of Danby, Charles at last
wearily agreed to let the council make a public inquiry.
Since the plot was so much discredited, it could do no great
harm.

At the end of September Charles returned to London on
his way to Newmarket. The Privy Council was in possession of an even larger bundle of papers, this time drawn up
into the form of eighty-one articles, and submitted by
Dr. Tonge: whom the clerks supposed to be seeking a
deanery. The council proposed to examine the papers, and
Dr. Tonge, on Thursday, the 27th of September; but the
council had risen by the time they could send word to
him, and the examination was postponed. Through
Mr. Kirkby (now in such ill repute that the king did not
look at him when they passed each other) the council sent
word to Dr. Tonge that he must appear before them on
Friday morning. As for Dr. Tonge's informant – the man
behind him, the maker of all these accusations, whoever he

[1] They had all been cut from the same sheet of paper, and all written
by the same hand. Charles commented, 'There is some contrivance in
this; but I am confident I can find it out. I have seen a handwriting not
unlike this. I would compare them together.' – The Duke of York's
memoirs in Clarke's *Life*, i, 517-518.

might be – let him rest within call, in case he should be summoned. Until now he had remained unseen.

But there was a half-glimpse of him on Friday morning, before Dr. Tonge attended the council. These two, the hairy doctor and the informer, had business. Their eighty-one articles were to go before the council; but, to make certain that the affair should make a noise in the public mind even if the council dismissed it, they had decided to place a sworn copy of the articles in the hands of a justice of the peace. Once before, three weeks ago, they had approached a justice to swear to the truth of their depositions, without allowing him to read the articles. Now they meant to give him the depositions, allow him to read them, and let him act as he saw fit. The magistrate they had chosen was Sir Edmund Berry Godfrey.

It was foul weather. London got up before daylight; but in the gusty murk of that morning, when tallow-dips made windows stand out smeary against the rain, daylight looked like dusk. The two informers hurried over Charing Cross, that vast open space in the midst of which the statue of Charles the First on horseback stood up in blowing rain. The square was churned to mud, for this was a rural place as yet unpaved with those egg-shaped cobbles on which the City carts made such a din. Towards the north the Royal Mews, where the soldiers were quartered, showed a few furtive gleams; and from the east, out of the dark throat of the Strand, blew a hideous noise of all the street-signs clattering and banging and creaking in high wind. Dr. Tonge and his companion turned down into Hartshorn Lane, at the end of which, above the wood-and-coal wharf overhanging the river, was Godfrey's house.

Elizabeth Curtis, the maidservant, admitted them. She could not see them well. There was no light in the little passage, except what came from the damp front-parlour where Sir Edmund sat early at his papers. But, since this was the only light of a flaring wick in a dish of grease – Godfrey did not indulge the luxury of wax-candles – its flutter showed only that one of the visitors was little and hairy, and the other was bloated. Elizabeth Curtis opened the door of the parlour. The remains of breakfast were still on the table, and a small fire burnt in the grate over which the silver tankard stood on the mantelshelf. At his desk by the flary lamp, the blackish, ageing justice in his frizzy black periwig (seeming more lean and tall by reason of his own shadow on the wall) sat looking up over his spectacles, with a goose-quill in his hand. Elizabeth Curtis dodged out after she admitted the visitors. Of the bloated man she saw only a shadow, which seemed to make his face unpleasantly long, before the door was closed.

In a cubicle adjoining the parlour, Mr. Henry Moor, Godfrey's clerk, sat at his high desk among the boxes of affadavits. The door was ajar. Mr. Moor heard rolling footsteps on the boarded floor; and he heard a voice. It was a harsh voice, upraised by reason of Godfrey's deafness, but as arresting as a blow in the face, and with the same sort of jeer. It aped the mincing drawl made fashionable by the Earl of Sunderland, but its flatness would bleat through like a sheep's. Also, Mr. Moor smelt a bad smell. The voice appeared to be taking an oath. Then someone hurried to close the door.

Some half an hour afterwards, when Elizabeth Curtis peeped into the parlour to clear away the breakfast things, she found her master alone. He was sitting back in his chair, his black-stockinged knees apart, staring at the floor in a black study. He looked much older than his fifty-seven years, and longer and withered and more disturbed of countenance. When he caught sight of her apron out of the corner of his eye, he put up a bony hand and rubbed his eyes.

'Go out into the street,' says Sir Edmund, plumping out in his loud shaky voice, 'and fetch me a porter.'

'Is it for an errand you want one, sir?' says Mistress Curtis; 'for if it is, why not send Mr. Moor?'

'Go out into the street,' says Sir Edmund, 'and fetch me a porter.'

He did not seem to look or hear until she had gone. Then he reached over the pile of papers on his desk, and took up a pen. *'I must see you at once,'* wrote Sir Edmund; *'I have*

*something of great moment to communicate. For God's
sake do not delay, but if you can find time send me the usual
sign, that one clerk would speak with me; I will meet you
at Mr. Welden's, and believe that I am ever yours, E.G.'*
He folded and sealed it, so that the red wax dripped bright
when his hand shook in the light. Then he rose, and fell
to pacing up and down, wiping his mouth, muttering,
stamping on the floor, until a street-porter was hauled in out
of the wet.

'Do you know,' says Sir Edmund, 'the house of Mr. Edward
Coleman, behind Westminster Abbey? – Good. Then this
letter is for Mr. Coleman's hand, and for Mr. Coleman
alone; do you understand? Good. Be off, then.'

Whereupon the stooped giant resumed his pacing beyond
the lamp, his lean shadow opening and shutting on the wall
like a pair of scissors; while day broadened on the river
behind the little-paned windows, and, some quarter of a
mile away down along the mud-banks, a swarm of watermen
began to assemble their boats round Whitehall Palace stairs.

At Whitehall Palace, or in the mind of King Charles,
there was no such disturbance. The king meant to go to
Newmarket that day; he had contracted a touch of ague at
Windsor, which the rain and bad air of London did not
improve, and he was impatient to get out of town. When
the Privy Council met on Friday morning, he was too
impatient. Over the morning meeting he presided himself.
When one of the Secretaries of State, Sir Joseph Williamson,
produced the eighty-one articles, Charles remarked that he
had been told about this 'conspiracy' by Tonge on the 13th
of August; but that he had merely referred the matter to
the Lord Treasurer. Danby spoke of the mysterious letters
which had been sent to Father Bedingfield at Windsor, and
which he had tried to intercept. The letters were produced
at the council-board; several councillors pronounced them
to be forgeries. Then Dr. Tonge was called in.

Although he was assured that he need have no apprehension, the doctor was plainly fearful. He gabbled that he
himself knew nothing, but that all his information came
from – another. What other? An acquaintance whom he

had known only a brief time, said the doctor; a worthy gentleman who had once been chaplain of Sir Richard Ruth's ship in the navy, but who, in consequence of exposing some ill practices there, had been very hardly dealt with. Well, well, let his friend be fetched at the afternoon session, and he would be heard. Charles, frankly wearied, did not wait for the afternoon session. In his six-horse coach – that prodigy in an age of speed, when the public Flying Coaches running thrice weekly to the principal towns covered fifty miles in a day, a pace which made men's wits dizzy and provoked a pamphlet demonstrating that we were going to the devil – in his six-horse coach, with relays at Bishop Stortford and Chesterford, he hoped to reach Newmarket by supper-time. But he never got there. As a blustery afternoon drew on, a courier from Danby overtook the cavalcade, with its escort of fifty horse, and presented an urgent message for the king. Danby implored him to return. Nor was Danby the man to talk wildly. Charles reached Whitehall late that night, a foul night of rain, in time to see a file of soldiers splashing in the mud up King Street, with someone swinging a lanthorn among them. As the coach rolled into Pebble Court, he could see that lights were still burning in the council office. The council had just risen. Gloomy looks and an unquiet buzz stirred Whitehall. In his private apartments, Charles allowed his clothes to be changed, and talked easily with his Gentlemen of the Bedchamber; but in the background, where the reflection of firelight climbed the wall, he saw the grave faces of Lord Treasurer Danby and Sir Joseph Williamson. He dismissed the others, faced these two, and asked what the message meant.

'It means,' says my Lord Treasurer, 'that the very cabinet of hell is set open.'

From the man's expression, Charles could not tell whether he was alarmed or pleased. For Danby was just now being assailed by parliament, and the discovery of a Popish plot might turn their teeth away from him to bite someone else. Danby – sickly, flabby, and shrewd of eye – had been urging investigation. 'He is as stiff as any stake,

and leaner, Dick, than any rake; envy is not so pale. . . .'[1]
Yet the man was a trusted friend, and you might rely on
what he said. He nodded towards Sir Joseph Williamson,
whose hands were full of papers.

'My lord says true,' agreed Sir Joseph: that elderly, plea-
sant-spoken, rather pompous gentleman whose nervousness
was not concealed. 'I have never seen the council sit so
amazed. Mr. Coventry said to me: "If he be a liar, he is
the greatest and adroitest I ever saw. Yet," says he, "it is
a stupendous thing to think what vast concerns are like to
depend on the evidence of one young man –" And so it is.
You may depend on it, your Majesty, we have hooked a very
different fish from Dr. Tonge.'

'*Have* you hooked him?'

'Can we hook a sea-monster?' says Sir Joseph, who was
a leading member of the Royal Society and fond of scientific
imagery. 'Or a saint and saviour? I do not know, and I
plume myself on my knowledge of men. This man speaks
with authority. It requires courage to look him in the
face; he would outstare a bishop. His memory alone is
prodigious, for he cites by name – by name – one hundred
and two persons concerned in this plot against your
Majesty: twenty-four English Jesuits, nineteen foreign
Jesuits, twelve Scottish Jesuits, nine Benedictines, three
Carmelites, two Franciscans, nine Dominicans, fourteen
secular priests, four secular persons, four Irish ruffians, and
two archbishops; indicating also those Popish lords who
are to occupy the high places in the new government once
your throat is cut. . . . Did your Majesty see the soldiers
going towards the City? They are taking Jesuits.'

Charles turned on him. 'Taking Jesuits? By whose
order?'

'I signed the warrants,' replied Danby, bowing slightly
but looking the king straight in the eyes afterwards. He

---

[1] Said the lampoonist:
> 'He is as stiff as any stake,
>   And leaner, Dick, than any rake;
>   Envy is not so pale—
>   And though by selling of us all
>   He's wrought himself into Whitehall,
>   He looks like a bird of gaol.'

assumed his old persuasive tone. 'The council voted it. Your Majesty well knows that we have your interest at heart, and that we only try to safeguard your person. I have signed warrants for the taking of one William Ireland, procurator of the province of the Society of Jesus; one John Fenwick, agent of the College at St. Omers; Thomas Pickering, John Grove, John Smith, Thomas Johnson, and Dr. Fogarty. . . .' Then he burst out, though still humbly and with great persuasion. 'Have I not told you many times, God knows! that your Majesty's only true friends are here in us, and that there is always danger to be apprehended from these Papists? Are you like to forget that your own grandfather was murdered by a Papist?'

'No, my lord,' says Charles gravely; 'nor am I like to forget that my own father was murdered by Puritans. I will deal frankly with you: rebel for rebel, I had rather trust a Papist rebel than a Presbyterian one.'

'Your Majesty is pleased to confirm what I said,' replied Danby suavely. He had become curt, as his way was when dealing with papers. 'I said that your only true friends were in the Church of England. Shall I read you an abstract here, of what the Papists say of your father?' He took the packet from Williamson. 'Thus, sir, they jeer at St. Omers! They say – here – "King Charles the First was none of King James's son, but a bastard begotten of the body of Anne of Denmark by her tailor. . . ."'

'My lord, I had apprehended that *I* was the bastard.'

Again Danby bowed. 'Your Majesty's memory never fails,' says he. 'So you are also. That is article three: that the king is "no lawful king, but comes of a spurious race, and that his father was a black Scotchman". No, now: let us pass over this wild stuff. Doubtless there is much wild talk everywhere – among the Jesuits. But sure the whole Privy Council is not mad, and when this man spoke they were struck dumb. He is pat with every name and date. Armies rising, fifty thousand troops secretly waiting in London alone; forty thousand black bills stored away for an Irish army which shall pour in, after the Duke of Ormonde has been poisoned; one mighty flame of uprising

which shall sweep away our damnable heresy and burn on
blood as it burns on oil!' (Charles saw that Danby was
curiously shaken, and he began to wonder uneasily what
sort of man this new informer might be; for this was like a
spell on men's wits.) 'Mark how very circumstantial he
is,' pursued Danby, cocking an eye towards Williamson to
see how it had impressed him. 'On August 22nd he met a
man, one Conyers, who was to stab *you*. For this purpose
Conyers had bought a two-edged knife, a foot long, with a
buck-horn handle. (He names even the handle, you see;
ay, and the price, which was ten shillings.) Why was it so
long? he asked Conyers. Why, says Conyers, to stab under
cover of my cloak; through my cloak I will stab him —
thus! . . .'

My Lord Treasurer made the appropriate gesture.

'I heard of Conyers and his knife,' remarked Charles, moving over restlessly to hold out his hands to the fire, 'as long
ago as August 13th. This informant of yours now meets
him on August 22nd. Did he speak of sticking heretic pigs
as well?'

Sir Joseph Williamson interposed.

'The design of killing your Majesty, in all the various ways
you have heard — for,' says he, 'I think my Lord Treasurer
hath told you of them already? — the design for killing you
was formulated at a great Consult of Jesuits. This Consult
was held last April 24th, at the White Horse Tavern in the
Strand. . . .'

Charles did not turn round; he remained winking and
blinking at the fire, wriggling his dark wrists in front of it.
But he was startled, and had almost spoken out when he
heard this piece of information. For it was true. On the
24th of April there had been, in strict fact, a meeting of
Jesuits; not at the White Horse Tavern, but in the more
dangerous place of St. James's Palace, the residence of the
Duke of York. It was merely a meeting for transacting the
ordinary business of the Society; but their having met at all
was a secret which Charles had thought known to very few
people in the world. Yet here was this informer, with his
black bills and his black bastards and his black nonsense,

in some fashion stumbling slap over a piece of the truth.
Charles turned round, sharply.

'And this informer: who is he? What manner of man
is he?'

Danby hesitated, and seemed troubled. 'Of that your
Majesty shall have the opportunity of judging,' says he.
'There is a special session of the council called for to-morrow
morning. As for the man – he has been a Jesuit. That is
to say, he went among them, and pretended to become one
of them, in order to spy out their secrets and betray them
to your Majesty; since, he says, he had heard of a plot
against the Protestant religion. I own that in person he is
not attractive. He is like –'

'I will speak with him,' says the king grimly, 'to-morrow.'

All the same, he spent a troubled night. Danby might
find political capital in the affair, and set the parliament-
hounds baying to keep them off his own scent. But the
Lord Treasurer was a fool not to realise the dangers. Such
wild tales as these were exactly suited to the fears of the
age. What might happen, if this plot took hold of the
public mind, it made a man shiver to think of. And, when
my Lord Shaftesbury and his Green Ribbon Club learned
of it, they could and would turn it into a terrible instrument against the government. . . .

On the following morning, the 28th of September, the
galleries ran with rumours. Several Jesuits had been
clapped into Newgate overnight, it was known; someone
was tugging at boulders to start an avalanche. It was a
grey day, as dull as the old oak council-room when the
members gathered about the board. Usually their clothes
made a garden of colour, with the great periwigs nodding
above it as they whispered together; but to-day they looked
sombre. Only gay young sparks like the Duke of Monmouth, or gay old sparks like the flamboyant Lord Chief
Justice Scroggs, snuffling and wiping his nose as he chuckled
to Lord Grey of Werke, stood out. At the head of the board
sat King Charles, absently spinning a globe-map. Mr.
Secretary Coventry and Mr. Secretary Williamson sat on
either side at their papers, with grave lords and gentlemen

ranked round them; and at the foot of the board was Sir
Robert Southwell, Clerk of the Council. Everything took
on a great to-do of papers shuffled, pens dipped, hands
behind ears to catch portentous words. For much ink
should flow, much blood might flow; and the Duke of York,
at Charles's right, looked straight across, gloomily, at a
sweating Danby. The Clerk of the Council turned round
at the clap of a door.

'Mr. Titus Oates,' he said.

II

'DIED ABNER AS A FOOL DIETH?'

The Murder

'The instrument made use of by Providence, for the frustrating of this horrid Popish Plot, was MR. TITUS OATES, a name which (notwithstanding all the slanders and calumnies upon him, because of our religion's and nation's enemies) will be dear and honourable in future ages, as well as the present.'

> *The History of the Damnable Popish Plot,*
> by the AUTHORS OF THE WEEKLY PACQUET
> OF ADVICE FROM ROME, 1680.

'For my part, I call the fellow a lying knave.'

> KING CHARLES THE SECOND.

' *"Where is Sir Edmund Godfrey? He has not been seen at his house all this day. They say he is murdered. . . !"* '

I

'MR. TITUS OATES,' said the Clerk of the Council. In he came rolling on his bandy legs, no whit abashed. Up, Jenkins! Up, fool! Up, devil! The wind of the prophets blows with him, and Providence itself brays through his nose. When he saw the king, Mr. Oates went down on his knees for a moment. Then he got up briskly, as though with a duty over and forgotten, and came rolling forward with assured steps: taking the measure of the Council with his eye, and taking it shrewdly. His body was short, broad, and bloated; to their eyes he seemed to move in a luminousness, like a saint or a decayed lobster. His big hand was for ever being raised to take oaths, fervently. He wore a fair, woolly periwig, whose foretop bangs drooped over eyes sunk deep, but watchful. Out of his periwig came jutting a curious chin: a chin so long that his mouth seemed exactly in the centre of his lead-coloured face. The mouth moved. 'Your most gracious and glaarious majesty!' cries he through his nose. 'I have ventured my life for you at sea, and my soul for you on land, and I am now come to discover a hellish conspiracy.'

He stopped, and took a deep breath. The effect of that loud, harsh voice, the effect of that bull neck thrust forward, the effect of that little eye which seemed to know unpleasant secrets about everyone present, was to impress the council enormously. Then Mr. Oates turned with great briskness to the Clerk of the Council.

'My lord,' says he, 'I desire to be put upon oath.'

'Stay a moment, Mr. Oates,' said Sir Robert Southwell. 'You were put upon oath yesterday. That will suffice for the council-book.'

'My lords, you are pleased to put me in the wrong,' says Oates, with an injured huff. 'My lords, I understood it was the form. But doubtless there are those that do not desire me to be put upon oath. My lords, what do you wish of me?'

'That you acquaint his Majesty with the things you have already deposed before this council, Mr. Oates,' replied Mr. Secretary Coventry. 'In particular with some account of yourself, and how you came to become a Papist –'

'By God and His holy angels,' cries Oates, lifting up his hands, 'I did only pretend to become a Papist; I was not really one, I declare it. My lords, this is no subtle Jesuit you see before you, but a plain blunt man. My lords, I will acquaint you with something of what I know; but if I do not tell all, it is because the time is not come to reveal it. I was ordained of the Church of England, and was formerly a vicar at Bobbing in Kent, to which I came about the year 1672. But I left it (the air not being good), and was sometime minister near Chichester in Sussex. I served as chaplain aboard Sir Richard Ruth's ship in the navy; but in consequence of exposing some ill practices, I left. Then I became a chaplain in the service of the Duke of Norfolk, at Arundell House in the Strand. My lords, it was here I overheard some whisperings amongst the priests – with whom that family, if your lordships will give me leave to say so, is sufficiently haunted – that there was some grand design on foot. But I could not learn what it was in particular. I had heard from my Protestant friends (and now I remember it, which I forgot to mention before, from Sir Hamond L'Estrange's *History of King Charles the First*, and other judicious authors), that there had been for many years a design to introduce Popery with blood and fire. So, my lords, I longed to sound the depth of this horrid business, and if possible to countermine it.'

Mr. Oates's fluency had grown, the voice now braying loud and firm, interlaid with a nasal whine of outrage whenever he spoke of The Design. He stood squat and bandy-legged at the foot of the board, his blue face set in a cunning look as he nodded at them, and weirdly split in two by the mouth. But his little eye always rolled towards the king.

'Therefore,' says he, 'I entered into conversation with these priests, pretending to have some doubts in my mind. But these priests could not satisfy me; they were not men for my turn, not having any great degree of learning. But then, my lords, I became acquainted with some Jesuits – cah, and I soon found that *these* were men for my turn!' says the witness, nodding and rubbing his hands exultantly; 'cunning, politic men, who could satisfy me. I pretended to be convinced by their arguments, and was reconciled to them, and admitted to the order of the Jesuits. (But I must tell your lordships I did only pretend, as witness – for I know your lordships relish a jest – that I stole a box of their sacred wafers, which I called in the way of pleasantness a Box of Gods, and that I did seal my letters with them for above a year and a half.)' He chuckled. 'I was admitted to the order on Ash Wednesday, 1677. After I was admitted, the fathers told me I had some years upon me, and that I could not undergo the burdens they put on younger men. "But what do you think of travelling?" said they, "and going beyond sea to do our business?" I agreed to this, and in April, 1677, I sailed to Bilbao in Spain, with letters of recommendation, and thence proceeded to Valladolid.'

In ensuing times, after that long day when Oates talked ceaselessly until dark, King Charles could not get the bleating voice out of his ears. It was as though Oates swelled and changed and grew inspired as he saw the council agog at his words, and as the tale shifted from England to Spain to France. After his return from Valladolid, he said, he had carried treasonable letters to the Jesuit College of St. Omers in France. Everywhere it was the same: monks singing *Te Deum* for the death of the black bastard; all England honeycombed with fireballs; Johannes Paulus d'Oliva, Father-General of the Jesuits at Rome, Pedro de Cordubo, Provincial of the Jesuits in New Castile, and Father La Chaise, the French king's confessor, pouring out money to encompass the plot. As for Oates, he had been a great instrument or agent of the Jesuits, not only in England, but in France and Spain too. He had personal conferences about the murder of the king with Father La Chaise; and in Spain Don John, the Father-General, had admitted him into his presence, where with his own eyes Oates saw the money counted out for Sir George Wakeman to poison the king. . . .

'Stay a moment, Mr. Oates,' said the king very persuasively. 'You tell us that you are acquainted with Don John, and saw him face to face?'

'As clearly as I see your Majesty now.'

'I have heard much of him. Pray, what manner of man is he? Describe him.'

'Your Majesty, I will do so gladly,' says Oates with great promptness, and with a faint sneer. 'He is like most Spaniards. He is tall, lean, and black.'

'He is short, fat and of fair complexion, with brown hair,' said Charles, still gravely. 'I know him very well.'

Someone laughed, immediately scowled down by intent members of the council. Mr. Titus Oates remained casual and unconcerned, and looked Charles in the eye. 'Your Majesty is pleased to say so. I know many people, I have near worn myself out in penetrating this hellish plot against your Majesty's life; it is of no concern; maybe I thought of someone else. . . . My lords, maybe I have reason to keep secret about some things; maybe I have reason in not discovering all I know. . . .'

'You tell us you spoke with Father La Chaise. In what house does the king's confessor live?'

'Your Majesty may know where he lives. He lives in the Jesuits' house by the Louvre.'

'My friend, the Jesuits have no house within a mile of the Louvre; it is as though you said Gresham College stood in Westminster.'

'God bless your Majesty,' says Oates, lifting a heavy hand piously, 'your Majesty, being a good Protestant, would scarce know all the Jesuit houses – or so I think? My lords,' his voice assumed a braying earnestness and drawl, 'my laards, if your laardships please, any matter that is before you, I will answer to it; but I hope you will not call me to account for a matter of geography that makes scarce an inch on a map. My lords, I am not ashamed to own anything I have said or done; I own what is entered as my oath before your lordships; but I am not at all bound to say what does not at all concern this business. Besides, your Majesty, armed with your native goodness and innocence, will have no notion of how deep these men's devilish councils run, and what great men (whom you think your friends) are allied against you. And to show it you, I will name (though they torture me for it, as has been threatened) I will name those laypersons of quality who are to assume the great offices of the realm once your Majesty's government is destroyed and,' he turned to them, 'your lordships *butchered in your beds.* As, the Lord Arundell of Wardour is to be Lord Chancellor of England; the Lord Bellasis, Lord General of the Army; the Lord Powis, Lord Treasurer; the Lord Petre, Lieutenant-General; Sir Francis Ratcliffe, Major-General; Mr. Edward Coleman, Secretary of State – ay, this Mr. Coleman hath been the prime mover in the business of killing your Majesty, and this will be proved if you will be pleased to seize his papers –!'

Charles interposed sharply.

'You speak of my Lords Arundell and Bellasis. Those lords have served my father and myself faithfully for many

E

years; and I tell you that unless proofs against them are very clear, I will give no credit to them.' He stopped and considered. 'As for my Lord Bellasis, who is bedridden of gout and so infirm that he cannot keep his feet in any case – why, Mr. Oates, I do not think he was a good choice as Lord General of the Army.'

'Now God forbid,' cries Mr. Oates, standing a little and appealing to the roof, 'that I should accuse any man unjustly! I do not say they know it; only that they were to be acquainted with it. My lords, I am not ashamed of anything I have said or done, and I will own what is entered as my oath. . . .'

Charles rose impatiently. 'Well, gentlemen, do as you think fit,' says he. 'For my part, I call the fellow a lying knave.'

The councillors did not think so. Equipped with fresh warrants, that night for the second time Mr. Oates set out in the rain on a hue and cry of arresting Jesuits. First among his warrants was one for the arrest of Mr. Edward Coleman, and the seizure of his papers. This last precaution, the seizure of the papers, was nearly overlooked until the eager Danby remembered it, and sent Mr. Bradley, a king's messenger, flying after the escort with the warrant. Towards midnight buff-coats and steel caps came splashing with a lanthorn up to the door of Coleman's house behind Westminster Abbey, and woke the street in the name of the king. Coleman's wife, his secretary Jerome Boatman, and a minor secretary named Cattaway, were at supper. Mrs. Coleman, very white, declared that her husband was not at home. They scented the fact that he had gone into hiding; there was a look of haste and stir and overset about the house, Mr. Oates bawling out that some —— God-eater had warned him, and he had destroyed his papers. Mr. Oates, who when he had a free hand seemed less like a man than like a bad smell, hurried his bandy legs round the house sniffing for evidence. Upstairs, in the study, there was a find: some letters and documents in paper bags, which the messenger sealed up to take to the council. But this was not enough. It became evident that papers had been destroyed; but, in examining the fireplace for traces, they found a recess behind the chimney, which contained a bundle of letters in a deal box slightly nailed down. They might not contain any damaging matter, since they had been left behind when others were burnt. None the less, they were sealed up with the rest. Boatman the secretary, with the muzzle of a pistol at his ear, confessed that his master kept a large book of entries for his letters and news, which he had seen as recently as the day before. But the book could not be found. The matter lay beyond doubt: somebody had warned Coleman of his danger.

Mr. Oates's scouring-party had several Jesuits to clap into Newgate before morning, and they could not stop further. There was one sharp brush when they attempted to take Father Whitebread (or White), the Jesuit Provincial, at the house of the Spanish ambassador in the Strand. The servants of the Donnish dogs refused to let them in; baskethilts were whipped out, and there was a blind cut-and-slash on the steps before the doors were slammed and chained. Mr. Oates (who had hidden himself behind a buttress while the blades were playing) bawled out jeers when he saw the sergeant sucking a skewered wrist and cursing in the rain. When the old moustache turned on him, he hopped and lumbered back, bellowing that he would denounce the sergeant for a bloody Papist if he did not leave off. He himself, said Mr. Oates, had a pious horror of steel or firearms; he himself had been urged to murder the king, but he had refused on the plea that he was afraid to fire a gun. Then the party shouldered on, pulling Jesuits out of their burrows, and banging the town to alarm. . . .

A mile or so away, in a house on the south side of the little sylvan lane called Pall Mall, fiddles and harps were wandering into a more dreaming tune. The house was planted with lime-trees in front; its rear windows looked down over deep gardens, and beyond at the canal hid among trees in the green beauty of St. James's Park. Inside – from the satin supper-room with the portrait of the house's owner by Sir Peter Lely, to the upstairs room where stood the enormous bedstead gaudily crusted with silver ornaments

of kings' heads, crowns, eagles, slaves, cupids, and Jacob
Hall dancing on a rope of wirework – it was all a-rowdy. It
was littered with landskip fans, 'chaney' oranges at three-
pence each, old medicine-bottles, white satin petticoats, red
satin shoes for small 'Master Charles'; and in the cellar were
kidderkins of strong ale, as thick as the coaches and sedan-
chairs now waiting under flaring links outside the door.
For to-night Mistress Eleanor Gwyn was entertaining at
supper.

It was a notable thing, regarded with amusement by
Charles, that most of Nelly's most joyous friendships were
among high members of the Opposition Party. Her motives
were no more political in entertaining them than in eating
a China orange; she liked the flighty Duke of Buckingham,
she liked my Lord Dorset who had been her first protector,
and she tolerated my Lord Shaftesbury. Charles made no
protest. To the contrary, he found profit in having a place
to meet the enemy on a neutral field, and he knew that he
should find several of them here to-night. There came
Nelly herself, skittering and scampering down the oak stairs
in the candlelight. On the landing she stopped to drop
him a curtsy, holding wide the skirt of her lavender-
brocaded gown; then down she came bouncing the rest of
the steps, running up to him, furiously fanning her plump
face that was somewhat flushed with wine, and rattling on
breathlessly in her usual fashion.

'Charles, I hope I shall have your company at night, shall
I not? I have been utterly dismal since I have lost you,' says
she. 'I have a thousand merry conceits to tell you. My
lady mother has got the megrims again at Chelsey, and
must give up brandy for a whole week. The Mail has been
a dismal place since you were not there, and I have lost
Sir Carr Scrope, never to be recovered again, for he told me
he could not live always at this rate, and so began to be a
little uncivil, which I could not suffer from an ugly *baux
garsçon*. Brrh! Mr. Montagu is in town swearing against
my Lord Danby, and saying he will have his head in six
months. Our little James is gone into France; and pray
how is that fat whore, the Duchess of Portsmouth, and I

hear you have got a pox from her? I spit – so. Come upstairs, angel. My Lord Pembroke is here, who is a worse
ugly one, but I must suffer him for Bucks's sake. Mr. Shadwell is writing a new play. Our Charles remembers his
sarvice to you, but he is at school.'

From upstairs jigged a noise of fiddle-music; Nelly would
have brought the whole pack of fiddlers from the music-
house in Villiers Street, and would be plying them with
strong ale until they scarce knew one note from another.
The upstairs rooms were pretty well filled. The music was
in one, and in another a crowd playing at Basset, that new
game introduced by Madame de Mazarin: a craze of the
ladies, but with stakes so ruinous that in France it had been
altogether forbidden. Nelly led him to still another apart-
ment, a supper-room with a crystal blaze from the ceiling,
walls of white satin patterned in gold, and a great carven
chimneypiece. And the place was a nest of Opposition
men, several of whom flaunted their rosettes of the Green
Ribbon Club. Straddle-legged before the fire stood stout
boisterous Buckingham, in claret silks, with his rapier tilt-
ing up the skirt of his coat behind like the feathers of a
fighting-cock, and his double-chins drawn in for grave
oratory. On either side of him, their periwigs wagging,
stood Mr. Aaron Smith the lawyer and Mr. William Harbord the agitator. In a chair before the fire (permitted to
sit down in his Grace's presence, by reason of his great
stoutness) was wedged a jovial Falstaff of a fellow, all belly
and chuckles, as true a shaped drunkard as heart could
wish. Make way for

> 'Og from a treason-tavern rolling home
> Round as a globe and liquored every chink;
> Goodly and great he sails behind his link!'

Which was still descriptive though not yet written, since
Mr. Dryden (who wrote it) was still his friend. For this
man was Honest Tom Shadwell the playwright, the famous
playwright, whose comedies were applauded even more
loudly than those of Mr. Wycherley or Mr. Dryden; who
was patted on the head by great wits like my Lord Rochester

and Sir Charles Sedley; and who – now so altered, so sharp was the turn of political times – had already joined the Green Ribbon mutineers as poet of the opposition to the court. His presence was a portent. There he sat rolling, his periwig askew, smoking a long pipe and declaiming to nobody in particular.

'Egad!' roars Honest Tom. 'Let friend John write his *All for Love*; 'tis a noble work I grant you, and true tragedy. But what of comedy, gentlemen; I say, what of comedy, hey? I tell you that true comedy signifies more than the putting-out of candles, kicking down of tables, falling over joint-stools, impossible accidents and unnatural mistakes (which the poetasters absurdly call plot). 'Tis the opinion of the best poets that the story of a play ought to be carried on by working up of scenes naturally; by design, not accidents. I have endeavoured to do it in this play I am writing now; and I doubt not but the scene in the second act, wherein Lady Busy would persuade Isabella to be kept, will live when the stuff of such scribblers shall be consumed in groceryware, tobacco, bandboxes, and hat-cases, and erased out of the memory of man – I do indeed! Eh? Whist, gentlemen, whist for God's sake! Here's his Majesty. . . .'

Charles sauntered in among them, and stopped the genuflexions. 'No, no,' says he; 'in Nelly's house let us make our usual pretence that I am not here, and that I do not overhear anything you say.' He bowed to Buckingham. 'Your servant, George. Your servant, gentlemen.'

Buckingham regarded him with heavy and grinning indolence, teetering before the fire. Yet you might feel that there was uneasiness in this room, uneasiness and tension in no more than the rustle of brocades or the creak of a buckled shoe. It may have been the silence.

'The Father of his people,' says Buckingham, with ponderous gallantry, 'is always welcome in a nursery of good patriots. We were about to drink your health.'

'Will *you* drink my health, my lord?' says the king, turning towards the sideboard across the room.

My Lord Shaftesbury was there, leaning one elbow on the sideboard. In contrast to Mr. Shadwell's exuberance, he was cool with a coolness which moved and stirred and was alive in the flushed room. But the pigmy body looked very withered, looked very old. His long confinement in the Tower seemed to have sharpened his long features, and made larger and more watchful his eyes. King Charles saw, with a curious surprise, that he now wore a faint fluff of moustache, like a boy's down, on the clever, suspicious face. As thought to flaunt his principles in the same way that the brittle arm would shake a sword, he wore a green surcoat and pantaloons. There was no change in his great flaxen periwig. But it was the agile intelligence which peered out of heavy-lidded eyes, moved, and was dangerous.

Just beside him stood his young friend Philip Herbert, Earl of Pembroke. Pembroke was as big as Shaftesbury was little; Pembroke was as dark as Shaftesbury was fair; Pembroke was as drunken as Shaftesbury was sober, for this young roysterer frequently had no notion of what he had been doing for days at a time. They were two subjects for a painter, against the white satin walls and the massed silver of the sideboard. But it was the little man who took the eye: one hand on a glass of barley-water, the other hand making play with a lace handkerchief.

'Will *you* drink my health, my lord?' says the king.

It appeared that the other gentlemen breathed freer, if more noisily, when my Lord Shaftesbury smiled with great gallantry, and lifted his glass.

'I am permitted only barley-water,' he answered. 'Lodgings in the Tower are not good for gout. But what a loyal patriot may drink, I do drink, with all my heart.'

'Damme, but you have the right of it!' suddenly bawled out my Lord Pembroke, slapping his sword-hilt and almost on the point of blubbering. It was difficult to tell whether this young man's crooked brain, sunk in a bath of liquor, would move towards tears or violence. '*I* was in the Tower too, rot my guts but I was! *I* was in the Tower once myself, bound over to keep the peace; I was in the Tower twice, now I think of it, but his Majesty let me out. I forgive him; there's only one man I don't forgive, rot me! Drink his health, I say. Here, damme, let's drink it kneeling!'

'You will not fare so well next time,' says Charles sharply.
He turned to Shaftesbury. 'Come, my lord, I am glad to see
we may meet as friends,' says he in the same easy pleasant
tone. 'These are troubled times, as I do not need to remind
you. They tell me you Green Ribboners set a good table at
the "King's Head". I hope you are not cooking any new
dish for me?'

'Hath any man,' says Shaftesbury in an equally low tone,
'ever attacked my principles, or said that I did not believe
in them?'

'Never, my lord, except when you are pleased to call them
ideals.'

'Yet they are ideals,' says the other, calmly, 'notwithstanding. I tell your Majesty that the day will come when this
people of yours shall be truly free, free in thought and free
in action, and even the worms shall feed on good earth. The
day will come when no holy oil shall anoint you sweeter
than any of your subjects; nor a stoat-skin robe and a pound
of diamonds hide the truth that you are even as other men.
Your breast is as amenable to daggers as mine or Tam o'
Bedlam's; your own barber could cut your throat any morning, when he shaves you; and therefore why should your
hand have more power in the state than the barber's, or
snatch up a larger portion of bread and cheese? The day
is not yet; but it will come.'

'It has come, my lord, and gone. We heard this talk in
'41, when both of us were boys. And this I should like to
know: in the new day, what becomes of you and your kind?'

'I and my kind will govern,' replied Shaftesbury, with
complete simplicity. 'Because we are not kings, but the
law-makers.' He smiled, brilliantly. 'However, you asked
me of our affairs at the Green Ribbon Club. Now bear
witness that it was not *I* who first spoke of this topic. It was
not *I* who first lugged out and cried, "Guard!" Or. if you
will put the matter in terms of cookery: parliament meets
on the 21st of October. Then we shall see what dishes are
set out. . . . I hear that there is a great noise being made at
Whitehall just now, of a Jesuit plot discovered, or the like?'

'You will know what I think of it,' says King Charles with

great gravity, 'when I tell you that I mean to go to Newmarket the day after to-morrow, and forget the business
altogether. What does your lordship think of it?'

He picked up an orange. Shaftesbury regarded him with
a pale smirk. 'I care just *that* for it,' cries he, contemptu-
ously, and tossed up his handkerchief. 'Your Majesty is
right. The thing is a contrivance of the Earl of Danby – all
of it – and I wonder he can make use of such poor strate-
gems. There may be those who can demonstrate that my
Lord Danby is not such an honest patriot as he would have
us believe; and he sows this false scent to lead them off.'

Charles tossed back the orange into the bowl. 'Now I
confess I had not thought of that,' he said, with sleepy
admiration. 'So you do not credit the plot, or wish to cry
it up? I applaud your good sense, my lord.'

He blessed the company ceremoniously, wheeled round,
and sauntered out with Nelly chattering on his arm: dark
and cryptic as ever, humming the tune of the fiddles. My
Lord Shaftesbury remained in the same place, and gently
dabbed his lips with the lace handkerchief. He appeared
very thoughtful when Buckingham and Mr. William
Harbord went uneasily to him.

'Now there,' says Shaftesbury in the same easy tone,
'there walks the second most black-hearted rougue who
ever –'

'Hush, my lord, for God's sake!' cries even the irrespon-
sible Buckingham, and seized his arm. 'If someone
should –'

'And this is the glass I drank from,' continued the other,
taking it up from the sideboard. Suddenly he flung it down
on the floor and smashed it; then the high sharp shoe-heel
of his sound foot pounded and dug at the pieces. He did
all this without apparent fury, except for the blood in his
shrunken face, or the great starved look of his eyes.

'What did you speak of?' asked Buckingham, very plainly
disturbed. 'The plot, beyond doubt?'

My lord was restless. 'Ay, the plot. I told him I gave it
no credit, and that I would not try to push it. I do not
think he was such a cull as to believe me. We have been

sent a gift from heaven, gentlemen,' says he, almost tenderly, 'and before that heaven I swear to you I will make Mr. Titus Oates the saviour of the nation. Draw your swords, gentlemen!' cries my lord, stung and shaken to exultation. 'Draw your sw—, or no; perhaps you had better not; but think of drawing 'em; *think* of drawing 'em! That's the thing. If Mr. Oates lies, we must cover up his lies as well as we may, or suggest others. The sign has come that all high-principled men have looked for; I have a mighty work to do before I die, and now, by the splendour of God, I will fry these Popish hogs in their own grease. Let my Lord Treasurer Danby cry up the plot as much as he likes. I'll cry louder, my good Bucks. I'll cry louder.'

II

Within a week the cry swelled through London. If Shaftesbury looked for a sign from heaven, he appeared to get it. On the following morning, September 30th, Mr. Edward Coleman, hearing that there was a warrant out against him, voluntarily surrendered himself to Sir Joseph Williamson. He was ordered before the council in the afternoon. Mr. Coleman had already sent a private message to the French ambassador: 'Be easy; there will be nothing found in my papers to embarrass me.' He faced the council with such angry openness and apparent truth that a few people had doubts. These doubts were strengthened in the afternoon – a grey afternoon, so that candles were brought into the room – when Coleman was confronted with Oates before the council-board.

'Do you know this gentleman, Mr. Oates?' asked the Clerk of the Council.

'No, my lords, I do not know him; I never saw him before,' said Oates, and went on to other matters.

When, presently, the name of the gentleman was conveyed to him, Oates burst out whining that his sight was bad by candlelight; that Coleman was cunningly altered in habit and wig; and that he himself was so weak and ill with running up and down two nights after Jesuits that he scarce

knew what he was doing or saying. For he recognised
Coleman well enough, declared Oates, as soon as he heard
the man speak. So far his charges against Coleman
amounted to the specific one that Coleman had paid Sir
George Wakeman, the queen's physician, £5,000 for poisoning the king; and the cloudy general one that 'if Mr. Coleman's papers are searched, there will be found that in them
which will cost him his neck'. The council hesitated.
Coleman, with his wasted blazing face and nervous hands,
looked like a plotter; he had the air; he was a known Papist;
and they believed Mr. Oates. But Coleman spoke like an
honest man. For the moment they did not commit him to
Newgate, though a blank warrant was drawn up; they committed him to the care of a messenger, until his papers
should be examined.

Neither, for the moment, was Sir George Wakeman imprisoned. He underwent a similar experience: summoned
before the council and confronted with Oates, the latter
declared he had never seen this man before. Afterwards
Oates cried the same excuses of weakness and bad eyesight.
But the plot had caught on; it was being shouted through
the town in thickening rumours. Then a committee of
the council began to examine Coleman's letters – and the
town exploded.

Coleman was done for: you might see him already on his
way to the rope, the disembowelling knife, and the quartering-block. Judged through the fears of the time, the contents of those letters amounted to high treason. In the
paper bags and the deal box were found about two hundred
letters, notably a very wild and very insane correspondence
between Coleman and Father La Chaise in France, and
Cardinal Albani, the Papal Internuncio at Rome. The letters were all dated between June 1674, and September 1676;
later correspondence, it was evident, must have been hurriedly destroyed. The remaining letters were written in
cipher, and might have baffled the council if Coleman had
not considerately left the key to the cipher among them.
Even so, all these dark references to 'trees' and 'gardeners'
and 'the East India Company' caused confusion for some

weeks, evolving terrible images in the minds of the readers.

The letters showed no such plot as Oates claimed, or any thought of one. But they did show that Coleman had been scheming indiscreetly, with a feverishness which annoyed those whose cause he was advancing, to advance the Catholic religion in England. First it was to be done by bribery of the king, so that the Duke of York might be pushed forward (with Mr. Coleman as master of ceremonies, a sad piece of grandiloquence), and then the dissolving of the anti-Catholic parliament with French gold. But it was the ranting wildness of some of his phrases which stung the council to alarm.

'We have here,' Coleman had written to La Chaise in the autumn of 1675, 'a mighty work upon our hands, no less than the conversion of three kingdoms, and by that perhaps the utter subduing of a pestilent heresy which has domineered a long time over a great part of this northern world. There never were such hopes of success since the death of our Queen Mary, as now in our days; when God has given us a prince,' – *i.e.*, *the Duke of York* – 'who has become (may I say a miracle?) zealous of being the author and instrument of so glorious a work. But the opposition we are sure to meet with is also like to be great, so that it imports us to get all the aid and assistance we can, for the harvest is great, and the labourers but few. That which we rely on most, next to God Almighty's providence and the favour of my master the Duke, is the mighty mind of his most Christian Majesty,' – *i.e.*, *Louis the Fourteenth* – whose generous soul inclines him to great undertakings. So I hope you will pardon me, if I be very troublesome to you on this occasion. I must confess I think his Christian Majesty's temporal interest is so much attracted to that of his Royal Highness (which temporal interest can never be great, except upon the growth and advancement of the Catholic religion) that his ministers cannot give him better advice, even in a political sense, than that of Our Blessed Lord: "Go seek first the kingdom of heaven, and the righteousness thereof, that all other things may be added unto him." '

That letter alone might have hanged any man. No bogy

was omitted, even to the mention of that bogy called Bloody Mary. With such a name cherished in glory, none of the council-members could have any doubt that the subduing of the pestilent heresy would be done with pincers and bonfires. If you listened well, you might hear the sharpening of Popish knives. Now every cloudy parable in Coleman's words became full of danger. The king had gone off carelessly to Newmarket; Coleman was hustled to Newgate; and Oates stood confirmed. As not infrequently happens, the fool had confirmed the liar.

The town went into fits. On every mouth was the challenge: '*What! Is there a plot or no?*' when anyone was disposed to ask prying questions 'What, is there a plot or no: or are you a bloody Papist, to deny it?' One lawyer noted gloomily that a man might have denied Christ with less contest than the plot. Mr. Evelyn, himself half-believing, wrote in his diary: 'Oates is encouraged, and everything he affirms taken for gospel.' Great times had come for Titus Oates and Israel Tonge. They were lodged in Whitehall under a guard to protect them from Popish murderers, and to keep them at hand so that they might themselves protect his Majesty's life with fresh discoveries. Mr. Oates had begun to strut in a clergyman's habit: silk gown and cassock, and great shovel-hat. He was now giving out that he was Doctor Titus Oates, created so by the University of Salamanca in Spain. Doctor Oates's conversation, it is true, turned some men's stomachs; for he did not swear as honest human beings swear, with good Anglo-Saxon oaths; he merely took up kennel-filth, rolled it into his talk in a casual sort of way, and flung it in your face; and if you did not like it, he pointed that finger of his: 'You're a Papist; I'll remember you!' That bustling divine, Dr. Gilbert Burnet, went to call on Tonge and Oates at Whitehall. He found little Tonge so lifted up and exalted that he seemed to have lost the little sense he had. Then Oates poked his blue face into the room.

'Oates came in,' Dr. Burnet later told his friend Adam Angus, 'and made me a compliment: that I was one that was marked out to be killed. He had before said the same to Stillingfleet of him; but he made the honour too cheap when he said that Tonge was to be served in the same manner because he had translated *The Jesuits' Morals*. He broke out into a great fury against the Jesuits, and said he would have their blood. To divert him from that strain, I asked him what were the arguments that prevailed on him to change his religion, and go over to the Church of Rome. Upon that, he stood up, and laid his hands on his breast, and said, God and His holy angels knew he had never changed; but that he had gone among them on purpose to betray them.'

But Oates's rich days were only beginning. The fever on men's minds alternately quickened and sank during the first twelve days of October. During those twelve days – a critical time, as too many people afterwards remembered – all his friends observed that there was something wrong with Sir Edmund Godfrey.

He had never, of course, been of a boisterous or genial turn. Even when he took a little relaxation, by going into the country to spend a few days at Windsor, he did not mingle with the local gentry or take exercise with them on the bowling-green. He played bowls with someone's foot-man, and with the man who rolled the green. 'I cannot get along in your company!' cries he, to a friend who remon-strated. 'I bowl and exercise with those people so that I may run up and down, and recover myself, and do what I can to divert this cursed melancholy fit –!'

But now, since Oates's revelations, it was observed that he looked more black and gaunt than he had ever looked before, stumping along the kennels and muttering to him-self over something that gnawed at his mind. People made way quickly to give him the wall. It was known that he had taken Oates's depositions, and they pointed and whis-pered that there walked a man in danger from the Papists. It was not known (what very few people knew) that, as soon as he received the depositions, he had hurried to warn Mr. Edward Coleman of the danger; he had shown Coleman the articles, and given him a copy to take to the Duke of York.

Still, it was said he had dropped a few remarks indicating

that he did not believe in the plot. It was observed that he seemed to make no move in the business, to investigate or press the charges against the Catholics, as his duty was in his magistrate's capacity. If he had not been known as so honest a justice, the cry of Popery might have been raised against him. As it was, he was thought to go in terror of being stabbed by the Pope's murder-men.

For beyond doubt he went in fear of something, perhaps several things. To Dr. Burnet, whom he met in the street, he said suddenly that he believed he should be knocked on the head. When he was pressed to get a good servant to attend him in his walks, he could only talk querulously of the idle habits of servants in London; and how they got into ill company from attending their masters. He was walking with an old schoolfellow of his, Mr. Thomas Robinson, and Mr. Robinson was questioning him in a guarded fashion about the depositions, when Godfrey roused himself out of his absent staring and wiping his mouth. 'We have not sounded the bottom of this business yet,' growls he. 'Upon my conscience, I believe I shall be the first martyr. I do not fear them, if they come fairly! No, and I shall not part with my life tamely. . . .'

Mr. Robinson, though he forbore to question further, assumed that Sir Edmund referred to the Papists. But it was in his own home that his disturbance showed most, in a restlessness, a burning of papers in the grate, a counting of money. Mrs. Judith Pamphlin, his housekeeper, noticed it. So did Mr. Henry Moor, his old clerk. So did Elizabeth Curtis, the maidservant. Above all, it caused concern to his favourite cousin, Mrs. Mary Gibbon, who came to fuss over him (with her home-made jellies) and rebuke him for his bad health. Thus, finding him drinking whey with brown bread in it, she bursts out: 'Sir, I make jellies for you one day, and you drink whey another.' Whereat he pushed the spoon one way, and the bowl another, and muttered something about his father's melancholy being upon him.

But it was to Mrs. Mary Gibbon that he came, in the dusk of a Tuesday in October, when the autumn winds blew hard. She lived in Old Southampton Buildings, thrusting up against the pleasant gardens of Staple Inn, with a court leading in from Holborn on one side and Chancery Lane on another.   There was already a sick-room smell in the house, for Mrs. Gibbon's mother was dying there, and the family had gathered round the bed.   Justice Godfrey called her out of the room, so great was his desire to speak with her alone, and took her up into another room. Although it was nearly dusk, some little light came through the small-paned window and the sooty drizzle over the chimney-pots outside: and she could see that he was bolting the door behind him.   Then he turned round.

'Have you heard,' says he, with his old abruptness, 'that I am to be hanged?'

'Now God ha' mercy!' says Mrs. Gibbon, and felt her heart turn over within her.   For a moment (being a stout common-sense gentlewoman, in her matron's neat hood, and having troubles of her own besides) she wondered whether he jested; but she was quickly disabused.   He stood looking at her fixedly and terribly in the twilight, breathing hard, his hands snake-veined; and she could hear the window-frame rattling to the din of wagons and street cries along Holborn.

'Hadn't you heard I was to be hanged?' he demanded again.   'Hadn't you?   All the town is in an uproar about me.'

'But for what?'

'Hanged by the government.   I took Oates's and Tonge's examinations; but, all this time, though I have often since been at dinner at my Lord Chancellor's, and at Sir William Jones's – that is the Attorney-General – I have never told *them* about the plot, or divulged it.   That is why I am like to be –'

'What plot?' inquired Mrs. Gibbons, who was a matter-of-fact lady.   She thought one of his fits had come back on him again; she would have soothed him.   But he only looked at her, and then looked out of the window.

'No matter,' says he.   'No matter.   It may come to nothing. Oates has forsworn himself; Oates is a liar; it may come to nothing.'

She was called away at that minute, and he took his own leave, saying in a rambling way that he would return to tell her more. She sympathised with him, but there was her mother a-dying, and all this worrit and dither about plots passed her by. Godfrey opened himself more freely to one of his most intimate friends, Mr. Thomas Wynnel, a few days later.

They were going (as Mr. Wynnel later remembered) about some legal business, to see a counsellor at law who lived near the Temple Gate. They turned out of Harts-horn Lane into the Strand; but in the Strand – or beyond it into Fleet Street, or thence up into the darkest City – you might shout secrets at the top of your lungs and never be overheard, because of the cries of the street-hawkers. From here to farthest Eastcheap, under the painted gables, rolled a din of barter and brawling. 'Flounders! Who'll buy my flounders! Two a groat and three for sixpence!' 'Lily-white vinegar, lily-white vinegar!' They cried rotten fruit, jars of usquebaugh, and scrofulous-looking sausages. They hawked mackerel and rosemary, and their voices rose harsh as the clank of passing-bells out of the sooty dimness. 'Have you,' bawls a tinker, after furiously banging on a brass kettle with a stick, 'have you a brass pot, iron pot, skillet, kettle, or frying-pan to mend?' – and overhead the shop-signs, painted, gilded, carven to great goblin shapes, swung and banged in the wind, in tune to the crash of coach-wheels on the cobbles. A philosopher might find music in the note of the pig-killer's horn, or a pleasant melancholy at hearing the dirge of that sad and solemn voice in which you were asked whether you had any chairs to mend. It was the poetry (or, if you like, the inferno) of London, which drove countrymen and foreigners mad. For no sooner were you quit of this din after dark, and attempting to sleep, when, ecod! out clash and clang the funeral bells to wake you up; and at two in the morning the bellman comes a-dinning under your window, shouting dismal rhymes; and after him people with tooting instruments to serenade other people, worse than the noise they make at the playhouse when they flourish for an entrance of witches.

F

All this restlessness, all the black looks of the mobile, centred round Somerset House in the Strand. Somerset House was the residence of the Popish Queen Catherine, the nest of bold and busy Papists, where mass was heard openly in the queen's chapel. Mr. Thomas Wynnel and Sir Edmund Godfrey passed Somerset House on that prophetic morning walk. It was a vast stone palace, covering many acres. It fronted on the street with a line of stone pillars built round a spacious square court; behind this were other courts, connected by stairs of freestone, and descending by terraces and staircases to the deep gardens along the river below. About these gardens hung gloom and beauty: the beauty of fountains and statues, the gloom of thick foliage shadowing little cracked stairs when a mist rose off the river. To the people in the Strand outside those masking pillars, it was a place of dread: even in the echo that haunted the gardens. From the Strand there were only two entrances into the palace.[1] One was the main entrance, through the great centre court. The other was a large gate at the western end of the long line of pillars, abutting on the Savoy. This latter gate, with a wicket in it, was called (for some reason) the 'Water-Gate'. It did not lead to any water-gate; it led down a flight of steps into a railed courtyard round which were the queen's stables, storerooms, and coach-houses, with houses belonging to minor officials of the palace.

Sir Edmund Godfrey's companion was slightly acquainted with Henry Berry, the Porter or Keeper of the Water-Gate; and stout Berry pulled off his hat to him as they passed. Since the rising of the unrest, the guards about the place had been doubled. There was a sentry at every door, and a company of foot-guards lodged inside. Outside the Main Gate, from the middle of the street, the tall Maypole with its gilded crown and vane towered up into the smoke; and below the cobbles rang to the tread of red-sleeved sentries in breastplates, their pikes on their shoulders, pacing before the long grey line of pillars.

[1] If the reader is following this narrative as a detective story, he is urged to remember these details. They will become important.

'They take precautions too, it seems,' said Mr. Wynnel. (One, two, three, four, five, six, *chump*! turn!) 'I wonder how the Popish lords fare? All the talk yesterday was of the lords – Arundell, Bellasis, Petre, Powis, and Stafford – who were to have the high places of government after the king's throat is cut. Come, sir! Sure the lords could not be such fools as to think of such a thing? What power has the Pope in such and such a case?'

Justice Godfrey looked down. 'No; he has none. The lords are as innocent as you or I. Coleman will die, but not the lords.'

'Coleman!' says the other violently. 'There is matter for wonder in that. They say Coleman was forewarned, and destroyed his papers. Granted; but, if you admit it, then why did not the man destroy *all* his papers? Sure a man does not "overlook" two hundred letters. They say there must have been that which was damnable in the letters he made away with, and doubtless they say true. But why did he leave all this talk of crushing out pestilent heresies, enough to hang a bench of bishops? – and, in sober truth, what could he have writ that would be worse? You say Coleman will die. If so, where are we then?'

'Oates is sworn and is perjured,' cried the magistrate doggedly, and struck his cane on the cobbles.

'Speak the truth! Tell me the meaning of that.'

'Why, the Jesuits have consults about a toleration for them; nothing against the king. But there is a design against the Duke of York,' says Sir Edmund cryptically, 'and this will come to a dispute among them. You may live to see an end on't, but I shall not. This much I tell you: I am master of a secret, a dangerous secret, and it will be fatal to me. My security in the business was Oates's deposition. Before Oates came to me, he first declared it to be a public minister; and then Oates came to me by that minister's direction. And then again – but no matter!'

The words puzzled his companion at the time; and afterwards, when he came to give his testimony on oath, he still did not understand them. They have never been fully explained. But Mr. Wynnel remembered his friend strid-ing rapidly, with the black mood on him, but still a strong and hearty and kindly old man.

Two days later – on Saturday, the 12th of October, 1678 – Sir Edmund Godfrey left his house early in the morning, and was never again seen alive.

III

The evidence about that Saturday was confused and misted; too many tougues clacking, too many ways for a man to die. But what most impressed his household was The Letter. It was as though affairs took a sharp, ugly turn, and there came probing a new finger of danger that had not hitherto presented itself to Godfrey's bemused mind. Mrs. Pamphlin the housekeeper and Elizabeth Curtis the maid-servant both took notice, and were affrighted afterwards, about that Letter.[1]

The Letter was delivered to Sir Edmund on Friday, October 11th, as he sat by the parlour fire. It was delivered at the door from the hand of a private messenger who was seen by Elizabeth Curtis, Mrs. Pamphlin, and Mrs. Pamph-lin's daughter. The messenger stayed for an answer, out-side in the passage. Sir Edmund opened the letter and read it. Afterwards he remained shading his eyes with his hand, and staring at the fire in a wild, troubled fashion before he roused himself. He refused to give an answer. 'Tell him I don't know what to make of it,' says he, and hastily threw the letter into the fire. He did know what to make of it. It marks the turn. From this point onwards he was no longer sunk in mazy forebodings without a name. He was

---

[1] Lest it should be thought that too much is being made of this letter, it will presently be demonstrated – by a note written from Newgate by one of the suspects – that Godfrey's household considered this letter to be the key to the whole affair. Also important will be the outburst of Elizabeth Curtis at the trial of the accused men, over a point on which she had not even been questioned. Any murder-investigation must begin at home. It has always seemed curious to me that in this case the testimony of the man's household, those who lived with him and saw him clearest, has been so strangely overlooked. Because so many public issues were involved, it does not follow that the man had no private feelings or private life. But this is not, gentlemen and connoisseurs in murder, to anticipate.

looking on a tangible warning of his end, and he showed it in his behaviour.

The grave is dug; this man is going to die. He now moves, and speaks, and opens his waistcoat to warm his grizzled breast at the fire, but *we* know that he will be very cold presently. Perhaps he thinks there may be a way out of it, a coin-spin chance for his life, but we know that he is already moving towards the ditch on Primrose Hill. Thenceforward we can watch the shadows closing around him, and mark each minute by the Dutch clock, and measure every falling sand. For some men must die, that other men may feel pleased with themselves. Mark what the stubborn narrow-mind does, as soberly and heavily as once he walked into a plague-house to collar a felon, or as once he defied a king for thirty pounds.

He went that Friday evening to a meeting of the vestry-men at the Church of St. Martin's-in-the-Field, of which he was 'the mouth'. There he took aside the churchwarden who kept the parish accounts, requiring the settlement of some debts which he owed the parish, and the parish owed him. After the meeting he went with the parish-officers to the house of Mr. Welden: the same house where, two weeks earlier, he had met Coleman to show him Oates's depositions. Though he seemed more agitated than the company had ever known him – insisting on flinging off his coat despite the cold weather, and talking heavily of his conscience – he was at the same time more careful, more dogged, more soberly determined. He meticulously settled up each debt, and breathed deep afterwards. When Mr. Welden the host pressed him to dine there next day, saying that their mutual friend Mr. Wynnel would be present, he answered like a duellist on the eve of a meeting: 'I may be able to come. I cannot tell, yet,' says he grimly, 'whether I shall.' He did not mutter. On the contrary, it was the harsh voice: 'You ask what news? Why, I'll tell ye: in a short time you will hear of the death of somebody.' When they saw that this was some close danger bearing down, and they urged him not to go abroad next day except in company, his reply grated with harsh arrogance: 'I want no company. I fear nobody.' It was idle defiance. The Dutch clock had already ticked off a few hours less to live.

He went home that night, where he burned an armful of papers in the parlour grate. Until late the household (as restless as himself over this new development) heard him tumbling over his trunks and boxes, tramping endlessly up and down. The next morning, Saturday, he was up much earlier than usual. He put on his customary flannel waistcoat, black breeches, black stockings, and buckled shoes; and he adjusted the white linen band round his neck. He put on his good rings and his silver-hilted sword. After some troubled hesitation, as though debating two courses, he put into his pockets a very large sum of money: seven guineas, four broad-pieces, and four pounds in silver. Then – being in the parlour – he called to Mr. Moor, his clerk, to help him into his new camlet coat. But after he had put it on, and adjusted the black periwig on his head, he changed his mind.

'No, take this coat off,' says he grimly. 'I'll wear the old camlet coat. It will serve the day well enough!'

He carefully put on his broad-brimmed hat with the gold band, and the clerk handed him his cane and gloves. Then he went down the path to the gate in the little yard giving on Hartshorn Lane, very tall and stooped in that wet day. 'And at the gate,' ran Henry Moor's clipped testimony afterwards, 'going out of the yard into the lane, he suddenly stopped, and turned himself towards this deponent, and looked seriously upon him, as if he would have said something to this deponent; and in that posture stood a small time, but immediately went his way, not speaking to this deponent; and after that time this deponent never saw him alive.'

When he did not return to the house that night, the alarm of the household grew, although he *might* have spent the night with his mother in Hammersmith. That letter had contained either a notice of personal danger, or some threat which impelled him to suicide. Murder or suicide was in the air: while handling such gloomy thoughts, men usually incline to the first belief, and women to the second. But it was not alone their own disturbance. As Saturday wore on, all over town there were flying curious half-rumours whose source no one could trace, sometimes only a wink and a nod in a coffee-house, sometimes a hint on 'Change: 'Godfrey is missing.' It was incredible; at that time, it would seem, not even his own household could have known he would not return; yet it was true. In Saturday's post, news-letters took into the country the same rumour: 'Godfrey is missing.' From 'Garraway's' off Cornhill to the 'Greyhound' off Charing Cross, the rustle over the long pipes and drinking-jacks was, 'Where is Godfrey? He has not been seen at his house all this day; they say he is murdered by the Papists.'

On Sunday old Henry Moor hurried out to the house of Godfrey's mother at Hammersmith, to find that he was not there. Then he communicated with Sir Edmund's two brothers, Michael and Benjamin Godfrey, who lived in the City. There was a familiar family scene. 'God have mercy on us, I pray we hear good news of him!' The brothers inclined to the belief that he was deeply in debt, and had hidden himself away to escape creditors. They did not believe, or like to believe, that his melancholy had driven him to suicide; for in that event his estate would be forfeited to the Crown. All day Sunday and Monday they searched for him: especially at Mrs. Mary Gibbon's house, declaring that he *must* have stayed the night there. 'He is not here; why should I deny it, if it were otherwise?' Mrs. Pamphlin wept, and Brother Michael cried out that they were ruined. But the counsel of the brothers was the counsel of respectability, which is the same in any age: Hush, hush, keep all things dark. Keep all things dark, while the town was caterwauling with rumour, and the very watermen called reports to each other when their boats passed on the Thames. On Tuesday, October 15th, the brothers had the disappearance publicly announced at a big funeral on the steps of St. Martin's-in-the-Field. It was out.

By Tuesday the great Plot, which had been sickening a little due to certain ugly truths bruited about concerning 'Dr. Titus Oates', was refreshed again. On Tuesday and

Wednesday every sort of conjecture ran hourly. Godfrey was found: he had suddenly married a lady of fortune, and had been found in bed with her. No, he had been found fuddled in an ale-house, in bed with a drab. No, he had gone overseas to escape his creditors. No, he had killed himself. But these rumours were small and contemptible as compared with the great burden: '*The Papists have made away with him.*' Bewildered Catholics walked in fear while each fresh rumour was circulated as to just where the great magistrate had last been seen in life. He had last been seen at the Cockpit in St. James's Park, the Earl of Danby's residence, which made even that good Protestant shake in his harness. He had been seen at Arundell House, the Catholic Duke of Norfolk's residence. He had been seen at St. James's Palace. He had even been seen at the royal palace at Whitehall; he had been seen anywhere and wherever you like, but where was he?

In this muddle, the source of the original rumour about his disappearance was lost. Afterwards Mr. Welden, who had invited Sir Edmund to dine with him on the Saturday, thought that it had been started by the brothers of the missing man – Messrs. Michael and Benjamin Godfrey. He stated that the brothers had happened to call on him on Saturday morning; that he had mentioned Sir Edmund's wild apprehensions of the night before; and that the brothers had cried, 'The Papists have been watching for him for a long time, and now we are confident that they have got him.' (These brothers always seem to speak as 'we', like the Cheerybles or the Siamese twins.) Others, however, could not believe that such a casual exclamation, uttered in the obscure home of Mr. Welden at York Buildings, could have swept from mouth to mouth until it was all over London before evening. These others had a more startling explanation as to the origin of the rumour. Be that as it may, for the moment: let us keep away from useless confusion. During those mysterious five days, Saturday to Wednesday, there was nothing but mad conjecture.

About two o'clock on the afternoon of Thursday, October 17th, a worthy Scottish curate named Adam Angus was browsing through a book-shop in St. Paul's Churchyard. Across from him the great scaffolding had begun to go up round that new St. Paul's which Sir Christopher Wren was building, to replace the fire-gutted ruin of the old, and the shop lay in its shadow. The day was miry, the light bad, and Mr. Angus in his gown and shovel-hat was standing close to the window. He was bending over the counter to read some printed papers there, when someone clapped him on the shoulder from behind. A young man in a grey-coloured suit – Mr. Angus, to his knowledge, had never seen the man before – was poking his head through the door, and looking upon him as though exultantly. 'Have you heard the news?' says this man. 'What news?' 'Sir Edmund Berry Godfrey is found,' says the other. 'He has been found in Leicester Fields, at the Dead Wall, with his own sword run through him.'

Then the man was gone, with the same abruptness. Mr. Angus, 'discovering himself surpris'd', as he relates, stared a moment distractedly before he tumbled out into the street; but the man had disappeared. There was nothing outside but the trudging figures, the cries, the hell-carts struggling up Ludgate Hill in the rain. It was all the more ghostly because the curate's friend Mr. Oswald, who was in the shop with him, had not seen the man or heard a word. Yet the matter seemed of such urgency that Mr. Angus bundled the skirts of his gown into a coach, and hurried off to tell the news to his omniscient clerical friend Dr. Burnet. For Leicester Fields was a very fashionable square of noblemen's town-houses, with pleasant gardens in the centre where fashionable gentlemen could fight duels by moonlight. Dr. Burnet communicated with another prominent clergyman, Dr. Lloyd, who in turn dispatched a servant to Sir Edmund Godfrey's house to ask whether or no they had heard it. They had not heard. But the murder was out before midnight.

Late that evening, a convivial company drinking the soot-black delicacy at Mrs. Duke's Coffee-House, next to Northumberland House, heard a body of horsemen clatter into Hartshorn Lane. Word went up to the coffee-room that these were constable's men, and that there was news of Godfrey. When the company tumbled downstairs to hear, they found two of the constables sitting outside on muddy horses under the flare of a link, while the others rode on down the street to the magistrate's house. The news was true. Godfrey had been found; but not in Leicester Fields. His body had been found in a ditch at the foot of Primrose Hill – a piece of country waste-land some three miles out of town – with his own sword through his heart.

They did not, know, at the moment, that the sword had been thrust through the body of a man already dead from being strangled.

III

'THE ENGLISH NATION ARE A SOBER PEOPLE'

The Terror

'It is not possible to imagine what a ferment the artifice of some, and the real belief and fear of others, put the two Houses of Parliament and the greatest part of the nation into.'

SIR JOHN RERESBY, *Memoirs.*

'One might have denied Christ with less contest than the plot. . . . It is not easy to imagine what a consternation, as well as fury, this spectacle,' the parade with Godfrey's body, 'caused in the minds of the common people. . . . The crowd was prodigious, both at the procession and in and about the church; and so heated that anything called Papist, were it a cat or dog, had probably gone to pieces in a moment.'

ROGER NORTH, *Examen.*

'The wished occasion of the Plot he takes,
Some circumstances finds, but more he makes.'

JOHN DRYDEN, of Shaftesbury,
Absalom and Achitophel

I

ABOUT the middle of that Thursday afternoon, two men were crossing the desolate waste at the foot of Primrose Hill, to drink something warm at the White House Inn in St. John's Wood. Towards the north, the great slope of the hill rose far on a grey sky; some distance away to the south was the small village of Paddington, with Paddington woods; and far away down to the east, if you cared to go up the hill in the teeth of the wind, you might make out the gables of London. There were shaggy farmhouses in the brown valley, hooded in trees with the hues of autumn; the line of Mary-bone Conduit, the lean shape of Tyburn gallows on the road to Oxford; and, far to the south, the Great West Road where three times a week the six-horse Flying Coaches galloped to Bath and Bristol. It was good land, rich land, except for this waste ground over which the two men stumbled now. A place of thickets, with no life except the bushes and brambles and a few trees; surrounded with closes; fenced in by high mounds and ditches; with no roads near except some deep miry lanes made for the convenience of driving cows, and these lanes not coming within five hundred yards of the place; swept by the east wind, with curious patches of green grass in the brown.

The two men were John Walters, a blacksmith, and William Bromwell, a baker, and they hurried against the cold. They were still half a mile from St. John's Wood when Bromwell stopped, touching his companion's arm, and pointed. It was in the region of a large pond of water, with a black tree or two about it. Not far away from the pond was a deep ditch shielded over with thickets and brambles. And in the brambles on the edge of the ditch lay a long cane, a pair of fringed gloves, and an empty sword-scabbard.

Now the two men looked at each other. But, although they hesitated, they did not meddle or even go to look closer. It might be one thing, it might be another; still, with the law and traps and dangers as thick as ghosts after dark, it behoved honest men not to meddle with anything whatever, lest the terrible red judges catch them. So they kept on their way, and presently splashed through the dead leaves to the door of the White House Inn in the wood. It was a fine thing to see firelight moving on a sanded floor; and black-bellied tuns, rich cheeses, nets of lemons under the rafters. But they could not get out of their minds those three things by the ditch, with the wind stirring the brambles above. They plumped down on the oak settles by the chimney, and John Rawson the innkeeper came bustling to serve them. While they drank their hot ale, winking and trembling to warmth before the blaze, and listening to the chimney growl under a cold sky, they fell to talking of what they had seen. The landlord was alert. 'I'll give you a shilling to go and fetch them!' cries he. 'Stop; I'll go with you myself.' All three were somewhat unwilling, and in the meantime a shower of rain had come up, so it was past five o'clock when the three of them set out across the waste in the twilight. The cane, gloves, and scabbard were just as they had been: William Bromwell noticed that the bank on which they lay was green. Rawson the landlord bent over to pick them up; in doing so he looked down into the ditch, and then started back with one cry:

'My God, there's a man murdered!'

They were not alone in the twilight. The body of a tall, lean man in black lay on its face at the bottom of the ditch, as though in a very long grave, with six inches of a sword-point protruding from the back just under the right shoulder-blade. Its posture was slightly crooked, because of the thick brambles on which it had been flung; so that in places the body did not touch the ground, and lay partly on its stomach against the left side of the bank. The left arm was doubled under the head at the bottom of the ditch, with the head resting on it as though in sleep; and the right hand was a little stretched out, touching the other side of the ditch. The knees touched the ground, but brambles had prevented the feet from falling, and upturned the soles of the shoes. The dead man's hat and periwig lay at the bottom of the ditch a little way ahead of his body. He had either been run through from the front – or else he had killed himself by putting a sword against his chest and falling forward on it. Of his face, twisted in the crook of the arm, they could see very little except a patch of something bluish and bloated, and one blood-filled eye. His shaven skull was white.

Now the wind went rustling again, and these three men awoke to terror. Nevertheless they must go and fetch John Brown, the constable. Without meddling with anything, they set off across the fields to the constable's house. They came on one figure, walking the hill against a mottled sky; but it was only a cow-herd whom they knew, and who cried to them that they had best let the business alone, or they would get into trouble. The constable, with several of his neighbours – some on horseback, some afoot – returned to the ditch with them. By this time it was well past six o'clock, growing into a tempestuous night, and so dark that it was barely possible to see. They gathered round the grave to look. 'It is a tall man,' said one voice in the gloom. 'I pray God it be not Sir Edmund Godfrey,' said Brown the constable, who knew the magistrate well. 'Take particular notice of everything, how the sword and the body are.'

He climbed down into the ditch, bestriding the body so that he could feel under it to find how the sword was placed. The pommel did not touch the ground. Protected thickly by brambles and bushes, the bottom of the ditch was completely dry. The body, though it was not wet under those overhanging bushes, was as cold as damp mud and as stiff as baked clay. Brown called to the company to hand it up out of the ditch. Still, though they rolled it over on the ground outside for Brown to look, he could not make certain of the man's face in the dark: the body must be carried to John Rawson's tavern.

'But,' the constable later gave evidence, 'I concluded that it would endanger breaking the sword, to carry the body all the way with the sword in it, so it was resolved rather to take out the sword. So thereupon I pulled it out – it was somewhat hard in the drawing, and crashed upon the bone in the plucking of it forth. Upon this, they laid the body across two watchmen's staves, and so carried it to-rights up to the 'White House', where they laid him down upon the floor in the house,' and they saw that it was Sir Edmund Godfrey.

John Rawson's beer is drawn, John Rawson's gin warms the guts, and it is always a business of great interest to look upon a murdered man, even upon a suicide. Though Brown forbade meddling, the company gathered close. The constable first caused the contents of his pockets to be examined and entered into a note, with a duplicate note taken to prevent any mistake. He was an officious soul, was John Brown – bustling about waving the dead man's sword, and giving directions with it – but he took great pains. If Sir Edmund Godfrey had been murdered, it became plain that he had not been murdered for robbery. He wore three good rings, and his sword was silver-hilted. In his pockets was the large sum of seven guineas, four broad-pieces, and four pounds in silver.

They took up the body, and laid it upon the table in the low inn-parlour. It was a somewhat helpless business, as one observer remembered it: the Watchmen on guard with their staves, the innkeeper's wife in her cap peeping round the stairs, the brown parlour with its sanded floor and its pewter tankards hanging from the rafters, and a wet company crowding to gape at the black man in the light of tallow dips. There were queer things here. On the dead man's black breeches were many spots of wax – not droppings from a common tallow dip, but from fine wax candles which were used only by people of quality, or priests. Despite the marshy state of the fields outside, his shoes were very clean and shining. The only sign of anything missing (Brown observed) was that round his neck he had no linen band, or cravat, such as he commonly wore. To the contrary, the collar of the dark camlet coat was buttoned up round his neck. It was, they observed, a very high stiff collar.

But there were other things to muddle the watchers' brains a little, though they did not wonder overmuch. The dead man's congested eyes looked at the roof out of hollows in a swollen face, and he was almost too stiff to be knocked into the proper shape. Yet, if you pressed on the neck, the neck became so limber that you might turn the chin and set it on either shoulder. Above all, on the breast of his coat where the sword had been driven in, there was no blood whatever. There was no blood, although there were two punctures in the left breast of the coat. The constable, though he told people not to meddle, wondered about it. On the dead man's back, where the sword had been pulled from under the shoulder-blade, there was a dripping of serum and putrefying blood. Brown remembered that there had been such an effusion, accompanied by a bubbling kind of noise, at the first plucking-out of the sword; another flow when the men carrying the body to the tavern had tripped over some stumps; and a third when, on entering here, they had by accident jerked the body against the door-post. But no blood on the front of him?

They were no surgeons, these ragged-hats sipping their ale round the board, and muttering likewise: but why didn't he bleed? Pigs bled when you stuck them, cows bled, sheep bled; ecod, why didn't a good Protestant magistrate bleed, unless the devilish Papists had put a magic on him? They did not much like to touch him until the strict Brown, who had ordered them not to meddle, went out after horses so that they might ride into town with the news. Then one of them – anticipating the surgeons by twelve hours – unbuttoned the coat to see whether there might be any blood inside.

There was no blood, but there was something else. The flannel waistcoat and Holland shirt were open to the waist, exposing the chest. And the body, from neck to stomach, was a mass of black bruises as though someone had stamped upon him or beaten him with a blunt weapon. Round his neck was a fissure worn deep into the flesh, folded over in purple creases, where some band or rope had been; there was a hard swelling under the left ear, as of a knot tied. He had been stamped upon, then strangled, and his neck broken at the end of it – a savage vision. The neck would not even lie upright on the table. As for the sword-punctures, there were two of them; one through the heart, and a shallower one under a rib two inches below; and both were bloodless. Hastily the watchers buttoned up the coat again.

Someone said, with a fury which was to sweep through all England: 'The Papists have done this. They murdered him, and then they ran him through with his own sword, to make people believe he did it himself.'

It was rising even now, like the clatter of hoofs when Brown with seven men galloped into Hartshorn Lane, carrying the news to Godfrey's house. When two riders stopped at Mrs. Duke's Coffee-House to spread the report, there rose up a howl even against these bearers of news: 'These are the rogues that murdered him themselves, and would make people believe he did it himself!' A friend of the Godfreys, who had been at the coffee-house, ran into the house just ahead of the constable to give warning. Then

Brown was admitted by the tall, gaunt Elizabeth Curtis and
the stout weeping Mrs. Pamphlin; and Brown, fumbling
at last before what he had to tell those faces, could only
say:

'I desire to speak with the justice.'

He was told that Sir Edmund's brothers, and a kinsman
named Plucknet, were above-stairs. So he waited for a
space in a parlour with a cold grate, until Messrs. Michael
and Benjamin Godfrey came downstairs to hear how their
brother died. Though they had some of the same angu-
larity of feature, they were stouter and more prosperous in
the comfortable way of City merchants: with gold chains,
brown velvet jump-coats, and grave fur gowns. Instead of
periwigs, they had satin skull-caps over hair worn long.
Michael had a handkerchief, Benjamin a snuff-box. Michael
seemed to be the choleric one, Benjamin the silent. They
were solid, lip-pursing gentlemen, who never went a-scour-
ing to smash windows at night, or cheated their doxies with
gilt shillings. With them was a leaner gentleman of the
same sort, named Plucknet; and behind them hurried little
old Henry Moor the clerk, in black small-clothes, with his
spindle shanks and his spectacles. Every man-jack of them
had been weeping, as the fashion was. They trembled and
they looked round the parlour while Brown told his story,
and outside in the passage Mrs. Pamphlin howled.

'Oh, God, I feared it!' cries out Mr. Michael Godfrey, and
began to stamp on the floor. 'D'ye hear, Ben? I feared it;
I told it. The Papists have made away with him. I heard
something of it this afternoon, from Mr. Angus, that he
had been found run through with his own sword; and
elsewhere, I can't remember how, I heard that he had two
wounds.'

'How,' asked Mr. Benjamin Godfrey, 'how are you sure it
is Sir Edmund's body?'

'Sir, I know him very well,' answered the constable.

'And of course,' says Mr. Benjamin sharply, and rapped
on the lid of his snuff-box, 'you *are* sure he was made away
with by Papists, or the like, and did not fall on his own
sword?'

G

'Sir, I cannot tell.'

'When he went from here on the Saturday,' says the clerk, nodding rapidly, 'he had then a linen band about his neck. Was it Primrose Hill you found him on? Ay: when I went to the funeral on Tuesday, to make his disappearance known, I met one Mr. Parsons – a coachmaker of St. Anne's, may it please you, gentlemen – and he told me that on the Saturday last Sir Edmund met him in the street and asked him the way to Primrose Hill, or Paddington Woods, or thereabouts. I even went there to look for him; on the Tuesday, I think it was.'

Michael Godfrey turned on him flaming. It was plain he did not like this imputation that Sir Edmund might have walked to Primrose Hill and taken his own life; else the estate would be forfeited to the Crown. And therefore, 'Did you, sirrah?' cries he. 'I counsel you not to say so, my friend; I counsel you not to say so. For maybe you are a cunning Jesuit yourself, hid away among us to spy on us? Maybe you dogged him to Primrose Hill yourself, and maybe *you* murdered him? Pah, you ninny-hammer! Did he walk to Primrose Hill with clean shoes? Did he fly there? Depend on it, they murdered him in another place, and carried his body there, and threw it into the ditch. (Ben – Plucknet – a word with you aside.) Depend on it, the Papists made away with him.'

'The Papists made away with him,' was what they were crying in the street, running up and down like distracted Black-Guard boys, those brawling street-urchins who throw dice by day and carry links by night. Every dog in the lane was barking at the stir. Godfrey is dead, Godfrey is butchered. The coffee-houses are ringing with it. Shortly the crier will be bawling in from Soho to Cripplegate, in rhymes worse mangled than Godfrey's body – just as, two nights later, he clanged his bell through the streets to cry the verdict of the coroner's jury over the body:

'That certain persons to the jurors unknown, a certain piece of linen cloth of no value, about the neck of Sir Edmund Berry Godfrey, then, and there, feloniously, wilfully, and of their malice beforethought, did tie

and fasten; and therewith the said Sir Edmund Berry
Godfrey, feloniously, wilfully, and of their malice beforethought, did suffocate and strangle; of which said suffocation, and strangling, he the said Sir Edmund Berry
Godfrey then and there instantly died.'

II

'*21° die Octobris, Anno Regni Serenissimi Domini
Nostri Caroli Secundi,*' on the twenty-first day of October,
in the year of the reign of Our Most Serene Lord Charles
the Second, '*Dei Gratia, Angliae, Scociae, Franciae, et
Hiberniae, Regis, Fidei, Defensoris,*' by the grace of God
King of England, Scotland, France, and Ireland, Defender
of the Faith. . . . Thus rings the stately proclamation,
solemn as a bell, when on that same 21st of October parliament met in the midst of such a panic as had never before
been known in the history of England.

The intervening days between the finding of the body
and the meeting of parliament, between Thursday the
17th and Monday the 21st, were the days of frantic rumour.
On Friday an inquest was summoned to meet at the White
House Inn under the direction of Mr. John Cowper the
coroner. It sat for two days, adjourning on Saturday to a
tavern in St. Giles's, and returned a verdict of wilful murder
by a person or persons unknown. The verdict was chiefly
influenced by the surgeons' evidence. Two surgeons and
five apothecaries examined the body. At the end of it all
the evidence collected stood thus:

1. Sir Edmund Godfrey had been strangled – presumably with his own linen band, since none was found on his
body and his clerk testified that he had worn one on Saturday morning. After being strangled, his head had been
wrung round so savagely that his neck was broken. Before
death, someone had stamped on his chest, or beaten it with
a blunt weapon, so as to produce bruises from neck to
stomach.

2. At some time subsequent to his death, his own sword
had been thrust through his heart. There were two

wounds, evidently the result of two attempts to drive in the sword smoothly. In the first wound, the sword had penetrated as far as a rib and had been stopped by it. Hence the blade had been drawn out and driven in once more.

3. When the body was found, he had been dead about four or five days.

4. At the examination by the surgeons, the body was so stiff that the shirt had to be torn off before an examination could be made.

5. He had not been robbed.

6. The spots on his clothes had been made by droppings from a wax candle. He did not use wax candles in his own house. Such candles were used only by priests and people of quality.

7. His shoes were very clean, almost shining: demonstrating that he could not have walked to such a muddy place as Primrose Hill. If he committed suicide, he must presumably have done so on the Saturday, when he vanished; and that Saturday had been very wet.

8. By testimony of those who had passed over the field during the week, there had been nothing in the ditch on Tuesday, October 15th.

9. Two fields away from the ditch, there was found in a lane the track of a coach.

10. Upon examination of the stomach, it was discovered that he had eaten no food for two days before his death.

These latter two facts were not, at the moment, made public. An attempt was made to trace Sir Edmund's movements on the Saturday when he vanished. Yet despite this evidence of the polished shoes, the evidence collected then, and later, indicated that on Saturday morning he *had* gone in the direction of Primrose Hill, although he returned to London by noon. Thus:

1. Early in the morning he had been seen going up St. Martin's Lane. Here he seems to have met one Parsons, a coachmaker, of whom he inquired the way to Primrose Hill, or Paddington Woods, or thereabouts. On the following

Tuesday, when his disappearance was made public, Parsons gave this information to Henry Moor, the clerk. Whereupon (says Moor) the clerk went to search for him in that vicinity on the Tuesday, but found nothing.[1]

2.   At nine o'clock on Saturday morning William Collins, one of the jurymen, had seen Sir Edmund talking to a milk-woman at Mary-bone Conduit, not far from Paddington Woods. This was about a mile away from Primrose Hill.

3.   At about ten o'clock Thomas Mason – who knew Sir Edmund very well, and bought his coals of him – had seen him returning from Paddington to London. He met Sir Edmund in the fields between Mary-bone Pound and Mary-bone Street, and they passed the time of day. Later Thomas Mason added a curious bit of testimony: 'As I was walking with my wife under a hedge near my house on the *Monday* morning, next after the Saturday,' says he, 'there came a short man in black clothes, in appearance above fifty years of age, to inquire of me whether I had seen his master, Sir Edmund Berry Godfrey, in the fields since Saturday last. He was very sad, and told me that he was Sir Edmund's clerk. He said he had lost his master, and knew not what was become of him.' Here is a conflict: Henry Moor stating that he had heard on Tuesday of Godfrey's having inquired the way to Primrose Hill, and on Tuesday had gone there to search for him; and Thomas Mason stating that Moor had come there the day before. Doubtless it is a slip of the tongue or memory on Mason's part, but it is worthy of notice in passing.

4.   Between twelve and one o'clock on the Saturday morning, Sir Edmund had returned to London again. Joseph Radcliffe, one of the vestrymen of St. Martin's Church, saw him pass Radcliffe's house in the Strand near Charing Cross. Joseph Radcliffe pressed him to come in, but Sir Edmund replied that he was in great haste, and

---

[1] This, of course, is hearsay evidence – not of Parsons himself, but of the clerk, and delivered afterwards to Sir Roger L'Estrange. L'Estrange's collection of evidence must be taken with caution, it is true; but on this point there seems no reason whatever to doubt it, since by the testimony of first-hand witnesses Godfrey *did* go in that direction.

could not stay. He spoke very earnestly and with a secret air, as though hurrying towards an appointment about which he was uneasy.

Here is an end; the trails flicker and vanish; the rest is dubious. Sir Edmund Godfrey went towards Primrose Hill in the morning, he returned to town at noon – and then he disappeared, into the terror and fury of England.

'On the twenty-first day of October, in the year of the reign of our most serene Lord, Charles the Second, by the grace of God King of England, Scotland, France, and Ireland –' the stately words toll like great bells in the House of Lords' Journals, when on that day parliament met at last. Bad bells, dangerous bells, to be heard above the rustling of robes. The House of Lords met in the Painted Chamber, where parliaments were opened or conferences of both Houses were held. It was a spacious place, with Gothic windows overlooking the river, a gilded and fretted ceiling, and hung with five great tapestries representing the siege of Troy. The Chronicler of the House wrote, 'His Majesty sitting in his royal throne, adorned with his royal crown and ornaments (the peers being likewise in their robes), commanded the Gentleman Usher of the Black Rod to give the House of Commons notice, "That it is his Majesty's pleasure that they attend him presently, with their Speaker." ' There was movement; there was danger; set open the windows, and you might hear a mob howling.

King Charles, the only calm man in either House, but also the most troubled, watched them as inscrutably as ever. He watched them from his robes, as behind a barrier. His brief, written speech lay on his knee: he was not an easy talker in the formal fashion, which he disliked, and as a rule he read haltingly, raising and lowering his eyes from the words. He disliked this ceremony, and much preferred to go down among them, lounging by the fire, singling out each man for a familiar word or gesture, spinning his politics with that growl tuned to mirth. But he must hold them with his authority to-day. He had returned to London from Newmarket two days before Godfrey's body was discovered; he had felt the cold of the Terror; he had heard the voice of Doctor Titus Oates, the Saviour of the Nation, now braying loudest in the land. It drove out sleep. Dr. Oates was deified. Dr. Oates could spit in the face of whomsoever he liked, for he was fawned upon even by the lords of the Country Party. Charles had heard along his own private ways a few truths about Dr. Oates. Dr. Oates had not even honest vices. When he had been a vicar at Hastings, and a chaplain on a warship, he had been expelled from both places for sodomy. And that, God's fish! *that* was the Saviour of the Nation! He had never told the truth in his life, and he had kept out of jail only because (as he jeeringly knew) he could give more trouble to honest men in prosecuting him than in letting him alone.

King Charles knew that he himself must hold this parliament with his authority to-day, for he was alone. Look about you – in particular when the House of Commons filed in to join the Lords, and rustled, and settled down – look about you, and you would see the same faces round the bear-pit watching for the kill. They were dogged men, simmering men, even in most cases thoroughly honest men: and they believed in Doctor Titus Oates as they believed in salvation. That was the pity, as it was the helplessness. They waited now to hear the king's speech; through painted windows the sun fell on them with bloodless colours, as they whispered behind their hands; a sea of eyes came to the foot of the throne; and in the two great fireplaces of the room you might hear the fires thrumming up the chimneys. They believed. Charles knew that his own Lord Chancellor, the Mouth of the King – Heneage Finch, Earl of Nottingham – 'the English Cicero', the gouty old honest gentleman with the peaked beard, believed in the Plot. Well, perhaps they had reason! First Coleman's letters, and now Godfrey's death. When Charles had first heard of Godfrey's death, he had one sharp opinion. 'This Godfrey,' he remembered telling the French ambassador, 'is a kind of fanatic, and I believe he killed himself.' But when the facts were brought to him by those who had gone to see Godfrey's body lying on the table at the 'White House', he had known it as murder. It was murder skilfully contrived, skilfully set in motion, skilfully made public; and it came, like a miracle, at exactly the right time.   A reward of £500 had been offered by the government for the apprehension of the murderer, so that doubtless there would be enough knights of the post, or informers, mustering before long. It would be of no value, now, to speculate as to just how far Doctor Titus Oates would have been able to cozen the nation with lies unsupported by proof – to cozen the butcher, the baker, and the Lord Chancellor alike – if this murder had not supplied his proof.   Without that, even the support of my Lord Shaftesbury's party could not have upheld him for ever.   No matter: the miracle had happened, and my Lord Shaftesbury's party had begun to dress the corpse with all the terrors at their command.

Now that parliament had come to sit, they could make their first drive against the Duke of York.   Already the existing penal laws against the Catholics – those laws which made it a hanging, drawing, and quartering matter to be a priest, and gave perpetual imprisonment to any Catholic who would not take the oath of allegiance to the Anglican Church – were being sharpened to the exact letter.   Every night new doors were being smashed open; new Catholics plucked out and haled off to Newgate; but this was only the beginning.   The weight of my Lord Shaftesbury's attack would be against the Duke of York, who now sat grimly upright and looked parliament in the face; but the popular fury would be against any Jack, Dick or Tom who could not defend himself, as popular fury always is.

King Charles cleared his throat.

'My lords and gentlemen!' he said.

They strained to listen as the heavy voice began.   Now, what a pox was this?   He was not speaking of Popery at all. He was speaking about the long prorogation, he was speaking about the preservation of peace in Flanders, and the army, and money. . . .

Then he looked at them.   'I now intend to acquaint you, as I shall always do with anything that concerns me,' he went on abruptly, 'that I have been informed of a design against my person by the Jesuits – of which I shall forbear

any opinion, lest I may seem to say too much, or too little.'
My Lord Shaftesbury, over there under the glow of one
window, would not of course dare utter the least whisper
of derisive mirth at this confiding of Fresh News, or this
casual treatment of the topic; but such, the Green Ribboners might feel, was Charles Stuart's fashion of handling
all his policies. 'But I shall leave the matter to the law,'
the king continued, 'and, in the meantime, will take as
much care as I can to prevent all manner of practices by
that sort of men (and of others too), who have been tampering in a high degree with foreigners, and contriving how to
introduce Popery amongst us.'

That was all. Whether there was a veiled sting or hint
in that last sentence, nobody might know except the urbane
gentleman who smiled on them, and concluded with a few
words about his lack of revenue. He brushed Popery aside
without another word, carrying it off in such fashion that
both Houses sat dumb. 'The rest,' says he, with his usual
formula, 'I leave to the Chancellor.'

Then up from the Woolsack rose Lord Chancellor Nottingham, gouty, golden of voice, and spoke in vague,
soothing fashion of nothing. He mentioned undefined
dangers. He made the customary references to troubled
times, and the ship of state, and avoiding shoals; but he was
confident that everybody would get on very amicably with
everybody else. 'My lords and gentlemen, you now find
the king involved in difficulties as great as any government
did labour under. And yet his Majesty doth not think
there be many words to bespeak your zeal and industry
in his service; for things themselves speak – and speak
aloud.'

He was a master of unconscious truth. The same order
and solemnity held, though at point of bursting, until the
two Houses separated to go about their individual business.
In the House of Commons, they even began motions to
debate the king's request for money, when one irate member of the Country Party leaped to his feet.

'Now I admire this!' roars he. 'I admire that none of
these honourable gentlemen who have spoken – nor any

others of the House who hold great places at court – should speak one word of the Plot! This, though his Majesty's life and government are in peril; this, though our property, our liberty, our lives, and, dearer, the religion of us all are in peril; and let the blood of two martyred Kings of France testify that no army, no money, in whatever sums, can protect a prince from the daggers of Popish assassins. I call up their blood! Is Coleman, then, so inconsiderable? Is Godfrey so inconsiderable? Let one of his Majesty's spaniels be lost, and inquiry is made in the *Gazette*; but here's a Protestant magistrate done to death under high noon, and not a whisper goes out in search of his murderers. Is the Privy Council cold in its pursuit? Then let justice be taken up, as it should be, by the great council of the land!'

A touch and the tornado; all their voices rose together, both in the Commons and in the Lords. For the next ten days they set about it. Dr. Titus Oates was examined before the bar of both Houses. He came waddling in with his doctor's robes and his woolly periwig, swelled up now to a high pitch of vanity and insolence, and told his story with fresh discoveries. Also, he wanted money. They had better give him money, he told them, setting his long chin against his shoulder and peering up triumphantly; they had better give him money, or he would be forced to help himself. They awarded him a pension of £1,200 a year; the finest lodgings at Whitehall; royal physicians to look after his health, and a royal guard to protect him while he sniffed out Papists. At his call the Lord Chief Justice, Sir William Scroggs, was summoned to take his examination; and the Lord Chief Justice began business by sealing warrants for the arrest of all the leading Catholics he had named. Among them the five Popish lords – Arundell, Bellasis, Powis, Petre, and Stafford – were taken and sent to the Tower. A bill was prepared to prevent any Catholic from sitting in parliament, and another commanding all Catholics who were not already in the crowded jails to depart ten miles from London. But there were sinister fears that even now the wily Jesuits might strike back. Sir Edward Rich declared he felt it in his bones that both Houses of parlia-

ment were to be blown up. Householders near Old Palace
Yard had heard at night a terrible knocking that seemed to
come from under the vaults, and brought dreams of Guy
Fawkes prowling again with his torch among the kegs of
gunpowder. Down hurried a committee to examine this,
with the dapper little Sir Christopher Wren to advise them;
Sir John Cotton was ordered to remove the coals and
faggots from the cellar under the Painted Chamber; and
Wren's committee found the vaults a dangerous maze of
tunnels winding from the Thames under Westminster
Hall, where in twenty-four hours a thousand powder-kegs
could be rolled from near-by cellars under Popish robes.
Night or day, sentries patrolled the vaults with lanthorns
and drawn swords; outside parliament's doors, sentinels
stood guard under the command of the Duke of Monmouth
himself. Cannon were planted round Whitehall, where
no cannon had been seen since the decaying battery of five-
pounders set up there in Oliver's day. Posts and chains had
been dragged out to be tied on hooks across the streets,
and barricade the ways in case of a massed attack. Houses
round Westminster were ransacked to find Papist arms.
Back from his country home rushed Sir William Jones –
'Bull-faced Jonas', the Attorney-General and great public
prosecutor – to order all the coals and kindling in his own
house conveyed from the front cellar to the back, in case
Papists should fling in fireballs from the street.

Panic is a fireball. And of all those who were busy on
committees, the busiest was my Lord Shaftesbury. He was
the prime mover, the prime agitator, of the Lords' Committee which had been appointed to inquire into Godfrey's
death. He ruled a small Committee of Secrecy within this
larger one, along with his friend Buckingham. But, even
added to this work, his work as Lord of the Green Ribboners carried everything before it.

His work lay in the City, where minds were easily turned
to violence by a skilful play with Godfrey's corpse. My
lord moved between his great house in Aldersgate Street
and his political headquarters at the King's Head Tavern
near Temple Bar, the whispering-hole out of which

breathed each new rumour. Before the ten days had
elapsed he had got the mobile party into such a state of
mind that if anything Catholic had appeared on the street,
be it only so much as a dog or a cat, it would have been
torn to pieces in an instant. Ballad-singers and street-poets
inflamed the passers-by. Medals and woodcuts showed the
Pope directing Godfrey's murder, the Pope plying the
bellows while London burned, the Pope gloating over
Protestants stretched on the rack. Powerful preachers
clawed the air over their sermons. A cutler issued a 'Godfrey' dagger – a sharp toy to keep off murderers, with *Remember the murder of Sir Edmund Berry Godfrey* engraved
on one side of the blade, and on the other *Remember religion* – and sold three thousand of them in one day. Even
the ladies trembled in this new dance. My Lady Shaftesbury, under the instruction of her husband, had made for
herself a pair of small pocket-pistols which she carried in
her muff, and never went abroad without them. Portraits
of Titus Oates, the Saviour of the Nation, appeared on
ladies' snuff-boxes, ladies' handkerchiefs, ladies' fans. Out
from the Green Ribbon Club couriers sped with the fresh-
est news. An omen from heaven had shone down, uplifting
all Protestant hearts and bringing tears to all Protestant
eyes, when there was found at Oatlands an old stone inscribed with the words, 'Oats shall save the nation from
destruction.' 'And what else d'ye hear, friend, in God's
name?' 'A troop of monks hath arrived in England to sing
Te Deum for the success of the Plot. The Pope himself
may be here, they say.' And still it was only beginning. . . .

At the King's Head Tavern, in the tall upstairs room with
the balcony looking out over the street, my Lord Shaftesbury
smoked his long pipe of tobacco and ordered his moves as
in a game at chess. His motives were pure. The means
to accomplish his end, it is possible, may have been dubious;
but his motives were pure, and he dreamed dreams of
liberty when the Duke of York should be driven from the
land. To that end the pageantry was carried with such
splendour as the late Sir William Davenant at the Opera
never matched. On the 31st of October the height of the

public spectacle was attained when they buried Sir Edmund Godfrey in the Church of St. Martin's-in-the-Field.

For even as yet the poor clay had not been able to rest. It had been nearly three weeks since Godfrey had been found missing, and two weeks since he had been found, very much like a dog in a ditch, but not quite so painlessly killed. Still the clay could not rest, though it rotted, because there was a use for it. It is useless to talk of the dignity of death, or say that the grave is private, when the high khans want votes. Suppose it be tumbled about a little, like a doll in a nursery, or its head grow a trifle chipped in the process? What's the difference? *he* won't feel it. So the body was borne back to London, exposed in the magistrate's house, and then for two days exposed in the streets – with all the pomp of palls, and soldiers with bowed heads over their swords, and the flesh crying for vengeance, while every person in London who could fight his way thence filed past to look at it. It swelled the apple-seller's grief, the link-boys' rage, causing them thenceforward to carry a deeper hate of the Pope. On the 31st of October the body was borne high in a vast procession of (says one chronicler) ministers and substantial citizens, stepping slow as the toll of the bells, to St. Martin's. Seventy-two clergymen walked before the bier. The church was packed, and the streets black with people for half a mile in every direction from St. Martin's Lane. Then up rose the great Dr. Lloyd to preach the funeral sermon; and, as a shrewd touch of the spectacular, there mounted into the pulpit on either side of him a 'thumping divine', two strong-bodied parsons to guard him from being killed by the Papists while he was speaking. Dr. Lloyd's powerful voice reached out across the assembly.

'My text,' said he, 'is from second Samuel, the third chapter and the thirty-third verse: *"Died Abner as a fool dieth?"*

' "And David said to Job, and to all the people that were with him: Rend your clothes, and gird you with sackcloth, and mourn before Abner. And King David himself followed the bier.

‘ "And they buried Abner in Hebron: and the king lifted up his voice, and wept at the grave of Abner; and all the people wept.

‘ "And the king lamented over Abner, and said, Died Abner as a fool dieth?

‘ "Thy hands were not bound, nor thy feet put into fetters. As a man falleth before wicked men, so fellest thou. And all the people wept again over him. . . .

‘ "And the king said unto his servants: *Know ye not that there is a prince and a great man fallen this day in Israel?*

‘ "And I am this day weak, though anointed king; and these men the sons of Zeruiah be too hard for me; but the Lord shall reward the doer of evil according to his wickedness." ’

From the crowd a moan rose up, shaking the twinkle of candles in the Church and moving out across all that throng whose breaths smoked in the cold. As Dr. Lloyd inflamed them with a furious attack on the Catholics, and pointed to the magistrate's wounds, most were weeping openly with grief or rage. Here was the whole tale unfolded in the Bible: the weak king, the man who would have served him struck down at the gate. This day the sons of Zeruiah had hidden themselves, trembling, in their houses; had anything Catholic appeared in the streets, be it so much as a cat or a dog, it would have been torn in pieces. Hang! Smite! Kill! Thus the mob swayed; and over Charing Cross the drizzle turned to first winter sleet, and my Lord Shaftesbury wept for joy that the devil was snared, and they buried Abner in Hebron.

III

They brought Mrs. Mary Gibbon, Godfrey's kinswoman, to be examined before the Lords' Committee at Wallingford House.

The Lords' Committee, whose mouth and heart were my Lord Shaftesbury and the Duke of Buckingham, had been hard pressed with work. Informations, depositions, rumours of all degrees of credibility poured in on them, and my lord burrowed eagerly at the reports. The stage-show was all very well; but the opera of terror now swelled with full-throated chorus, with brass and wood-notes; and so it behooved them to find a definite victim. This murder must be laid to the Papists, else it was of no value whatever. Let Dr. Israel Tonge, if he liked, demonstrate as a sign from heaven the fact that the letters 'E-d-w-a-r-d C-o-l-e-m-a-n' could be rearranged in the form of an anagram to make, 'Lo, a damned crew'; or that 'Sir Edmundbury Godfrey' spelt out the accusation, 'Dy'd by Rome's reveng'd fury'. It was a good discovery, and struck the populace with awe. But nevertheless a murderer must be found.

Along one line of investigation, however, they had the good fortune to be able to avert a danger towards themselves. Early in their burrowings they had discovered, with disquiet and (it would seem) with surprise, that Godfrey and Coleman had been close friends; and that Godfrey had even warned Coleman, and showed him Oates's deposition, on the crucial 28th of September. When Mr. Welden – at whose house the two had met – testified to this before the Lords, the committee stirred in alarm. It was not alone that this sudden discovery of Godfrey as being hand-in-glove with the Catholics, and therefore the last person in England they would be likely to kill, might weaken the case against the Catholics if it were made known. But my Lord Shaftesbury's chief lieutenants, members of this committee, had lately been receiving King Louis's bribes at the hands of Coleman. If Coleman, now kept in irons at Newgate, should from one cause or another choose to *talk* – damme, gentlemen! the result would be awkward, at its most civil interpretation. Mr. Edward Coleman must be hustled off to the quartering-block as speedily as might be; and the sooner Jack Ketch boiled his head afterwards, then the better it would be for certain Green Ribbon men. In the meantime, this source of information must be stopped up as tight as a tap. As soon as the committee heard of the Godfrey-Coleman alliance, they hurried off a message to Captain Richardson, the Keeper of Newgate, instructing him that Coleman must be kept solitary, and must on no account be allowed to communicate with any person whatever.   A sub-committee, headed by my Lord Shaftesbury, was appointed to examine Coleman with regard to Godfrey's murder.   They spoke with him at Newgate, behind inscrutable doors: but what he said to them, or they said to him, they never told.   Over Newgate the windmill whirled, trying to drive clean air through this stone den; an iron door opened and closed for ever; but no word from Coleman ever crept out.   The matter was dropped.

'But with regard to the matter of bribes,' Mr. Harbord afterwards admitted, with an ill-advised straying into candour, 'the committee were careful to take no names of Mr. Coleman; it being in his power to asperse whom he pleased, possibly some gentlemen against the French and Popish interest.'

Since all dangers were sealed up, the committee pursued their evidence with zeal.   My Lord Shaftesbury was tireless. He even recorded on paper the statements of boys of sixteen and seventeen years old, concerning what had been said to them by a child of six.   He did not, it is true, press the investigation of one magistrate's report that (on the Saturday of his disappearance) Sir Edmund Godfrey had been seen at a house in St. Giles's, close to a great mansion in Leicester Fields.   But he may have overlooked it.   For (since there must never come to the outer world any hint of Godfrey's having been in danger from any hands except the Papists') my lord had got into a paroxysm over Mrs. Mary Gibbon's evidence.

At the insistence of her husband, Mrs. Mary Gibbon had put on paper an account of Sir Edmund's last speech with her: of how he had come to her in agitation at the time her mother lay dying; of how he had taken her upstairs, bolting the door, and muttered his fears that he was in danger of being hanged by the government because he had tried to conceal Oates's deposition.   Well, in all sanity it was plain that he had not been hanged by the government; in an official fashion, at least.   The government adorns its stranglings with more pomp, with a festival to Tyburn, and javelin-men

high-stepping round the cart, and a pine coffin for Jack o'
Newgate to sit on. Doubtless it had been Godfrey's ever-
gnawing conscience, which would not rest if twopence were
misplaced. But my Lord Shaftesbury could not bear this
hint of friendliness towards Papists. Therefore, when Sir
John Bankes – a friend of Mrs. Gibbon – in an unwise
moment delivered the paper containing her deposition to
my lord, he ordered her to be summoned before the committee.

Mrs. Gibbon was a housewife after the German fashion,
not concerned with plots when there was bread to be baked,
but she was terrified of meeting the great Green leader.
And she had forgotten her spectacles again. They took
her into a big, low room, where all the walls and the
furniture were polished; there were a number of men in
it, but she saw only my Lord Shaftesbury, who sat by the
candle.

Then my lord pounced.

'You bitch, you damned woman,' cries he, shaking the
paper aloft, 'what devilish paper is this you have given us
in? *I'll* have the truth out of you. You bitch, you shall be
put on oath. Here, Wildman, put her on oath. *I'll* have
the truth out of her, so help me Goad.'

There was that in the expression of my lord's eyes which
started the woman in a-blubbering. 'My lord, I was upon
oath when I said it,' says she. 'My lord, it is the truth.
He –'

'Ah, but you were not on oath before us,' says my lord,
nodding with a sort of terrifying kindliness. 'Before us,
who are the guardians of the king's domain, and the keepers
of his awful majesty; and before Goad, who shall roast you
in the fire everlasting. I tell you now, there is a Stone
Hold in Newgate for such as you. I'll tell you what you
shall do,' says he, with an air of inspiration. 'You shall
swear to us here, you shall confess it, that you were set on to
write that paper by Sir John Bankes, and Monsieur de Puy,
and Mr. Pepys that is a servant of the Duke of York. And
if you do not confess that they set you on to write it, you
shall be taken hence and in my sight you shall be torn to

pieces by the multitude. You shall be torn in pieces by the multitude, and you shall be worried as dogs worry cats –'

'Hold hard, my lord,' said a voice querulously; 'the damned woman's in a fit.'

But even more than quieting such evidence, it was necessary to persuade someone to fasten the murder on the Catholics. A shrewd stroke of business would be done if he might induce the two men who had found the body – William Bromwell the baker, and John Walters the blacksmith – to say that they were set on to find it by some great Roman Catholic. Both were haled before the committee. Both were promised £500 and a free pardon if they would confess. 'And if any man ever was hanged,' my Lord Shaftesbury told Bromwell, 'you shall be hanged if you do not confess it.' But Will the baker and Jack the blacksmith were either not inventive enough, or too much afraid, or even too honest, for they could only stammer that they knew nothing of it. So they were taken off to Newgate and put underground in irons, in the hope that a few days without air would refresh their memories. When Walters was hoisted out again, my lord had become all captivating bluffness and friendliness. He took Walters aside into a by-closet, clapped him on the shoulder, and addressed him with the familiar or condescending 'thou'. 'Honest Smug the Smith,' cries the little cock-sparrow, heartily, 'thou lookest like an honest fellow – thou shalt shoe my horses, and I'll make a man of thee! Come, tell me now: Who murdered this man, and who set thee to find him out? What Papists dost thou work for?' Honest Smug the Smith, with his head a trifle turned, said he still did not know.

But, although nothing was pressed out of Bromwell or Walters, the Leader took fire with new hope when they brought him word of the next discovery. One Francis Corral, a hackney coachman, had been overheard making some professional remarks about the carrying of Godfrey's body to Primrose Hill: here, it was thought, they might have snared the very man who drove the coach. In he was hurried, to face a Leader grown feverish with long search after some murderer.

'I would ask you,' says my lord, 'if you carried Sir Edmund Berry Godfrey to Primrose Hill, or know who carried him?'

'My lord, I did not,' answered the coachman Corral, who was a weak man physically, and shook before that eye. Whereupon my lord took a handful of silver out of his pocket, letting it rattle on the table, and roll and gleam while he looked out over it.

'If you will swear the truth,' says he, 'you shall have five hundred pounds. Ay, and you shall have a room near the court itself, if you are afraid of anybody that set you to work. And you shall command a file of musketeers, to guard you if any of those that employed you should try to do you mischief. But if you do not tell the truth? We are the peers of this land; and if you will not confess, there shall be a barrel of nails provided for you, to put you in, and roll you down a hill. Eh?'

'My lord,' cries the other distractedly, 'what would you have me say? I know nothing of the matter. . . .'

'Then thou shalt die,' says my lord, with pleasant familiarity.

They took him to Newgate, and tried the treatment of an underground cell without air to turn its filth. As they took him out, he remembered hearing my Lord Shaftesbury say to Buckingham, with a decisive nod, 'The Papists have hired him, and he will not confess.' But Whip the Coachman had not so strong a frame or lungs as Smug the Smith, and after a couple of hours underground they must pull him out and revive him with brandy. This, be it pointed out, was no cruelty or anything out of the way; it was the customary fashion of protecting the king's sacred person; and, if a man had the ill-luck to be caught in the feelers of the law, or pulled into Newgate – why, he must expect what he got, anyone in the street could tell you, and be thankful for no worse. Let's have no maudlin speech, gentlemen. For if, while the Popish Plot was blossoming, passers-by heard screams coming even through the walls of Newgate – why, doubtless it was a woman in childbirth; nothing more. Anyhow, Whip the Coachman was well-favoured. This scent of the fox had grown so warm that my Lord Shaftesbury did not care to wait before he attacked Whip again.   For after only a few hours the coachman had his manacles taken off, briefly; he was bundled into a coach along with big Captain Richardson, the Keeper of the Jail, and taken by Holborn way to a house in Lincoln's Inn Fields.   There Shaftesbury had gone after the meeting of the committee, with a few of his lieutenants, to have private speech with Whip.   My lord greeted him this time in a blaze of triumph.

'Now, you rogue,' says he, 'here's one that will justify he saw you!'   My lord pointed and stabbed at a man standing in a corner, but the coachman's wits were still fuddled, and he did not well observe the witness whom my lord now addressed: 'Did you not see this Corral whip his horses, and go down by Tottenham Court?'   'Yes, my lord,' replied an obedient voice.   Whereupon Shaftesbury turned to the coachman again.   'Sirrah,' cries he, clapping his hands together, ' what's the reason you will not confess?   Why do you put us to all this trouble?   If you will not confess – Richardson, take him away, and let him be starved to death.'

Then the coachman, whose nerves were gone, found himself weeping: an absurd spectacle, doubtless, on which my lord made comment.   'Ah, rogue, you look through your fingers!   There's never a tear comes down, is there?' says he playfully.   'By Christ's mercy, my lord!' shrieks out Whip, 'I know no more than a child unb –' 'That's a Popish word,' says my lord quickly, and pointed at him, and nodded at those round about.   'He has consulted with the Papists, and will not confess.   I have no more to say. Richardson, take him back. . . .'

They did not starve him to death; they kept him, as a matter of fact, only four days without food.   Since he still could not think of anything to say, he remained for six weeks in the Condemned Hold; and afterwards, to lighten the punishment, he was removed to the Common Side, where he had a board floor to lie on instead of a stone one. Bromwell the baker, among others, kept him company. But by that time they had little to fear, since the committee had forgotten all about them. Long before that time there had come new, agreeable, amenable witnesses to stimulate the zeal of the Lords' Committee, and an arrest had been made for murder.

IV

'WITH A DARK LANTHORN –'

The Knight of the Post

'Good store of good claret supplies every thing,
And the man that is drunk is as great as a king.'

CONTEMPORARY SONG.

Duke of Buckingham: 'Oh, he'll confess nothing; he expects a pardon.'
Lord Shaftesbury: 'I'll secure him from that, I warrant you! There's
three hundred to one.'

SAMUEL ATKINS'S account of his examination before the Lords' Committee,
State Trials.

I

'I WOULD not have,' cried one excited member of the House of Lords, 'so much as a Popish man or a Popish woman remain here, not so much as a Popish dog or a Popish bitch, not so much as a Popish cat to purr or mew about the king.' The sentiment was generally endorsed. While Godfrey was being buried, both Houses were engaged in passing a bill ordering all Popish recusants to depart ten miles from town; and both Houses issued a resolution, 'That there has been and still is a damnable and hellish plot contrived and carried on by Popish recusants, for assassinating and murdering the king, and for subverting the government, and destroying the Protestant religion by law established.'

And late in the afternoon of the first day of November – a Friday – a first arrest was made for complicity in murder.

This arrest presently ceased to be important; it was the first of several false stabs made by the government, as suspicion moved from one person to another. But it had more dangerous implications than any, and it was a brilliant move

118

on the part of my Lord Shaftesbury. My Lord Shaftesbury, whose wits were never nimbler than at this moment, had seen an opportunity of fastening Godfrey's murder almost directly on the Duke of York.

Several times before we have met Mr. Samuel Pepys, former Clerk of the Acts to the Admiralty. But we have met him as a merry companion. The little, dark-faced, jovial, garrulous man, with his brown periwig, his some-what protuberant eyes and thick lips, has bustled every-where in a sparkle of gossip – even rating himself soundly because he does not hear enough gossip: for he treats both pleasure and work with the same diligence. You can hear the earnest voice, *'But, Lord!'* that such-and-such a thing should be true. Yet during eighteen years, since the old days when he recorded gleefully that he was worth all of £300, he has grown heavier in both senses; he has risen to a high place in the world, and become a rich man.

Since May 31, 1669, he had ceased to keep up that inti-mate diary of his, for he had been having such trouble with his eyes that he feared he was going blind. The last news-entry made in the diary ends exuberantly enough, with the stating of his accounts: 'Had another meeting with the Duke of York, at Whitehall, on yesterday's work, and made a good advance: and so, being called by my wife, we to the Park, Mary Batelier, and a Dutch gentleman, a friend of hers, being with us. Thence to "The World's End", a drinking-house by the Park; and there merry, and so home late.' It foreshadowed the future, despite the gloomy appre-hensions about his blindness. He had now risen to be Mr. Samuel Pepys, Secretary of the Navy; and no man in England was a more faithful friend or servant of the Duke of York.

In his employ at Derby House, the Admiralty office, Secretary Pepys had a clerk named Samuel Atkins. Samuel Atkins was just twenty-one years old, and had remained with Mr. Pepys for four years despite certain tumbles from grace. For he was inclined to be a gay young blade, fond of a ripe damsel and a bottle of Canary; and Mr. Pepys tended to be a martinet, 'the severest man in his house in

the world,' Atkins sadly admitted.   Nevertheless, easy-going
Young Samuel was not lacking in wit, courage, or ability
at his work; and he was as devoted to his master as Mr. Pepys
was to the Duke of York.   Both were tested.   At the end of
October the Privy Council at Whitehall was roused and
refreshed to receive information which accused Samuel
Atkins the clerk – and possibly Samuel Pepys the master –
of complicity in the murder of Sir Edmund Godfrey.

The accuser was one Captain Charles Atkins,[1] son of Sir
Jonathan Atkins; former commander of a frigate, but ousted
from the navy for cowardice in battle.   Although Captain
Charles was a bad hat, he was a vacillating bad hat.   He had
little of Titus's taste and rich talent for perjury; his wits
were none too clear; and afterwards he could only make a
piteous plea to Young Samuel that, if the latter would only
see reason in this business, they could both make their fortunes.   He was well acquainted with Young Samuel, having come sometimes to Derby House to borrow money from
him.   In private, regarding the accusation he made, he
shuffled and struck his flag before the clerk as he once struck
his flag before the Turks.   But he had little need of his own
inspiration: his inspiration and strength came from outside.

Regarding the deposition which Captain Charles made
accusing Secretary Pepys, it is to be noted that he made it
to his own uncle, Sir Philip Howard – a friend of Shaftesbury and zealous fellow-member of the Committee of
Inquiry – after a close conference with that same uncle.
There is no actual proof that my Lord Shaftesbury instigated this, but, wherever you turn in this case, it is impossible to get away from traces of my lord's fine Italian hand.
He bobs up out of every chest; he springs from each drawer
of papers like a jack-in-the-box; he is omnipresent.   If
nobody had been tampering with Captain Charles, assuredly
his evidence was a light from heaven.   It was the one thing
which the Green Ribbon leaders most hoped for.   To accuse
Mr. Pepys of Godfrey's murder was to accuse the Duke of
York.   Between the Green Ribbon leaders and their worst

---

[1] They were not related.   To avoid useless confusion, Charles Atkins
will be referred to as 'Captain Charles'.

enemy stood only two people: Young Samuel Atkins and Old Samuel Pepys. If Atkins could be persuaded or terrified into denouncing Pepys, it might not be difficult to persuade or terrify Pepys into denouncing his own master: 'for,' the Tory Roger North later thought, 'Mr. Pepys was an elderly gentleman,[1] who had known softness and the pleasures of life.'

It was a very frightened young Atkins whom Secretary Coventry's man tapped on the shoulder at five o'clock of a foggy November afternoon. 'I was not to show you my warrant,' the man confided, 'unless you refused to come.' But Atkins, though he burst into wild denials, agreed to go without fuss — looking round nervously, as much in fear of Mr. Pepys as of the law. He was taken to the great house of my lord Marquess of Winchester, where in an upstairs room, snug with fire and candles, sat the awesome gentlemen of the Committee of Inquiry. That scene has almost the air of a schoolboy being taken before the headmaster: say, Young Samuel before Busby, the headmaster who so valued his terrifying reputation that he refused to remove his hat even in the presence of the king, lest it should lower him in the eyes of the boys. My Lord Shaftesbury sat at the head of the table, with his aide-de-camp the Duke of Buckingham. My Lord Essex was there. So was Henry Compton, Bishop of London, that aggressive prelate who had begun life as a soldier, and who (the Duke of York used to complain) still talked more like a colonel than a bishop. But Shaftesbury played Busby. Not only was he in a suave good humour, but he spoke politely and with a sort of sinister patience. Indeed, all of them carried matters in a spirit more of sorrow than of anger, as at a young soul to be rescued from error.

But it was a hanging matter nevertheless.

'Pray, Mr. Samuel Atkins,' says my lord, in the buttered-toast-and-cane fashion of the study, 'do you know one Mr. or Captain Atkins?'

'Yes, my lord,' says Young Samuel, finding his voice.

[1] He was only in his forty-sixth year, but he was a veteran — as his enemies were shortly to discover.

'How long have you known him?'

'About two or three years, I think, my lord.'

'Are you related?'

'No, my lord; only for namesake have been called cousins.'

'Do you know or believe,' pursues my lord, pursing out his lips, and looking up and down suavely from his papers, 'he had any reason to do you a prejudice? No? Now, did you ever tell him, upon discourse about the plot, that there was no kindness – or want of friendship, I think it was,' says my lord, again consulting his papers with a mild frown, '– or want of friendship betwixt Mr. Pepys and Sir Edmund Berry Godfrey?'

The other found his voice rising. '*No*, my lord! I never mentioned Sir Edmund Berry Godfrey's name to him in my whole life, upon any occasion that I remember; nor ever talked with him about the plot!'

'Do you know one "Child"?'

'No, my lord,' says the other, trying to reflect, and feeling his wits becoming unstuck. 'I have heard of such a man's being concerned in the victualling of the navy, but to my knowledge never saw him.'

My lord shut his eyes and opened them in a mildly pained manner; and Essex interposed snappishly: 'No, no, not the victualler; this is another sort of man, and one whom you will be found to know very well.'

At a signal they brought in the man called Child, and Samuel was still more perplexed. Child was an ordinary-looking seaman, who stood still and said nothing: another lad for the study. Samuel strenuously denied ever having seen Child, and Child (whether or not to the surprise of the committee) denied ever having seen Samuel. Matters were going just a little wrong, and so Captain Charles was brought in to make them more brisk. Captain Charles had a sea-dog's swagger, and a customary long pipe of tobacco in his hand; but he looked, you conceive, a trifle too foolishly like Mr. Dick in a periwig (occupied with perhaps the same sort of thoughts about King Charles the First's head), and he kept his eye fixed on my lord.

'My lord,' cries Captain Charles, 'Mr. Samuel Atkins told

me there was a difference betwixt his master and Sir
Edmund Godfrey; and I asked him, "Is Sir Edmund Godfrey
a parliament man or no?" He said, no. I asked him whether
their difference was upon an occasion of Mr. Pepys being
formerly accused for a Papist in the House of Commons? —
and whether Sir Edmund Godfrey might not be concerned
in doing that? He answered, no, and that it was upon this
occasion.'

This struck even Samuel as being singularly muddled,
like an ill-learnt lesson. 'He answered, no, and that it was
upon this occasion.' What occasion? What did they mean?
Whereat my Lord Shaftesbury turned round triumphantly.
'Now,' says he to the clerk, 'didn't you ask Captain Atkins
whether this "Child" was a man of courage and secrecy?
And didn't you bid him send Child to Derby House, to
inquire for your master; but be sure not to ask for you?'

Now the clerk felt all the eyes in the study fixed on him.
All he could be certain of was that they were trying to put
a bubble on him: that they wanted him to say he had sent
Child to Mr. Pepys, and that Mr. Pepys had sent Child to
murder Sir Edmund Godfrey. Whereupon Young Samuel
did what was, under the circumstances,· probably the best
thing to strengthen his wits; he lost his temper. He
embarked on a long and rather remarkable tirade, recalling
the minutest details of his last conversation with Captain
Charles. He pointed out as the most important feature of
the conversation that Captain Charles had attempted to
borrow a crown, and had got it (a point over which he felt
ill-used); and that he, Samuel, had even possessed the delicacy to wait until another person was out of the room before
he slipped the coin into Captain Charles's hand.

My Lord Shaftesbury spoke in a tone between wheedling
and sharpness, as one who wishes to go to business at last.

'Come, come, Mr. Atkins, you are a seeming hopeful
young man, and, for aught I can see, a very ingenious one.
Captain Atkins has sworn this positively against you, to
whom he bears no prejudice or malice, but has acknowledged several obligations to you. And, to tell you truly, I
do not think he has wit enough to invent such a lie. Come,

be ingenuous with us, and confess what you said!   Indeed, we believe Captain Atkins to be a man that has loved wine and women, and been a debauched man; but whence would you have us think him to be a rascal?'

'Why, my lord,' says Samuel, 'I would offer this: how far is a coward to be reckoned so?'

'Pray, Samuel Atkins,' says my lord abruptly, 'what religion are you of?'

'I am a Protestant, sir, and my whole family before me.'

He was asked whether he had taken the sacrament; he had always been intending to take it, he reminded himself (his intentions were for ever good); and he jubilantly recalled a promise to the rigid Mr. Pepys that he would take it on the coming Sunday. 'Ah, but now,' says my Lord Shaftesbury, with dry sarcasm, 'now I am sure you won't do so: you can't forgive Captain Atkins?'

'Yes, my lord,' replies Samuel, with solemn heat, 'I assure you I can and do, and to show it to you, I also remit to him the money he owes me – about fifty shillings.'

Still they kept their tempers.   In all conscience the best course was to flatter and cajole this fellow until his head was turned, because a willing witness was what they aimed at when a clerk accused his master.   In the case of witnesses with clean periwigs and clean records, a willing witness was worth a bushel of hangdogs who had to have testimony screwed out of them with irons.   If cajolery failed, the other course could be used.   So they applied butter; they addressed him in sorrow and urging; and it was the jolly Duke of Buckingham, bursting through them like a sun, who spoke as one man of the world to another.   'I see,' cries Bucks jocosely, laying his finger on Samuel's forehead, 'I see the great workings of thy brain.   Come, for thine own sake, declare what thou knowest.'   Honours?   Preferments? He was jounced and jostled and oiled, never conceiving that great men could be so civil, but he still knew nothing; and they were compelled to send him out of the room while they debated it.

He crouched in the outer room.   And, though he would not admit it in the long, solemn, and rather pompous statement he later drew up for Mr. Pepys (who, he felt, would not understand), he was miserable. He wanted to go home, even to be lectured to by the Secretary. He was loyal to Mr. Pepys. Besides, something stubborn drew up at the back of his Puritan head, and said: Don't give way to this fellow who borrows your money and then tells lies about you. Don't let him put this bubble on you. To tell the truth, he was nearly as much afraid of Mr. Pepys as he was of the great lords in their foretopped periwigs. He would never have dared to speak back to the Secretary as he had spoken back to my Lord Shaftesbury. Out of that poor pride began to come an unshakable determination that he must say nothing, and tell no lies. If only he could communicate with Mr. Pepys, Mr. Pepys would fetch him out of this. Maybe even the lords would believe him, if he could convince them that Captain Charles was a liar. They were civil gentlemen, and *they* wished him no harm; they had said so.

But they appeared to believe that liar who took your money and betrayed you. That was an awful thing. He would try to explain to them, next time. All the same, the worst cut of all was that these plots and murders and great noises of state were no concern of his: he had not even known Sir Edmund Godfrey was thought to be murdered by the Papists, until a friend of his had told him. The friend had been astonished at his dullness, but it had been no affair of his. Now, if he had been accused of something he had in truth done – such as getting drunk, and staying the night with a lewd woman, and trembling for ever lest Mr. Pepys should come to hear of it – then he would have cause for fear. His mind went back to a pleasanter day, two weeks or so ago, when he and a couple of ladies had been rowed to Greenwich to visit the hospitable Captain Vittells of the yacht *Catherine*. They had stayed aboard the yacht drinking until half-past ten. Then he dimly remembered being lowered into the yacht's wherry to be rowed ashore, along with the women, and a Dutch cheese, and half a dozen bottles of wine. He had a faint recollection of how the tide had run so fast that the wherrymen could not make

London Bridge, but had been obliged to put them all ashore at Billingsgate, and tumble them into a coach; still, he had been very much fuddled, and slept most of the way up.

If such a matter as that debauchery ever came to the certain knowledge of Mr. Pepys, he would indeed have cause to tremble. The doors of Derby House had been shut against him before this, for staying out all night. But this! – when he or his master had seen Sir Edmund Godfrey only once, to his knowledge, and then they had been very civil to each other. No: sure the lords would not believe that lying, wheedling Captain Charles. The lords, he thought almost tenderly, were his friends. It was all a mistake. He wanted to go home.

He was not going home; he was going to Newgate.

II

Newgate Prison. . . .

On the night before each hanging, the great and doleful voice of the crier must go calling past the cells of the condemned: *'You prisoners that are within, Who for wickedness and sin,'* it intones, accompanied by twelve solemn tolls of a hand-bell, with double strokes, 'after many mercies shown you, are now appointed to die to-morrow in the forenoon, give ear and understand, that to-morrow the greatest bell of St. Sepulchre's shall toll for you in form and manner of a passing bell, as used to be tolled for those at the point of death; to the end that all godly people hearing that bell, and knowing that it is for your going to your deaths, may be stirred up heartily to pray to GOD to bestow his grace and mercy upon you while you live. I beseech you,' it sings weirdly, 'for JESUS CHRIST'S sake, to keep this night in watching and prayer for the salvation of your own souls, while there is yet time and place for mercy; as knowing that to-morrow you must appear before the judgment of your CREATOR; there to give an account of all things done in this life, and suffer eternal torments for your sins committed against Him, unless upon your hearty and unfeigned repentance you find mercy through the merits, death, and passion of your only mediator and advocate, JESUS CHRIST, who sits now at the right hand of GOD, to make intercession for as many of you as penitently return to him. . . .'

Newgate Prison, the 'foul, heynouse jail' of the chronicle; since the time of King John a hold for felons; in origin a real gate, or gatehouse, in the city wall. Whittington's Newgate, where there was no water-supply at all until a philanthropic grocer caused the waste of a cistern to be diverted there for the relief of the prisoners, was almost destroyed in the Great Fire of 1666. But on these ribs there was rebuilt a prison which in twelve years had become as noisome as the old. Its great arched gateway – flanked by six-sided twin towers, battlemented and with statues in niches over the gate to give good moral effect – looked out over Snow Hill, where the refuse of the butchers' stalls ('guts, dung, and blood,' Doctor Swift was to write some years later) poured down the gutters to Fleet Ditch: as though the two places sympathised with each other for their similar purpose. Up over the gateway a windmill churned feebly in smoke, for there is small fresh air inside the place except what that windmill brings, and all the corridors have to be lighted by links. There is a water-supply now, but only two years ago there was a great to-do about water being refused to the prisoners unless they paid for it.

For here the rule of management is simple: it consists of extortion. The office of Head-Keeper (now held by Captain Richardson) is one of the most profitable in England, and is only to be obtained by a dear penny or much weight in high places. To the Keeper come all the profits from the drinking-cellars, the ward-fees, the cells with beds, the imported food, the entrance and discharge fees. His chief jailer and assistant turnkeys batten in their own turn on the prisoners, just as the prisoners batten on new arrivals. A new arrival must pay 'chummage' to his mates, unless he wishes to be beaten until he is more friendly; or have his clothes stripped off and distributed to better men.

If you are ever dragged into this place (which God forbid), it is well to know the ways. First there is the lodge at the gateway. Here you are clapped into irons, as a matter of form, until you pay 'easement'. If you are clearly penniless and without friends, they will either knock off the manacles or keep them on, according to the humour of the moment. But in any case you will go into the underground Condemned Hole – 'where,' writes one who has experienced it, 'you may repose if your nose suffers you to rest,' – until you have paid half a crown, no great sum, to get out. Then arises the question of whether you shall lodge in the Master Side or in the Common Side of the prison.

Of course, if you have plenty of money, and are openhanded with it, this unpleasantness can be avoided at the beginning. In this case you will have chosen the Master Side. Each felon or debtor pays 14s. 10d. on his entrance for fees and 'garnish money', 1s. 6d. for coals, and 1s. to be spent among the prisoners in the ward. Beds in the long room cost extra per week, and sheets still extra; but there is a common fire there in cold weather, and the Master Felons' Side is just over the uproarious drinking-cellar with brandy at fourpence a quartern. A nobleman or even a flush highwayman can lodge in the almost comfortable Press Yard. But the customary shrunken crew shovelled in from the Sessions House must go to the Common Side, already swollen to its grated doors, and on the Common Side they cannot reasonably expect air or light or coals or blankets.

Most of all, in this hive of link-lit passages, you will be aware of the din. It never ceases. Some prisoners, the turnkeys say, do not mind being shut up, so long as they can guzzle and crack jests in good company. Some grow mad, and are comic or a nuisance according to your mood. Some only sit still, but this is not usual. The women are the worst. Since they know they are not there for long, with transportation or the gallows as may be, they do not take the trouble or clean themselves or their wards, and lie like sows; their talk pales all others' for the ripe oath or the sexual simile; and the end is a scream of mirth. All mix and mingle in this pool. It is in the air. For the strongest-headed, as he ducks past the by-closet where the limbs of quartered men lie waiting to be boiled with bay-salt and cummin-seed, the strongest-headed must check himself, or his imagination will sicken, and behind his own cell-door he will begin to see a cluster of small mad faces peering in.

'You prisoners that are within, who for wickedness and sin,' cries the weird and wandering voice accompanied by the bell, 'after many mercies shown you, are appointed to die to-morrow in the forenoon. . . .' This of itself must strike terror to any wretch who hears it for the first time, when he is dragged into Newgate at night. Samuel Atkins, taken there by Captain Richardson himself, was fortunate in having little taste of the usual treatment. He was to be urged gently, until he should see the wisdom of keeping his eye on the main-chance.

Therefore, though he was put into solitary confinement without writing materials, he was at least kept in Captain Richardson's own lodgings. Here he brooded for five days, feeling that he must speak to the lords, and convince them, once he had got a grip on his defence. On Wednesday, November 6th, he sent an urgent message to the Lords' Committee asking to be brought before them again.

The Lords were elated. Time now to dip pen into ink, and eagerly await disclosures from the clerk. This time Samuel was not taken to Lincoln's Inn Fields; he was taken to my Lord Privy Seal's room by Parliament House, to a room with a polished floor, and great chairs of carven oak, and brocaded hangings to the windows; and here the committee sat in full dress, smiling upon him. 'Well, now,' says my Lord Shaftesbury, 'we hope you have better considered, and are ready to give the committee some light into this business?' But at the clerk's ominous words, 'I have considered, my lord, and I desire to clear myself –' the Green leader leaned forward sharply and struck upon a bell. 'Nay, Mr. Atkins,' says he, 'if you come to that, we must send for the captain. And the captain says he has much more against you, and you will appear the worst man living.'

When Captain Charles was fetched, with his pipe of tobacco in his hand, Samuel plunged into a defence. As

I

to Sir Edmund Godfrey's being a parliament man (i.e., of the Country Party as opposed to the Court Party), he had not known what Sir Edmund's politics were, and still did not know.   Captain Charles accused him of speaking of a quarrel between Mr. Pepys and Sir Edmund Godfrey, and added that it was 'upon this occasion'.   Captain Charles meant, did he not, that these remarks about a quarrel were made by him (Samuel Atkins) on the occasion of the last conversation between them, when Captain Charles had borrowed the crown?   That was the meaning of 'on this occasion'?   Yes.   But the last time he had seen Captain Charles was about the middle of August, a little before Bartholomew's fair time, and long before any discovery was made of the plot.   Therefore he could not have spoken of the plot, as Captain Charles said he did.   In fact, he had not even known that Sir Edmund Godfrey had taken any depositions at all, until after he had heard the magistrate was dead. . . . At this point the lords set up a cry of incredulity. What!   You work in an office of business, and did not hear of Dr. Oates's depositions until then?   Oh, that's impossible, young man.   Good God, what a generation of liars we live among!   Come, come, for the good of your soul. . . .

Samuel looked round him.   'My lord,' cries he, 'what if out of the pure invention of a lie, as it must be, I did say as the captain swears?   What if I said the captain's lies were truth?   What then?'

'Nay,' says my lord gently, 'leave *us* to make the use.   Do you confess it; then you shall be safe, and we will apply it.'

'My lord, I can't do it.'

'Indeed, Mr. Atkins, ten may swear against you, and for aught I know belie you,' says the other with great briskness. He added dryly: 'Are you innocent?   You're most unfortunate, and Captain Atkins must be the worst man – Pray, look one another in the face!'

This bantering was a slight mistake, and my lord, in satirically urging the wrong Captain Charles might do if he lied, presently went too far.   The captain was no hardy starer; his food or his sleep had disagreed with him; and he held hard to his pipe while he looked at Samuel Atkins from the other side of the table. The latter pounced. 'Look, my lords, for God's sake! – he's as white as a cloth!' There was a rustle and a pause. 'Where?' says my Lord Marquess of Winchester, blandly; 'where? I don't see it.' Whereupon Samuel Atkins looked around the council-board, discovering that Buckingham was staring at the candles in the wall-brackets, and Essex at the table, and Halifax at the roof, and the Bishop of London looking pity-ingly upon him, and Shaftesbury smiling. Captain Charles flung down his pipe on the table. 'Why should I say so, my lords, if he did not tell me?' cries he. And at last it pene-trated through Samuel's Puritan skull that here was as broad a hint as examiners ever gave: that these gentlemen meant him to tell lies: that they had him in their fingers, and meant to squeeze him dry.

They sent him back to Newgate, after a further examina-tion in which they told him they would prove he was a reputed Catholic, a great favourite of Mr. Pepys, and that he read Popish books to his master. This was enough to brood on, especially when the Bishop of London touched another fear by asking with great quickness: 'Are you given to drink and debauchery?' After this second lesson, he accompanied Captain Richardson back to the (at least) pass-able room in Newgate which he knew he could not expect to occupy much longer. The committee had begun to close its fingers. Samuel spent two sick, scared nights in solitary confinement before a new move was made.

Early on Friday morning he was awakened out of bad dreams by a rattle of rings, and saw his bed-curtains being drawn aside. Against the dingy light he saw Captain Charles Atkins, with Captain Richardson beyond his shoulder. Captain Charles wore the usual red breeches, broad belt, and tucked-up periwig, as much the mark of your seaman as the gunpowder spot on his hand; but his ex-pression belied it. He seemed in great agitation, firing off volleys of brandy-sighs, and his face was puffed with tears.

'Oh, good morrow,' says he hollowly.

Samuel leaped out of bed. 'Good morrow,' says he, and hurried after Captain Richardson in his shirt. 'Hold, captain,' says he, 'a word with you. For God's sake don't leave me with this man alone; he'll positively go and swear God knows what against me!'

'I have orders from the Lords' Committee to leave you alone with him,' declared Captain Richardson, who hurried out discreetly, and clapped the door shut behind him. Samuel Atkins turned back, shivering, to his companion. Captain Charles had fallen to stamping and wringing his hands as though with the cold. He greeted the clerk by crying: 'Oh, Samuel Atkins, we are all undone!'

'How, undone?'

'Oh, Lord, there's a man,' groaned the captain, 'there's a man come last night who has sworn positively against you that you were at the murder, or was to have been there.' He drew himself up more soberly, and looked at the clerk. 'This is an honest man; I know him slightly; he comes not out of the country. This morning he has sworn before the Lords' Committee that he knows those who did the murder; and that the murder was done in Somerset House, on the Saturday. And he has sworn that two nights later in Somerset House, by the light of a dark lanthorn, he saw you standing by Sir Edmund Godfrey's body. . . . My good uncle, Sir Philip Howard, has bade me come and tell you of it at once, so that you may repent before it is too late.'

III

For once Captain Charles's information was true.

Early in that week, on the day after Samuel Atkins's arrest, Mr. Secretary Henry Coventry was both perplexed and excited to receive a mysterious letter sent from Bristol. It was written by a certain Mr. *William Bedloe:* who lived in London but appeared to have gone out of town in a hurry. The letter was full of hints about terrible matters ready for discovery, and references to 'those people that sent him out of town'. He begged the Secretary to be allowed to return to London and see him clandestinely; but at the same time he asked for a public Order to the

Mayor of Bristol, so that his being brought back to town might be assured.

'These two things,' Mr. Coventry wrote back courteously, 'seem to be inconsistent. You may, if you think fit, come up of yourself, as privately as you can, without the knowledge of the mayor or any other person; being under no restraint, as I suppose you are not. But if you judge it convenient that Mr. Mayor should be acquainted with your coming, I have written to him a short letter here enclosed, and have sent you a copy of it, that you may consider whether you will make use of it or no. I know not whom you mean by "those people that sent you out of the town"; but, when you come to town, I will take the most effectual course I can for your safety and protection.'

No one had yet come forward to claim the reward for exposing Godfrey's murderers, and this appeared to be a bid for it. The unknown Mr. Bedloe had also written to the other Secretary of State, Sir Joseph Williamson. On November 5th Mr. Bedloe had himself taken up, with great public show, at Bristol. And on the afternoon of the 7th — the day following Samuel Atkins's second interview with the Lords' Committee — he was brought to London. That same afternoon Secretary Coventry sent word to the king to beg his Majesty's presence at the examination of Mr. Bedloe before the principal secretaries of state.

That request found Charles in his own apartments, restlessly a-prowl, so that even Chiffinch trod softly and looked in concern. For two weeks, ever since that first florid session of parliament, Charles had been gloomy and disquieted. Only this day there had been another bad scene in the House of Commons, when some of Coleman's letters were publicly read. Coleman, Coleman, Coleman! God's fish, the fellow had created more trouble than even the longest head could have predicted! Charles's overheated thoughts wandered away to his brother James. James had sworn to him (which his brother believed) that he knew nothing of Coleman's correspondence, or anything treated of in the letters; and he was asking his friends in both Houses to declare it for him. But even now James did not

seem fully aware of the danger in which he stood.   And
again Charles registered to himself a vow which had become
the strongest force in his life, all that he could hold in the
wreck.   He had said it to Danby yesterday.   'I would be
content enough if something were enacted to pare the nails
of a Popish successor,' he told the Lord Treasurer; 'but, by
Almighty God, I will not suffer my brother to be taken away
from me, nor the right line of succession to the Crown interrupted.'

Ay, they all trembled; but *he* must not tremble.   Thus
far, let it be admitted, my Lord Shaftesbury was not only
winning this game at chess: he was sweeping the board.   He
never made a mistake.   From his opening gambit he had
in sober truth forced Charles's rooks and knights to with-
draw, and put his queen and bishops in distress.   Presently
he might be in a position to overset the board altogether,
and call for a set of chessmen whose crowns were cut according to his pattern.

My lord had frightened the court: the women were the
worst.   Oddly enough, the staunchest was Queen Catherine,
dusky-pale as ever, growing thin with the hard years, shut
up among the priests at Somerset House as a target for every
knave's arrow, but still determined.   Louise was in tears of
fright.   Even the sensible Duchess of York, in the terror
after Godfrey's murder, had thought of fleeing to Holland.
And the murder of Godfrey. . . .

It was touching the murder of Godfrey that a message
from Mr. Secretary Coventry was brought to him, and he
went out to join the two Secretaries of State.   Again the
council was assembled, as it had assembled to welcome Dr.
Titus Oates; the old papers shuffled, the old clearing of
throats, the old eagerness when the doors were opened.   But
it was a very different sort of man from Titus whom they
brought in through those doors now, and whom they announced as Captain William Bedloe.

A handsome harsh fellow, this captain, with a decided
air.   If his manners had not now been a little on the humble
and wheedling side, as though from a strong attack of conscience which had prostrated him, you might have felt that

these manners would have been overpoweringly distinguished. He was tall, with a figure set off by a military campaign coat flopping with much gold braid. He wore a basket-hilted rapier rattling against the leg of one gambado boot, and swept a feathered hat across his breast when he bowed. His darkish periwig accentuated the handsome, sharp features; his eyes shifted under darkish eyebrows which met above them like the top of a cross; and he coughed a little to adjust his voice, which was mellow when it found its proper level. After he had made his obeisances, he stood at a dignified attention tempered by humility and the horrors of conscience.

Thus entered the second great accuser of the Popish plot: William Bedloe, late of Chepstow and the great world, cobbler, stable-boy, swindler, and horse-thief. 'Captain' William Bedloe, who never saw a battle, and whose apochryphal rank was gained by fraud from the Prince of Orange. In Flanders he had swindled an airy passage as 'Lord Newport', in France as 'Lord Cornwallis', and in Spain as 'Lord Gerard': for he had been a servant in the household of the Catholic Lord Bellasis, and he possessed the air. As Lord Newport he had slipped away, but Lord Gerard was thrown into jail for getting money under false pretences and Lord Cornwallis had been under sentence of death for a robbery in Normandy. He had got out of that, just as he had recently got out of Newgate with the smell of a £500 reward in his nostrils. Like Oates, he had been befriended by Jesuits, and like Oates he betrayed them. He was a less unpleasant rogue than Titus, and doubtless a merrier; more cautious and less have-at-you, except when he began to boast; but with as broad a talent at sending men to death for the Rhino, and a snarler when you crossed him.

Now he looked round at the assembled council, with a hollow yet bluff and manly eye to convince them of his honesty, and was sad. His difficulty was that he did not know what Oates had already sworn to,[1] as regards its exact

[1] This has been conclusively demonstrated by Andrew Lang, *The Valet's Tragedy*, and Father J. Gerard, S.J., *The Popish Plot and its Newest Historian.*

details, and he must support the Great Titus if he were to gain credit at all.   But he took the plunge, beginning with the account of a Popish plot to take Chepstow Castle, with twenty thousand religious cut-throats to be imported from Spain to be commanded by Lord Powis, and twenty thousand more from Flanders to be commanded by Lord Bellasis.

'. . . for I was born at Chepstow (may it please your lordships),' declared Mr. Bedloe, 'descended from no indifferent a great Irish family, if I may say so, though bred up an indifferent scholar.   My friends have all been Protestants since the world began.   True – I do not deny it! – I have been among Jesuits, else how could I unfold these things? But I went into the Prince of Orange's army, and there, finding the religious houses kind and obliging, I hearkened unto their arguments, and so was persuaded.'

'And thus,' said Mr. Coventry, 'you bore the rank of captain there?'

Mr. Bedloe tacked quickly.   He assumed a gruff air. 'My lords, I was not, in strictness, an officer in the Prince of Orange's army.   I was designed to be lieutenant to Vaudepert, a captain.   I employed some time to make levies in England from Holland; but, knowing the Jesuits by being four years among them, I learned of their designs.   I have travelled for them to Madrid, bearing letters.   It was Cave and Le Faire, Jesuits, who sent me –'

'Yet you are in England now, I think?' says Mr. Coventry. 'Where do you lodge, Mr. Bedloe?'

'Sir, I lodge where Captain Charles Atkins lodges,' says Mr. Bedloe, and seemed perplexed at the interest shown at mention of this name in one or two listeners: 'where Walsh the priest lodges, near Wild House.'   But something appeared to stick in the witness's throat, which he must get out.   He seemed to be working up a design of his own, and this mention of lodgings brought him nearer to it.   'Where Walsh the priest lodges,' he repeated, 'and near there lodges the priest Le Faire.   *Le Faire*: that is the man I would speak of, my lords.   Ay, Le Faire.   Le Faire is an Englishman, who calls himself a Frenchman. . . .   My lords, did I not say, as I tell you now, since it has pleased God to work upon my heart, that I could make a discovery concerning the horrid and damnable murder of Sir Edmund Berry Godfrey?'

It was over and out, and they were silent, while Mr. Bedloe watched them. He took his risk: 'My lords, I cannot but tell the truth, may Christ in His mercy pity me! I was offered two thousand guineas to be in the murder – in *a* murder, for they did not tell me who was to be killed. I was offered it by three of those who did the murder: by Le Faire; and by my Lord Bellasis's gentleman; and by the youngest of the waiters in the queen's chapel, one that wears a purple gown, and is employed to keep the people orderly.'

Nobody spoke at this evidence, which reflected towards the queen. Nobody dared speak, or turn an eye towards the king, who sat without moving. But Bedloe's laced finery shook about him, and his own eye took courage when he roared:

'They murdered him in Somerset House. They murdered him in Somerset House, in the corner room: the left hand as you come in, near Madame Macdonnel's lodgings, and near the room where the Duke of Albemarle lay in state. But they did not tell me they had murdered him until after he was dead. I would not join with them. . . .'

'Stay a moment, Mr. Bedloe,' says Sir Joseph Williamson. 'Who were the actors in this, that did the murder? I have one Le Faire; and a servant of my Lord Bellasis; and a chapel-keeper at Somerset House?'

'There was one other. There was Walsh, the priest, that lodges where I lodge. These four strangled him.'

'This chapel-keeper at Somerset House – how is he named?'

'Sir, I do not know his name, but I know the man. He wears a purple gown.'

'My Lord Bellasis's gentleman: how is *he* named?'

'Nor do I know that for certain,' replied Bedloe, knocking his fist against his head, 'but my Lord Bellasis's gentleman is he that waits upon him in his chamber, and none other dresses him but he. He is of middle stature. He has little whiskers like a Frenchman.'

'Well, go on.'

'The trappan,' said Bedloe eagerly, 'was managed thus. They persuaded Justice Godfrey that, if he would go a little way into the Strand, they would make a great discovery to him. Justice Godfrey called a constable, and appointed the constable to meet him at Strand Bridge, with power to take into custody. In the interim of which, they persuaded Justice Godfrey to walk into Somerset House. And while he was walking with two of them – my Lord Bellasis's gentleman and a certain Jesuit whom I know not – then others hurried out with gloves, and stopped his mouth, and hurried him into the room. There they stifled him with a pillow; and then, since he struggled, they tied a cravat about his neck and so strangled him.

'This was in the Saturday afternoon, the 12th of October. When it was done, Le Faire sent for me – by a footman in blue livery – to come to Somerset House in the walk under the dial. And when I had come there, Le Faire told me they had done it. Le Faire, and my Lord Bellasis's gentleman, and the chapel-keeper offered me two thousand guineas if I would help to carry the body away at night.'

Heads were gradually turning in the direction of the king. The Privy Council was not so zealous in finding evidence as was the Lords' Committee, but here was as flat an accusation as you might find. King Charles did not betray any of that fury which possessed him when any reflection ever touched on his wife or his brother: and Charles's genuine rages were such that no one who faced him ever forgot it. The worst thing you might do in his presence was give any hint which so much as brushed the queen. But he still remained silent, his sardonic eyelids moving a little, looking upon Bedloe; and Bedloe had grown so confident that he almost returned the look.

'And pray, Mr. Bedloe,' asked Secretary Coventry, 'did you help to carry him off?'

'No, my lords. I would not do it. It was the chapel-keeper carried him off. They carried him off in a sedan-chair about Piccadilly, and so on to the fields.'

'Did you see Sir Edmund Godfrey's body after he was dead?'

'No, my lords, I did not see him. They told me he was in Somerset House.'

Here Charles intervened curiously. 'Now why, Mr. Bedloe,' he asked, 'was Sir Edmund Godfrey to be killed?'

The other was prompt. 'Why, may it please your Majesty, 'twas done in hopes that the examinations he had taken would never come to light.'

'Was it so? But pray, Mr. Bedloe, where was the good of that? The parties that gave the informations are still alive to give the same informations again.'

This was a bad one, but Bedloe met it. 'Why, 'twas in hopes that the second informations taken from the parties would not have agreed with the first; and so the thing would have been disproved, and made it not to be believed. Ay, and for this reason my Lord Bellasis advised it. Mr. Coleman and my Lord Bellasis,' added the witness, growing bolder, 'advised to destroy him.

'And my conscience was upon me, and I could not abide it. Wherefore,' he said hoarsely, 'I escaped yesterday fortnight by coach from the "Talbot" in the Strand to Bristol. And, upon coming to Bristol, I sent for my dear mother; and upon her blessing she charged me to discover whatever I knew. My lords, I will take my oath and the sacrament of all this. I have had the racks of all this for a whole year in my conscience. For I would have got the truth of their designs three months ago, when the king was at Windsor, they about that time whispering something: but not so as to let me know it. But I come before you now a little eased of this horrid weight, to crave God's pity and your pardon.'

There was more discursive talk, of plots and accusations in general, before the king concluded the meeting by ordering Bedloe to the bar of the House of Lords next day. Charles left the council-meeting in wrath. In many respects this deposition of Captain William Bedloe was an ever greater tissue of nonsense than that of Titus Oates. 'Why did the Jesuits murder Justice Godfrey and steal

Oates's depositions?' 'It was in hopes,' replies Bedloe, 'that the second informations taken from the parties would not have agreed with the first; and so the thing would have been disproved.' Here was sublime absurdity. Were even the House of Commons such culls as to believe that, after the second set of depositions had been taken, the Jesuit murderers would then triumphantly produce the originals, saying, 'Ha, ha! Here are the original depositions, which we stole from Godfrey when we murdered him, and now you can observe that the two don't agree?'

Well, but there were other things as well. It was possible (considered Charles, who had been wrought up to a pitch by this indirect accusation of Catherine) that good Captain Bedloe had gone too far, and might be trapped. Charles had a mazy recollection, which as yet he could not confirm, that he himself had been at Somerset House on the Saturday afternoon when Bedloe said the murder took place, though he afterwards remembered he had been at Newmarket. But above all Bedloe had made a flat statement: 'They murdered him in Somerset House, in the corner room: the left hand as you come in, near Madame Macdonnel's lodgings, and near the room where the Duke of Albemarle lay in state.' Now this was not exact; there were many rooms to choose from thereabouts, in such a large place. But it was possible that Bedloe might choose ill, and that he might select some chamber which was so full of people all day long that you might as well speak of doing a murder in the Stone Gallery at Whitehall. Therefore let him be tested. To-morrow let him go before the House of Lords, and commit himself publicly on oath. Afterwards let him be taken to Somerset House, in the company of some good Protestant – say Charles's own son, the Duke of Monmouth, who was the idol of Shaftesbury's party; and (taking no chances) a guard of musketeers to see fair play – and there let Bedloe point out the room. It was possible that cautious Captain B. might have planned well. Nevertheless, if he had not –

But the next morning, which was Friday, November 8th, Captain Bedloe brought a fresh surprise to everyone.

They took him before the bar of the House of Lords; and he made a great impression. Lean and buttoned up in campaign coat, his harsh eyebrows lending a pleasing Puritanical touch to his face, he pleaded for pardon like an honest man. The first part of his story was, in main essentials, very like the story he had told the day before. Le Faire, Walsh, the chapel-keeper, and Lord Bellasis's servant were still the murderers; Godfrey had still been lured into Somerset House, and stifled between two pillows (he said one pillow yesterday, but the point is too small for a quibble); Godfrey had still been killed or kept 'either in the room or the next where the Duke of Albemarle lay in state' (which was slightly different from yesterday's story, but nothing important); finally, Godfrey's body had still been carried away by Somerset-House retainers on Monday night.

Then occurred the surprise. Yesterday he had sworn that he had not seen Godfrey's body after the magistrate was murdered. To-day he swore he had seen the body, before it was carried out at night. And – after a conference with the Lords' Committee – he now wove a sinister story of prowlings and mysterious tappings on doors at Somerset House after dark. He told of how he was taken by the hand, and led to a dim place where the body lay; there the slide of a dark-lantern was thrown back, so that by its light he saw two men standing over Sir Edmund Godfrey's corpse. These two men were Lord Bellasis's servant, *and Samuel Atkins, Mr. Pepys's clerk.*

'Now surely,' said King Charles meditatively, 'this man has received a new lesson during the last twenty-four hours?'

He had. Though Captain Bedloe had not spoken or thought a word concerning Samuel Atkins the day before, still it was not to be expected that the Lords' Committee (after all their trouble) would fail to find a way of including their most valuable prisoner in Bedloe's story. With a little ingenuity, Samuel could be fitted into the tale somehow. Bedloe, by a happy chance, lived in the same house as the redoubtable Captain Charles, and was well acquainted with him: so that the two worthies concocted a sound story with the assistance of Sir Philip Howard. If Bedloe had never met Samuel, still Captain Charles could supply any necessary information. And Bedloe was agreeable, though cautious. With this addition, Bedloe's story could not be bettered in any way. It was a grenade with a double charge: one charge exploded against the actual Jesuit murderers, and the other charge blew up through Atkins, through Pepys, to the Duke of York.

Thus the ends of the tale converge, the destinies cross. Bedloe from one side, Captain Charles from another, the Lords' Committee from still a third, all come together to shut in Samuel Atkins. They have got him, and he cannot get out: the thing has an air of inevitability about it. Thus, on that same morning of November 8th, Captain Charles was sent hurrying to wake up Samuel with news of Bedloe's discovery; there to rave and blubber with crocodile tears that they were both undone; there to insinuate promise of rewards if Samuel would only confess. The whole drive of the plot-hunters now centred round a dingy room in Newgate Prison, where a white-faced clerk sat on the edge of the bed in his shirt, and red-breeched Captain Charles stalked about the room with alternate tears and threats.

'Ay,' repeated Captain Charles, 'my good Uncle, Sir Philip Howard, has bade me come and tell you of it at once, so that you may repent before it is too late. And,' says he, with a confidential leer and a nod of dark secrecy, 'didn't you once tell me – come, now! – that your master was a concealed Papist, and had a house at Rouen? And you know you desired me to impeach Mr. Pepys about this murder, because then he would take the blame for it, and keep it from being laid to the Duke of York?'

IV

Samuel Atkins got up. 'Oh, God,' says he, 'when did you swear to *that* lie?'

'What should I swear it for? But you know you told me,' answered Captain Charles coolly. 'Come,' he said presently,

'I am sent by the Lords' Committee. You cannot be hurt, but shall make our fortune, and what should you care for your master? Come! We are both young men, and we ought to lay hold on this fair occasion of making our fortunes.'

Thus the clerk was left to reflect on the matter. In the afternoon Captain Richardson came upstairs and put him into manacles, for better show when he was taken before the Lords' Committee. Again they went to Westminster. The season of black fogs had come on, mingling with a sooty drizzle from chimneys, so that from under the arch of Newgate little was to be seen except occasional smears from fires where the sellers of hot baked apples and pears stood screaming their wares, or a stray tallow-dip in a window, or the loom of ever-splashing crowds. Fog muffled the din of wagons down Old Bailey Hill. Fog crept through the series of ponderous grated doors which the turnkeys clanged and thudded, one after the other, to let them out, with a fall of chains and clank of bolts which sounded like companies of soldiers grounding musket-butts on stone. One turnkey chuckled at another's joke that it was growing proper cold, and in another month it would be merry times for any prigster in ill rigging who should be clapped into Old Susie without rib or prog.

Young Atkins was not yet familiar enough with Alsatian cant to understand that it would be merry times for any ill-clad jackanapes who should be put into the underground Stone Hold without bread or meat. But he had heard of Old Susie, and of the fetter-hold for refractory prisoners. His mind was not easy when Captain Richardson took him out of Newgate, down Old Bailey Hill past the Sessions House, across Ludgate, and down Blackfryars to Blackfryars stairs, where they took wherry for Westminster.

The contrast was still greater at the meeting of the Lords' Committee, where all was pomander-scent and the ease of life. A large committee sat to greet him: the Duke of Buckingham was feeding sugar-plums to a wolfhound, and my Lord Shaftesbury was pleasantly weary as with a riddle solved at last to satisfaction. Samuel Atkins felt his heart sink when he saw, across the table from my lord, a tall, dignified, stern-browed stranger in a blackish periwig and military campaign coat – who saluted him civilly on his entrance, as though he knew him.

'Ah,' says Shaftesbury. 'Now, Mr. Atkins, you don't deny you know this gentleman, do you?'

'My lord, I never saw him before in my whole life!'

'And what say you, Mr. Bedloe?'

Mr. Bedloe's native caution, in the face of the young man's still-defiant glare, evidently made him hesitate a little, as though he wished to make sure no bubble was being put on *him* by the lords; and therefore he felt his way gingerly. He turned a reproachful look on the clerk, and spoke with a degree of sadness. Said he: 'I believe, sir, I have seen you somewhere, I think, but I cannot tell where; I don't indeed remember your face.'

My Lord Duke of Buckingham sat up with some abruptness. 'Is this the man, Mr. Bedloe?' he asked warningly.

'My lord,' answered the other, 'I can't *swear* this is he. 'Twas a young man, and he told me his name was Atkins, a clerk, belonging to Derby House; but I cannot swear this is the same person. The light being bad –'

'But to the best of your knowledge,' insisted Shaftesbury sharply, 'you verily believe this to be the man?'

'Yes, my lord.'

'And he told you his name was Atkins, a clerk, belonging to Derby House?'

'Yes, my lord,' declared Bedloe, and took a firm stand.

'That will suffice. . . . Now, Mr. Atkins,' says my Lord Shaftesbury, with grim gentleness, and tapped his finger on the table, 'here's a positive oath, here's positive evidence, that on the Monday night of October 14th, between the hours of nine and ten o'clock, you were standing beside Sir Edmund Godfrey's dead body in Somerset House. Good God, what more would you have? If you were not in Somerset House at that hour, where do you say you were?'

'My lord, I don't know! How can I know? It being so long ago –'

There was a general nod of satisfaction, and they sent

Bedloe out of the room so that matters could be dealt with more frankly. Shaftesbury was at the end of his patience with this useless playing round the mouse. He leaned over the table and made a flat offer. 'Mr. Atkins, if you are innocent, you are the most unfortunate creature alive. Now I'll tell you what: here's good news for you: here's but one way to save your life, and you may now have it. Confess all you know, and make a discovery in this matter, and your life will be saved. . . .

'Nay, now, won't you "tell a solemn lie to the prejudice of anyone?"' says he, mimicking as the other burst out. 'Now that's most gallant of you, Mr. Atkins, and you deserve a reward, and I'll tell you what: you'll be either hanged or knighted. If the Papists rise and cut our throats, you'll be knighted. If not, you'll be hanged.'

He stated the evidence coolly, making point after point on his fingers, and a chorus sustained him. There were others concerned in this plot, he announced, whose names Mr. Bedloe had not yet chosen to make public: ay, and (put in the Duke of Buckingham) all of them were now in custody. If one of those persons confirmed Bedloe, as they must, then all the world could not save Samuel Atkins.

'My lord, nobody more than I would be glad of true discoveries,' says the clerk, 'but I cannot suffer by things being misplaced. . . .'

There was a pause, and they sat back, looking at him. 'Oh, he'll confess nothing,' said the Duke of Buckingham. 'He expects a pardon.'

'I'll secure him from *that*, I warrant you!' snarled my Lord Shaftesbury, and got up. 'There's three hundred to one. Call Captain Richardson. Take him back to Newgate.'

It was the end. The clerk knew it, and sat huddled up on the return journey. They took him back, and set him away in hand and leg irons, and all night he remained awake looking at the dark. He was charged with having been seen standing over the dead body of Sir Edmund Godfrey: whom he had only seen once in his life, when the magistrate came to confer with Mr. Pepys over some business. He was

K

accused of being seen in Somerset House on the night of Monday, October 14th, between nine and ten o'clock. He would not have believed, truly, that people could tell lies like that.

It seemed to Samuel Atkins that he had grown very much older in one week. He was not now concerned with little Captain Charles, who took your money and betrayed you; he was concerned with larger, and more perplexing and maddening things. It was not that he much minded, one way or the other, but he would not be put upon. It was the mere bigness and overbearing calm cheat of this business, as though a tapster should swear you had not paid a reckoning when you had paid it, that determined him to fight: the calm fashion in which they told you you had better swear away your master's life, and no nonsense about it. God rot 'em, anyhow! thought the mouse, and began to nibble at his bonds. Ay, fight: but how prove he was not in Somerset House on the Monday night, when they all swore he was? How did a man prove where he was on such-and-such a date, unless he had some cause to remem –

Samuel Atkins stopped writhing in his manacles, and in the gall of the cold: for the darkness seemed to have a window in it. He saw a trim yacht riding at Greenwich, against the bleak low shore in October. He saw a cabin with wine-bottles on the table, and the laughing faces of women half-boozy, and the captain a-chuckle, and himself shouting out toasts. He felt himself being lowered like a sack into the wherry, as foxed as ever a man was, while the rowers strained against the tide. He remembered that: just as it had come into his mind, in fear, when they first arrested him; and the night of that debauch had been the night of Monday, the 14th of October.

Little by little, here in terrible doubt, there in-assurance, he became certain of it. Monday, October 14th. On that afternoon, at half-past four o'clock, he and the two women had arrived at Greenwich, and gone out in a little boat to the yacht. They drank until seven, at which time they had supper; and he, determining to stay on, had sent back the little boat. After supper they had resumed the merriment, until half-past ten at the very earliest. Then ensued that cloudy journey in the wherry, with a Dutch cheese under one arm and a woman under the other. An hour afterwards he was stumbling into a coach at Billingsgate, with a lass speaking encouragingly; ay, and now let him admit to more, this his conscience, that he had stayed the night with her. To-day that damned rogue in the blackish peruke had sworn he was in Somerset House between nine and ten. Well, but, if need be, he could produce a dozen good Protestant witnesses to swear in open court that he had been drunk and a-roystering instead.

He could think of the whole world raising its hands in horror at such debauchery; but he lay back and cried a little nevertheless, for he knew now that he was not going to be hanged after all.

. . . And some mile and a half away, in a very different sort of room and a very different sort of bed, another man (who had a conscience less sensitive on the matter of claret and willing dames) lay contemplating the underside of the bed-canopy with equal satisfaction. The room was not altogether dark. There was a fire of Scotch coal burning under the hood of a carven chimneypiece. Its light showed that the bedstead was of a somewhat more gaudy form than the man would have chosen himself, being crusted with silver ornaments of cupids, crowns, slaves, and Jacob Hall dancing on a rope of wirework. The light also showed that this room was in some disorder, with a land-skip fan lying on the floor in the glow, and a red satin petticoat imperfectly hung on a chair.

This man lay with his hands behind his head, regarding the roof with satisfaction which was a relief to old bones. He was not acquainted with Samuel Atkins, nor had he heard of him until this day, but he was reflecting (at this particular moment) on much the same matters.

His test had been a success. That afternoon he had sent Captain William Bedloe, with a guard, to point out the room at Somerset House in which Sir Edmund Godfrey had been murdered and hidden. The test had been rendered a dozen times simpler by Captain Bedloe's swearing to-day that he not only knew of, but had actually seen with his own eyes, the room where the body lay. And the result had been satisfactory, for Captain Bedloe had chosen a room where it was most certain to everyone's eye that none of these things could possibly have been done. The room he had selected was the queen's backstairs, the place where the footmen waited all day, the common passage for all the queen's servants, the place through which even her food was carried. In the face of such a regiment of witnesses, to say nothing of the sentries at every door and the foot-company stationed inside, not even the most violent Attorney-General could hope for a verdict if he prosecuted on this particular reconstruction of the murder. They would have to devise a very different story.

It was the first time one of my Lord Shaftesbury's gambits had been stopped. His stroke into the queen's territory, with a knight of the post, had been stopped with mere pawns. True, it was no great set-back; the Green lord lost nothing; and he would return with fresh traps before you could say Titus Oates. But it gave a space for thought. Thus this man lay drowsily contemplating the roof, and listening to light breathing not far away while he smiled.

'Yes, my lord,' says King Charles musingly, to the silver figure of the rope-dancer on the bedstead; 'you will have to try again. You will have to try again.'

AN INTERLUDE FOR CONNOISSEURS IN MURDER

The Evidence

' "Pon my word, Watson, you are coming along wonderfully. You have really done very well indeed. It is true that you have missed everything of importance, but you have hit upon the method, and you have a quick eye for colour." '

Adventures of Sherlock Holmes

'THEIR club,' – we return to De Quincey again – 'is styled, The Society of Connoisseurs in Murder. They profess to be curious in homicide; amateurs and dilettanti in the various modes of carnage; and, in short, murder-fanciers.'

We are now to follow the great Thomas's example, and initiate a similar club or council-board to debate the solution of Sir Edmund Godfrey's murder. Ours need not be a club of such rowdy meetings as those described by De Quincey: we need have no such members as that sinister character, Toad-in-the-Hole, who concluded the meeting by firing pistols all over the place and calling for his blunderbuss. Nor need we carry matters in such a spirit of ferocious waggery; in fact, when you read the minutes of De Quincey's society, you have sometimes an uncomfortable suspicion that you have strayed into a club of real murderers, and that Thurtell (as he claims) was really its first president.

But take a long library, lined with all the books that will be needed for this investigation, with shaded lamps and a rare print or two of curious crimes; let the time be a spring night, so that the windows can be set open to suggest life and change in a fresh-scented world; let the rafters be old and mellow, the chairs comfortable, the glasses filled, the cigars lighted. Therefore there will be outlined twelve suggested solutions to the riddle of Godfrey's death, with the

principal arguments in favour of each. A round dozen
should be enough alternatives for anyone's taste. All of
them have been hazarded at one time or another, from 1678
to 1936; most of them have had the backing of one distinguished historian or another; nevertheless, we do not now
sit as historians, but as detectives. After the evidence has
been placed before us, the historian shrugs his shoulders
and in most cases intimates that our guess is as good as his,
and our analysis likely to prove as valid: since we are like
to sit in a much longer library, and in much more distinguished company t'other side the Styx, before ever we learn
the truth.

Now, in outlining these twelve theories, no attempt will
be made at the moment to offer *objections* to them, or pull
them to pieces: that will be done later: at this point we only
offer as strong a plea as is possible for each case – as, in the
course of two centuries and a half, some person or other has
done for each. In some instances we shall see the fallacy
almost immediately; other instances are apt to seem strong
and plausible cases. In any event, it is well that we should
stop at this point for consideration. Matters have now been
carried up to the end of the first fortnight of November,
and before long the authorities will themselves have chosen
those whom they believed to be the murderers. So let us
first sketch out our Bloody Dozen, which are:

I

*That Sir Edmund Godfrey committed suicide, by falling
upon his own sword.*

First of all, it will readily be admitted that, if all the
other *physical* contradictions of the death could be explained naturally – the crease in the neck, as of a cord or
band; the bruises on the chest; the complete absence of
blood; and certain other points – then this theory is not only
tenable, but is among the strongest on the ground of motive.
Sir Edmund's father had died suicidally mad, after several
times attempting to take his own life. That his son had
inherited this melancholy taint was common knowledge;

Sir Edmund did not deny it, and it is confirmed by his own words and behaviour.   At this particular time, moreover, he was in a morbid state ripe for suicide: in bad health, on the verge of a breakdown, imagining himself to be beset by vast dangers: and, above all, with his conscience hag-riding him.   He was the close friend of Coleman, an apparent traitor; he had warned Coleman, he had concealed information from the government.   Not only had he vio-lated for ever his public reputation as an upright justice, but he was in danger of ruin and disgrace even if he were not sent to Tyburn.   Mark his actions on the eve of his disappearance: his wildness among his friends, his insistence on settling up all his accounts to the smallest debt, his remark to his friends, 'Shortly you will hear of the death of somebody,' his burning of papers, even his grim remark to the clerk when he determined to wear his old coat instead of the new one when he went out on Saturday: 'It will serve the day well enough.'

Very well.   On Saturday morning he sets off for Primrose Hill, determined on suicide.   And here it may be well to consider those curious droppings of a wax-candle on his breeches, which had so ominous a suggestion in any theory that he was murdered.   But it may be remembered that on Friday evening, before he went to Mr. Welden's house, he had attended a meeting of vestrymen at St. Martin's-in-the-Field; in other words, *in a church*.   There is no place where we may more reasonably expect to find wax-candles, and Sir Edmund, in the overwrought state of mind to which every witness agreed, may reasonably both have got those spots upon himself and have failed to notice them.   On Saturday morning, then, he goes to Primrose Hill: but it is a dark jump he is contemplating, that plunge from life, and even then he cannot make up his mind to it.   By noon or one in the afternoon, he returns wretchedly to town: hence his agitation when he passes Mr. Radcliffe's house in the Strand, and his refusal to stay to dinner.   The day has been miry, and he has been walking through the fields with mud nearly to his ankles; altogether aside from his prim, neat nature, a man who has been plodding in such fashion will not wish to have so much mud clogging his ankles like weights. He has his shoes cleaned by one of the street shoeblacks with which London abounded, using their mixture of soot and rancid oil; he goes to a tavern or coffee-house, he broods wretchedly, and he makes up his mind again to the act. But he is an old man. He cannot face again that three-mile walk to death; so he takes a hired coach, and bids the coachman take him into the far lanes, and then be off. Hence the clean shoes, and the track of a coach a little way off from where he was presently found.

Here he sits for a long time, trying to make up his mind. His intention has been to hang himself with his own long cravat, from one of the stunted trees in that place by the pond of water. For this purpose he has taken off the cravat, buttoning up his coat-collar against the October wind. Yet he cannot face that slow choking. When he sees near by a ditch on whose edge a sword can be propped point upwards, so that a man may tumble on swift death, he throws the cravat aside, and makes up his mind at last.

Although this accounts for the minor points of the pattern, it may readily be admitted that so far it rests mainly on conjecture. But the major points – the bruises from neck to stomach; the absence of blood from a living body; the circle round the neck – can, medically speaking, be explained on clear grounds.

Every medical man is familiar with the process known as *post-mortem hypostasis*: the gravitation of the blood to the lowest part of the body, which takes place after death, and produces blue-black marks indistinguishable from bruises. A curious parallel to Sir Edmund's case is to be found only a few months before (February 4, 1678), when a Mr. Nathaniel Cony died – of being kicked to death, the prosecution alleged – after a brawl at a tavern in the Haymarket. The marks on Mr. Cony's breast and stomach were almost exactly similar to those on Sir Edmund Godfrey's; at the trial for Cony's murder, the defence produced surgeons to demonstrate that the apparent bruises were in reality caused by post-mortem hypostasis or suggillation.

Again by present-day medical evidence, the absence of blood on the clothes or in the ditch is not at all impossible. Haemorrhage, in the event of a sharp straight wound, can be restrained by a block caused by adhesion of the tissues on either side of the heart cavity, so that the wound is stopped as though by a tap, and the flow of blood is very small. It must be remembered that, after the sword had been withdrawn from Godfrey's body by Brown the constable, there *was* a flow of blood; unfortunately, the sword had been taken out in the dark, as the witnesses' entire first examination of the body had taken place in the dark; and, as a result, no one is in a position positively to state that this small quantity of blood was not already on his clothes when he was found.

Finally, the deep crease round his neck, as though from a strangling-cord, was later explained by one of the very surgeons who first examined the body. At the trial Dr. Richard Lazinby gave it as his opinion that the circle had been caused by a cloth or cord; but afterwards, from whatever cause, he gave a very different verdict. 'I went to see the body of Sir Edmund Godfrey,' said he, 'at the "White House" near Primrose Hill, where it lay upon the table with the collar not yet unbuttoned. But, going out of the room to refresh myself after my walk, and leaving a crowd of people there, I was soon after called back again to see the neck of the body, his collar being then unbuttoned. And, being asked what I thought of the two marks above and below, being just the breadth of the collar, which was a deep stiff collar: I gave it as my opinion that they were the marks of the edges of the collar. I said further that the swelling of the neck and the breast was so great above and below the collar that it occasioned those marks like a ring upon a swollen finger. . . . I later observed that the swelling of the breast had discharged itself into the lower crease, so that the crease was hardly perceivable.'

Since this view was agreed in by another surgeon, Dr. Thomas Hobbes of St. Clement Danes: since, if these marks were in truth caused by a tight stiff coat-collar biting deep into over-swollen flesh, the whole theory of strangling must be repudiated: then we have an apparently plausible support for the first solution.[1]

II

That Sir Edmund Godfrey committed suicide, by hanging himself; and that afterwards – to prevent his estate being forfeited to the Crown – his two brothers, Michael and Benjamin Godfrey, arranged other trappings to suggest murder.

Such a belief was strongly held by many at the time, to such an extent that a question was asked about it by the Lord Chief Justice at the trial. Its motivation is strong, and it has at least one piece of convincing corroborative evidence. If this hypothesis is to be accepted, the course of events must have been precisely the same as that indicated in the first solution – up to the point that Sir Edmund returned to Primrose Hill on Saturday afternoon, and there hanged himself with his band to one of the trees near the pond, as Sir Thomas Clifford had hanged himself some years before in Devonshire.

Now observe that one piece of evidence, which made a meaningless contradiction at the inquest, fits into place to explain everything. Henry Moor, Godfrey's clerk, stated that on Tuesday, October 15th – when the justice's disappearance was publicly announced – one Mr. Parsons, a coachmaker, told him that on Saturday Godfrey had in-

---

[1] This is a sort of synthesis of the seventeenth-century theory of Sir Roger L'Estrange and the able modern explanation of Mr. Alfred Marks in *Who Killed Sir Edmund Berry Godfrey?* – with an addition or two of which I am guilty. Hume and Lingard are inclined to concur in the suicide verdict. Hume says: 'The murder of Godfrey, in all likelihood, had no connection one way or the other with the Popish plot; and, as he was a melancholy man, there is some reason to suspect, notwithstanding the pretended appearances to the contrary, that he fell by his own hands.' And Lingard: 'After an inquiry of two days before the coroner, the latter opinion (i.e. murder) was adopted by the jury, but chiefly on the authority of two surgeons whose testimony betrays their profound ignorance of the phenomena consequent on sudden and violent death. Even at the time, the verdict was deemed so unsatisfactory that other medical practitioners solicited permission to open the body, but to this the brothers of the deceased made the most determined opposition. They were aware that a return of *felo de se* would deprive them of the succession to the estate, and on that account had laboured during the whole investigation to impress a contrary persuasion on the minds of the jury.' – Mark this latter statement, which will become very important in our next theory.

quired the way to Primrose Hill: therefore, the clerk says, he went there himself to look for Godfrey on Tuesday afternoon. But Mr. Mason, who knew Godfrey well, positively states that he met Moor in the fields near Primrose Hill on *Monday*.

Observe also that up to this time (viz., Monday afternoon) both of Godfrey's brothers had strenuously opposed any attempt to make public Sir Edmund's disappearance. Their almost frantic counsel had been to keep all things dark. But on Monday evening they suddenly and inexplicably changed their minds, and blared forth the disappearance at a public funeral on Tuesday morning. How are we to explain this swift change? Surely the most reasonable answer is that Henry Moor went to Primrose Hill on Monday afternoon, and found his master hanging; and that afterwards, to conceal the fact, he used Parsons's information to pretend he had not gone there until a day later.

This Primrose Hill is a lonely spot, where for two days a man may prowl or a body hang without discovery. Moor finds the body – a suicide, as he had suspected – he cuts it down, and then runs back to town to find out from the brothers what they must do. They are business men, not assassins or stage-showmen; and hence their efforts to arrange the trappings of a murder, so that Sir Edmund's estate may not be forfeited, partake of the clumsiness which seems to pervade this whole crime. Since the linen band with its knots and loose end would demonstrate that he had hanged himself to the tree, the band is cut off and taken away. The collar is buttoned up round the neck, in a forlorn hope that the creases can be covered up. Remember, in their favour, that there were no bruises on the chest: these 'bruises' were the result of hypostasis after the body had been thrown into the ditch. Now occurs the problem of the counterfeited murder: how are they to manage it? Within miles there is no weapon they can use – except a sword, and the dead man's sword at that. Even if they wore swords themselves, neither could be foolish enough to leave such a damning souvenir skewering the body. So they thrust, but it is their own brother they are thrusting: they are nervous, they bungle it: and hence those two wounds, as though a shaky hand had first jabbed the blade against a rib before a clean stab was made. Since it would be difficult and highly dangerous to move the body, they tumble it into a ditch. But now it will be understood why they are so eager to publish the disappearance. Until that body is found and decently buried, until they can be sure no man saw them at work in the fields, they will not sleep sound at night.

Thus far, gentlemen, in dealing with theories based on suicide, we have dwelt chiefly on the physical evidence; the bloodstains and wax-stains, the material shapes which can be put under a magnifying glass. But now we go on to murder, to motives, opportunities, outer indications, to thinner and more subtle signs. The material evidence must wait, for consideration at the end of the summing-up, in order to determine which hypothesis it best fits. We have next:

III

That Sir Edmund Godfrey was murdered by his brothers, Michael and Benjamin.

Of what their relations were with the justice, of what they privately thought of each other, nothing is known. We have no convenient domestic *mise-en-scène* so useful to fiction: no high words in the parlour or deep debts on 'Change, no servant to testify that their relations were anything but amiable. Nevertheless, we do have certain circumstantial evidence which might have roused the authorities if they had not been so intent on crying up a purely political murder, and which would have been the first thing to be investigated by a present-day detective.

Murder, like charity, usually begins at home. Now one of the most curious points in this case is the origin of the rumour – mysteriously set rolling on Saturday morning, before Sir Edmund had been gone from home for more than two or three hours – that he had already been captured and murdered by Catholics. At this time not even his own household could have known that he would not come back to midday dinner in the ordinary way; he had simply gone out for his morning walk, according to custom. Yet the report was all over town, and Saturday's news-letters carried it into the country. Mr. George Welden, Godfrey's close friend, at whose house the justice had secretly met Coleman and whose truthfulness has never been questioned, states that this report was started at noon on Saturday by Michael and Benjamin Godfrey. If they knew he had been snared, how did they know it, and why did they blurt it out so soon? – unless they were too eager to blame on the easy Catholic scapegoats a murder they meant to commit themselves.

IV

That Sir Edmund Godfrey was murdered by Jesuit priests, because of a dangerous secret which had indiscreetly been communicated to him by Edward Coleman.

This is not the loose and easy theory that, in Macaulay's words, 'some hot-headed Roman Catholic, driven to frenzy by the lies of Oates and the insults of the multitude, and not nicely distinguishing between the perjured accuser and the innocent magistrate, had taken a revenge of which the history of persecuted sects furnishes but too many examples.'[1] Now, that casual explanation is all very well, it is easy, it is possibly even true. But it cannot be argued, because there is no evidence either way; there is nothing either to attack or defend. You cannot murder a man with a generalisation, nor can you convict a specific person of that murder merely by saying that he must have been a fool if he did it. This effort to bring thirty thousand people into the dock at once must be ruled out of court; but our fourth theory – that Godfrey was murdered by certain Jesuits, for a certain definite reason – is a legitimate and powerful one, demonstrating, as Mr. John Pollock points out, that 'his death was no ludicrous act of stupid revenge, but a clear-headed piece of business'.[2]

When Godfrey received Oates's written examinations on September 28th, he immediately warned his friend Edward

[1] *History of England* (1849 ed.) i, 237.
[2] *The Popish Plot*, 155. See pp. 149-166.

Coleman. He met Coleman at Welden's house, where they
read the papers together, and afterwards a copy was sent
to the Duke of York. So much has never been denied; so far
he had earned only the extreme gratitude of the Catholic
party. But here enters the furious indiscreetness of Mr.
Edward Coleman. How are we to explain that remark of
Godfrey's to Mr. Wynnel, *I am master of a dangerous
secret, which will be fatal to me,*' his suspicion that he was
being dogged, his fear of being knocked on the head, his
fear of being 'the first martyr'? What secret? He knew
nothing that was not already known to the king, the council, and any one of the many who had read Oates's depositions. There never was any secret about Oates's depositions.
Godfrey's remark is explicable only if, during that significant interview at Welden's, Coleman himself let this secret
slip out. And there is a direct clue to what the secret must
have been. Hidden in Oates's tissue of nonsense and sick
malice there was one lonely half-truth: it was impossible
that even Titus Oates could write sixty-eight folio pages
without inadvertently telling the truth somewhere. He
declared that on April 24, 1678, there had been a great consult of Jesuits at the White Horse Tavern in the Strand, for
the purpose of debating ways to kill the king. Though in
reality it had been for transacting the ordinary business of
the society, there really had been a consult of Jesuits on that
date – not at the White Horse Tavern, but at a much more
dangerous place: St. James's Palace, the residence of the
Duke of York. And thus Coleman, coming on that item in
Oates's narrative, told Sir Edmund Godfrey the truth.

If this knowledge had ever come out, 'To Shaftesbury
the knowledge would have meant everything. Witnesses
of the fact would certainly have been forthcoming, and
James's reception of the Jesuits in his home was a formal
act of high treason. The Exclusion Bill would have been
unnecessary. James would have been successfully impeached and would have been lucky to escape with his head
on his shoulders.'

Such was the gunpowder entrusted to a conscience-racked
magistrate who already felt that he had been remiss in his

duty. It was his business to tell the government: hence his mutterings, his forebodings, and the explanation of every word he uttered. It was the Jesuits' business to take the only way of making certain that his conscience would not send him to betray that secret.[1] His death was a cruel necessity. His friends must kill him in order that he might not kill them. Of all solutions to the mystery, this is at least the most ironical, and runs exactly in line with the ingenuity of modern detective-story writers. A person, or group of persons, shall be accused under damning evidence at the beginning of the story; half-way through the book they are triumphantly cleared, by alibis or plain facts, and forgotten. But at the *dénouement* the change is rung again, the alibis are proved to be no alibis, the plain facts no facts, and the forgotten suspect bobs up as guilty after all.

v

That Sir Edmund Godfrey was murdered at the instigation of the Earl of Danby.

Again, before examining the real and solid case against this suspect, we must clear away one accusation which is manifest rubbish. In all the years of the Popish Plot, the person most frequently and violently accused of Godfrey's murder (aside, of course, from the Catholics) was the Earl of Danby. During the years 1679-81, when he had fallen from power, he was accused in a spate of pamphlets and letters to parliament. In 1681 he was actually indicted for the murder by a Middlesex grand jury, although the case was never brought to trial. This indictment was the result of a charge trumped up by one Edward Fitzharris, a known rogue. It stated that Danby had known of the plot before Oates disclosed it, and had tried to stifle it; that the upright Protestant magistrate Godfrey grew suspicious of his hushing-up, investigated it, and was about to reveal the Lord Treasurer's treason in protecting Papists, when Danby had him murdered.

This is demonstratably absurd, not only from what we

---

[1] Sir Edward Parry (*The Bloody Assize*, 27-88) agrees with this. See also C. R. L. Fletcher *An Introductory History of England*, iii, 42-43.

know of Godfrey – who himself did the hushing-up and protecting – but from what we know of Danby. Danby was
loudest of all in crying up the plot. His whole adminis-
tration was based on a hatred of Popery and France. More,
he was at that time in such danger from attacks by parliament that the plot seemed to come as a miraculous boon, to
turn their attention away from him. It is significant that
at the beginning even Shaftesbury believed the whole scare
to be instigated by Danby himself. Therefore we ought
carefully to consider the possibilities opened up by this,
especially since there is a certain remark of Godfrey which
indicates that the secret assassins he feared were the Earl
of Danby's men.

In discussing the theory before this one, we spoke of Godfrey's declaration, 'I am master of a dangerous secret, which
will be fatal to me,' together with his fears of being
knocked on the head in a dark lane, and we explained it
on the grounds that the place of the Jesuits' conference on
April 24th was told to him by Coleman. This is all very
well: but it does not go far enough. In his conversation
with Mr. Thomas Wynnel he did say, 'I am master of a
dangerous secret,' but it was not *all* he said; the full conversation has been given on p. 83 of this book. Sir Edmund
said: 'There is a design against the Duke of York, and this
will come to a dispute among them. You may live to see
an end on't, but I shall not. This much I tell you: I am
master of a secret, a dangerous secret, and it will be fatal to
me. *My security in the business was Oates's deposition.
Before Oates came to me, he first declared it to a public
minister; and then Oates came to me by that minister's
direction.'* Then Sir Edmund checked himself.

This puts an altogether different complexion on the
words. To begin with, 'There is a design against the Duke
of York.' Whoever had a design against the Duke of York,
assuredly it was not the Jesuits: therefore Sir Edmund
cannot have been referring to them. To whom did he refer,
then, in connection with this dangerous secret which would
be fatal to him? Who had a design against the Duke of
York; who was connected with the secret? The 'public

minister', and the only public minister who was in charge of the case, was the Earl of Danby.

Exactly what do these words mean?[1] Do they hark back to Sir Edmund's old fear – that, as he told Mrs. Mary Gibbon, he was in danger of being hanged by the government for warning Coleman, for stifling the plot, for never communicating Oates's narrative to the Attorney-General or the Lord Chancellor? Did he mean, in effect, 'My security would have been a zealous investigation of the charges in Oates's deposition. Oates first went to the Earl of Danby, who sent him on to me because he believed me to be an honest justice on whose quickness to investigate he could rely. Now that he has discovered I am in league with the Jesuits, my Lord Danby will have me hanged.'

But if this is the explanation of his words, then all Godfrey's fears turn into complete nonsense. He might well be afraid of being arrested for misprision of treason: but he could not conceivably go in terror of being knocked over the head by secret assassins. Everyone agrees that this is what he did fear. No public minister outside Bedlam, Danby least of all, would send cut-throats secretly to avenge a magistrate's neglect of duty, when he could immediately fling that magistrate into the dock in ordinary course of law. Moreover, public exposure would be a triumph for anyone crying up the plot; it would demonstrate that, when the best justice-of-the-peace in England had been corrupted by the wiles of the Jesuits, then no living soul was safe; and Godfrey in a dock would be very nearly as valuable as Godfrey in a coffin. Finally, if this is the explanation, what becomes of that 'dangerous secret' which has been the whole point of the debate? It has evaporated; it will not fit anywhere into the scheme; and so this solution to the puzzle of Godfrey's fears must be discarded.

Now observe that, in speaking of a design against the Duke of York and our old *monstrum horrendum* the

---

[1] See the very interesting discussion of this point in Andrew Lang's *The Mystery of Sir Edmund Berry Godfrey*, part three of *The Valet's Tragedy*. Here still another explanation is given of Godfrey's words, but it does not supply any explanation of the 'dangerous secret' which is the whole point of the dispute.

dangerous secret, Godfrey mentioned only two people: Oates – and Danby. Why? Godfrey knew Danby personally. At this time Danby was desperate. Ralph Montagu, former ambassador to France, had recently been recalled in disgrace; Montagu believed Danby to be responsible for this disgrace, and was promising trouble. For Montagu had still in his possession letters which Danby had written (at the king's direction, but in Danby's handwriting) asking for money from Louis the Fourteenth. If Montagu chose to produce those letters now, demonstrating before parliament that the anti-French, anti-Popish Danby had been asking for such money, then they would have the Lord Treasurer's head. It was not Danby's fault; but that is no consolation when you face impeachment; and he felt ill-used enough on every side to seize at any way out.

Then Tonge and Oates appear with their malodorous packet. Danby not only gives them strong countenance (this is beyond doubt); but he abets them, supplies fresh lies, and becomes himself involved in the sham. So he sends Oates to Godfrey; why should he, the Lord Treasurer, do any such thing unless he were determined to kindle a scare at any cost? Wouldn't that blatant jeer of Oates, 'I come from my Lord Danby,' show plain as a bloodstain how much the Lord Treasurer was involved? No sooner has the magistrate received the deposition, than he announces that Oates is sworn and is perjured. Danby knows that Oates has let drop a bragging hint, or much more than a hint, about his great patron; he suddenly discovers that Godfrey, the staunch Protestant, is an intimate friend of the Jesuits; and he believes, which is no less than the truth, that Godfrey has discovered evidence involving him. Godfrey's security was Oates's deposition, so long as he believed it. But when he learned that the Lord Treasurer was a plotter against the brother of the king, he had to die.

VI

That Sir Edmund Godfrey was murdered by Titus Oates.

Here is poetic justice. We may say with moderation that

Glorious Titus, if he was not 'the bloodiest villain since the world began', was at least the most thoroughly detestable bad smell which ever wandered through it. To apply the other term is to dignify him, to award him the robes and trappings of high crime; and Titus Ambrosius does not deserve such consideration. To convict him of this murder would not be altogether a pleasure, for it would endow him with a personal courage whose existence some have doubted. Nevertheless, the strong probability is that he did commit it. High legal authorities, including Sir James Stephen[1] and Lord Birkenhead,[2] have suggested this. Mr. Sidney Lee,[3] in his account of Godfrey, declares that it is the most probable solution. Glorious Titus has even figured as the murderer in fiction: notably in a skilful reconstruction by Mr. John Buchan, where the crime is made to take place in the Savoy. For of all people in England, Titus Oates had the most to gain by Godfrey's death.

At the time of the murder the Popish plot was almost cold in the mouth. Titus had been repeatedly trapped in lies by the king; his credit was diminishing, certain truths were being revealed concerning his past lying, and the great plot had begun to sicken. Something was needed to rouse the nation with a shock of horror; and this murder came, with an uncanny rightness never known outside fiction, at exactly the proper time. The clock strikes: Godfrey dies: Oates becomes the saviour of the nation. Godfrey thought that he was being followed by someone who always skulked out of sight – doesn't this sound like Titus? The wanton brutality of the crime, the stamping on the chest, the wringing of the neck – doesn't this sound like Titus? (Three years before the end of his life, when he was supposed to be somewhat sobered down, he was arrested for savagely beating a woman over, the head with a cane because she had

[1] *History of the Criminal Law*, i, 394.

[2] 'It is indeed doubtful whether there was a plot, but the probability is that some conspiracy was always on foot. . . . But an impartial observer is left with the uncomfortable feeling that Oates and his colleagues, or unscrupulous men behind them, may perhaps have committed the murder in order to rouse popular feeling against the Catholics.' – *Famous Trials*, 70.

[3] *Dictionary of National Biography*.

plucked at his sleeve.)   That he would have had the
courage, unfortunately, cannot be questioned: when after
his long career of success King James caught up to him, and
thrust the last lie down his throat, he showed that he could
endure pain with amazing coolness.   Finally, after he had
strangled the magistrate, his disposal of the body was exactly
in line with Titus's style of cunning.   He thrust a sword
through the body, because unwary Catholics might then
say the death was suicide; but it would be obvious to a child
that it was not suicide, and the statement would rebound
on them with an accusation of guilt.   In fact, the very first cry
that did go up – not an hour after the finding of the body,
and merely from a group of idlers in a coffee-house – was,
'They murdered him, and then they ran him through with
his own sword, to make people believe he did it himself.'

But this next leads us to a corollary theory, which is:

VII

*That Sir Edmund Godfrey hanged himself; and that
Titus Oates, who had been shadowing him for purposes of
blackmail, came on his body and arranged a 'murder' to
give credit to the plot.*

A very good case indeed, which is based on the question:
Why had someone (it appears) been consistently dogging
the magistrate?   Suppose someone had learned of his connection with Coleman, saw the rich possibilities of blackmail it unfolded, and therefore spied on the magistrate to
get full evidence – and who but Glorious Titus?   Mr. David
Ogg[1] sets forth as a slight indication: 'Still another reason
for suicide may be suggested.   Oates was an absolutely unscrupulous man who probably knew just a little of Coleman's activities and of his relations with Godfrey.   This
would be sufficient for a blackmailer, and so Oates may
have chosen Godfrey for this purpose. . . .   The theory of
blackmail is compatible with the hypothesis that, at least
after the fatal 28th of September, the magistrate was being
shadowed, whether by Oates or by someone interested in

[1] *England in the Reign of Charles II*, ii, 583-4; see pp. 579-584.

his movements; hence, the man or men on his trail may have been the first to come upon him while he was still hanging. If Oates or an accomplice made this discovery, he may suddenly have realised that, for the purposes of the plot, more could be made of Sir Edmund dead than alive; and as it is likely that the discovery was made in a solitary place, it would not be difficult to pierce the body with the sword, and leave it in a position which would suggest a death as spectacular as the other incidents retailed in the depositions. This hypothesis attributes to Oates a genius for propaganda, a not unreasonable attribution; nor is it inconsistent with the little we know of Godfrey's life and temperament; and it accepts consistency of motive as the principle inspiring the actors in the drama.'

VIII

That Sir Edmund Godfrey was murdered by the friends of Edward Coleman.

This solution is based on blackmail of a somewhat different kind, and intimated by Sir John Hall.[1] It supplies the answer to a question which must have puzzled us: how did Godfrey and Coleman come to be such close associates? What did these two, the sober magistrate and the showy babbling fanatic, have in common? Why did the magistrate risk his neck for the plotter, when his duty and his inclinations lay in the other direction? And assuredly the answer can be that Godfrey (like others) had been taking bribes of Coleman.

It is not at all improbable.[2] Whoever studies the political history of this reign must be moved to mirth or profanity, according to his nature, but at least to a dazed

[1] *Four Famous Mysteries*, III, 87-136. The aim of Sir John Hall's excellent discussion is to 'point out the unconvincing character of certain theories which have been advanced to explain his murder and to suggest the direction in which the truth probably lies.'

[2] In fact, one modern historian states that modern economic authorities have been curious about Godfrey's method of managing his wood and coal business, which appears to indicate that in his earlier years the magistrate may have been something of a crook. G. N. Clark, *The Later Stuarts*, 1660-1714, IV., 89.

surprise, at the nonchalance, the airiness, even the *naïveté*, with which everybody appears to be taking bribes from everybody else. On the surface it presents a spectacle of such incredible crookedness that it seems to belong to farce rather than to life. Take again the analogy of comparing these people to children. Now we need not derive our ideas of children from Christopher Robin; children are realists. They lie and cheat and indulge in shady transactions: but they stoutly deny that they do these things, and they are absolutely merciless to any of their number whom they catch at it. With the people of the seventeenth century, who despite their ingenuity and shrewdness were in many respects children, this curious but quite natural code prevailed. Mr. Pepys, as honest a man as ever worked at the Admiralty, records how he accepted a bribe; but he adds delicately that he took it without looking at it, 'that I might say I saw no money in the paper.' That stately old Cavalier the Duke of Ormonde, pattern of ancient virtues, took bribes. Even that austere republican Colonel Algernon Sidney, who once shot a favourite horse because Louis the Fourteenth had insisted on possessing it, ('It was born a free creature, it has served a free man, and it shall not now be mastered by a king of slaves!') was, despite this high-falutin, secretly in the pay of King Louis as one of Shaftesbury's lieutenants.

This motivation must be understood if we are to make sense of the political history of the time, and affords sufficient answer to those who have displayed so much pious horror at Charles the Second's 'selling the country' to France. Some bribes, of course, were mere indiscretions. Dutch bribes, Protestant bribes in general, held no deep taint, and came almost within the province of legitimate business. The great danger was dealing with Popish France. At the height of anti-Catholic agitation, when the mob stoned Nell Gwyn's coach under the impression that it was Louise de Kéroualle's, Nelly put her head out of the window and turned the tumult to cheers by saying, 'Good people, pray be civil: I am the *Protestant* whore.' They did not object to the whore, but to the Pope; just as they did not so much object to the bribes, as to the Popery. Very nearly everyone was taking Louis's money, and it was no great shame provided you were not caught; but if you *were* caught, then look to yourself! – for you were apt to find your head on a spike over Temple Bar.

Under these circumstances a probable explanation of Godfrey's association with Coleman is that he had been so unwise as to take a part of the money Coleman was doling out. Hence he was stuck fast in the intrigue, and Coleman's friends or allies reasonably thought he could never get out. He warned Coleman of the danger, yes; but what happened? Coleman was flung into Newgate just the same. Did they suspect Godfrey of treachery? Or did they expect him to help Coleman beyond his abilities; to take his place now as their helper; to, in Sir John Hall's hypothesis, 'fulfill some promise or redeem some pledge'? Godfrey refused; there was a meeting and a furious altercation, culminating in the struggle that killed him. They may even have kept him prisoner – thus accounting for the fact that he had eaten no food for two days before he died – under these threats; and then, finding that they had gone too far, the only refuge was murder.

IX

That Sir Edmund Godfrey was murdered by Christopher Kirkby.

In any well-constituted detective-story you will find the 'most unlikely person'; sauntering innocently along the verge of the action with his hands in his pockets, amiable, helpful, and open to no suspicion so long as it does not occur to anybody to wonder why he is sauntering there at all; but, at the unmasking, the unlikeliest person is discovered to have the likeliest motive of all. So with Mr. Christopher Kirkby. Examine his status: you will find that, if it is possible to make out a strong case against Titus Oates, it is also possible along different lines to make out an equally strong case against Oates's dupe.

That Kirkby assisted Oates and Tonge in preparing their lies, that he was party to the sham, cannot be believed for a moment. He was a much more dangerous person – a dupe and a fanatic. He believed, deeply believed, in every vaporing of Titus's imagination. He saw London in blood and ashes. He had been the first to warn the king; with what result? That he was exposed to complete scorn; that the king did not believe him; and, it may be remembered, when the king passed him in the Park, Charles cut him dead. His favour at court was irretrievably gone: through no fault of his own, but because, like a persecuted saint, he could not persuade his patron of the truth. He must have wished desperately for some means, any means, by which the snares of Babylon could be exposed in their wickedness.

But a worse thing happens. They have taken their depositions to that stern Protestant, Sir Edmund Godfrey, and Kirkby may rest secure in the knowledge that Sir Edmund at least will sound the depth of this devilish business. But the whole world is mad; the whole world is under the spell of Jesuits; for here's Sir Edmund not only cursing at honest Mr. Oates, but going to the Jesuits like a Protestant Judas and warning them. Here's treachery. And if any man ever deserved death, it was Justice Godfrey.

In connection with this theory, there are a few points which deserve to be considered very carefully. Kirkby, as has been remarked, wore a suit just like Oates's, and a fair woolly periwig like Oates's. In fact, on the important occasion of the revelation of the plot, Kirkby had been mistaken for Oates.[1] Now, ever since the murder there has grown up a rumour that Oates was the assassin; originating nobody knows exactly where, formless, but certainly contemporary before it was put into words; one of those mysterious current reports that are so often true. Suppose, then, that someone saw the murder done? And suppose that for the

---

[1] 'One Bedingfield, a Jesuit, deeply concerned in the plot, who had got (as is said) to be confessor to the Duke of York, had related in a letter to Blundel, another of the gang, that his Royal Highness had intimated some such thing to him, *viz.*, That a gentleman in *such-coloured habit*, and a minister, had been with the king and made some discovery. Now it happened that Mr. Kirkby, when he waited on his Majesty, had on a suit much of the same colour with what Dr. Oates then usually wore, which created such their mistake.' – *History of the Damnable Popish Plot*, 1680. See also Christopher Kirkby, *A Complete and True Narrative of the Manner of the Discovery of the Popish Plot to his Majesty*, 1679.

second time, on a critical occasion, Kirkby was mistaken for Oates?

Again, there is the question of that mysterious letter which arrived for Godfrey on the night before he disappeared, and which troubled his household so much. It is not conceivable that a minister of state, with Godfrey's death in mind, would write a letter making either a threat or an appointment: he would not be such a fool, considering that the letter might not be destroyed. Nor is it conceivable that hired bravoes would indulge in any such formality: they would wait for their quarry in a dark lane, and seize him: the more unexpectedly, the better. But it is precisely the course that would be pursued by a private person (and an incautious, fanatic private person) laying a trap.

And there is that recurring point of Godfrey's having taken no food for two days before he died. It has been argued that this supports the suicide theory: that Godfrey, broken down and on the verge of taking his own life, could eat nothing in the wretched days before he made up his mind. But this complete starvation seems unlikely, to say the least; and, fortunately, we have one piece of evidence which seems to refute it; for we know that, at Mr. Welden's house on the night before he disappeared, he did at least drink a glass of beer. And, *since the meeting ended with an invitation to dinner for the next day, which he tentatively accepted,* his friends (to say nothing of his household) observed no signs of a hunger-strike. Thus, whatever our whole solution of the mystery may be, we must agree that he was captured and kept somewhere in secret for two days before he was murdered. Was he refused food by his captors? But what if, on the other hand, it was he himself who refused food; because he did not dare eat it; because he knew it was meant to do away with him smoothly, without fuss; because he knew it was poisoned; and the murderer only adopted violent means when he refused the drug.

For Christopher Kirkby, it will be remembered, was a chemist.

X

That Sir Edmund Godfrey was murdered at the instigation of the Earl of Shaftesbury.

Here we have it; here's the most overwhelmingly strong solution of all.

Now we need not adopt the sweeping view, advanced by Dalrymple in the eighteenth century, that the whole Popish plot was a contrivance of Shaftesbury.[1]   But, on the other hand, we need not slur over his connection with it as did Christie,[2] his official biographer.   Even so sympathetic and lenient a critic as Osmund Airy admitted not only his 'unscrupulous violence' in the matter, but the streak of cruelty that ran through his nature;[3] and we have observed in his treatment of innocent witnesses that he was prepared to stop at no underhand measure, however horrible, to advance the credit of the plot.   All this lies beyond doubt: he admits it in his own words.[4]

[1] 'Shaftesbury framed the fiction of the Popish plot in the year 1678 in order to bury the duke and perhaps the king under the weight of the national fear and hatred of Popery.   Shaftesbury was stimulated, too, by offences both given and received.   For the king having said to him, "Shaftesbury, thou art the greatest rogue in the kingdom," he answered, bowing, "Of a subject, sir, I believe I am."

'It has been much doubted whether Shaftesbury contrived the Popish plot, or if he only made use of it after it broke out.   Some papers I have seen convince me he contrived it, though the persons he made use of as informers ran beyond their instructions.   The common objection to the supposition of his contriving the plot is the absurdity of its circumstances. When Shaftesbury himself was pressed with regard to that absurdity, he made an answer which shows equally the irregularity and the depth of his genius.   An account of it is in North's *Examen*, p. 95.   A certain lord of his confidence in parliament once asked him what he intended to do with the plot, which was so full of nonsense. . . ."It is no matter," said he; "the more nonsensical the better; if we cannot bring them to swallow worse nonsense than that, we shall never do any good with them." ' – Sir John Dalrymple, *Memoirs of Great Britain and Ireland*, i, 43-44.

See also a modern view.   'Was he a co-conspirator from the very beginning?   The answer must be in the affirmative, for in the list of "Worthy men" and "Men worthy" (to be hanged), found in his study in 1681, the name of Andrew Marvell appears among the former.   And Marvell died, on August 18th, 1678, while Oates and Tonge were concocting their articles.' –J. G. Muddiman, *The King's Journalist*, 211.

[2] W. D. Christie, *Life of Shaftesbury*, ii, 287-293.

[3] *Dictionary of National Biography* (1887 ed.), xii, 112; 124-125.

[4] 'But the Earl of Shaftesbury could not bear the discourse: he said we must support the evidence, and that all those who undermined the credit of the witnesses were to be looked on as public enemies.' – *Burnet*, ii,163-164.

Well, in the murder of Godfrey, *cui bono*? Who did stand to gain the most by it?   Oates certainly, or any knight of the post who could gain a few pounds for the pleasant and easy labour of bearing false witness; but then mightier issues were involved than the deification of one liar, or of letting Titus strut in gown and bands at Whig dinner-tables. Titus becomes merely Gulliver playing among the tea-cups of Brobdingnag. The very Throne itself was involved. A vast political party was coming into being, and growing strong enough to believe it could upset the legitimate succession, and it would not be far wrong to say that Godfrey's murder gave it more support than any other single act of the latter seventeenth century. *Cui bono?* Not the man whose stake was a shovel-hat and £1,200 a year, but the man whose stake was England.

This is merely negative evidence: there are positive indications that Godfrey was a terrible menace to Shaftesbury's party, and might kill it before it was many years old. We have been talking much of the 'dangerous secret' – which, it is suggested, was told to Godfrey by Coleman, and concerned the Jesuits' consult at St. James's Palace on the 24th of April. But there was another sort of secret, and one a dozen times more explosive. This has been pointed out by one of the ablest and most brilliant writers ever to deal with Stuart times, Mr. Arthur Bryant. Mr. Bryant says:[1]

'If Coleman ever confided to Godfrey the perilous knowledge of the Jesuits' meeting at St. James's, it is likely that he revealed to him an even more damning fact: that Shaftesbury's chief lieutenants, including Pepys's sworn foe Harbord, had been receiving at his hands secret pensions from the French King in return for their Navy-wrecking activities of the previous summer. If so, it lay in Godfrey's power to bring against these men, who posed as patriots and sworn foes of France, charges that amounted to high treason, and no one who knew his courage and probity of character could doubt that he would do so.'

There you have the most natural explanation, even the most humanly natural one. Wouldn't most human beings

[1] *Samuel Pepys: The Years of Peril*, ch. VIII, 218.

blurt it in the way Coleman probably did? – 'So *I* am accused of treasonable doings, am I? Well, let me tell you what *they* have been doing.' Also, it is the most natural explanation of Godfrey's forebodings. Here was no religious secret, which did not weigh greatly with Godfrey. If he had already risked his neck to warn Coleman and the Duke of York, he was not likely to execute a complete about-face merely because a consult of priests had met at one place rather than another: especially since, if he were to explain how he got the information at all, he would convict himself of misprision of treason. Here, be it repeated, was no religious secret; it was a matter of ordinary business honesty, the thing that admittedly did weigh most heavily with him. He had once walked alone into a plague-house to collar a felon. He would walk that same lonely road now. He had once defied the king over a bill for thirty pounds. He would not fail to defy the Earl of Shaftesbury over a bill for services rendered in treason. But out of it we hear again that tortured cry, 'Upon my conscience, I believe I shall be the first martyr!'

Again, there is that question of the rumour of his death, set flying through town before he had barely gone from his home. It has been suggested that it was started by his brothers, and this is possible. The only question is whether that report could have grown so widespread; could have swept through every tavern from Westminster to Moorfields in the space of an afternoon; unless many tongues were set clacking for a purpose: unless, in short, there was an *organisation*, like Shaftesbury's Green Ribbon Club, ready to set it going at the leader's signal.

With regard to the actual murder, another intimation might be made here; but I shall not deal with it because I believe it was a purely private matter, in accordance with the suggestion made by Mr. J. G. Muddiman, and had no connection with Shaftesbury; and for still another reason which will presently become clear. But, 'Even if . . . the Jesuits were seeking to put Godfrey and his secret out of the way for ever, they would presumably have done so directly, and not have kept him in duress and without food

VERITAS EX CINERIBVS REVIVISCIT

ÆTATIS SVÆ 57

P. Vanderbanc Sculp.

Are to be Sold at Thomas Cherets in James Street Couent Garden

The true Effigies of that worthy and never to be forgotten S.ᵗ EDMOND BURY GODFREY Knight and Iustice of the Peace who was MURTHERED by Papists the 12.ᵗʰ day of October An. Dom. 1678.

SIR EDMUND BERRY GODFREY

OF all souvenirs now remaining of the Popish Plot, perhaps the most curious, and certainly the most interesting, is the pack of playing-cards here reproduced. Here are depicted some of the outstanding scenes and bogies, as they appeared to a contemporary artist. To arrange the cards in chronological order is a matter of some difficulty, since thirty-one of them depict purely imaginary events, and others—like the nine of diamonds and the deuce of clubs placed at the end—are mere comments on the plot. " Mr. Everard in the Tower " has no actual connection with the plot ; but Edmund Everard may be called the forerunner of the informers, since in 1674 he was imprisoned on a charge of attempting to poison the Duke of Monmouth. Again, the artist has not always been accurate in picturing real events. The execution of the men accused of Godfrey's murder, for example, shows a triple hanging ; whereas two of the victims were hanged on February 21st, 1679, and the third a week later. But here is the living terror as it was then felt, and this pack may well have been shuffled and cut by Green Ribbon mutineers round their table at the " King's Head."

The Plot first hatcht at Rome
by the Pope and Cardinalls
&c

D.r Oates receiues letters from
y.e Fathers to carry beyond Sea.

Whitebread made
Provintiall.

Severall Iesuits receiuing
Commissions to stir the People
to Rebellion in Scotland

I

The Consult at the
white horse Taverne.

VIII

The Conspirators Signeing ÿ
Resolve for killing the King.

VIIII

The Consult at
Wild House.

Knave

Pickerin attempts to kill ÿ
K. in St. Iames Park.

Ashby received instruction of
Whitebread for the society to
offer Sr George Wakeman 10000

The Consult of Benedictine
Monks & Fryers in the Savoy

Whitebread writing letters
concerning the state of Ireland

Mr Langhorn delivering out
Comissions for severall Offic.rs

Coleman writing a declaration
and letters to la Chess.

Coleman giveth a Guiny to
Incourage ye 4 Ruffians.

The Irish Ruffians going
for Windsor.

Exstirpate Heriticks rootg branch

Father Conniers Preaching against
ye Oathes of Alejance & Supremacy

The Confult att
Somerfet houfe.

Gavan inform the Fathers of the
affairs in Staffordfhire.

Dr Oates difcouereth ÿ Plot
to ÿ King and Councell.

The Seizing feverall
Conspirators.

Sr. E. B. Godfree takeing Dr.
Oates his depositions.

The Club at ye Plow Ale house for
the murther of S. E. B Godfree.

Sr. E. B Godfree dogg'd by
St Clements Church.

Sr. E. B. Godfree is perswaded
to goe down Somerset house yard.

Sr E.B. Godfree Strangled
Gerald going to stab him.

Sr E.B. Godfree Carrying up
into a Roome.

The Murtherers of Sr E.B. Godfr.
are diverting themselves at
Bow after the murther.

Mr Dugdale in Staffordshire
reading several letters relate:
ing to the Plott.

VII

The body of Sr E.B. Godfree
is shew'd to Capt. Bedlow &
Mr. Prance.

VI

The dead body of Sr E.B.G
Conuey'd out of Sommerset
house in a Sedan.

V

The body of Sr E.B.G. carry'd
to Primrose hill on a Horse.

II

The Funerall of
Sr E.B. Godfree.

♣ King

Capt. Bedlow examind by ye
secret Comitee of the House
of Commons.

♣ X

Capt. Bedlow carrying letters
to Forraigne Parts.

♥ VII

Coleman examind in New:
:gate by severall Lords

♥ III

Dr. Oates discovereth
Gauan in the Lobby.

VII

Sʳ William Waller burning Popish books Images and Reliques.

VI

Mʳ Coleman drawn to his
execution.

Queen

Redding endeavouring
to Corrupt Capᵗ Bedloe.

VI

Capᵗ Berry and Alderman
Brooks are offer'd 500ᵗ to cast
the Plot on the Protestants.

Gifford and Stubbs give mony
to a Made to fire her Masters
house.

M.ʳ Prance discouⁱers the murther
of S.ᵗ E.B. Godfrey to the Kinge
and Councell

Ireland and Growe drawn
to their execution.

The Execution of the mur
therers of S.ᵗ E.B. Godfrey

Knave ♣

Reddin standing in ye Pillory.

Queen ♦

Mr. Ieninso examin'd by ye Prvy Councell.

VI ♦

Pickerin Executed.

V ♣

The Execution of the 5 Iesuitts.

The Tryall of S.r G. Wakeman &
3 Benedictine Monks.

Fenwick at Dover, sending
Student to S.t Omers.

M.r Everard imprison'd
in the Tower.

London remember
the 2.d of September } 1666

for two days before killing him. The facts revealed at the inquest suggest that it was someone who wished to obtain a statement from him than someone who wished to destroy him promptly who covered his breast with bruises and, after holding him captive without sustenance, strangled him.

'It is not inconceivable that those who brought about Godfrey's death did so by accident while pressing him with fiendish cruelty to swear to that which they wished.' Or, we may say, to find out what he knew, and whether he knew dangerous things. 'Come: speak up! What did Coleman say to you? Did he say anything to asperse gentlemen in our places?' If it really was Shaftesbury who spoke, can't you hear his voice in that? Don't our minds go back to a certain interview with Whip the Coachman? 'My lord, what would you have me say? I know nothing of the matter.' 'Then thou shalt die,' sings a voice coolly, and after a new attempt: 'If you will not confess – take him away, and let him be starved to death.'

Starved? Yes; but in Sir Edmund Godfrey's case that was too slow, and lasted only two days or so until the murderers lost patience. If this is in truth the explanation, then whatever happened in some secret room below ground, however the spots of wax-lights fell upon him as he lay trussed up under their candles, whoever thought of thrusting his sword through him after he had been turned into the first martyr, still one thing at least cannot be denied. The republican leaders (like certain other gangsters we have heard of in our own time) at least gave him a magnificent funeral.

XI

That Sir Edmund Godfrey was murdered by the three men who came to be accused by the government, and who were tried for it on February 10th, 1679.

This need not be discussed here, for it will be dealt with fully in following chapters. We shall attend the trial at Westminster Hall and listen to Lord Chief Justice Scroggs roaring from the bench, as well as Sir George Jeffreys ably seconding Sir William Jones for the prosecution.

XII

That Sir Edmund Godfrey was murdered for a private reason, by some private person who has not yet been suspected.

Here is merely the theory of X, always put forward in any good detective story, and usually is the correct solution. It is introduced for the benefit of those crafty connoisseurs who do not altogether credit any of the foregoing explanations; it is left deliberately vague so that they can fill in the lineaments of any characters whose leer they consider suspicious; but it may be said that there *is* internal evidence, which those same connoisseurs doubtless have already noticed.

In any event, gentlemen, there is our Bloody Dozen, an alternative for each member of the jury. It is not all the possibilities that might be opened up; but it is enough, it will serve; or else the club may find its wits whirling and go away muttering the query of Jesting Pilate.

One question alone remains, which must be left to you, the jury, before we discuss it at the end: which of these solutions does the physical evidence best fit? It will have been remarked that some of the foregoing examples, good enough as far as they go, suffer from the same embarrassment which comes of attempting to introduce a quart into a pint pot. It goes in smoothly enough; each cranny is filled and the head is neat-looking; the only difficulty being that there is a pint of beer left over. Others suffer from the difficulty of attempting to fill a quart pot with a pint: not to say with a drop in the bucket. Still others appear sound. You shall judge; and, meanwhile, let us return to the gustier air of the seventeenth century; to walk once more in the company of King Charles the Second; and, for a few brief hours, to light up again the dark house of the past.

V

'THEY EAT THEIR GOD, THEY KILL THEIR KING, AND SAINT THE MURDERER'

The Feast of the Lawyers

"'Tis vain to dispute it further; there must be an end. . . . I do remember you once more, that in this matter you will not be deluded with any fanatic hopes and expectations of a pardon, for the truth is, Mr. Coleman, you will be deceived; for we are at this time in such disorders that, though the king should be inclined that way, I verily believe both Houses would interpose between that and you.'

> LORD CHIEF JUSTICE SCROGGS, in sentencing Edward Coleman, Nov. 28th, 1678, *State Trials*.

'Come, Mr. Blunder, pray bawl soundly for me at the King's Bench; bluster, sputter, question, cavil; but be sure your argument be intricate enough to confound the court; and then you may do my business. Talk what you will, but be sure your tongue never stand still; for your own noise will secure your sense from censure: 'tis like coughing or hemming when one has got a belly-ache, which stifles the unmannerly noise. Go, dear rogue, and succeed; and I'll invite thee, ere it be long, to more soused venison.'

> WILLIAM WYCHERLEY, *The Plain Dealer*.

I

'OYEZ! Oyez! Oyez! If any can give evidence on the behalf of our Sovereign Lord the King, against *William Stayley,* let him come forth and he shall be heard!'

'The prisoner stands indicted as not having the fear of God before his eyes, being led by the instigation of the devil, not minding his allegiance, but traitorously endeavouring the death and destruction of Our Sovereign Lord the King: he did on November the 14th, in the thirtieth year of the king, falsely, wickedly, and traitorously compass, imagine,

devise, and invent killing the king; that he did maliciously
contrive (I say) the death of Our Lord, the King of England.

'To this he hath pleaded *Not Guilty*. You are to try
whether he be guilty, or not.'

'Call the witnesses to prove the offence.'[1]

And now began the feast of the jurists, the new All-
hallowtide revels, the thunderous and stately silly-season of
the law.

For some time the courts had been preparing to grind,
with so many Papists in Newgate awaiting trial for treason;
and, just two weeks after Captain William Bedloe's arrival
in town, the first cause was tried. It was not, of course, for
the murder of Sir Edmund Godfrey. Too much Jesuitical
rabble and rubble had to be swept away and carried to Jack
Ketch – the newly-appointed Mr. Ketch, who has been
patron saint of hangmen ever since – as a preliminary. Besides, although Captain Bedloe was still swearing oaths, and
though day by day his discoveries had grown with his bold-
ness until he now rivalled Doctor Oates in wealth of invention, still the government had not been able to lay hands
on those people whom he had named as Godfrey's murderers. But there were others to be dealt with. They must
begin by hanging, drawing, and quartering the small fry.
For, as the Attorney-General pointed out at the trial of the
first man, in explaining why they chose to commence with
this fellow when there were others of greater quality and
devilry to be had: 'There are a sort of men in the world,'
says Mr. Attorney-General, 'who endeavour what they can
to cry down this discovery of horrid and damnable designs
against the king's person and the Protestant religion. It is
true: some are so charitable as to think the Roman Catholics
in England do promote the Roman Catholic religion; but
that the design against the king's person is a fiction. But
they shall do well to take warning by the trial of this man,
and the imprisonment of so many offenders.'

---

[1] In all the accounts of trials herein, the speeches of witnesses, counsel.
and judges are, of course, taken word for word from the *State Trials*
except where the spoken word has confused the sense: in which case a
tangled sentence has been slightly altered in order to make clear what the
person was trying to say.

'And,' said Lord Chief Justice Scroggs, with a sinister look at the jury, 'you shall do well to begin with this man, for perchance it may be a terror to the rest.'

It undoubtedly was. Of all the brethren of the long robe, who prudently kept wooden bowls on their desks – for you must pay in advance, and drop good guineas into that wooden bowl, before your cause would be taken up – the most zealous in prosecuting Papists was that same Attorney-General, Sir William Jones. 'Bull-faced Jonas' was a thoroughly honest man, who believed in every tag of the plot, and who had gone roaring from one great man to another to say it was thought Sir Edmund Godfrey had been done to death by the Papists. 'Bull-faced Jonas' was inclined to be peevish and sour-tempered, glowering under his black coif, but that was because he was a fighter; and, at the same time, his tongue could run with every honeyed guile of counsel. Mr. Roger North (himself no mean lawyer, for his income was £4,000 a year dropped into the wooden bowl) observed that none stood so cunning as Sir William Jones at laying traps for the judge. 'Now if, my lord,' says Sir William persuasively, 'we prove so-and-so, then surely so-and-so must be true?' And if the unwary judge said, 'Ay, if you prove that indeed –' then counsel knew that provided he could charm the jury into thinking he had proved *that* point, he would carry his cause no matter what its other merits.

Behind the Attorney-General, with full briefs for prosecuting Papists, stood a battery of other adepts. Nearly all were of fiery honesty. There was Serjeant Maynard, nearing eighty, 'the best old book-lawyer of his time,' the cunningest of all at trapping and stalking, who used to chuckle over his saying that the law was *ars bablitiva*. There was Sir Francis Winnington, the Solicitor-General, a bull-dog at a brief. There was the slippery Serjeant Stringer. Or there was the nimblest of the young tongue-lashers, Sir George Jeffreys, whose talents at scourging or toadying had brought him to be Recorder of the City of London while still only thirty, and whose yell of fury made even Bully of Alsatia shake in his rags at the Sessions House.

M

For when young George Jeffreys preened it in The
Temple (if you wanted him now, he was to be found in
number 3, Hare Court, Inner Temple), students of the law
were not afflicted with too much dull nonsense about study.
Buttressed away from Fleet Street, in a tangle of ill-paved
walks that straggled down the slope between the low brick
buildings and the misty gardens along the river, these
cloisters and courts were noisy with a pack of robust students as formidable as the Alsatian cut-throats next door.
Without doubt, there must have been somebody of studious
habits, as Roger North says his brother Francis was. Tucked
away up two pairs of stairs, in an airless petit chamber with
a tallow dip, you might have found an earnest young man
poring late over Littleton, Manwood on Forest Law, Coke's
Pleas of the Crown and Jurisdiction of the Courts, Fitz-
herbert's *Natura Brevium*, and other delectable manifesta-
tions of *hic, haec, hoc*. And this was a very exemplary
fellow, who kept vast commonplace-books, practised putting
causes in the Commons, had a weak smile and fluttery hands,
and never got drunk except with a judge. Sir Francis North
was always exemplary. When he came to possess a fine
house in Chancery Lane, he even had strong notions about
sanitation, and disliked the way in which the houses of
office so continually filled up his cellar. So he had it all
pumped out into the street, and forced his neighbours to do
likewise.

But your men of the temple in general (or of Lincoln's
Inn or Gray's Inn), being three-bottle lads, owned to broader
views. They paid their five pounds' entrance fine to get
five years' sport before they assumed wheedling airs and a
scarlet gown at Westminster Hall. If an officious Bencher
tried to make them behave, he was held under the pump.
Even the Lord Mayor, who assayed an entrance in full
panoply with his sword of state borne before him, got his
sword of state beaten down and himself booted out, and
provoked a riot for whose quelling he must appeal to the
king and whistle up the train-bands. (Still, it is not to be
denied that my Lord Mayor got his revenge: for, when there
was a fire in the Temple, he blandly refused to call out the

fire-engines.) These Templars were great patrons of the fencing and dancing schools. They were fond of a hand at ombre over a late pipe of tobacco and half a dozen of claret; and if presently they came to argue a cause with no well-defined notion of the law, after boozing until the small hours with a favourite blowen at Mother Cresswell's, still no great harm was done. In the first place, they could rely on their native fluency, the *ars bablitiva;* in the second place, it was possible that His Lordship would have an equally hazy idea of the points at law, or an equally muddled head from having been drinking all night at the same place; finally, they could rely on the extreme flexibility of the criminal code.

For the criminal code, especially as it applied to trials for treason, was very much what His Lordship the judge cared to make it. 'I hate precedents at all times!' Jeffreys once roared some years later, when he himself came to sit on the bench as Lord Chief Justice; and precedents could be made according to the current political views of the judge. In trials for treason, the principle of the law was simply this: that the king's person must be protected. Here's a man indicted for treason, and it would be folly to give him the benefit of the doubt: the safest course is to hang him and take no chances. 'I have been told,' declared His Lordship sententiously, 'curse not the king, not in thy thoughts, not in thy bedchamber, or the birds of the air will carry it.' And thus we have the spectacle of a man being condemned to death on the testimony of a witness whose confirmation is no stronger than that A Little Bird Told Him. What the little bird said was evidence.

The code was a quite honest one: it seemed necessary for the preservation of the domain: 'for you know as well as I do that the practice of the law is so, and the practice *is* the law.' To begin with, the accused was kept in close confine-ment from the day of his arrest. He was allowed to see no one; consequently, he had no means of knowing what evidence had been given against him, who swore to it, or how he might combat it. In this condition he was haled into court, to make what defence he might on the spur of the moment against a case suddenly put before him by experienced lawyers who had been preparing it for weeks. He could call for witnesses – if any could be found on the spur of the moment. For, says Sir James Stephen, 'He was not allowed as a matter of right, but only as an occasional exceptional favour, to have either counsel or solicitor to advise him as to his defence, or to see his witnesses and put their evidence in order.'

Again, 'there was an utter absence of any conception of the true nature of judicial evidence on the part of the judges, the counsel, and the prisoners'. In theory no hearsay evidence was admitted, and two witnesses were required to prove treason; 'but, subject to these small rules, the opinion of the time seems to have been that if a man came and swore to anything whatever, he ought to be believed unless he was directly contradicted'. On one occasion one badgered Catholic prisoner broke out in a frenzy: 'All the evidence that is given comes but to this: there is but saying and swearing! I defy them all to give one probable reason to satisfy any reasonable, uninterested man's judgment how this could be!' The Lord Chief Justice warmly pointed out that the witnesses were on oath, and had kissed the Book: wasn't that enough?

For the strongest advocates in the prosecution were the judges themselves. My lords sat up aloft, under the crimson canopy and the gilded sword of state, their hands behind their ears, waiting to pounce. It was the practice, and the practice was the law. More than sixty years before, that eminent jurist Sir Edward Coke had wagged his finger at Sir Walter Raleigh in the dock, and declared: 'Thou art the absolutest traitor that ever lived!' Nowadays it was still their business, as guardians of the king's person, to bulldoze or trap witnesses, and then direct a significant glance at the jury. If the witness would not be trapped or bulldozed, 'You're a Papist,' says my Lord Chief Justice Scroggs, pointing; 'so you may say anything to us.' 'This is a mighty improbable business,' chimes in Mr. Justice Dolben darkly. Then my lords look at each other with an air of sinister enlightenment, and down under their spectacles at the jury, and across at the prisoner in the dock. Thus the jurymen – though for eight years they have been secure against the possibility that, if they should return a verdict not to the judge's taste, His Lordship may fly into a rage and throw the whole jury into jail – are most concerned about the celerity with which they can return a verdict of guilty.

It was not that anyone objected to returning such verdicts. On the 21st of November, 1678, when the first of the trials for treason in the Popish plot took place at the Court of King's Bench, Westminster, a great mob pelted towards Westminster Hall. Here was a good show on nearly any day that the King's Bench, the Chancery, or the Common Pleas sat in that vast stone-ribbed hall by the river, where the remains of Cromwell's head still hung over the south porch. It was bleak weather; most of the crowd chose to refresh themselves at the underground drinking-cellars – Hell, Purgatory, Paradise, and Heaven they were called – before stumbling inside. The great stone jug was dim enough inside, for fog obscured the windows up under the peaked roof; but first of all a visitor's ears were struck ringing by the din of the place. Ranged along the left-hand wall were the shops of the haberdashers, the booksellers, the mathematical instrument-makers, the sempstresses, all abroil with their own clients. At the further end were the two courts of King's Bench on the left, and Chancery on the right. They were set up on a sort of scaffolding, divided by a shaky flight of steps which led up to the entrance to both. Though they were enclosed by boards to a tolerable height, like a pen or a bear-pit, still they were not covered over at the top; and any barrister pleading his cause must have powerful lungs to make himself heard above all the other voices in the hall.

Between here and the Court of Common Pleas abutting on the right-hand wall, the 'daggled gowns' hurried with their green bags. Here were the professional knights of the post, who would swear to anything for a shilling. Here were the old crones who sat witch-like in corners, entrusted with minding the fine beaver hats of the lawyers while they were in court.   Here a very plump young sempstress made eyes at a very thin young clerk; there a formidable widow, with a mania for a dozen law-suits at once, stood screeching in a ring of barristers and solicitors.   'Godsbodkins, you puny upstart in the law!' screams the widow, her cap shaking over her eyes; 'you green-bag carrier, you murderer of unfortunate causes, the clerk's ink is scarce off your fingers! – you that newly come from lampblacking the judge's shoes, and are not fit to wipe mine: you call me ignorant and impertinent!'   They are a collection of Hogarth sketches mouthing and gesturing, their breath going up in smoke under the dry war-banners that hang from the roof.   But in the Court of King's Bench sat fat Lord Chief Justice Scroggs, with a foggy nimbus round his head, bidding the crier make an Oyez for the trial of William Stayley on a charge of high treason.

William Stayley, the son of an eminent Catholic goldsmith, had been arrested on November 15th.   He had been arrested on the information of two Scotsmen, Messrs. Carstairs and Sutherland.   These gentlemen stated that on November 14th, being in a cook-shop in King Street, they had overheard Stayley in a conversation with a Frenchman named Fromante.   They stated that they were in the next room, the door being open, face to face with Stayley only seven or eight feet away; and that Stayley had been crying in French, 'The King of England is a grand heretic.   The King of England is a great heretic, and the greatest rogue in the world: there is the heart, and here is the hand, that would kill him.'

By a statute passed shortly after the Restoration, it was enacted that if any person should compass, *imagine*, devise, or intend death to destruction to the king; or bodily harm leading to death or destruction, or imprisonment or restraint of the king's person, or to deprive or depose him; and such compassings or imaginings should express, utter, or declare by any printing, writing, preaching, or malicious and advised speaking: then every such person, being lawfully convicted thereof upon the oaths of two lawful and credible

witnesses, should be adjudged to be a traitor, and suffer the
pain of death. Thus on November 15th the two lawful and
credible witnesses, Messrs. Carstairs and Sutherland, summoned Stayley out of his shop for a private talk. They informed him that they had overheard him speaking treason,
and had written down the words; they intimated that, unless
a good price for silence were forthcoming, they would inform the authorities. 'You see what the gentleman reads,'
says Carstairs; 'I would advise you to look to it.' When
Stayley declared that he had never spoken any such words,
and would not be put upon, Carstairs ran out in a fury and
fetched a constable.

The arrest caused some wonder among those who were
acquainted with the witnesses. Carstairs was well known
in Scotland as a liar and forger who made his living as a
government spy on conventicles. Dr. Burnet attempted to
interfere.

'When I heard who the witnesses were,' said Burnet, 'I
thought I was bound to do what I could to stop it. I sent
both to the Lord Chancellor and to the Attorney-General
to let them know what profligate wretches these men were.
Sir William Jones, the Attorney-General, took it ill of me,
that I should disparage the king's evidence. I had likewise
observed to several persons of weight, how many incredible
things there were in the evidence that was given. I wished
they would make use of the heat the nation was in, to secure
us effectually from Popery; but I wished they would not
run too hastily, to the taking men's lives away upon such
testimonies. Lord Holles had more temper than I expected
from a man of his heat. Lord Halifax was of the same mind
– but the Earl of Shaftesbury could not bear the discourse.
He said we must support the evidence, and that all those
who undermined the credit of the witnesses were to be
looked on as public enemies.'

The trial, as the Attorney-General explained, was intended chiefly as a warning to those who discredited the plot.
It was not in the least sensational. It was short and even
rather dull. Stayley, in a mood of cool despair, made so
lethargic a defence that he could strike very little fire from

Scroggs. The prosecution was conducted with great scrupulousness (except that Fromante, the other party to the alleged conversation in the cook-shop, had been put into prison so that he could not testify on the prisoner's behalf); and it is quite possible, even probable, that Stayley did speak the words. But Lord Chief Justice Scroggs required a more truculent prisoner than this young man to rouse his own eloquence, and he coined only a few of his celebrated epigrams. 'Excuse me if I am a little warm,' he told the jury, after a heated discourse on the iniquities of Papists; 'but it is better to be warm here than at Smithfield.' And again, when a witness on Stayley's behalf testified that the young man had always shown the strongest loyalty towards the king: 'That,' retorted the Lord Chief Justice, 'was when he spoke to a Protestant.' The jury with one voice returned a verdict of guilty. 'Now you may die a Roman Catholic,' said Scroggs; 'and, when you come to die, I don't doubt you will be found a priest too.'

It is not recorded that the spectators set up their usual great shout of applause, for this was much too tame, and it was difficult to conceive of Stayley as a deadly plotter. The first fireworks were touched off on November 27th, just after Stayley had been hanged, drawn, and quartered at Tyburn. On that day Edward Coleman came to his trial – and a day later Titus Oates, before the bar of the House of Commons, accused Queen Catherine of high treason.

II

Doctor Titus Oates had now grown so swollen up with the attention of the Green Ribbon lords that he could well consider himself a law unto himself. He was the greatest man in England. The Archbishop of Canterbury received him as an equal, and abroad his health was drunk next to that of the king. The heralds had traced his descent back to a noble family of the fourteenth century. Money was to be had in plenty from the Green Ribboners; gentlemen fought to dress him and hold his basin in the morning; odes were composed to him; throngs wept at his sermons. And the extent of his information about the plot now had no limit whatever. Before he cried up his accusation of the queen at the House of Commons, he had already tested it out on the Privy Council, with the king in attendance.

He intimated, piously, that there was some excuse for the queen. She had been for so many years insulted by the king's infidelities, so many times reduced to tears of shame by having her bed defiled, that she could endure it no longer: and therefore she determined to have Charles poisoned. Oates told the council how, in the preceding July, he (the omnipresent doctor) had been summoned to Somerset House along with several Jesuit fathers. The fathers went into a room where the queen was waiting, while Oates himself remained in the ante-room: and there he heard a woman's voice saying that she would assist the Catholic religion with all her estate, that she would stand these violations of her bed no longer, and that she would assist Sir George Wakeman in drugging the king's posset. Afterwards Dr. Oates was taken in to see the queen, and she gave him a gracious smile.

The council had reason to sit amazed. The king was white with rage; and Oates should have observed this. Charles had given him permission to speak, because above all things he must know how far the man dared go, but the doctor would have been wiser to confine his accusations to a statement before the Privy Council alone. Oates – after his singular triumph at the trial of Edward Coleman on November 27th, when he was saved at a moment of danger by the luck that never deserted him – knew he could say what he liked.

They brought Mr. Coleman to the Court of the King's Bench amid a crowd howling for his death. Sir William Jones led for the Crown, well supported by Mr. Serjeant Maynard and Sir George Jeffreys. Coleman stood holding to the rail of the dock, his face still more wasted after his confinement in Newgate, his nose sharper, his eyes more hollow. He had cause to lick dry lips, since this was the trial for which every man-jack in packed Westminster Hall had been waiting, and the crier must keep bawling his Oyez so that any man might be heard.

After the business had been opened by a discussion between the prisoner and the Lord Chief Justice, in which Coleman spoke with a wrangling humility and querulousness which boded ill for his chances, the prosecution called Titus Oates as its first witness. Oates stood with his blue face upturned towards the judges' bench, his bow-legs planted apart, and poured out such a torrent of new accusations that even Scroggs was startled.

At his examination by the Privy Council in September, Oates had made no charges against Coleman except the general hint that, if his papers were searched, there would be that in them which would cost him his neck; further, the doctor had not recognised Coleman when the two were confronted. Now he revealed himself as one of Coleman's closest brothers-in-arms. He carried intimate letters for Coleman, he had intimate talks with Coleman. He had been with Coleman at Wild House, after the Jesuit consult in April, when it was determined to murder the king. Coleman at a later conference in the Savoy wished to have the Duke of Ormonde poisoned. When the four Irish cut-throats were sent to Windsor in August to kill the king, Coleman with great thoughtfulness had asked Father Harcourt what provision had been made for the Irishmen's expenses; and, when the father pointed to £80, mostly in guineas, lying all spread out on the table, Coleman had been so enthusiastic that he gave the messenger a guinea to hurry off with their pay. When it was proposed to give Sir George Wakeman £10,000 for poisoning the king, Coleman said it was not enough, and advised adding £5,000 more to make the business sure. Dr. Oates had even seen Coleman receive the patent appointing Coleman to the Secretary of State, in a letter endorsed by the Pope: for this letter had been opened in Oates's presence, and he heard Coleman say it was a good exchange.

This evidence drew enough hums and hisses from the spectators; but it seemed to fret or perplex the Lord Chief Justice. Scroggs turned ponderously.

'If the prisoner at the bar be minded, he may ask him any question?'

Mr. Edward Coleman appeared to conquer a shaky throat, and got his grip of the railing round the dock, and pointed to a gentleman standing a little distance away.

'My lord, I am mighty glad to see that gentleman, Sir Thomas Dolman, in court,' he cried. 'I think he was present at my examination before the Privy Council. And this man that now gives evidence against me, at the council told the king he never saw me before. But he is extremely well acquainted with me now, and has a world of intimacy.'

Oates was contemptuous. 'My lord,' he retorted, 'I said I would not swear that I had seen him before in my life, because my sight was bad by candlelight, and candlelight alters the sight much. But when I heard him speak I could have sworn it was he, but it was not then my business. I cannot see a great way by candlelight.'

'The stress of the objection,' said Scroggs, frowning again, 'lieth not upon seeing so much – but how was it that you laid no more to Mr. Coleman's charge at that time?'

Dr. Oates replied that he did not wish the prisoner to know beforehand all the damning evidence against him, or the prisoner might bring false testimony to refute it. 'My lord, I was not bound to give more than a general information against Mr. Coleman. Mr. Coleman did deny he had correspondence with Father Le (*sic*) Chaise at any time; and I did then say he had given Father Le Chaise an account of several transactions. And, my lord, then I was so weak, being up two nights, and having been taking prisoners – upon my salvation, I could scarce stand upon my legs.'

It became evident that Scroggs's neck was swelling a trifle, and that Titus's slipperiness was commencing to irritate him despite his duty against the prisoner. He began to press Titus with questions, as to why the informer had not said more about Coleman before the council; but Titus neatly evaded each one. Presently, after a wrangle in which the most inconspicuous figure was the dazed prisoner – alternately turning from one to the other, and opening his mouth without getting in a word – then an angry Scroggs returned to the question of whether or not Titus had failed to recognise the prisoner at the council-board.

'Mr. Oates, did the king, or the council, or the Lord Chancellor, ask you whether you knew Mr. Coleman or no?'

'They did not ask me,' says Titus coolly.

'Mr. Oates, answer the question in short, and without confounding it with length. WERE you demanded if you knew Mr. Coleman?'

'Not to my knowledge.'

'He said he did not know me!' cried the prisoner weakly.

'But you seemed, Mr. Oates,' pursued Scroggs, in a soft growl like a gentle tiger, 'you seemed to admit to me a moment ago that you had been asked this question. And you gave me no answer, because at the time you were doubtful whether it was the man, by reason of the inconveniency of the light, and your bad sight.'

'I must leave to *the king* what answer I made Mr. Coleman,' jeered Titus, playing the boldest stroke he had yet dared. '*He* wonders I should give an account of so many intimacies.'

This appeared to rouse the Lord Chief Justice to his position in the case, for assuredly he was there to prosecute Coleman; but he turned to Coleman nevertheless. 'Was he asked whether he was acquainted with you, Mr. Coleman?'

'I cannot answer directly,' said the prisoner, faltering in an agony of verbal precision when he was within an ace of having the game in his hands. 'I do not say he was asked if he was acquainted with me; but I say this, that he did declare he did not know me.'

'Can you prove that?'

'I appeal to Sir Thomas Dolman, who is now in court, and was then at the council-table!'

Scroggs directed his eye towards this new witness. 'Sir Thomas, you are not upon your oath, but are to speak on behalf of the prisoner: what did he say?'

'That he did not well know him,' answered Dolman.

'Did he add that he did not well know him by candle-light? But,' said the Lord Chief Justice, turning back to

Oates, 'but, Mr. Oates, you said that when you heard his voice you knew him. Why did you not come then and say you knew him?'

'Because I was not asked,' snarled Titus, setting his feet firmer.

'But, Sir Thomas, did Mr. Oates say he did not well know him *after* Mr. Coleman spake?' demanded Scroggs. 'Was it before or after Mr. Coleman spake that Mr. Oates said he did not well know him?'

It was afterwards, Sir Thomas Dolman declared, and again for a brief moment the game veered into Coleman's hands. Titus had declared that he had not known Coleman by candlelight, but that he had known him as soon as the man spoke: whereas it now appeared that he had first heard him speak without recognising him. Despite his loud braying, Titus had already got himself into a muddle over his dozen fresh discoveries about the prisoner. Three minutes more, and the saviour of the nation might have been on the run. Through the mind of any friend of Coleman at the trial might have rung silent advice: Pin him down, you fool! – pin him down now, while you've still got the favour of the judge! Amid the uproar, shrunken-faced Mr. Coleman stood opening and shutting his mouth, looking appealingly at the bench. Scroggs himself became involved in putting a question whose elaborate phraseology twisted his tongue, and Mr. Justice Dolben intervened to help him out when he sputtered.

'Sir Thomas,' said Justice Dolben, 'did Mr. Oates say he did not well know Mr. Coleman, or that he did not well know that man?'

'He said he had no acquaintance with that man.'

Whereupon Scroggs found his voice, for he had just seen near the bench a man who could resolve these difficulties – Sir Robert Southwell, Clerk of the Privy Council.

'Sir Robert Southwell,' appealed the Lord Chief Justice, 'you were present at Mr. Oates's examination before the council. In what manner did he accuse Mr. Coleman then?'

The reply was very calm and very precise. 'My lord, the question is so particular,' answered Sir Robert Southwell, 'that I cannot give the court satisfaction. But,' says he sharply, 'other material things then said are now omitted by Mr. Oates. For Mr. Oates did declare against Sir George Wakeman that £5,000 was added to the sum Sir George was to receive for killing the king; and that Mr. Coleman had paid five of the fifteen thousand pounds to Sir George in hand.'

Titus was saved. Here, at the timely intervention of Sir Robert Southwell, was proof of his honesty. For it appeared that Mr. Oates *had* made a strong accusation, a definite accusation, against Coleman at the original examination: he had accused Coleman of paying £5,000 to Sir George Wakeman. But so extreme had been his fatigue at that time (exactly as he said) that this accusation had completely slipped his mind – *so that he had not even made it among the others at this present trial.* Was honesty ever better vindicated? Here was faithful Titus, swearing at this trial that he had been weak and ill with running zealously about pious business: so that his bemused eyes could not firmly identify Coleman, or his bemused wits remember all the accusations against him. In fact, so cloudy had been his mind that he did not even remember now what a sharp charge he had laid against the prisoner. In itself it answered all their infamous doubts not only about his bad memory, but about his bad eyesight.

Titus was not to be beaten. His luck never deserted him. He screwed his face into an expression of virtuous contempt; his little eye, sunk deep in the rolls of flesh, wandered round the bench, the smirking jury, the spectators craning their necks in that dingy bear-pit of a court-room open to the roof of Westminster Hall; he settled the low-crowned hat on his woolly periwig, and somewhere in the middle of his face appeared an equal smirk. My Lord Chief Justice Scroggs turned a face radiant with relief.

'This answers much of the objection upon him,' said Scroggs, and turned sharply on Coleman. 'The court has asked Mr. Oates how he should come now to charge you with all these matters of poisoning and killing the king, and yet how he mentioned you so lightly at the council-table.

But it is said by Sir Robert Southwell he did charge you with £5,000 (for poisoning the king) to be added to the £10,000 – and he charged you expressly with it at the council-table.'

Afterwards the prosecution had no trials. Afterwards came William Bedloe (an effulgent Bedloe, now dressed in the blaze of fashion, with Venice-point and fringed gloves) with some remarkable new stories. He was not cautious now. He blared after the fashion of Oates, he threw out his chest. But his tales against Coleman were not necessary, for Coleman's own letters would have hanged him in any event. They were read at great length, and in sober truth they were enough to condemn any man according to the legal interpretations of the time. Scroggs, in his summing-up, worked himself up in a pitch of genuine eloquence against the Papists. Judged purely as rhetoric, there are few speeches which ring more powerfully than those of William Scroggs. His peroration rose:

'Have we so soon forgot our reverence to the late king, and the pious advice he left us? A king that was truly a DEFENDER of the FAITH, not only by his title, but by his abilities and writings. A king who understood the Protestant religion so well that he was able to defend it against any of the cardinals of Rome. And when he knew it so thoroughly, and died so eminently for it, I will leave this characteristical note: that whoever after that departs from *his* judgment had need to have a very good one of his own.

'These Popish priests have indeed ways of conversion and conviction – by enlightening our understandings with a faggot, and by the powerful and irresistible arguments of a dagger. But there are such wicked solecisms in their religion that they seem to have left to them neither Natural Sense, nor Natural Conscience. Not Natural Sense, by their absurdity in so unreasonable a belief as of the wine turned into blood; not Natural Conscience, by their cruelty which turns Protestant blood into wine.

'*Tantum religio potuit suadere malorum?* Mr. Coleman, in one of his letters, speaks of rooting out our religion, and our party. And he is in the right, for they can never root out the Protestant religion, but they must kill the Protestants. But let him and them know: if ever they shall endeavour to bring Popery in by destroying the king, they shall find that the Papists will thereby bring destruction upon themselves, so that not a man of them shall escape. *Ne Catulus quidem relinquendus!* Our execution shall be quick as their gunpowder, but more effectual.'

He sat back, blowing, and wiped a hot forehead. The day was dying behind those little windows: he noticed it in his last remark to the jury, and added in a more sober tone: 'Gentlemen, if your consultation shall be long, then you must lie by it all night, and we'll take your verdict to-morrow morning. If it will not be long, I am content to stay a while.'[1]

'My lord,' said the foreman gravely, 'we shall be short.' And indeed there was not time for a change in the darkling light, or a change in the posture of the bent muttering figure in the dock, before they returned.

III

Titus was now invincible. The next morning both Oates and Bedloe went before the bar of the House of Commons, and the door was locked so that none might intrude after them. Bedloe, now as close as a boil to Oates's skin and confirming him at every point, had been supplied with a story concerning the queen's design to poison the king. Though he told it at his rich best, though his stern earnestness made an impression, still he had not that flair which made the mob follow breathlessly after every creak of Titus's square-toed shoes. They go waddling and creaking down the years, those square-toed shoes; the long chin juts out of the periwig as he peers over his shoulder, and the face is set in that expression the secret of whose power no man will now ever solve.

The Commons waited, and Titus appeared: a martyr with his mouth pulled awry, now dreading that he himself

[1] Coleman's trial lasted from nine in the morning until five in the evening. – Narcissus Luttrell, *A Brief Historical Relation of State Affairs*.

would be poisoned. But he told his story with a brave blatter, throwing himself upon their mercy and help. Without a dissentient voice they gave him a vote of confidence. The House then voted an address, after hearing Oates's accusation against the queen, that Catherine and all her household should be removed from the king's person.

Now of all the dirty dogs in the kennel called Oates's Plot, this particular canine was among the mangiest. The conduct of the queen during these bad days had roused only admiration. The English people had come to feel for her something like affection, that affection reserved for foreigners who have become institutions. Although they might believe that Papists meant to burn down London and cut a hundred thousand Protestant throats, they could not swallow so grotesque a charge as that the queen would poison her husband. Angriest of all was Charles himself.

'They think I have a mind to a new wife,' he snapped; 'but, for all that, I will not see an innocent woman abused.'

First of all he must go to her, and assure her that he did not believe one word of it. This accusation, the notion that anyone in the world might credit her with desiring to kill the man she had never ceased to love, came close to breaking Catherine's courage. She had held on for a long time, but this nearly ended it. So he must go to her, and stand over an ageing woman while she wept, and pat her shoulder gently. And it came to him most strongly, whilst he stood by the dim clock-lamp at her bedside: If ever he could get himself into a position to have a reckoning with the gentlemen who had managed this, then God in heaven! but it should be a terrible reckoning.

For the first time he left off his veiled tactics in dealing with his enemies. When the Commons' address for the removal of the queen came to be debated next day in the House of Lords, Charles led the attack himself. Despite protests from Shaftesbury, the Lords by eight votes refused to confirm the address. Dr. Oates, to his stupefaction, found his papers seized and himself shut up in his room. Whereupon Oates was in a martyr's rage and astonishment: he even complained that the Yeomen of the Guard outraged his feelings by smoking tobacco in his rooms. The furious Commons would not permit such indignities to their favourite, so Oates had to be let out, to readjust his ruffled plumes and ruffled sneer.

The Green Ribbon attack was driving Charles each day a step nearer the wall. Already a move to dismiss the Duke of York from parliamentary councils, the first step towards excluding him from the throne, had been narrowly beaten. The Green Ribboners would return to that: they were steadily circulating their whisper that the Duke of Monmouth was legitimate, was the true heir to the crown, and once they had fully set him up as a dummy Protestant champion it would not be too difficult to overset James. The Duke of Monmouth, who had all his father's easy airs but none of his father's intelligence, made no objection. He wore these honours from Shaftesbury complacently and admiringly, as he might wear a ring on his finger. Already Charles, for want of money, had been compelled to disband the army in Flanders. On November 30th parliament edged a trifle nearer, by proposing a bill to place the militia under parliamentary control. To put the militia in the hands of parliament was asking for civil war, just as it had been a quarter of a century before. 'My father lost his head because of such measures,' Charles said grimly. 'I will not let the militia get out of my hands, not even for half an hour.'

The terror was not diminishing: on the contrary, the sky over England looked more lurid. Two thousand men lay under arms all night. Wealthy merchants hastened to send their families abroad, in case there should be fighting. While parliament put forward the militia bill, they were engaged at the same time in removing Catholic members from both Houses according to the most recent Test Act. This purging harked back to the days of Cromwell, whose head still hung askew over Westminster Hall. On December 1st the Commons voted an address to the king representing the danger that came of his following private counsels rather than those of his faithful parliament: they meant Lord Treasurer Danby, and they meant to have Danby's head. This resolution was favoured even by some of the court's supporters; if Charles had been less steady he might have believed that even his friends were melting away from him when Lord Shaftesbury pressed on to triumph. On December 3rd Edward Coleman was butchered at Tyburn amid caperings of delight from the crowd. It was the opinion of some who saw him drawn along on the sledge, or at his prayers among the spectators, that he expected a reprieve; and when it came time to begin the business, some said he muttered, 'There is no faith in man.' The story is dubious: it smacks too much of official last-words and a mummified scene in a picture-book. In any event Coleman died bravely. Two days later the five Catholic Lords – Arundell, Bellasis, Powis, Petre, and Stafford – were impeached for high treason.

One by one they were going. Five other and less high-placed Catholics were to come up for trial later in the month: there would be no rest for Mr. Ketch. Charles, up that flight of stairs in the little room which was the only place where he could be alone, must look fairly upon the situation and decide what he could do. These men were innocent: he knew that. He held the royal right to pardon. These were human beings, who felt pain as much as he did; they were members of a religious faith that had befriended him, and for which he cared as much as he was capable of caring for any. He could pardon them. And to pardon one Catholic meant civil war.

He was not of the stuff of which martyrs are made. The issue did not touch him deeply enough. For personal relationships, for a wife or a brother or a close friend – Father Huddleston, the priest who had saved his life after Worcester fight, he had protected by a royal proclamation – for these he would risk whatever he must. But in his heart he was puzzled and a trifle angry that so much fuss should be made over religious matters; let his subjects be Protestants or Catholics or Quakers or whatever they pleased, so long as they lived at peace, with food in the larder and no high-souled knaves to steal the fowls in their gardens. True enough, this religious scare was merely being used by Shaftesbury and the grandees as a weapon: *that* was what he must fight. But he would not do it with pardons. If these men were condemned, he resolved quite frankly to let the law take its course. He would fight in council as long as he could to save them; he would even, characteristically, put off signing the death-warrants as long as he could: yet if they had to die he would go no further. But even his old cynicism could not sustain him; for the first time he wavered; for the first time we hear his words become clumsy and bewildered. 'Let the blood lie on them that condemn them: for God knows I sign with tears in my eyes!' He had put it off again.

But the sample of knavery which most roused him was the trial of the 'five priests' – Thomas Whitebread, William Ireland, John Fenwick, Thomas Pickering, and John Grove – on December 17th. It was not held at the Court of King's Bench, but at the terrible Sessions House in Old Bailey: where jail-fever blew out of Newgate, and struck at the judge on the bench so often that he must muffle himself round with sweet herbs, sprinkle the place with strong vinegar, and carry a bouquet of flowers under his nose.

Though it was a cramped enough hole, the largest part of it being a dock big enough to accommodate more than forty prisoners at once, still there was a noble feature in the room upstairs from the court. This was the judicial dining-hall. Here were held the great feasts offered to the judges during each sessions by the Lord Mayor and the Sheriffs. Here, at stated intervals during the trials, repaired the judges, the counsel, and any distinguished guests who happened to be present. It was not uncommon for His Lordship to reel back to the bench and pronounce sentence of death while three parts gone in drink, with the chaplain rocking tipsily beside him. Whether or not this atmosphere was more congenial to Scroggs than that of the King's Bench, at the trial of the Jesuits he was in a mood of playful ferocity. He cracked jokes with Oates (now a favourite of his), and was exceedingly waggish at the expense of the prisoners, so that he did not work himself into a full state of rage until he fell under the spell of his own eloquence at the summing-up.

Of the prisoners, Pickering and Grove we have met before; they were the men who had so often attempted to kill the king with silver bullets in screw-guns, but who for a variety of reasons had so often failed. Thomas White-bread, a man of sixty, was provincial of the English province of the Society of Jesus. John Fenwick was the London agent for the college at St. Omers, Thomas Ireland was procurator of the province. All were men of intelligence and education, somewhat hampered by the fact that they had no knowledge of what charges were to be brought against them in court, and, when they got there, none except Ireland was allowed to present evidence or witnesses in his own behalf.

After proceedings had been opened by Serjeant Sir Samuel Baldwin, Sir Cresswell Levinz, and Mr. Finch, Titus Oates again stepped forward as the first witness. He told his old story of intended massacre (his own part, he said again, was to murder Dr. Tonge for having translated *The Jesuits' Morals*): of Fenwick's design to stir up rebellion in Scotland and Ireland, of Whitebread's sealing commissions for officers in the Popish army, of everyone's signing the resolution to kill the king. As a reward for killing the king, Grove was to have £1,500, and Pickering was to have thirty thousand masses: which, at a shilling a mass, came to the same sum. They had cut teeth in their silver bullets so as to inflict an incurable wound. On one occasion Pickering had suffered a penance of thirty lashes for bungling a good opportunity to fire.

Oates went on at length, while Whitebread and Fenwick attempted to pin him down to definite dates or places. 'My lord,' said Whitebread, 'before I forget it, I desire to say this. He says that at such and such consults in April and May, he was present, and carried the resolutions from one to another. There are above a hundred and an hundred that can testify he was all that while at St. Omers.' And presently he spoke more gravely: 'My lord, I am in a very weak and doubtful condition as to my health, and therefore I should be loath to speak anything but what is true. We are to prove a negative, and I know 'tis much harder to prove a negative than to assert an affirmative. But truly, I may boldly say, in the sight of Almighty God before whom I am to appear, there have not been three true words spoken by this witness.'

This was unfortunate, for it gave Scroggs an opportunity to point out that, being Papists who had a dispensation to say anything, they must not expect to be believed. Then Oates set out to demonstrate his intimacy with Grove and Fenwick, on the strength of money borrowed from them.

'. . . and I will put him in mind of another time when he and I were in company,' brayed Titus, pointing his finger at Grove. 'Someone brought us a note of what was done in the House of Commons, turned into burlesque: for they used to turn all that was done at the council, or at the parliament, or at the courts in Westminster Hall, into burlesque; and they then translated it into French, and sent it to the French king, for him to laugh at too,' declared Titus, as sober as an owl. 'But that by the way! Twice more he drank in my company, at the "Red Posts" in Wild Street – and once more when he owned to me that he had set fire to Southwark.'

The Lord Chief Justice sat up. 'Now by the oath that you have taken, did he own to you that he had fired Southwark?'

'My lord, he did tell me that he, with three Irishmen, did fire Southwark; and that they had a thousand pounds given them for it, whereof he had four hundred pounds, and the other two two hundred pounds apiece.'

'Now for Mr. Fenwick!' said the Lord Chief Justice. 'Now, Mr. Fenwick, do you know Mr. Oates?'

'Yes, my lord, I do,' said the agent for the college at St. Omers.

'Were you well acquainted with him? Speak plain.'

Oates interposed. 'He was my Father Confessor, my lord!'

'I believe,' said Fenwick grimly, 'he never made any confession in his life.'

'Oh, yes: he hath made a very good one now,' retorted Scroggs jocosely. 'Were you of his acquaintance, Mr. Fenwick? Speak home, and don't mince the matter.'

'My lord, I have seen him.'

Scroggs stared. 'I wonder what you are made of! Ask a Protestant – an English one – a plain question, and he will scorn to come dallying with an evasive answer.'

'My lord, I have been several times in his company.'

'Did you pay eight shillings for him?'

'Yes, I believe I did.'

'How came you to do it?'

'He was going to St. Omers.'

'Why,' says the Lord Chief Justice, opening his eyes in a gay good humour, 'were you the Treasurer for the Society? No? You never had your eight shillings again, had you? Did Mr. Oates ever pay it again?'

'No; sure he was never so honest.'

Scroggs pressed the point, for some obscure reason, with several more questions. 'Why did you not ask Mr. Oates for it?'

'He was not able to pay it.'

'Why did you then lay it down for him?'

'Because I was a fool,' said Fenwick with gloomy candour.

'That must be the conclusion always,' returned Scroggs; 'when you can't evade being proved knaves by answering directly, you will rather suffer yourselves to be called fools.'

'My lord, I have done more for him than that comes to; for he came once to me in a miserable poor condition, and said, "I must turn again, and betake myself to the ministry to get bread; for I have eaten nothing these two days"; and I gave him five shillings to relieve his present necessity.'

Oates was outraged. 'My lord, I will answer to that!' he bawled. 'I was never in any such straits! – I was ordered by the provincial to be taken care of by the procurator.'

'You brought no such order to me.'

'Yes, Mr. Fenwick,' cried Oates, wagging his finger, 'you know there was such an order! – and I never received so little in my life as five shillings from you; I have received twenty, and thirty, and forty shillings at a time, but never so little as five.' On the point of his condition he added: 'I have indeed gone a whole day without eating, when I have been hurried about your trash . . . but I assure you, my lord, that I never wanted for anything among them.'

'Perhaps it was fasting-day,' suggested Scroggs waggishly.

'My lord,' interposed the Lord Chief Baron, with an arch legal smile, 'their fasting-days are none of the worst.' ·

'No,' agreed Titus, 'we commonly eat best on those days.'

Here it is conceivable that there was laughter in the court. With such merry conceits (witty or not, according to your taste and generation), Scroggs conducted the case until Whitebread demanded to be heard on a relevant point of their defence. Oates, he said, had stated that he (Titus) was present at several sinister consults of Jesuits in April or May; it could be demonstrated that during those months Oates had never left the college of St. Omers in France. Would that suffice to answer Oates? 'Ay, if you can prove otherwise pray do,' agreed Scroggs.

'My lord,' said Fenwick, 'we can bring an authentic writing from St. Omers, under the seal of the college, and testified to by all in the college that he was there all the while.'

'Mr. Fenwick, that will not do!' declared Scroggs; 'for, first, if it were in any other case besides this it would be no evidence; but I know not what you cannot get from St. Omers, or what you will not call authentic.'

'Does your Lordship think there is no justice out of England?' demanded Fenwick. 'It shall be signed by the magistrates of the town.'

'You must be tried by the laws of England, which,' said Scroggs, 'sends no piece of fact out of the country to be tried.'

'But the evidence of it may be brought hither?'

'Then you should have brought it,' said Scroggs triumphantly. 'You shall have a fair trial; but we must not depart from the law or the way of trial to serve your purposes. You must be tried according to the law of the land.'

Having been kept in prison without opportunity to find any witnesses, they could produce none. Whitebread, turning this round, demanded if Oates himself could produce two witnesses to show he was in London in April or

May. Titus turned the question off by declaring that he
could narrate some circumstances to prove it; and, after
some wrangling, Scroggs suggested that after his labours
Mr. Oates had better sit down and have some refreshment.
Whereupon the prosecution called William Bedloe as a
witness.

Once more Bedloe split up his evidence. With either
the caution or the artistic restraint which often characterised him, he would not swear boldly to all five prisoners.
He said he was acquainted only with Ireland, Pickering,
and Grove. Against these three he swore flatly, as one who
would not go the whole hog but would be very downright
about frying half of it: and he described in detail a meeting,
during the previous August, at which all three had spoken
enthusiastically about murdering the king. As to Whitebread and Fenwick, he would say nothing except that they
were spoken of 'as being very active in the plot'. With
regard to Ireland, Pickering, and Grove, Ireland pressed
him very hard, and drove him from point to point: 'Mr.
Bedloe, can you produce any witness that you ever spoke to
me before in your life?' But Bedloe stood on his testimony.
He kept making references to Le Faire, Le Faire, Le Faire,
as he usually did, and presently he roused the curiosity of
Scroggs. 'Where is that Le Faire?' inquired the Lord Chief
Justice. 'You would do well to produce him.'

But it became clear that the case against Whitebread and
Fenwick had collapsed. To prove treason against them, two
witnesses were required; and Bedloe would not swear to any
treasonable words or actions on their part. Though he
added zest by a fresh tale of a plot to murder the Earl of
Shaftesbury, the Duke of Buckingham, the Earl of Ossory,
and the Duke of Ormonde, and though Oates hurried to his
assistance with a wealth of detail which attempted to pull
Whitebread into this plot, still the case remained the same.
The prosecution then attempted to use a letter as consti-
tuting a second witness. But the letter made no mention of
Whitebread's name or Fenwick's name, and Scroggs very
fairly refused to allow it. Then he ordered that Whitebread
and Fenwick be taken back to Newgate.

'You must understand,' the Lord Chief Baron interposed, to Captain Richardson, 'they are in no way acquitted: the evidence is so full against them by Mr. Oates's testimony that there is no reason to acquit them. It is as flat as one witness can be. The king hath sent forth a proclamation for further discovery; and, before the time therein prefixed, no doubt there will be more evidence come in. Therefore keep them as strict as you can.'

Whereupon Ireland, Pickering, and Grove were called on to make their defence. Ireland, who had been allowed to see his sister the day before the trial, did well: he had got a couple of witnesses through her, although there was no knowledge beforehand of what testimony they must rebut, and there was no time to get anyone else. They attempted to prove that Ireland had been out of town in August,[1] when he was supposed to have met with Grove and Pickering to discuss the murder of the king. But they underwent considerable knocking-about from the bench (Ireland already being in disgrace for having called Mr. Oates a paid liar to his face), Oates was protected by the judge when matters grew warm, and one crown witness testified otherwise. As a final hope on Ireland's part, there was in court a gentleman from Hastings who had been in that town when Oates was convicted on a charge of malicious lying – the good Dr. Oates had brought against the Hastings schoolmaster a charge of sodomy, Oates himself being the one who was really addicted to this practice – and a certificate setting forth the facts had been brought from the Hastings town-council. But the bearer of the certificate himself hastily disclaimed all intent to take away the credibility of good Mr. Oates, and Scroggs with equal haste refused to allow the town-council's document to be read. 'I do not think it authentic evidence,' said Scroggs.

All three prisoners saw that there was no hope whatever, and that no hope had existed from the first. Ireland, whose father and uncle had been killed in Charles the First's service during the war, saw that loyalty would carry no weight. Whereupon Scroggs summed up to the jury in what is

---

[1] They were telling the perfect truth, as was later demonstrated.

probably the most tremendous philippic launched at the
time of the Popish plot. Read it as a piece of mob-excite-
ment, and it is not difficult to understand Scroggs's success
as a criminal lawyer.

'If they had not murdered kings,' he bellowed, again on
his favourite subject of Catholics in general, 'if they had
not murdered kings, I would not say they would have murdered ours. But when it hath been their practice so to do:
when they have debauched men's understandings, over-
turned all morals, and destroyed all divinity, what shall I
say of them? When their humility is such, that they tread
on the necks of emperors; their charity such, as to kill
princes, and their vow of poverty such, as to covet kingdoms
– what shall I judge of them? When they have licences to
lie, and indulgences for falsehoods (nay, when they can
make him a saint that dies in one, and then pray to him,
as the carpenter first makes an image and afterwards wor-
ships it) and can then think to bring that wooden religion
of theirs amongst us in this nation, what shall I think of
them? What shall I say to them? What shall I do with
them? . . . They eat their God, they kill their king, and
saint the murderer! They indulge in all sorts of sins, and
no human bonds can hold them.'

There was some twenty minutes of this, after which the
jury again promised to be short, and again kept its promise.
Ireland, Pickering, and Grove were found guilty. Scroggs
gathered up his papers in satisfaction.

'You have done, gentlemen,' cries he to the jury, 'like
very good subjects, and very good Christians – that is to say,
like very good Protestants – and now much good may their
thirty thousand masses do them!'

The court adjourned until sentence should be pronounced that afternoon.

IV

Mr. William Bedloe left the Sessions House in a gloomy
state of mind. In the street he hesitated, well bundled up
in his great outer-coat; then he crossed the Old Bailey.
Pulling his broad-brimmed hat well down on the periwig

so that he might not be recognised, he turned to the right and entered a tavern in Black-and-White Court. Here he called for a private room, with a good fire and a candle, and a jug of that good strong potation called Go-by-the-wall. In his private room, in an elbow-chair drawn close to the fire against freezing weather, he sat him down to consider his position.

Scroggs's words remained in his mind: 'Where is that Le Faire? You would do well to produce him.' And Scroggs was in the right. Bedloe had begun to lose his place. He was not losing credit: under the circumstances, no knight of the post could do that: but he was slipping and sliding away from importance in the great scheme of the plot. To-day, in order to make half of himself secure and prepare a way for retreat, in order to say to a small inner prompting that he was not telling *all* lies, he had let two prisoners slip away. But that was not the important thing. The important thing was that he had been lauded and lifted up as the exposer of the Papists' most damnable act, the murder of Justice Godfrey – that very proof of the whole plot, worth as much as all Oates's screw-guns and thirty thousand masses together – but as a discoverer he had failed.

'Where is that Le Faire? You would do well to produce him.' Ay: if only he could produce him! As the murderers of Godfrey he had named Le Faire, Walsh, a chapel-keeper, and a servant of Lord Bellasis. For nearly six weeks a royal proclamation had been out against them: but Le Faire and Walsh had hidden themselves beyond pursuit, and the other two, of cloudy status at the very least, could not be found or identified. In that respect the great discovery was stillborn.

Then, at the suggestion of the Lords' Committee, he had worked Mr. Samuel Atkins into the business, as having been seen standing over the magistrate's body in Somerset House between nine and ten o'clock on Monday night. But now, only a few days ago – on December 13th – Bedloe had learned that this was a bad blunder. Since November, Atkins had been kept heavily ironed in Newgate. Leading

Green Ribbon men had gone to threaten or cajole him, but still he remained obdurately silent. 'Samuel Atkins,' declared Sacheverell, 'is one of the most ingenious men to say nothing I have ever met.' This ingeniousness in the young man looked so suspicious that it had convinced the Lords' Committee of some trap. So they had allowed the clerk pen, ink, and paper to compose his defence; and, once he had put enough into writing, his papers were seized. From these papers they discovered to their wrath that the clerk could bring unshakable evidence to prove his whereabouts on the night of October 14th, when he had been tippling aboard a yacht at Greenwich. The Lords' Committee hastily summoned the witnesses named in the papers, Captain Vittells of the yacht *Catherine* and five of his men, to a private inquiry; and they had discovered that to convict him would be impossible. All the witnesses were Protestants, all were of good character in the king's service. Let a judge do what he liked, let counsel plead as they liked, such flat testimony could not be disproved. Mr. Bedloe's whole case was swept away.

It was not only that four of the men Bedloe had accused were not to be found, and the fifth beyond touching. But he had described as the scene of the murder a room in Somerset House where it could not conceivably have taken place. The men, the place, the motive were all equally weak. In addition to which, he had varied his evidence so often in the course of these weeks that the most astute counsel might find it coming to pieces in court.

My Lord Shaftesbury had come to look upon him angrily. If he were not careful, he would lose favour altogether. It was true that he had brewed up a variety of fantasies to confirm Oates's testimony of the plot in general: and that was useful enough: but in his own particular domain of the plot, the damnable murder, he had failed so far. A victim must be discovered – not a hazy name or a slippery soul who could not be found, but a solid man who could be clapped in irons, exhibited to the mob, and hanged for their satisfaction – or every resounding scare-horn of the Green Ribbon Club would die to silence.

Bedloe realised that he had already committed himself about the names of the murderers. He himself could not change it, unless he slurred it over and added more people to the list. But on one point his caution had not allowed him to commit himself altogether, and he blessed it with a prayerful curse. He had been cautious about the persons he said he had seen standing over Godfrey's body in Somerset House on the Monday night. That part was vague; he had not even been willing to swear definitely about Samuel Atkins. If he could get his hands on somebody whom he could swear he saw by that dark lanthorn, it would be just as good as naming one of the actual murderers. And the Lords' Committee would smile again.

But he must take great care. If he selected someone to accuse, there were certain necessities, for he must not make the same blunder twice or he would be undone. First, the victim must be somebody who could not prove his whereabouts on Monday night. Second, it must be a Papist. Third, it must be someone who was well acquainted with Somerset House. Fourth, it must be a man of trembling disposition, who could be frightened by a few snaps of Shaftesbury's fingers: they must catch no more Tartars like Samuel Atkins. After this fellow was caught, let the Lords' Committee deal with him – let them terrify him into confessing the crime – let them supply the details according to their own taste – let them suggest a proper scene for the crime, if they thought they could manage it so well. Plainly, thought Bedloe, they must stick to Somerset House as the place where the murder was done. *He* didn't mind. If he lent a little assistance to the committee and the victim, they might be able to select a few more murderers, preferably two or three low-born Papists without wit to defend themselves.

That depended on the victim; and first he must find a suitable fellow to fit into the light of the dark lanthorn. He had been having an unpleasant time, had Captain Bedloe, what with the ill graces of the Lords' Committee and his own wabbling nature under that bluff exterior; and now it soothed him to sit by a snug fire, drinking a hot potation of rum, white wine, and spices, while he considered the phantom figure he was building up. For some weeks he had been considering it. He must come to a decision, and make a choice – if he could find one. He was no ineffectual fellow. If it became necessary, he could scold or accuse or stick to a flat statement as well as Titus Oates. He had flung it out at Edward Coleman, he had flung it out to-day: though assuredly he had expected his brother to help him more than his brother did. William Bedloe was a superior person, (thought Mr. William Bedloe); he wore distinguished manners along with the nobility; he had some knowledge of Latin and mathematics, and was even contemplating the writing of a play: yes, he could yet supplant Titus as the saviour of the nation if he kept his eye on business and chose the proper sort of victim as Godfrey's murderer. Sipping his hot drink by the fire, easing his scratched vanity with savage resolutions for the future, it occurred to him to wonder who *had* killed Justice Godfrey after all.

This was the afternoon of December 17th. Two days later, while Bedloe was still prowling and puzzling near Westminster, he heard news of the uproar in the House of Commons. It had come so suddenly, this turn of disaster, that the Court Party scarcely knew how to meet it. It meant the end of Danby, and, darker spirits muttered in the lobby, the end of the king as well.

For some time the Green Ribboners had been reserving a shot which might do the business. There were rumours of it; Sir John Reresby had already warned Danby to look to himself, and the possibility had existed for some months. Mr. Ralph Montagu, former ambassador to France who had been dismissed from his position in disgrace, at last made use of Danby's letters. The French government hated Danby no less than Shaftesbury and the Green Ribbon mutineers hated him; so they had conspired, in their old alliance, to expose Danby as one who had secretly asked money from France. In Montagu's possession there was one particular letter, dated March 25th, 1678, which fully set forth the secret negotiations. It contained such explosive material as, 'The king (of England) expects to have six millions of livres a year for three years . . . because it will probably be two or three years before the parliament will be in humour to give him any supplies after the making of any peace with France.' Montagu was going before the House of Commons to read this. And at the foot of the letter, in Charles's handwriting, appeared the words, '*I approve of this letter. C.R.*'

On the evening of December 18th my Lord Treasurer sought out Charles to tell him what would happen next day. This, the king felt, was a final bedevilment, but he tried to put a good face on the matter. He saw Danby privately, and the Treasurer was much agitated. The Treasurer saw that all doors were closed before he spoke.

'Your Majesty,' he went on hurriedly, 'I can affirm, and you can bear me out, that ever since I have had the honour to serve you up to this day, I have delivered it as my constant opinion that France was the worst interest you could embrace, and that they were the nation in the world from whom I did believe you ought to apprehend the greatest danger, and who have both your person and government in the last degree of contempt –'[1]

'Make yourself easy, my lord,' said Charles shortly. 'The letter was writ by my order. My name is upon it.'

'That is what troubles me most: that the matter must reflect chiefly on you!' cried Danby, and threw out his hands. 'Sir, you know how true a servant I have been to you. I do not think Mr. Montagu would dare –'

'How came you to take no precautions against this? Had you any warning?'

'Sir John Reresby,' admitted the Lord Treasurer, 'acquainted me a month ago that the Commons would certainly fall upon me. He had it from Monsieur du Cros, the Duke of Holstein's resident, and also from Mr. Montagu himself, who is his cousin. But I rejected this. I did not think Mr. Montagu durst impeach me, for I have letters from him as well as he has letters from me. I have

---

[1] Danby's words are derived from the speech he made before the House of Commons, Dec. 23rd. See also Reresby, November 18th.

letters to show from him, whilst he was ambassador in France, endeavouring to persuade me to accept the French king's money: but I refused it.'

'But you are certain he will impeach you?'

Danby stared at the wall, curiously. 'When it is too late, your Majesty,' he said, 'I learn how he is bought by M. Barrillon and my Lord Shaftesbury. The French king hates me. My Lord Shaftesbury's party hate me. I do not know why my own countrymen should hate me. I entered upon an empty Treasury almost six years ago. I have added thirty new ships to the navy, of bigger dimensions than before; I take upon me the vanity to say so by the payments I have made to the navy and the seamen, beyond former times, and by the paying-off of the greatest part of the debt which was stopped in Exchequer; nor will I say anything of the sum, above a hundred thousand pounds, which now remains in the Treasury after all this. . . .' He stopped, and was much puzzled. 'I have served the Treasury faithfully, I think. I do not know what these gentlemen would have.'

'When does Mr. Montagu go before the House?'

'I think to-morrow. There may be,' said Danby, his sallow face growing brisker, 'if your Majesty will give me leave, a means of preventing him. If your Majesty will give me leave to seize his papers, on the grounds that he has been corresponding with the Pope's nuncio without commission from you –?'

Charles gave the permission, but he spent a troubled night nevertheless. Ralph Montagu was no fool ('*peu dangereux pour sa figure, mais fort à craindre,*' Grammont had written long ago, '*pour son assiduité et par l'addresse de son esprit*'),[1] and he must have anticipated such a move.

---

[1] This Montagu was a very ingenious fellow, and a terror among the ladies. He would have been brought more fully into this chronicle if there had been room for him. In his later days he courted the very wealthy and very mad daughter of the Duke of Newcastle, and among a crowd of suitors won her hand by convincing her that he was the Emperor of China. An envious suitor wrote:

> 'Insulting rival, never boast
> Thy conquest lately won;
> No wonder that her heart was lost—
> Her senses first were gone.'

He had anticipated it. Danby got all his papers except the important ones, notably that letter of March 25th, and when it was read out next day an observer records that it put the House of Commons into a flame. It was moved that Danby ought to be impeached for high treason. There were two days of furious debate. On the second day Danby counter-attacked with strong charges of treason against Montagu, but the Treasurer had so many enemies that the whole reflection and violence was only against himself. Six articles of impeachment were read against him. It was put to a vote whether the proceedings should be taken to the House of Lords for impeachment, and carried by forty-nine votes.

Thus Danby's packed parliament, whose little members he had kept loyal for so long with bribery, crumbled under him. Though no outward use was made of those damning words at the foot of the letter, 'I approve – C.R.,' everyone knew what was meant. The secret was out, and, without any over-statement, the kingdom was tottering. One more push from Shaftesbury, and there would be an end of things: it was almost certain that James would be sent to travel, it was possible Charles might be sent as well.

The Green Ribbon leaders had reason to ask themselves complacently: Could Charles Stuart, could any living human being, hope to extricate himself from the position into which with deadly inevitability they had at last forced him? And if so, how? In August 1678, Charles had rested easily with a tractable parliament, a large army at his command, and nearly a million pounds in his pocket. Before Christmas in the same year, they were very nearly in a position to wrest away from him every one of his prerogatives: to exclude his brother from the throne, to banish his queen, to indict his prime minister for high treason, and to take over his command of the army. Not one minister of outstanding ability now remained to him. Not one way of raising money remained to him, except the dubious assistance of a none-too-friendly Louis the Fourteenth. Against him were ranged the most brilliant politicians of the century, led by Shaftesbury, Buckingham, and a man whose influence in Green Ribbon matters was gradually becoming almost as great as theirs – George Savile, Lord Halifax,[1] probably the most gifted orator in English history.   Shaftesbury, Buckingham, and Halifax led a formidable organisation of a hundred fluent tongues, and were supported by all the wealth of the king of France.   They faced one man, alone and jeered at, whose only asset was his personal popularity among the ordinary people of England.   It was the last test.   It was the darkest hour.   And all this had come about because one ageing magistrate, of no particular importance in the great scheme of things, had been found murdered in a ditch.   And all because of an insignificant killing, probably in a private cause.   And all for a few drops of candle-grease, a pair of polished shoes, an absence of blood on a shirt.   And all for the want of a horseshoe nail. . . .

In this state of bedevilment, on Saturday, December 21st, Charles met Mr. William Chiffinch hurrying in with fresh news.

'Bedloe –' said Chiffinch.   'Bedloe,' he went on, 'has made a fresh discovery.   There was a man they took in custody last night, on one charge or another.   They had him to-day in a little room by the lobby of the House of Commons; and Mr. Bedloe, coming past to see him, all of a sudden sets up a great cry and to-do, pointing to the man, and cries, "*This is one of the rogues that I saw with a dark lanthorn about the body of Sir Edmund Godfrey, but he was then in a periwig.*"   This hath an ill look, your Majesty.'

---

[1] There was no cooler, more urbane mind or manner in England than that of Halifax, the first 'Trimmer'.   It is indicated in one of his replies to Burnet on the matter of his religious views: 'I believe as much as I can, and I hope that God will not lay it to my charge if I cannot digest iron, as an ostrich does, nor take into my belief things that must burst me.'   His temper is summed up in his own maxim: 'To know when to leave things alone is a high pitch of good sense.'

VI

'YOU HAD BETTER CONFESS THAN BE HANGED'

The Accusation

'Courage, friend, to-day is your period of sorrow,
 And things will go better, believe me, to-morrow.'
'To-morrow?' our hero replied in a fright:
'He that's hanged before noon ought to think of to-night.'

MATTHEW PRIOR, *Ballad of the
Thief and the Cordelier.*

'One of the best-known legal maxims, which oral tradition hands down from one generation of law-students to another, is that there are three degrees of perjurers: "the liar, the damned liar, and the expert witness".'

SIR EDWARD PARRY, *The Bloody Assize.*

I

LUCK, so long angelic at the elbow of Titus Oates, had turned to William Bedloe, and indicated the proper victim for his purpose. In Prince's Street, Covent Garden, lived a Catholic silversmith named Miles Prance. A man of considerable intelligence, but of weak and uncertain temperament, Mr. Prance enjoyed a modest living in his trade. He had frequently been employed by the queen at Somerset House, and was intimately acquainted with that palace. Also he had done silversmith's work for several Jesuits, with whom he was friendly; and his brother was a priest.

Whereupon coincidence, always moving ironically in this case, laid hands on Prance. In his house he had a lodger – one John Wren – who owed him fourteen months' rent. Wren was pressed to pay up; there was trouble between tenant and landlord, concluding with threats against Prance. Wren, casting about for some means of executing them, stumbled upon the knowledge that Prance had spent a couple of nights away from home about the time of Sir Edmund Godfrey's disappearance. In point of fact, as it was later proved, this had been well before Godfrey's disappearance, and had no connection with it; but nobody was in a particularly critical frame of mind, and the words 'about the time of Sir Edmund Godfrey's disappearance' made a satisfactory accusation. Furthermore, it had been brought to Wren's attention that – about the time Pickering, Ireland, and Grove were on trial – Miles Prance, in liquor at a tavern, was overheard to say, 'They are very honest men.' Thus on St. Thomas's Eve, information was laid against him by Wren and two others, accusing him of complicity in the murder of Godfrey, and putting in a claim for the reward.

He was taken into custody; he was carried to the lobby of the House of Commons; and William Bedloe, having heard of the arrest, heard every prayer answered as well. Here was exactly the man for Bedloe's money: here was one who fulfilled every qualification as a victim. He could prove no alibi. He was a Catholic, and the friend of priests. He was intimately acquainted with Somerset House. He could doubtless be made to see reason without great difficulty. After a private view of the prisoner, Captain Bedloe did not take a long time to make up his mind. In Miles Prance he saw a thin, rather stooped man with fair hair – he wore no periwig – and a short fair beard, much frightened by the condition into which he had been thrust. Bedloe denounced him in a ringing voice, like Charles Hart at the playhouse: 'This is one of the rogues that I saw with a dark lanthorn about the body of Sir Edmund Godfrey, but he was then in a periwig!' And Mr. Miles Prance, set upon in the hue and cry, was carried before the full Lords' Committee.

He answered their questions as best he could. Wasn't he a Papist? Yes, he had been a Papist, but he was now a Protestant, and had taken the oaths. Did he know these Jesuits who had just been sentenced to death: Ireland, Pickering, and Grove? – or Fenwick and Whitebread either?

There was some shuffling, but Prance admitted that he had wrought in his silversmith's trade for Grove, Fenwick, Pickering, and Ireland. Didn't he say, the Sunday after they were arrested, that they were very honest men? Yes: he said that, but he was drunk when he said it. People had taken offence at it, and threatened to complain of him to the council-board; and he had hidden himself out of the way to avoid being questioned.

Ah, but hadn't he hired a horse to ride out of town? After more shuffling, which promised well, Prance admitted this. He then declared earnestly that he had not slept away from his house for more than two or three nights in a year, nor attended the queen's chapel once a month, though his wife was a Papist. And then they began upon the question of Godfrey's murder.

'May I be damned to the pit of hell,' cries Prance, 'if I know anything of the murder, or the plot either! The Monday night Sir Edmund Godfrey was missing, I slept at a neighbour's house. And as to seeing me with a dark lanthorn, in Somerset House, and wearing a periwig, that could not be. I once had a light flaxen periwig made of my wife's hair, but I do not ever wear it. My lords, may I be damned to the pit of hell if I know anything of this!'

The less astute of the full committee then began to press him with regard to confirming Bedloe's evidence; the less astute failed to perceive that it was Bedloe's evidence about the murder which he must *not* confirm. Nevertheless, he was asked whether he knew Le Faire and Walsh, whom Bedloe had accused of the actual murder; and Pritchard, who Bedloe swore had taken a hand in it. Miles Prance denied knowing any of them.

The old game was played again. He was taken off to Newgate, and lodged in the underground hole.

That turnkey who, a month ago, had said it would go ill with anyone who was clapped into Old Susie with such weather coming on, spoke no less than the truth. It was the bitterest weather in years, well below freezing. It caked the water-buckets, it stiffened the clock-weights, it deadened the ears of passers-by when an aching east wind raked up

Newgate Street: inside and outside, old Newgate itself wore a frosty rime even above ground. Christmas was coming on, with all its holly and merriment. At Christmas, alone of all times of the year, a fire would be lighted for one day in the chimney of the Common side, and beef would be given to the Common felons. The prisoners, stumbling about the prison in their irons (for all must wear irons wherever they went, since otherwise it would be impossible to distinguish between prisoners and visitors) could look forward to this treat of a wedge of beef. Outside the carol-singers prepared to strike up, the flageolet-man piping an experimental note or two on his instrument, and winding his ragged scarf round his neck. Business, too, was brisk at the Sessions House just down the way: the Christmas sessions was in swing, so that every day Recorder Sir George Jeffreys staggered away from the bench with a throat sore from sentencing malefactors. But Miles Prance, after they had loaded him with irons, saw the frozen cell into which he was being taken underground, and screamed.

Miles Prance was of no tough fibre. This thin, fair-haired, imaginative man, his fluency of speech now gone and his thin hands plucking at his beard, had always lived tolerably well. Without fire or light in that underground hole, on the eve of December 21st, he nearly died in one night. Presently the cold half stupefied him, but he kept on endlessly thinking over Bedloe's charges.

He lay there until early in the morning of Sunday, December 22nd. And then he heard footsteps coming down the ladder into the cell.

Prance dragged himself back as well as he could, fearing that this meant the end of him. He saw no light. The foot-steps descended; he made out a vague shape, which bent over; and he heard a rustle as something was placed on the floor. Then the person, whoever it might have been, ascended the ladder without a word. Presently he heard steps descending again, and he saw the light of a candle. This candle was placed on the floor, and Prance's muddy eyes observed that what had been put first on the floor was a sheet of paper closely written. When the unknown person had gone up again, still without speaking, Prance dragged himself over painfully to read the paper by the light of the candle. He was so numbed that it took him a long time to read.

'You had better confess than be hanged,' said the paper tersely. It went on to indicate that Prance had better discover a great knowledge of the plot. So many Popish lords should be mentioned by name; fifty thousand men to be raised, commissions given out, officers appointed. Bedloe's evidence about Godfrey was summed up and abstracted in it too – as regarded the viewing of the body by the light of the dark lanthorn.

Prance, jolted out of even his misery by this hint, pondered the contents of the paper. It was a contrivance of my Lord Shaftesbury, offering pardon or the rope. Prance prayed as he liked: still, one taste of Old Susie was enough to press any words through his rattling teeth. His soul would be damned, perhaps. But at least he could see his wife and children, at least he could get out of this terrible place; and, once he did get out, he could worry about his conscience afterwards. By his bellowings he roused the keepers upstairs, and he demanded to be taken to my Lord Shaftesbury, that he might speak with the Republican leader. At a little past five o'clock that evening he was taken out, and carried to Thanet House in Aldersgate Street.[1]

[1] Here we are on debatable ground, and reasons must be offered for the description of events centering round Prance's 'discovery'. The account here given is derived from Prance's own words, in the confession he made nearly ten years later to Sir Roger L'Estrange, and printed in *The Mystery of the Death of Sir E. B. Godfrey Unfolded*, 1688. Some writers have doubted the truth of this confession: on what seem to me to be insufficient grounds.

First of all, let us establish the one point on which all writers now agree. All writers now agree that the 'discovery' Prance made, his accusation under pressure of the three men who were tried for the murder, was false. All writers agree that these three men were innocent, and that Prance was a liar in denouncing them.

Very well. The reason why some people have doubted Prance's confession to L'Estrange, as to who prompted him in concocting his tale, is this: That, though he received a paper summing up Bedloe's evidence and was urged by the Lords' Committee to confirm Bedloe, still the story he invented was very different from that of Bedloe. Bedloe had accused one set of men; Prance accused still another set. Bedloe put the place of the murder in one part of Somerset House; Prance put it in still another part. Therefore, it is argued, if Prance's account of the paper received from

Prance, as he later admitted, was not taken before the full Lords' Committee. Captain Richardson took him to my Lord Shaftesbury's house in Aldersgate Street; and there, in a low parlour, sat only four men. There was a great bowl of Christmas punch on the table, of which Shaftesbury's three friends had partaken freely, and the Green leader himself was a little uplifted in liquor. Two of his companions were military-looking gentlemen, my lord's henchmen Major Wildman and Colonel Scott, and the third was the big and drunken Earl of Pembroke. Pembroke did not often stray so far into the City from his great house in Leicester Fields, though punch would draw him anywhere. But Shaftesbury's attention was directed towards Prance.

He began with his usual attack of Rogue and Rascal. 'You will discover this plot,' says he grimly, and pointed. 'There are great ones concerned in it, and you must discover

---

Shaftesbury be true – if, in short, Shaftesbury put him up to the 'discovery' – why didn't Prance confirm Bedloe?

But surely it is obvious that to confirm Bedloe, with regard to the actual murderers of Godfrey, was the one thing which Prance must *not* do. If he did so, Shaftesbury's whole scheme fell to the ground. For seven weeks a royal proclamation had been out to arrest Le Faire, Walsh, the chapel-keeper, and Lord Bellasis's servant: they could not be found, and were not likely to be found. If Prance merely accused them and corroborated Bedloe, there would be no victim at all: a complete failure to arrest anybody, and a failure of Shaftesbury's whole case. Similarly, Prance must not agree with Bedloe as to the place in Somerset House where the murder took place, for this could be easily disproved.

The Green Ribbon leaders knew that. Clearly then, their demands of Prance that he corroborate Bedloe could have had reference only to what took place *after* the murder; that is, the disposal of the body in Somerset House, the dramatic scene with the dark lantern, the various priests skulking about it. Here Bedloe's tale could be fitted in with that of Prance to make a perfect whole. And this is proved by the fact that, at the trial, Bedloe swore to just this course of events.

Nobody is in doubt that Prance lied; the only question that remains is who put him up to accusing the men he did accuse. It seems most probable that Prance, being so intimately acquainted with Somerset House, and knowing so many of the attendants there, himself concocted the story during his interview with Shaftesbury, and had the approval of the Green Ribbon leader – who suggested amendations and drilled Prance until the silversmith was parrot-perfect in repeating it. Whether Shaftesbury or Prance originated it, it at least gives evidence of Shaftesbury's thorough methods in schooling the witness about everything he must say. Prance's story was neat and artistic; Shaftesbury had perceived that it must be, for they must make no more blunders in delivering somebody to the hangman.

them too. Little ones will not serve our turn. Damn
you for a rogue,' cries he, 'for crossing Bedloe's evidence
and swearing you were not at Somerset House and did not
see Sir Edmund Godfrey's body there! Will you discover
this plot now? Speak up!'

A curtain goes down on that scene; we have no more.
What was said in that low parlour; how the story was concocted between them, if in fact it was concocted there at
all: these things we do not know. But we know that the
secret interview behind a locked door went on for more
than five hours, until eleven o'clock at night. Then Prance
was carried back to Newgate. Next morning he sent a
message to the House of Lords, saying that he was ready to
make a discovery of the plot. Not only would he make a
discovery of the plot, but he was prepared to give evidence
concerning the murder of Sir Edmund Godfrey, if he could
have promise of a full pardon. It was granted. The Duke
of Buckingham and several other committeemen went to
Newgate to take his examination, it having been ordered,
'No other person, lord or commoner, should be present at
the said interview, but the said lords and the prisoner.'
The House of Commons also appointed that their Committee of Secrecy, or any three of them, should wait upon
the penitent Prance. No record remains of what Mr.
Prance said to them, or they said to Mr. Prance, but the
meeting was satisfactory.

Thus on the day following – Christmas eve, of the year of
grace 1678 – Miles Prance was taken before the Privy Council in the presence of the king. Here he made his denunciation, accusing *Robert Green, Henry Berry,* and
Lawrence Hill, together with two Irish priests, of the
murder of Sir Edmund Godfrey.

II

It was a shrewd choice. All three men were servants
at Somerset House: men of low station, small learning,
and little ability at defending themselves. Through his
acquaintance with Somerset House, Prance knew them

well. And the choice showed how a better place for the murder to have occurred (in Somerset House) had been ingeniously selected.

For *Henry Berry* was the porter of the great Water-Gate at Somerset House. As has already been indicated, it was not a 'water-gate', but a wicket in the Strand leading down a flight of stone stairs to a courtyard beside the queen's stables and the lodgings of Somerset House dependents. Though there were sentries at every gate – this could not be helped whatever part of the palace you chose – still it was more secret than any other place. Berry, a stout comfortable man of middle-age, had complete control of opening and shutting the water-gate; and, in addition, he supplemented his wages by keeping an ale-house not far away. He was a former Protestant who, in order to keep his good position at Somerset House, had been reconciled to the Church of Rome.

Robert Green was an Irishman, son of a Catholic mother and Protestant father. He was a small, shrunken, and elderly man, who commonly wore a curious reddish-coloured periwig, and a crucifix hanging at his girdle. He could neither read nor write. For some years he had been employed as a cushion-layer, a sort of minor carpenter, at the queen's chapel; and was the closest one Prance could find to that vague figure of a 'chapel-keeper' so often mentioned.

Lawrence Hill was the servant of Dr. Godwin, treasurer of the queen's chapel. The son of a shoemaker, Hill possessed some little ability more than the others. Before coming into the employ of Dr. Godwin at Somerset House, he had been servant to a Recusant lady of some wealth, and had done some business for her. A tall, powerful man with a black beard, Hill had lived in the servants'-lodgings of Dr. Godwin's house – these lodgings being just off the courtyard below the Water-Gate – and there he occupied one tiny room with his wife and baby. He was of quiet habits, noted as a good family man and a good servant. In October he had left these lodgings for a house of his own in Stanhope Street.

These three: the stout porter, the tiny carpenter in his reddish peruke, the big black-bearded manservant: these were the men accused by Prance, together with two priests named *Girald* and *Kelly*, who could not be found. On December 24th Miles Prance was led before an agitated Privy Council to tell his story of the murder.

Prance was determined but very pale. They had brushed him up, and started the blood stirring in his veins by putting him in front of the fire, and combed his hair and fair beard; but he was nervous in such noble company. At the very beginning he made a bad blunder in his lesson. By a slip of the tongue, he declared that Godfrey had been waylaid on Monday, October 14th, instead of Saturday the 12th. But he corrected himself well, by saying he meant either the end or the beginning of the week, and went on with increasing fluency.

About a fortnight before the murder, said Prance, he had been approached by one Father Girald, an Irish priest, with the proposal of killing a man – at that time, he did not know who the victim was. But a week later he learned it was to be Justice Godfrey. Girald, Green the carpenter, and Hill the manservant had said savagely that they would commit the murder: Godfrey was an enemy to the queen and her servants, and had used some Irishmen very ill.

'And,' went on Prance coolly, 'Girald owed an old grudge to Sir Edmund besides, about a business of parish-duties. They all told me that my Lord Bellasis would see our action rewarded, if we did kill him. My lords, they watched and dogged Sir Edmund for a week before his death. Green called at his house that very Saturday morning. And Green, Girald, and Hill dogged him that day, until they caught him.

'My lords,' continued the witness, both his voice and his eyes warming, 'it was about nine of the clock – that same Saturday night – that Sir Edmund was passing along the Strand on his way home from St. Clement's Church; and Green, Girald, and Hill were following him. But Hill made haste to pass ahead of him: Hill stopped at the wicket of the great Water-Gate at Somerset House. The wicket was open, and Hill stepped inside, and looked down as though he had seen something there. Then he turned back, and called to Justice Godfrey: "Sir, there are two men quarrelling within here! They will soon be quieted if once they see you; you must come and stop them."

'Whereupon Sir Edmund entered through the wicket, and after him crept Hill, and Girald, and Green. And down the stairs they all went to the courtyard, till they came to a bench that is at the bottom of the deep descent. This bench is joined to a railing next to the upper end of the stables on the right-hand side –'

'Pray, Mr. Prance,' interposed Sir Joseph Williamson, who was taking short notes of this, 'where were *you* then? Were you there?'

'Yes, my lord, I was,' said Prance with pale earnestness. He had none of the 'God-help-me' declarations of Oates or Bedloe, nor their playhouse flourishes. He spoke soberly, with quick nods of his head, and a slight tightening of the eyelids as he seemed to grope after each detail. 'Yes, my lord, I was. I was sitting on that bench I spoke of. I sat on that bench I spoke of; and with me there was Henry Berry, the porter of the gate; and an Irishman that lodges at Green's house – I do not know his name.[1]

'My lords, by the time those others had come half-way down towards us, Justice Godfrey being followed by Green, Girald, and Hill, I rose up and went to the wicket. I was to stand at the wicket and give warning in case anyone should come down. At the same time Henry Berry went in another direction, and up another flight of stone stairs on the right, that leads to the Upper Court of Somerset House; he was to watch in that direction. . . . Then, my lords, when Sir Edmund Godfrey came down to that bench, the man Green leapt at him from behind, and put round his neck a large twisted handkerchief. Then they all fell upon him, and dragged him down suddenly into a corner behind the bench. And Green flung upon him, and throttled him, and beat him upon the breast, and twisted his neck until he broke it.'

[1] This was the other priest, Kelly.

'Did you see this done, Mr. Prance?'

'No, my lords. I was watching at the wicket. But about a quarter of an hour afterwards I came down to see what was done. And I found Sir Edmund was not quite dead; for I laid my hand upon him, and his legs tottered and shook, and then Green wrung his neck quite round.'

A mutter of horror went up from the council, a muttering and whispering at the scene this conjured up. That dank courtyard by the stables, with which many of them were familiar, had grown to be a cobble-stoned pit shut in by the houses of devils. It seemed all the worse that the most savage actor in the scene had been the tiny, ageing Green in his reddish periwig. In the midst of the muttering and whispering, Prance stood defiantly.

'Pray go on, Mr. Prance,' said the Lord Chancellor, the Earl of Nottingham.

'Then, my lords, I and all the others – Green, Berry, Hill, Girald, and the other Irishman – we took him up, and, and through a door on the left-hand side of the yard. This door leads up several stairs into a long dark passage opening at last into the Upper Court. And in this passage there is a door on the left hand: which, being opened, leads up with eight stairs into another house; but immediately upon the right hand, going up, there is a little closet, or square room. . . .'

'Mr. Prance,' interposed the Lord Chancellor, courteously but rather snappishly, 'we cannot follow by your description all these directions, left, right, left, upstairs or downstairs, as you would have it.'

King Charles spoke for the first time. 'No matter, my lord. Mr. Prance shall go presently and show to several of our number all these places he names. Tell us only what you did, Mr. Prance.'

The witness cleared his throat. 'May it please your Majesty: this little closet, or square room, was the place to which we carried Sir Edmund Godfrey's body. These lodgings are occupied by the servants of Dr. Godwin's household, and the little square room was formerly occupied by Hill himself. At the time I speak of, October 12th, he was still living in that room, and had not yet moved to his new house in Stanhope Street – which he did later.   We put the body in this room: and there we set it down bending, with its back against the bed.   There it was left for two nights, in Hill's care. . . .'

'And in Hill's room?'

'In Hill's room, my lords.   For two nights it was left there. But then, being afraid of discovery, on the third night Green, Berry, Hill, Girald, and the other Irishman, did take up the body and convey it away from there about nine or ten o'clock at night.   They carried it up further into another place in Somerset House: a room towards the Garden, I think it was.   There I saw it myself on Monday night, with a dark lanthorn, where it lay bended.   But on Tuesday night they took it to still another place in Somerset House – and on Wednesday they thought fit to remove it back again, to Hill's little room where they had first placed it.'

He was vivid in his detail: little flashes of light showing the frightened murderers peering over their shoulders – a scuffle and flurry as they carried the body, bent into a sitting position – and then the final disposal.   On Wednesday night at past twelve o'clock, Hill had procured a sedan-chair so that they might convey the corpse away from Somerset House.   They put the body into the sedan-chair, Prance and Girald carrying it; and Berry opened the wicket to let them out into the Strand.   Assisted by Green and the 'other Irishman' (Kelly), they carried the sedan as far as the New Grecian Church in Soho.   Here Hill met them with a horse. Taking the body out of the sedan, they forced open the legs and set this corpse astride the horse: Hill sitting behind to hold it in an upright position.   Green, Girald, and Kelly accompanied these two singular riders off to Primrose Hill. But Prance, fearing to be discovered missing at that bleak and weird hour of the night, hurried off home when the body was set on horseback.   The sedan – which had been left in one of the new unfinished houses in Soho – they picked up on their way home from Primrose Hill.

Prance ended rather breathlessly, his clever face uneasy

but his mouth dogged. The council was convinced. His recital had been so meticulous down to the last detail, so circumstantial, so persuasive with the easy air of truth, that they could not but believe him. As soon as he had finished, he was ordered to go to Somerset House in the company of the Duke of Monmouth and the Earl of Ossory (Sir Robert Southwell, Clerk of the Council, attending to take down notes of it), and point out the various places mentioned in his narrative.

In better fettle now that the worst was over, Prance led them to Somerset House almost with eagerness. They made a strange company for this artistic silversmith: the handsome, light-headed, heavy-faced Monmouth in all the grace of his laces; the stern, military young Ossory, son of the Duke of Ormonde; the hard-headed Sir Robert Southwell, together with all their attendant gentlemen crowding along in curiosity. Nor did Prance's performance disappoint most of them in regard to its zealous sincerity.

Outside Somerset House the red-coated guards still paced and wheeled before every door. Ossory noticed them, and seemed about to ask a question, but he checked himself when Prance ran on ahead. The wicket of the Water-Gate was opened: the group of gentlemen in their great cloaks stood looking down a steep flight of stairs into a great courtyard made even more damp and gloomy by the winter daylight. To their right stretched the long line of the stables, behind low iron railings. To the left was an open space, abutted on by a huddle of buildings which communicated with the spacious rooms of the Upper Court. Between the huddle of buildings on one side, and the stables on the other, they could see down a broad open vista to the river. But in this cobblestoned courtyard the air of the stable was strong; the horse-troughs were frozen over; and a few dispirited plane-trees grew round the coach-house along the left-hand wall.

When they descended into the courtyard, Prance ran forward with eagerness, directly and positively: 'as if,' murmured Sir Robert Southwell, 'anybody should walk to Westminster Hall door.' He pounced upon the bench he had mentioned, which was over in the right-hand corner by the rails; then he showed the place behind the bench where Godfrey had been pulled down. Next he indicated the stairs in the left-hand wall, going up to the Upper Court, where Berry had watched during the murder. All this made a great impression on the committee. Finally, in sober civility he led them over to a little door in the left-hand wall, by the coach-house. Now they went into the huddle of buildings, up some steps into a long dark entry, and thence to what Prance explained were Dr. Godwin's lodgings.

The committee found themselves looking up another flight of steps. A little way up were two rooms, one on the left and one on the right. The lodgings were low and badly lighted, but so small that there was no difficulty about making out any detail. It was to the room at the right of the stairs that Prance pointed. This room was only nine feet long by six feet broad; by the light of its one window they could see that it was crowded with a bed, a cupboard-table, two or three trunks, a little stool, and a number of corded boxes thrust under the bed.

'This, my lords,' says Prance, like an eager dog, 'is Hill's room, the room where we did put Sir Edmund Godfrey's body. That is the bed we sat it up against. It was facing the door, sitting down – thus.'

'It is an extraordinary little place,' observed Sir Robert Southwell, frowning and looking round. He looked across at the other room to the left of the stairs. 'And that room there, Mr. Prance: what room is that?'

'It is Dr. Godwin's dining-room, sir. That is where his family eat. In his family there is Dr. Godwin's niece, Mistress Mary Tilden, and his housekeeper, Mrs. Broadstreet. Hill waited on the table for them. There is also a maid called Catherine Lee. I know the family well.'

He stopped, growing a trifle nervous, for there were heavy waddling footfalls on the stairs, and down into the entry panted a stoutish old woman with a cap over her hair and a bunch of keys at her girdle. She was holding to her side, breathing hard, and she was clearly frightened at the presence of the committee; but, though she made them a very low curtsy, she burst out at Prance nevertheless.

'Mr. Prance, what is this you have been a-swearing to, Mr. Prance? You know all these things are false, Mr. Prance. God hamercy, I hear you have been swearing against Lawrence Hill, and Hill is took up or is to be taken up?' She seemed about to weep. 'Mr. Ravenscroft says that Hill defies and damns you and all your works: but you know all these things are false, Mr. Prance.'

'Now here there may be evidence too,' says my Lord Ossory. 'Who are you, woman?'

'Ann Broadstreet, may it please your lordships. I am Dr. Godwin's housekeeper.' She became even more angry at the look of sad and shaky indulgence which Prance gave her, as though he pitied her but had his eyes fastened too high on the truth to waver. 'My lords, he knows these things are false!' cries Mrs. Broadstreet. 'Lawrence Hill –'

'Do you know Lawrence Hill?'

'Yes, I do, my lord,' answered the woman aggressively. 'He served us for seven years, and indeed a better servant we never had.'

'Does he live with you now?' asked the Duke of Monmouth, shedding the beam of his handsome presence upon her, and looking very judicial.

'No, not now, may it please your lordships. He moved to a house of his own, in Stanhope Street, about the end of September last.'

Upon which statement Ann Broadstreet, in her haziness or flurry, had made a mistake in dates. Prance quickly seized upon it. 'I lay nothing against you, woman,' says he, with sad significance in the way he looked at the others; 'but that is not true. He did not leave his lodgings here until the middle of October, after Sir Edmund Godfrey's body lay in that room.'

There was a debate, the woman now thoroughly frightened, until Sir Robert Southwell cut it short. 'Well, well, all this can be proved later. You have more to show us, Mr. Prance. You said, I think, that Sir Edmund Godfrey's body was taken from here, and removed to a room towards the Garden? And that was the room where you saw it, on Monday night, by the light of a dark lanthorn? Well, show us that room.'

Here Prance went astray. For some half an hour he led them a long dance through the vast maze of rooms, courts, and galleries which formed the nobler part of Somerset House in the Upper Court. For, in searching after a room 'towards the Garden', he must be inordinately careful: the place was a-swarm with footmen and retainers of every sort. Prance moved in an agony of indecision, now rolling his eyes and now clapping a hand to his forehead; and at length he made up his mind. 'My lords,' said he as though with a burst of honesty, 'I am not certain of the room, and so cannot swear to it. I was never there but once, my lords; and then Hill conveyed me there with only the aid of a dark lanthorn. And so I cannot be certain which was the room, except that it was towards the Garden.' Still, there were murmurs of approval, for this was shrewdly like the testimony of an honest and truthful witness. In the eyes of the committee he was vindicated, and presently they took him back in triumph before the Privy Council, only the Earl of Ossory muttering that this business was a cheat. For on the most delicate point of his evidence he floundered a little.

'Mr. Prance,' he was asked, 'you say that the body was carried out through the Water-Gate, on the Wednesday night, in a sedan-chair: were there no guards or sentries in the usual places, at the carrying on of this work?'

'I did not take notice of any,' said the witness, after a pause.

But it was a triumph none the less. In the afternoon Green, Berry, and Hill were brought before the council – the constables were unable to find the two Irish priests who had been charged as well – and Prance faced them coolly. That odd parcel of plotters, the stout Berry, the little red-wigged Green, the tall black-bearded Hill, could do nothing but declare their innocence. Hill readily admitted that Prance was right about the date he had left his lodgings at Dr. Godwin's: he had not moved to Stanhope Street until past the middle of October: and this enhanced Prance's credit. Green even identified the second Irish priest whom Prance had mentioned as one Father Kelly, which appeared to be corroboration out of the very mouth of the guilty. Hill, who seemed the nimblest-minded of the three, and the most active in the murder since he had kept the corpse of Justice Godfrey in his own room (where, by the way, his wife and baby also slept), was taken off to Newgate to be put into the underground cell previously occupied by Prance. The other two were carried away protesting, Berry bewildered and Green waspish.

Mr. Miles Prance, a trifle puffed up, then rounded off matters by a long and fluent discovery concerning the Popish plot in general. He confirmed the evidence of Oates and Bedloe; for the dozenth time a hypnotised council heard of a Popish army to be raised, the names of its generals, the details of their commissions as approved by the Pope. In place of a frozen hole at Newgate, soft-boned Mr. Prance now saw for himself a bed of feathers and nightgowns of fine linen, a file of musketeers to attend him in honour, and a place as exalted as that of Titus Oates in the gratitude of the nation. He saw all this coming on him at once, amid the pattings of the lords, and his dreams grew lofty in an hour. He entered into matters with zeal. When their lordships should be pleased to set him at liberty, he promised them, he would make further discoveries and take into custody certain men whose faces he knew but of whose names he was uncertain. His head was a little turned with the suddenness of being exalted. And of course, he suggested (without a doubt of the reply), their lordships would be pleased to set him at liberty now. They were kindly, but at their reply he went white.

It had been all for nothing. He was going back to Newgate. And the nerve-strain of the day, the strain of the reaction afterwards, was too much: on the way back with Captain Richardson, he wept and blubbered in the coach. As the coach bumped along Fleet Street, he could hear the strains of *God Rest You, Merry Gentlemen* wavering up from pinched throats; and see the wenches with their was-

sail-bowls going from door to door; and smell the fragrance
of hot ale and roasted apples.   It was Christmas Eve.

III

Christmas went by in sharp frost, and Mr. John Evelyn
never saw the court so brilliant as during that season of
terror.   But Captain Richardson of Newgate was not easy
at the way in which Miles Prance was comporting himself.
Though Prance had been given a better cell, and was treated
with some consideration, he remained either apathetic,
staring at his Bible, or moaning and groaning in a corner.
Something had come over this sensitive gentleman, whether
a fit of conscience or what goad it was not within the province of Captain Richardson's wits to determine.   On Sunday, December 29th, when the captain came to him with
news that he was again to be examined by the council, he
found Prance sitting dull-eyed and looking at the wall.   But
when Richardson gave him the news, Prance started up in
some wildness.

'For God's sake,' says he, 'take me to the king.   I must
see his Majesty first: I have something of great importance
to tell him.   Captain Richardson, will you take me to wait
upon his Majesty?'

It was done.   That afternoon Charles gave an order that
he was to be summoned to William Chiffinch's lodgings
in the backstairs of the palace.   Richardson took the
prisoner there: Chiffinch was alone, narrow-eyed and suspicious, his hands on his hips.   The three of them waited
until the door of another room opened, and the king
appeared.

'Come in here, Mr. Prance,' said Charles, beckoning.

'Hold a bit, sir!' cried the careful Chiffinch; 'you would
be well advised to have another witness –'

'Come in here, Mr. Prance,' repeated Charles.   During
these latter days he had fallen into the habit of biting his
nails to the quick, to such an extent that the festering skin
gave him great pain; and loss of sleep had made him somewhat haggard.   Prance shuffled into the other room, while

the king looked at the other two grimly: then he closed the door against them. For some minutes Chiffinch and Richardson waited. Behind that door they could hear Prance's hysterical voice upraised. Presently Charles threw open the door. He wore a very grave face; and inside was Prance, on his knees, peering with smeary eyes over his shoulder.

'Now you had best come in, gentlemen,' said Charles. 'Mr. Prance has something, I think, which you ought to hear. Well, speak up, man! Tell these gentlemen what you have just told me.'

'I declare, and it is true,' said Prance, still on his knees, his hands clasped together, 'I declare the men I have sworn against are all innocent. That is what I have to tell. All I swore against them was false.'

Charles took him by the shoulder. 'Upon your salvation,' he suddenly roared, 'is this so?'

'Upon my salvation, the whole accusation is false!'

'Then that,' said Charles, drawing a deep breath, 'should suffice for my lords of the Privy Council.'

Afterwards Prance wavered; for he had no sooner gone out with Captain Richardson, wiping the corners of his eyes, than he begged the captain to take him back again. He was not sure he ought to have made that confession. But he plucked up enough courage next day to reassert it before the Privy Council, and declare that his evidence was perjured. Never were the Green Ribbon grandees, or even the more honest members of the government, in such a tall rage. As one man they uprose at him. 'Why did you swear against those men, then?' 'Who put you upon it?'

'My lords,' cried Prance, 'nobody prompted me. I only knew the men I swore against. I never saw Bedloe in my life before I was taken into custody. I know nothing of the plot, or the murder; my lords, I have never been guilty of shedding any man's blood. I could not bear it, I could not sleep or rest, for the story I told your lordships. . . .'

You rogue, you villain, you apostate! – that was the burden of the accusations now thrown at him, amid a great shaking of fists. 'Somebody has been tampering with him,' was the declaration. 'Ay,' agreed the dashing Duke of Monmouth, in a pettish temper, 'certainly they have let the priests and Jesuits come to him; else he could never have gone off like this.'

But it was Lord Chancellor Nottingham, that dignified and lofty-mannered gentleman called The English Cicero, who had the shortest suggestion. 'Let him have the rack,' said the Chancellor tersely.

That he was really put on the rack seems doubtful. There is no evidence of it, aside from some testimony of screams coming out of the underground cell where he was now confined. It is probable that he received no ill-usage beyond a little sharp knocking-about from the jailers, an ordinary business of being picked up off the floor in his irons and flung down on it again: for the cold of the dungeon was torture enough. But with the festal season of the new year, 1679, his malady took a new turn, and it was suspected that he was feigning madness. The council received reports of his conduct from two people who had gone to watch over him: Mr. William Boyce, a maker of glass eyes and an old friend of Prance, and Charles Cooper, Captain Richardson's servant. At times he spoke to Boyce sensibly enough: 'Here I am in prison, and I am like to be hanged. I am falsely accused.' But on other occasions he would lie at full length on the floor, his head in his arms, crying with weird and sing-song screeches: '*Guilty, guilty – not guilty, not guilty – murder, no murder. . . .*' They heard him in the upper part of the prison. And that uncanny voice, together with the rocking of his head from side to side as he intoned his litany, brought disquiet even into a house of the damned. Charles Cooper, Captain Richardson's servant, thought that he was only shamming: for Cooper observed that Prance thirstily drank liquor though pretending that he had spilt it, and could still tell one buckle of his shoe from another. So they left him alone for the cold to do its work.

On Friday, January 10th, the reverend Dr. Lloyd, afterwards Dean of Bangor, was commissioned by the council to go and urge the prisoner into a more pliant frame of mind.

In preparation for Dr. Lloyd's visit, Prance was hastily carried up to a much better room, and given a blanket to wrap round himself. Dr. Lloyd must be convinced that the prisoner suffered as little as possible under the circumstances. And afterwards Dr. Lloyd described that interview: it throws vivid lights and queer shadows across old Newgate.

'It was late on a Friday, in the afternoon,' said Lloyd, 'that I was called before his Majesty in council, and there ordered to go to Prance in Newgate; and it was quite dark before I got thither. When I came to Captain Richardson with my order, he brought me up into the room where Prance was. I never saw it before or since, that I remember; and I saw it then only by a small candlelight. It was walled strong and close, with great pieces of timber; and yet it was very cold through the extreme hardness of the weather.

'Prance lay in the furthest corner of the room from the door, wrapped up in a coverlet, or some such kind of thing. When the captain called him to get up, he seemed to have very little strength in him; but with much effort he came to me at the chimney, where I think there was a little fire: but I am not certain of this. The captain withdrew, and I said to Prance what I ought to say in obedience to the order that was given me. He at first denied his privity to the murder with which he was charged, and he confessed nothing of it at that visit. But at last he desired me to come again, and then he said he would tell me everything he knew.

'When I came the next day in the evening, he was brought down to the hall fire, where for a good while I spoke all that was said, and he did not answer a word to me. Perhaps he could not, for he seemed to be stupefied with cold. By degrees he seemed to come to himself, and then complained extremely of pains – at one time in his arms, at another time in his legs – roaring with it, till the natural heat came back. Then he seemed to be a new man, and of his own accord said to me: "I remember you were with me last night, and I promised you I would tell you all that I knew." And then he began to speak to me so freely, not only of the murder of Sir Edmund Godfrey, but of designs against the king's life, that I began to be afraid of him.'

The blood is coming back in pins and needles to Prance's veins; we see the lean man with the dishevelled fair beard nodding and winking before that fire, finding his voice again hurriedly to say that Green, Berry, and Hill were guilty after all. His denial of it had been all a sham. Such was his palsied zeal that he went on with an account of a plot to murder the Earl of Shaftesbury. Dr. Lloyd warned him to speak the truth, but he protested with raised hand that this was the very truth of truths. At the end of it he begged to have his irons knocked off: which was done; and he begged to be removed to a warmer room: which was done. Henceforward he had nothing to fear.

From January 11th 1679, matters could go with a rush towards bringing Green, Berry, and Hill to trial. The Attorney-General, Sir William Jones, had already been busy with mustering his witnesses. One point of Prance's evidence the prosecution set out to corroborate first of all. Prance had stated that on the morning of October 12th the prisoner Green had gone to Sir Edmund Godfrey's house, and asked at the door for him. To prove this by one of the members of Godfrey's household would be excellent contributory evidence. So the prosecution hurried to find Mrs. Judith Pamphlin, who had been Godfrey's house-keeper, and Mrs. Elizabeth Curtis, who had been his maid. Elizabeth Curtis's evidence would be much the more useful, since she commonly answered the door. These two women were taken to Newgate, to see whether they could identify any of the three prisoners.

Lawrence Hill, chained up to the boards underground, had been going over a number of bitter reflections. He could recall how, when he had first heard Prance was arrested for complicity in the murder of Justice Godfrey, he had grunted out that it was a good thing, and that he wished they were all arrested. And the very next night (damn them) constables had come banging at his door, and plucked him out of bed. In the meantime he had been given a warning that Prance would accuse him; but, like a

fool, he had refused to run for it and get out of town. He
had been content with telling the little silversmith to go to
the devil with all his works, and this was the result of it.
While he lay there trying to ease his bones, Hill blinked
before a light that was brought into the cell. Mrs. Elizabeth Curtis and Mrs. Judith Pamphlin were brought in to
see him. Hill had no notion of what was afoot, or why they
were there, but he described the incident in a note he was
allowed to write to his wife.

'On the Thursday after I came to this place,' he wrote,
'there came two grave men like justices to examine me.
They called me not a few rogues, and ordered me to be
chained to the boards; but I was set at liberty in the night-
time. The Monday afterwards they came again, and
brought two women with them: which I suppose were Sir
Edmund's servants. At first, when they came, the women
declared they had never seen me in their lives. *They said it
was a smaller man, and had another kind of face, that
brought the letter.* So I was sent up, but immediately sent
down again; and a barber sent for to shave me; and when
he had done, they whispered together. What they said
God knows.'

The italics are mine, for here is this mysterious letter –
the letter brought to Justice Godfrey on the evening before
he disappeared – bobbing up again. It stuck in Mrs. Curtis's
mind; it cannot be got rid of whichever way we turn; the
two women clearly considered it the most important thing
in the case. Though Elizabeth Curtis could identify none
of the three prisoners, and admitted as much to Mrs. Pamphlin, still the prosecution knew that there were means of per-
suading her to say something else at the trial.

But the prisoners were not too downcast. Though excited
and incoherent, knowing nothing of points at law, still they
felt with a few hopeful curses that they had a fighting-
chance of being acquitted. Outside the prison their wives
were working for them, and these ladies – especially the
aggressive Mrs. Hill – at least knew the value of proving an
alibi. The prisoners' hopes strengthened when they heard
what defence was being constructed for them. Mrs. Hill

(assisted by a gentleman named Ravenscroft, for whose brother Hill had formerly worked) was getting Mary Tilden, Dr. Godwin's niece: Mrs. Broadstreet, the house-keeper: and Catherine Lee, the maid, to testify positively that on the night of October 12th Hill had not stirred out of Dr. Godwin's house at any time. Robert Green's defence would also come from three witnesses – his landlord, the landlord's wife, and their maid – that at the time Prance swore the murder took place Green was eating his supper in their company, and did not go out all night. Henry Berry, the porter, put his hopes on the strongest card the defence had to play: the testimony of three sentinels at the Water-Gate, all Protestants and all of good character, that no sedan-chair had been carried out of that gate at any time on the night of October 16th. And these sentinels could further testify that Berry did not open the gate at any time. It was altogether a strong case, and if their witnesses would not be flustered or trapped they might walk out of that court free men.

But even though they knew they could prove all this, they were not made easy by the howling of the mob outside Newgate. Every day the mob grew denser and more violent, shouting for the blood of the three priests – Ireland, Pickering, and Grove – who had been condemned but whose executions were so long overdue. The executions had been postponed by the king himself. In council Charles fought to save their lives, against a united opposition led by the Lord Chancellor. But he could not keep up the battle for three guinea-pigs in a trap, for the whole government was crumbling about him. The impeachment of the Earl of Danby had gone so far that on December 30th Charles had been forced to prorogue a furious parliament. He had prorogued them until February 4th of the new year – having no money for the meantime – but when they came to sit again they would only renew their attack. If he were to save Danby's head, he must dissolve his parliament for good.

He had reason to bite his nails to the quick. To dissolve his Long Parliament, which had sat for seventeen years, meant a general election. And a general election was precisely what the Green Ribbon mutineers most desired. In the present state of the nation their candidates would sweep the polls. Only one sign of dissension appeared in the flushed organisation at the King's Head Tavern. Since the time was coming when they could exclude the Duke of York from the throne, they must speak out boldly and declare who they would put in his place to succeed after Charles's death. Shaftesbury's candidate had long been the Duke of Monmouth, if it were possible to brush up his mother's past and legitimatise him. But this view was not shared by Shaftesbury's ally, that nimble, cool, and dexterous orator Lord Halifax. Halifax agreed that royal authority should be destroyed and a form of republic established under some decorous pretence of a monarchy: 'the best definition of the best government,' he declared, 'is that it hath no inconveniences but such as are supportable:' yet still he did not care for a dummy monarch of such dubious antecedents as the Duke of Monmouth. As yet it was no great cause of dissension between them, for the populace must first be treated to a good meal of hangings in the banquet of the Popish plot.

Ingenious rumours kept the mobile excited: it was said that, in former times, Primrose Hill had been called Greenberry Hill, and thus the names of the murderers had been miraculously written upon the place where they threw the body of their victim. Godfrey's ghost was exceedingly spry, putting in electioneering appearances all over town, and even making its bow in the king's closet. Its most spectacular appearance was in February, when a great darkness overspread the face of London – carpers said that this darkness was only fog, a phenomenon sometimes observed in that town, but such carpers were hissed to silence – and in the midst of spectral gloom the ghost of Godfrey appeared floating over the altar in the queen's chapel while mass was being said.

The Duchess of Portsmouth was alleged to have swooned at this news, since she had assisted with her own hands at the murder, and had spat upon Godfrey's dead body. It

was she who had urged the prorogation of parliament, for
if the Houses had sat only a short time longer they would
have found out the whole hideous depth of the plot. Four
villains had been appointed to murder the Earl of Shaftesbury, and went continually with pistols in their pockets. A
new and particularly unpleasant knight of the post, named
Stephen Dugdale, had just come up out of Staffordshire
with news of his own part in the plot to murder the king:
the Pope was going to make him a saint if he succeeded.
In fine, a philosophical observer can state with moderation
that in his genius for the spread of inflammatory political
propaganda my Lord Shaftesbury could give any modern
whisperer cards, spades, and little casino.

On January 24th the king took his courage in both hands
and made a decision. He dissolved the old parliament, and
immediately writs were issued for a new one to meet in
March. Meantime there would be the contest of the general election. February, 1679, marks the entrance of a new
element in politics: for the first time in English history,
there was an election fought out along party lines as we
know them now. Strike up the band and kindle the red
flares! Shaftesbury's campaign-managers ordered fifty
thousand ribbons with *No Popery* printed on them in gilt
letters. M. Barrillon wrote to Louis the Fourteenth, asking for an immediate supply of money to buy beer for the
voters. Children, supporting the sides they heard preached
at home, prepared to give each other black eyes in the streets;
and under auspicious stars campaign-oratory was born.

Before two years were out these parties had been solidi-
fied into Whigs and Tories. They had their own oaths:
'God damme!' was the oath of the Tory, and the Whig imi-
tated Oates's bray with, 'So help me Goad!' They had their
own colours: your ribbon was blue if you favoured the Duke
of Monmouth, red if you favoured the Duke of York.
Coffee was (alleged to be) the favourite drink of the Whig,
while the Tory preferred any beverage that could get a
man sufficiently drunk. Thus the Whig 'plotted', the Tory
'sotted'. Each hoary lie, each bellowing platitude from the
candidate, was then a novel thing; there were no modern

cynics to write *hic jacet* over such promises after election; and to hear the first campaign-speech must have been awesome and startling, like eating the first oyster or seeing the first giraffe.

But in the first two months of 1679 this was only foreshadowed. On the same day that the king dissolved the Long Parliament, January 24th, Ireland and Grove were at last executed at Tyburn amid the hisses of a great multitude. Pickering still remained respited by order of the king, but this respite could not last long. And on Wednesday, February 5th, Robert Green, Henry Berry, and Lawrence Hill were carried before the bar of the Court of King's Bench to be arraigned for the murder of Sir Edmund Godfrey.

It was not the trial; the trial would not take place until several days after the indictment. But the solemn formality must have its course. All three prisoners found their hearts knocking and their legs shaky when they were herded into the raftered gloom of Westminster Hall, up before the tall bench where sat the full-wigged and red-robed justices who should presently judge them. There were three: Lord Chief Justice Scroggs, Justice Sir William Wild, and Justice Sir William Dolben. At one side, in a slanting of smoky light through the windows, stood the great lawyers who should presently prosecute them. There was the Attorney-General, Sir William Jones; there was Recorder Sir George Jeffreys; there was Solicitor-General Sir Francis Winnington; and there was Mr. Serjeant Stringer.

Only the night before Hill had written to his wife, 'Dear hart, keep up your courage; and by God's grace we will come through this alive.' Now the great voice of the Clerk of the Crown rose and fell with sonorous intonation under the rafters.

'Robert Green, hold up thy hand; Henry Berry, hold up thy hand; Lawrence Hill, hold up thy hand.

'You stand indicted by the names of Robert Green, late of the parish of St. Mary le Strand, in the county of Middlesex, labourer: Henry Berry, late of the same parish and county, labourer: and Lawrence Hill, late of the same parish and county, labourer; for that you three, together with – Girald, late of the same parish and county, clerk: and Dominick Kelly, late of the same parish and county, clerk – who are withdrawn:[1]   Not having the fear of God before your eyes, but being moved and seduced by the instigation of the devil, the twelfth day of October, in the thirtieth year of the reign of Our Sovereign Lord Charles the Second – at the parish of St. Mary le Strand aforesaid, in the County of Middlesex aforesaid, in and upon Sir Edmund Berry Godfrey, knight, in the peace of God, and of our said Sovereign Lord the King, then and there being feloniously, voluntarily, and of your malice aforethought, did make and assault; and that thou, the aforesaid Robert Green, a certain linen hand-kerchief of the value of sixpence, about the neck of the said Sir Edmund Berry Godfrey, then and there feloniously, wil-fully, and of thy malice aforethought, didst fold and fasten,' etc.

'How sayest thou, Robert Green: art thou guilty of the felony and murder whereof thou standest indicted, and hast been now arraigned, or not guilty?'

'Not guilty!'

'Culprit, how wilt thou be tried?'

'By God and my country.'

'God send thee a good deliverance.   How sayest thou, Henry Berry: art thou guilty of the felony and murder whereof thou standest indicted, and hast been now arraigned, or not guilty?'

When all three had been asked to plead, and had entered a plea of not guilty, Mr. Justice Wild directed that the trial should take place on the ensuing Friday, February 6th. But another strain awaited the courage of the prisoners. On Friday Mr. Attorney-General moved the court that the trial might be deferred until the following Monday, so that the king's evidence might be more ready.   It was granted. Green fingered his crucifix, Berry was pale, and Hill dogged.

On the night before the critical Monday, February 9th,

---

[1] Girald and Kelly still could not be found.   There is another name mentioned in the indictment, that of Philibert Vernatt, but as he has no real connection with the story of the murder, could not be found, and only adds another name to confuse matters, I have ventured to omit him.

Hill remained in his cell looking at the dark with wide-open eyes. A heavy-witted fellow at the best of times, he was not unduly disturbed except when he remembered the faces of the crowd outside Newgate, and he knew that the evidence would prove his innocence. 'Dear hart, keep up your courage; and by God's grace we will come through this alive.' One thing troubled him more than any other: not long ago he had cheated an acquaintance of his over a matter of a shilling. It so weighed on his conscience that he had even confessed it to Samuel Smith, the chaplain of Newgate; he knew that he must pay back that shilling somehow. Though he felt himself to be a great sinner, and phrases of repentance came easily to his lips, still he had a very close and clear feeling of his God, in whom there was refuge. It was a feeling that swelled the chest and made blind the eyes: 'Our Father, Which Art in Heaven.' Lawrence Hill did not believe that this Father, who saw even the bird's broken wing and the pain of the lame dog, would forsake the lame dog that licked His hand now.

VII

'WELL, WOMAN, WHAT SAY YOU?'

The Trial

'Little to do, and plenty to get, I suppose?' said Serjeant Buzfuz, with jocularity.

'Oh, quite enough to get, sir, as the soldier said ven they ordered him three hundred and fifty lashes,' replied Sam.

'You must not tell us what the soldier, or any other man, said, sir,' interposed the judge; 'it's not evidence.'

Bardell v. Pickwick.

Fiat justitia! Not for more than seventy years, not since the trial of the conspirators for the Gunpowder Plot, had Westminster Hall seen such a crowd. It overflowed into Westminster as far as the palace bowling-green to the north, and the slums beyond the Abbey to the south; no coach or sedan-chair could butt through it. Westminster Hall was in such a din and scramble that shopkeepers' stalls were capsized, pickpockets could scarcely get their hands out of their own pockets, and the light was dimmed by those who had swarmed high up outside to crane in at the windows. In the courtroom itself there was such a crush that it overflowed into the jury-box, so that nobody could tell which were the jurymen among the spectators; and the Clerk of the Crown ordered the Crier to make proclamation that all who were not jurymen must get out of the box on pain of a hundred pounds' fine. But so great was the volume of whistling, jeering, stamping, and singing that the Crier must bawl his Oyez, and bawl it again, and bawl until he was purple-veined in the face, before any word could be distinguished.

The prisoners were brought in, manacled together on a length of chain, the javelin-men forcing a passage for them. But all three prisoners found their fears relieved, their hopes beating high, when they looked into the lobby where their witnesses were waiting, and saw that the witnesses were there.   Berry saw the corporal and the three sentinels of the Water-Gate, together with others who could testify as to his whereabouts on the night of the murder.   Green saw Mr. and Mrs. Warrier, his landlord and landlady, who could give him his own alibi.   Hill saw not only Mary Tilden, Mrs. Broadstreet, and Catherine Lee of Dr. Godwin's household, but several friends who could speak as to his whereabouts for the entire day of October 12th.   *Now* the prosecution could not prove any dogging or following of Godfrey during that day.   Mrs. Hill had done well: but there was more.   Hill saw his wife waving her fingers to him, with hurried motions of her lips, and he was carried close enough past her to hear even more heartening news.

The king himself was going to help them.

From Elizabeth Hill's half-tearful cries, he gathered that she had gone to the king and obtained permission to put a powerful witness into the box on the prisoners' behalf. This witness would be none other than Mr. William Chiffinch, Page of the Backstairs, who would give an account of Prance's frenzied recantation in Chiffinch's lodgings.   In his own way, he was the king's personal representative.   It did not surprise Lawrence Hill that the king should put out a hand to shield three labourers from harm: as it surprised nobody who knew Charles the Second: for that, quite simply, was Hill's notion of what a king should do.   It was common knowledge that he had given the witnesses a gruelling examination the day before.   But every part of Lawrence Hill's mind fastened on the business of demonstrating what must be plain, what must be clear as the sun, that Miles Prance was a liar.

The three were herded rattling into the dock, in before the packed benches of the court, with smoky light shining down in slants on the bench where sat prosecuting counsel. The tumult quieted somewhat at the entrance of the judges. Scroggs, broad of mouth and broad of beam, was in good voice and good wit.   He towered over the other two: Justice Wild, sixty-eight years old, a small man, called by some 'an arrant perverse old snarler', but a very fair-minded judge; and Justice Dolben, a younger man with a heavy jaw, who was inexorable at pursuing the plot. The learned judges bowed to counsel, all standing, a civility which Attorney-General Jones returned with a grunt, Recorder Jeffreys with smiling obsequiousness, Solicitor-General Winnington and Serjeant Stringer with grave genuflexions. Amid much uproar, while Scroggs settled down and got his breath, the jury was called and sworn. There were no challenges, for the prisoners knew none of them. After a brief opening of the indictment by Solicitor-General Winnington, Sir William Jones rose slowly – setting his papers together with nicety – to open the evidence.

'May it please your lordship,' intoned Bull-faced Jonas, with a portentous glance round the court, 'and you, gentlemen of this jury, the prisoners who stand now at the bar are indicted for murder.

'Murder, as it is the first, so is it the greatest crime that is prohibited in the Second Table. It is a crime of so deep a stain that nothing can wash it away but the blood of the offender; and, unless that be done, the land in which it is shed will continue polluted. My lord, as murder is always a very great crime, so the murder which is now to be tried before your lordship is, it may be, the most heinous and most barbarous that ever was committed! The murder was committed upon a gentleman, and upon a magistrate, and I wish he had not therefore been murdered, because he was a Protestant magistrate.

'My lord, I will not spend much of your time in making my observations beforehand, because I must in this case crave leave to do it at the conclusion of the evidence. For I, that have made a strict examination into this matter, do find that I shall better spend my time in making observations, and showing how the witnesses do agree, after the evidence is given. Therefore, my lord, I shall at present only make a short narrative of the fact, to show you the course of our evidence, so that it may be the better understood and remembered by the jury.

'My lord, upon the discovery of the late horrid plot –'

Scroggs interposed. 'And the present plot too, Mr. Attorney,' he warned. 'But pray go on.'

Sir William Jones bowed, a trifle sour at being put off, and agreed. Then, without flourishes, and with a harsh-lipped sincerity which bore conviction to every listener, he outlined Prance's case. The prosecution would prove (he declared) that for some days Sir Edmund Godfrey had been watched by the prisoners. They would prove that, on the morning of October 12th, one of prisoners – Lawrence Hill – had called at the magistrate's house, in order to find out where Justice Godfrey was going that day. They would prove that another of the prisoners – Robert Green – had previously been at that house on the same errand. Next they would demonstrate, by the testimony of one of the actual murderers, how this crime had been committed: that Sir Edmund Godfrey had been returning along the Strand from a house near St. Clement's Church, about seven or eight o'clock on the night of October 12th: that he was decoyed through the Water-Gate of Somerset House, under pretence of stopping a fight going on inside: and that he was there murdered. It would be shown that afterwards the prisoners named in the indictment – Green, Berry, Hill, Girald, and Kelly – had all carried the body to Hill's lodgings. There the body lay until the night of Monday, October 14th, at which time it was carried to some other room high up in Somerset House. This point must be particularly mentioned (said the Attorney-General) because there the body was seen by another witness now present in court (Mr. William Bedloe), and this witness would tell how he saw it there by the light of a dark lanthorn.

Finally, they would prove that on the night of October 16th the body was removed from Somerset House. It would be shown that a sedan-chair was procured by Lawrence Hill: that the body was bent to fit into this sedan: that it was carried out of the gate by Girald and Prance, Berry having opened the gate for them: and that it was conveyed to the Grecian Church in Soho. There the body was set up on a horse, Hill sitting behind to hold it up, and carried to Primrose Hill.

'My lord, this will be the course of our evidence,' concluded Sir William Jones, still soberly and with terrible
conviction. 'And though your lordship and the jury will
easily believe that most of these particulars must come from
the testimony of one who was party to the fact – yet, my
lord, I will undertake so to fortify almost every particular
he delivers with a concurrent proof of other testimony; and
the things will so depend on one another, and have such a
connection; that little doubt will remain in any man's mind
that is come hither without prepossession, but that Sir
Edmund Godfrey was murdered at Somerset House, and
that the persons who stand now indicted for it were the
murderers.'

He pointed slowly at the prisoners, and sat down. Then
up with great briskness rose Sir George Jeffreys.

'My lord,' said the smiling Recorder, 'if your lordship
pleases, according as Mr. Attorney hath opened it, we desire
we may call our witnesses. And first we will call Mr. Oates.'

There was a great stir in the court as Titus lumbered forward, and the Crier administered the oath.

'Mr. Oates, lay your hand on the Book. The evidence you
shall give for Our Sovereign Lord the King, against Robert
Green, Henry Berry, and Lawrence Hill, the prisoners at
the bar, shall be the truth, the whole truth, and nothing but
the truth, so help you God.'

'My lord,' brayed Titus, after a genial word from the
bench, 'upon the 6th of September last, I did go before Sir
Edmund Godfrey, and there upon oath gave in several depositions. And after I had made oath of these depositions,
we took the record along with us home again. And on the
28th of September, after we had taken two or three copies
of this record, we went before Sir Edmund Godfrey again,
and swore all the copies we had taken. . . . And upon
Monday (which was, I think, the 30th of September), Sir
Edmund Godfrey came to me, and did tell me what affronts
he had received from some great persons – whose names I
name not now,' said Titus darkly, '– for being so zealous
in this business. . . . My lord, that week before Sir
Edmund was missing, he came to me and told me that

several Popish lords, some of whom are now in the Tower, had threatened him and asked him what he had to do with it. My lord, I shall name their names when the time shall come. My lord, that is all I can say: he was in a great fright, and told me he went in fear of his life by the Popish party, and that he had been dogged several days.'

'Did he tell you that he was dogged?' demanded Sir William Jones.

'Yes, he did. And I did then ask him why he did not take his servant along with him? He said the servant was a poor weak fellow.[1] I then asked him why he did not get a good brisk fellow to attend him. But he made no great matter of it. He said he did not fear them, if they came fairly to work. But he was often threatened; and he came sometimes to me to give him encouragement. And I did give him what encouragement I could – that he would suffer in a good cause,' cries Titus piously: 'and the like. But he would often tell me he was in continual danger of being hurt by them.'

Oates stood down, and his place was taken by a good witness who was known to many in the court. This was the old and respected Chief Prothonotary of the Court of Common Pleas, Sir Thomas Robinson. Sir Thomas Robinson had gone to school with Godfrey in boyhood, and had known him for more than forty years. He spoke decisively and positively of a meeting with the magistrate on the 7th of the preceding October, five days before Godfrey's disappearance.

'I said to Sir Edmund Godfrey,' he went on ' "I understand you have taken several examinations about this plot that is now made public?" "Truly," said he, "I have; but I think I shall have little thanks for my pains. I did it very unwillingly, and would fain have had it done by others." "Why," said I, "you did but what was your duty to do, and it was a very good act." Then I asked if I might see the examinations; but he did not have them about him; he said he had delivered them to a person of quality.

' " But," said I, "I should be very glad to understand, Sir

---

[1] Presumably Henry Moor.

Edmund, that the depth of the matter were found out." "I am afraid," said he, "that it is not:" and discoursing further, he said to me, "Upon my conscience, I believe I shall be the first martyr!" – "Why so?" said I; "are you afraid?" "No," said he, "I do not fear them, if they come fairly, and I shall not part with my life tamely." '

These were merely opening salvos for the attack, but there was a great sitting up and craning in the audience when Miles Prance was called. And this was Prance as he had been before the Privy Council, brisk, cool, and self-assured, but with an earnest humility which weighed much with the spectators. He cleared his throat, watching Scroggs with doglike devotion, and the prisoners (when he looked at them) with horror. Every word he spoke had a ring of truth.

'Mr. Prance,' said Scroggs, 'pray tell us the first proposals that were made to you to do this murder, and the first time it was mentioned: who they were that first mentioned it, and where.'

'My lord, it was about a fortnight or three weeks before Justice Godfrey was murdered. We met several times at the "Plough" Alehouse.'

'You met with whom?'

'With Mr. Girald, Mr. Green, and Mr. Kelly,' replied Prance, looking coolly at the furious men in the dock. 'Girald and Kelly did entice me into the plot, and told me it was no sin.'

Sir George Jeffreys took over the examination. 'Girald and Kelly – who are they?'

'Two priests. And they said it was no sin, it was a charitable act. They said he was a busy man, and had done and would do a great deal of mischief, and it was a deed of charity to do it; and so they told the rest besides.'

'Where was it they said this?'

'They said it at the "Plough", by the water-side,' answered the witness with great emphasis.

'Well said! – What other discourse had you?'

'There they resolved that the first of them that could meet with Sir Edmund Godfrey should give notice to the rest to

be ready; and so in the morning, when they went out on
Saturday, October 12th –'

'But before you come to that,' broke in the Attorney-
General, 'do you know of any dogging of him into the fields?'

'Yes. It was before that, I heard them say they would
follow him; and that they had dogged him into the fields.'

'Do you know of any sending to his house, or going to it?'

Prance considered, sharply. 'One time I do know of,' he
said, 'and that was Saturday morning. On Saturday morning Mr. Kelly came to give me notice that they had gone
abroad to dog him. And afterwards they told me that *Hill*
or *Green* went to his house and asked for him. But the
maid said he was not up out of bed, so he went away and said
he would call by and by.'

At this point Hill spoke out from the dock. 'What time
was that in the morning?'

'It was about nine or ten o'clock in the morning.'

Prance then went on at great detail into his story, beginning with the important statement that the plotters had
followed Godfrey all day on that Saturday. The impression
he made on the court was enormous. He was a good witness, almost a perfect witness. In all the great mass of small
particulars he outlined, he never faltered, never contradicted himself, and he was patient at carefully explaining
just what he meant. The story he told now tallied exactly
with that he had already given to the Privy Council, but it
had even more convincing details. Small effects like, '*And
when Sir Edmund was strangled, Girald would have thrust
his sword through him, but the rest would not permit it, for
fear it should discover them by the blood;*' his account of
the body seen by the light of a dark lanthorn with '*something thrown over him, but I could not tell what, for I durst
not stay long there;*' these effects caused Scroggs to beam.
It was a remarkable performance, and the excitement of the
spectators mounted in a series of hums.

He concluded with a new account of a gathering of priests,
shortly after the murder, in a tavern at Bow. This was a
hilarious meeting, at which the murderers had written a
paper describing their crime; and the paper was read by all

the priests, amid roars of merriment and delight. In substance the account was as lurid as any concoction of Oates,
yet the sober restraint with which it was told, the small
details – 'We had a barrel of oysters, and a dish of fish; I
bought the fish myself: it was Friday,' – left his listeners in
no doubt.

'I would now ask you a question,' said the Attorney-
General, half smiling in satisfaction, 'which, though it does
not prove the persons guilty, yet it gives a great strength to
the evidence. Do you know Mr. Bedloe, Mr. Prance?'

'I do not know him,' declared the witness.

'Had you ever any conference with him before you was
committed to prison?'

'Never in all my life.'

Sir George Jeffreys rose suavely. 'Now,' he said, 'the
prisoners may ask him any questions, for we have done with
him.'

It was several moments before Hill, at whom the others
looked, spoke up. The prisoners, trailing their manacles
over the edge of the dock, had been so coloured by Prance's
story, notably the waspish little Green in his red periwig –
that it was as though they felt the atmosphere and belief of
the court creeping into their own hearts. Hill was clearly
far from at his ease. His challenge did not ring out strongly.

'My lord, in the first place, I humbly pray that Mr. Prance's
evidence may not stand good against me, as being perjured
by his own confession.'

Scroggs sat up. 'Perjured? How?'

'I suppose, my lord, it is not unknown to you that he made
such an open confession before the king?'

'Look you, sir,' said Scroggs impressively: 'I will tell you
for that, I do not know that he ever made a confession to
contradict what he said upon his oath.'

'But, my lord, he was upon his oath before!'

'Ah, yes. Yes, he had accused you upon oath. But afterwards, you say, he confessed that it was not true – yet that
confession that it was not true, was not upon oath. How is
he then guilty of perjury?'

Hill discovered himself feeling a trifle dazed. He did not

understand this: all this was not so simple as he had hoped. The penetrating eye of the Lord Chief Justice appeared to have become mixed up with the penetrating words of the Lord Chief Justice. He said, trying to cling to what he could understand:

'My lord, if a man can swear a thing and afterwards deny it, he is certainly perjured?'

'If a man,' declared Scroggs, drawing in his chin weightily, 'if a man hath great horrors of conscience upon him, and is full of fears, and the guilt of such a thing disorders his mind so as to make him go back to what he had before spoken upon oath – you can't say that man is perjured, if he don't forswear it. But I believe nobody did credit his denial, because his first discovery was so particular that every man thought his general denial proceeded only from the disturbance of his mind.' At this point, Hill found himself looking round the court for Mr. William Chiffinch, but the Lord Chief Justice changed the subject quickly: 'Have you a mind to ask him any questions?'

'Try if you can,' suggested the heavy-jawed Justice Dolben, 'to trap him in any question.'

'Mr. Prance, what hour was it that I went to Sir Edmund Godfrey's house on the Saturday morning?'

'About nine or ten o'clock,' said Prance, facing him; 'I am not certain in the hour.'

'No, no, a man cannot be precise to an hour,' said Scroggs; 'but prove what you can. You, Mr. Berry: will you ask him any questions?'

Berry, in pursuit of a suggestion thrown out by Prance that the plot had often been discussed at the ale-house which Berry kept in addition to his duties as porter, tried to get a definite statement from him.

'Mr. Prance, who was in my house at that time you spoke of?'

'There was your wife there, and several other persons besides.'

'Who were they?'

'There were divers people; it is an ale-house.'

'But who? Can you name any of them?'

'There was Girald, and Kelly, and I.'

Scroggs interposed sharply. 'Why, did you not all know Mr. Prance? Didn't you, and Green, and Hill, all know Prance?'

'My lord,' said Berry, 'I knew him as he passed up and down in the house.'

'Good God, what answer is that?' demanded Scroggs, now settling down to the trial at last. 'What do you mean by his passing up and down in the house? Did you never drink with him?'

'Drink with him, my lord? Yes.'

'Yes? Well, people don't use to drink as they go along. . . . Was not Mr. Prance known by all you three? Which of you can deny it? What say you, Hill?'

'My lord, I knew him,' said Hill. 'I admitted it.'

'What say you, Green?'

'Yes, I did know him,' acknowledged Green, who seemed the most tongue-tied and feeble of the three.

'But yet, my lord,' instantly cried out Mr. Attorney-General, 'we shall prove in the course of our evidence that, upon their examinations before the Privy Council, they denied they ever knew him.'

Now this was a flat lie, or a misunderstanding on Mr. Attorney-General's part; someone beckoned to him, there was whispering and paper-rustling among counsel; but he straightened up again, not daunted, and ignored it. Had the prisoners cast doubt on Mr. Prance's story, on the strength of one recantation? Very well: they would now show, by the testimony of Captain Richardson, that Mr. Prance had only recanted before the king because he was in terror of being murdered by Papists. Whereupon they called Captain Richardson, who swore to this. 'Now you have an account, Mr. Hill,' said Scroggs complacently, ' how he came to deny, and how soon he recanted his denial.'

Then William Bedloe was sworn.

Bedloe's evidence was trimmed, so far as was possible, to fit that of Prance without completely denying all his former story. The edges of the two touched: Bedloe's task was to

supply suggestive faces for the gloom beyond the circle of
Prance's dark lanthorn. Again he produced his old bogies
of Le Faire, Walsh, and Pritchard. This time he declared
that these gentlemen had offered him £4,000 to assist in the
murder of someone: they never directly mentioned the
magistrate's name. 'Girald was one of their number, was
he?' asked Scroggs. No, admitted Bedloe, but they spoke
about Girald, and said they would introduce Bedloe to him.
On the night before the murder his Jesuit friends had told
him to come to Somerset House, for the business was to be
done then. But Bedloe, in horror at the design of murdering anyone, stayed away from Somerset House. On Monday
he met Le Faire in Red Lion Court, and the Jesuit berated
him for not keeping his promise. But Le Faire readily for-
gave him, saying that the murder was already done, and that
if Bedloe would come to Somerset House that night he
should see the body.

So (continued Bedloe) on Monday night he went to
Somerset House, being led by the hand through a dark
entry. Here he saw the body lying under a coverlet. There
were four or five persons standing about it, and there was a
small light. This was all he could swear. He had no direct
knowledge of Hill or Green, and could not swear he had
seen them about the body. Nor did he know anything
directly of Berry, although the priests had told him that the
porter was to open the gate for the body to be carried out.
This (concluded Bedloe) was the substance of his knowledge, until December 21st, at which time he had seen
Prance in the lobby of the House of Commons, and had
instantly identified him as one of the rogues who had been
standing about the body on the night of October 14th.

Bedloe was allowed to stand down. He had merely suggested that Le Faire, Walsh, and Pritchard had been other
priests concerned in the planning of the murder along with
Girald and Kelly, thus adding body to Prance's evidence
while deftly fitting it into his own. At the one important
point on which he was asked to confirm Prance – a bloody
gathering round the corpse on the night of October 14th –
he confirmed him flatly. For had he not apprehended

Prance afterwards? Blacker yet looked the case against the prisoners.

Next appeared the constable, John Brown, who had found Sir Edmund Godfrey's body in the ditch and examined it there. He gave an account of his information, declaring that the breast of the corpse was beaten, that there was no blood on the body or in the ditch, that the neck seemed broken, and that there was a great deal of silver and gold in the pockets. 'Ay, ay,' agreed Scroggs, 'for the Papists count theft as a sin, but not murder.' And Mr. Justice Wild helpfully explained matters to the jury: 'They left the money in his pockets to make men think he had murdered himself.'

Mr. Zachariah Skillard, one of the surgeons who had examined the body, was next called.

'Did you observe his breast?' asked Mr. Attorney-General. 'How was it?'

'His breast,' answered Skillard, 'was all beaten with some obtuse weapon, either with the feet, or hands, or something.'

'Did you observe his neck?'

'Yes; it was distorted.'

'How far?'

'You might have taken the chin, and have set it on either shoulder.'

'Did you observe the sword-wound?'

'Yes, I did. It went in at one place, and stopped at a rib; in the other place it was quite through the body.'

'Do you think he was killed by that wound?'

'No: for then there would have been some evacuation of blood, which there was not. And, besides, his bosom was open, and he had a flannel waistcoat and shirt on; and neither those, not any of his clothes, were penetrated with blood.'

'But are you sure,' insisted Mr. Attorney-General, 'that his neck had been broken?'

'Yes, I am sure.'

'Because,' persisted the other gravely, with a sidelong look at the jury, 'some have been of the opinion that he hanged himself, and that his relations, to save his estate, ran him through. I would desire to ask the surgeon what he thinks of it?'

'Sir,' declared the surgeon positively, 'there was more done to his neck than ordinary suffocation or hanging.'

Zachariah Skillard was followed by Nicholas Cambridge, another surgeon who had examined the body, and corroborated Skillard. Then, amid great interest in the court, Sir George Jeffreys announced that the prosecution would call Elizabeth Curtis, Sir Edmund Godfrey's maid. The lean woman, who still wore black, had been fluttering about the witnesses' lobby in a high state of indecision. A fellow-witness had warned her not to speak perjury, and she hesitated for a time. But now she took the oath steadily enough, showing large knuckles on the rail of the witness-box, and looked steadily at the prisoners.

'Elizabeth Curtis,' said Mr. Attorney-General sternly, 'look upon the prisoners, and tell my lord and the jury whether you know any of them or no.'

'My lord,' said Mrs. Curtis, 'this man that I now hear called Green was at my master's house about a fortnight before he died.'

'What to do?' asked Scroggs.

'I don't know, but he asked for Sir Edmund Berry Godfrey.'

'What time of the day was it?'

'It was in the morning.'

'What did he say?'

'He asked for Sir Edmund Berry Godfrey; and, when he came to him, he said, "Good morning, sir," in English; and afterwards spoke to him in French. I could not understand him.'

'Upon my soul, I never saw him in all my life!' cried Green.

'He had a darker coloured periwig when he was there, not that red one,' insisted Mrs. Curtis, staring hard; 'and he was about an hour talking with my master.'

'Are you sure this was the man?' asked Sir William Jones, amid a hum in the court.

'Yes, I am sure.' She pointed. 'And that other man, Hill, was there on the Saturday morning my master disappeared, and spoke with him before he went out.'

'That you will deny too?' inquired the Lord Chief Justice of the prisoners.

'Yes, I do!' shouted Hill.

Mrs. Curtis explained with firmness that she had been in the parlour, making up the fire, when Hill called. She had carried in her master's breakfast, and when she went out of the room she forgot her household keys. Presently she came downstairs again to fetch the keys off the parlour table, and Hill was still there.

'How long afterwards did you see him again?'

'Not till I saw him in Newgate.'

'How long was that afterwards?'

'A month ago,' said the witness rather absently. Again something was on her mind, and her wrinkled eyelids fluttered. 'But,' she added abruptly, 'that is not the man that brought the note to my master.'

'Note? What note?'

'A note that a man brought to my master the night before. . . .'

'What is become of that note?' demanded Sir William Jones.

'My lord,' said Mrs. Curtis, addressing him with shaky haziness, 'I cannot tell; my master had it. . . . There was a man came to my master's house, and asked if Sir Edmund Berry Godfrey were within. He said he had a letter for him, and showed it to me. It was tied up in a knot. I told him my master was within, but busy. "But," said I, "if you please, I will carry it in to him." He did so, and I gave it to my master. When I went out again, the man stayed and asked for an answer. I went in again and told my master that the man required an answer. "Tell him," said my master, "I don't know what to make of it." '

'When was that?' asked old Mr. Justice Wild.

'On Friday night, the Friday night before he was murdered.'

The Attorney-General grunted and brushed all this aside

for more important pressure. 'But you swear Hill was there on the Saturday morning?'

'Yes, he was.'

'What clothes did he wear then?'

'The same clothes that he has on now,' declared Mrs. Curtis, studying him and nodding vigorously.

The Solicitor-General, Sir Francis Winnington, rose in excitement and extended his hand towards the bench. 'Here is a great circumstance, my lord! We asked her what clothes he was in, when he came to Sir Edmund's, and she saith, "The same that he hath now." '

'Have you ever shifted your clothes?' asked Scroggs with interest.

'No, indeed, I have not,' said Hill grimly. He protested here. 'But she did say, when she came to see me in Newgate, that she never saw me in my life! And, my lord, I hope I have sufficient witnesses to prove where I was all that morning.'

'She says she cannot swear you were the man that brought the note,' Scroggs informed him.

The smaller witnesses for the prosecution now passed in quick order. Two witnesses swore that they had several times seen Green and Hill drinking at the 'Plough' Ale-house with Prance. Two more witnesses gave somewhat vague testimony to substantiate Prance's story concerning the merry meeting of priests at the 'Queen's Head', that meeting at which there had been so much mirth over the description of Godfrey's murder. A fifth witness tried to demonstrate that Berry had told a lie before the Privy Council. But though this attempt failed, and though the Attorney-General was also compelled to admit that none of the prisoners had ever denied knowing Prance, the case against Green, Berry, and Hill had been skilfully built up. The prisoners whispered to each other that their turn would come to make their defence, and disprove all this: 'So keep up courage,' growled Berry to the almost swooning Green. But a last great blow for the prosecution was delivered by Sir Robert Southwell. Sir Robert Southwell described how Prance had conducted the Duke of Monmouth and the Earl

of Ossory over the alleged scenes of the crime in Somerset
House.   He explained Prance's extreme readiness and
sureness, his surprising knowledge of every step inside the
house: and Sir Robert so clearly believed each word of
Prance's testimony that the court was carried away in
admiration.   Even Prance's hesitation about identifying
one room – the 'room towards the Garden', to which the
body had been conveyed on Monday night, and where
Bedloe had seen it by the lanthorn-light – even this drew a
roar of approval from Scroggs.

'Why,' cried the Lord Chief Justice, not without reason,
'his doubtfulness of the room does assert and give credit to
his testimony, and confirms it to any honest man in England!   "Here," saith he, "I will not be positive;" but,
having sworn the other things that he remembered positively, he is made the more credible for his doubtfulness of
a thing which he does not remember – which a man that
could swear anything would not stick at.'

Mr. Attorney-General bowed.   'My lord,' he said, 'we
have now done with our evidence for the king, and leave it
till we hear what the prisoners say.'

Now the trial would grow warm, now would come the
real cut-and-thrust.   Well, call the witnesses for the defence!
Hill, the first to be asked for his proof, began by attempting
to show that on the night of October 12th he was in Dr. Godwin's house by eight o'clock in the evening (at least an hour
before Godfrey was alleged to have been murdered), and
that he had not gone out afterwards.   To this end he called
Mary Tilden, Ann Broadstreet, and Catherine Lee.

Mary Tilden, Dr. Godwin's niece, was a nervous young
gentlewoman, not over-bright, very serious-minded, and
very good to look at.   She wore a blue bonnet and a great
swaddling coat.   In a steady voice she testified that Hill had
been a servant in her family for seven or eight years, and
was never out of the house after eight o'clock at night.   At
eight o'clock on the night of October 12th he was in the
house, and had not stirred out of it.   This seemed positive:
the judges conferred together, and adopted an attitude of
firm jocoseness.

R

'Pray,' said Scroggs, 'what religion are you of?   Are you a Papist?'

'I know not whether I came here to make a profession of my faith.'

'Are you a Roman Catholic?'

'Yes.'

Scroggs became more playful. 'Have you a dispensation to eat suppers on Saturday nights?'

Sir George Jeffreys looked from Hill to the girl, and assumed a shocked expression.   'I hope,' says he gently, 'you did not keep him company *all* night, after supper?'

Mary Tilden had gone scarlet.   'No, I did not – but he came in to wait on the table at supper.'

'But,' suggested Scroggs, 'I thought you kept fasting on Saturday nights.'

'No, my lord, not on Saturday nights.'

After a few more questions, the Lord Chief Justice began to lose his temper.   'Maid, can you say that he was always at home at night?'

'I can say he was never abroad after eight at night.'

'Why,' interposed Sir George Jeffreys, humorously pursuing a good subject, 'you did not watch him till he went to bed, did you?'

'We were always up until eleven o'clock at night.'

'And he was in your company all that while?' thundered Mr. Attorney-General.   'Was he in your company all that while?'

The witness turned round.   'I beg your pardon: if your lordship *saw* the lodgings you would say it were impossible for any to go in or out, but that we must know it within. We were constant in our hours of going to supper.   Our doors were never opened after he came in to wait at supper.'

Scroggs grew wrathful.   'Being a Papist, you may say anything to a heretic,' he declared, and Justice Dolben agreed, with an ominous nod: 'This is a mighty improbable business!'   The chase was continued.

'Who kept the key to your lodgings?'

'The maid, Catherine Lee.'

'Hath Hill never kept the key?'

'No, my lord – the maid.'

'How do you know but that the maid might not let him out?'

Here Mr. Miles Prance intervened, smugly, with a flat lie. 'My lord, Mrs. Broadstreet said at first there was but one key; but before the Duke of Monmouth she said there was six or seven keys.'

'Look you what tricks you put upon us to blind us,' said Scroggs, pointing. 'You come and tell us that he was every night at home by eight o'clock, and did not stir out, for there was but one lock and the maid kept the key; and yet there were three or four keys to it.'

'There was but one key to the lock that kept the door fast!' insisted the witness. She was growing flurried under this badgering, she swallowed, and the judges observed that before long she would be in the mood to make a slip. They went at it quickly.

'Mr. Prance,' said Justice Wild, 'what time was it that you carried the body out of Somerset House on Wednesday night, the 16th of October, the night it was carried to Primrose Hill?'

'It was about ten or eleven,' answered Prance. 'Hill went to fetch the horse.'

'We had never been out of our lodgings,' cried Mary Tilden, 'never after eight o'clock, since we came to town!'

'When were you out of town?'

'In October,' said the witness – and they had caught her.

'Nay, now, mistress,' beamed Justice Dolben amid the laughter, 'now you have spoiled all: for in October this business was done.'

'You have undone the man, instead of saving him,' agreed Justice Jones, and, when the witness protested she had made a slip, Scroggs turned heavily to Mrs. Ann Broadstreet, the housekeeper.

'You, woman! – what month was it you were out of town?'

'In September,' replied Mrs. Broadstreet.

'It is apparent you consider not what you say,' observed the Lord Chief Justice, 'or you have come here to say anything that will serve the turn.'

Mary Tilden protested. 'No, I do not, for I was out of town in September. I came to town the latter end of September. . . . And it is impossible, if the body was in the house as Prance says it was, that I should not see it, or somebody must. I used to go every day into that little room for something or other, and I must needs see him if he were there.'

Whereupon Mrs. Broadstreet was brought to be examined, with the challenge: 'Well, woman, what say you?' Mrs. Broadstreet, very fat and with her hands on her hips, spoke in one breathless rush.

'We came to town upon a Monday; Michaelmas Day was the Sunday following; and from that time neither Hill nor the maid used to be abroad after eight o'clock; we kept very good hours; and Hill always waited at supper, and never went abroad after he came in to wait at supper; and the lodging was so little that nothing could be brought in but that we must know it.'

Scroggs considered. 'This little room – Hill's room – is a lower room than the main chamber of the house, is it not?'

'It is even with the dining-room, my lord,' put in Prance.

'What say you, Sir Robert Southwell?'

'My lord, it is an extraordinary little place. As soon as you get up eight steps, there is a little square entry. And there is this room on the right-hand, and the dining-room on the left-hand, I think.'

'And must you go into the room to go to the dining-room?'

Mrs. Broadstreet answered him. 'No, no, it is a distinct room. But the key to the little room, where they say this body was kept, was always in the door; and every day somebody went in there for something or another.'

'For my own part,' declared little old Justice Wild, after a pause, 'I will not judge you. But that his body should be carried there about nine o'clock at night on a Saturday night, and remain there until Monday night –! It is very suspicious that if you were in the house, as you say you were, and used to go into that room every day, you must either hear it brought in or see it.'

'But we did neither, my lord!'

At this point Mr. Justice Dolben leaned over the edge of the bench, like Punch over the edge of the box, and fixed her with the most sinister leer ever seen outside a Punch-and-Judy show. 'It is well you are not indicted,' he said.

Mrs. Broadstreet fell back, like Judy. 'Mr. Prance, you know all these things to be false, Mr. Prance!'

'I lay nothing to your charge,' says Miles Prance coolly; 'but you said before the Duke of Monmouth that Hill had gone from his lodgings before the time of the murder, and we know he had not.'

Miles Prance was always more alert than the judges at finding traps for witnesses. Though here was a witness whose very definite evidence went to prove that the body could not have been placed in Hill's lodgings, Prance slipped nimbly ahead of the judges in finding a way to shake her credibility. He was right: she had made such a statement before Monmouth, Ossory, and Sir Robert Southwell. The matter was not important, since Hill himself had acknowledged that he had not left Godwin's house until past the middle of October; and, in fact, his whole line of defence here was based on the fact that he *was* still living there on October 12th, else he could have had no alibi.

But Prance's quick-wittedness had placed Mrs. Broadstreet neatly between Mephistopheles and deep water. If she now declared that she had said no such thing before Monmouth, Ossory, and Southwell, it could be triumphantly proved that she was a liar. If, on the other hand, she stuck to her original statement about the time Hill left Dr. Godwin's, she could give him no alibi for the night of October 12th. In either case she was, in the phrase Jeffreys whispered to Serjeant Stringer, well Trapanned. They pressed her, and the Attorney-General found an accusation almost as bad.

'Have you not a brother that is in the Proclamation: one Broadstreet, a priest?'

'I have a brother, whose name is Broadstreet.'

'Is he not a priest, and in the Proclamation?'

'I hope I must not impeach my brother here,' said the

bedeviled witness. 'But about the other matter,' she persisted, 'I said upon my oath that we came to town on Monday, and Michaelmas Day (the 29th of September) was the Sunday following, and Lawrence Hill went away a fortnight after.'

'She swore to us,' said Sir Robert Southwell, 'it was two or three days after Michaelmas Day.'

'I beg your pardon, I only said I could not tell the time exactly.'

'Well, well,' interposed Scroggs, uninterested now that this witness had been disposed of, 'have you any more to say?'

Mary Tilden broke in again, in very solemn and serious-minded mood. 'There never was a day but that I went into that little room for something or other, and if anybody came to see me there was so little space that the footmen were always forced to be in that room.'

'Were you there upon Sunday?' asked Justice Dolben.

'Yes, my lord, I was.'

Whereupon Mrs. Broadstreet and Mary Tilden stood back, and Hill called Catherine Lee, the maid. Two witnesses had been blown to pieces and scattered; Hill had reason to feel panic with the slow approach of the rope to his neck; but he looked hopefully at the maid. Catherine Lee was a neat little blowen with curls, and the judges took a fancy to her.

'My lord,' spoke up Catherine Lee, 'I did never miss Lawrence Hill out of the house at those hours.'

'Maybe you did not look for him?'

'I did go down every night to the door to see if it were locked,' said the girl positively, 'and I went into the parlour to see that things were safe there.'

'You are a Roman Catholic, are you not?'

'Yes, I am.'

'Might he not go out of the house, and you never the wiser?' suggested Justice Dolben persuasively, and even Captain Richardson weighed in with a helpful word, and Justice Wild summed it up: 'Have a care what you say, and mind the question I ask you. Were you there on the Sunday, in that room where they say Sir Edmund Godfrey's body was laid?'

'I cannot say that I was in that room, but I called in at the door every day, and I was the last up every night.'

Hill was still fighting. He called a series of witnesses to prove his whereabouts on the entire day of October 12th. His first witness, Daniel Gray, told little one way or the other, and provided the next failure. But the second witness – Robert How, a carpenter whom Hill had hired to do some repairs to his new house in Stanhope Street – testified that on the Saturday Hill had been in his company from nine in the morning until two in the afternoon. This would prove that Hill could not have called at Godfrey's house between nine and ten, as Elizabeth Curtis had sworn, and the prisoner stressed the point. Scroggs contemplated the witness.

'What religion are you of? Are you not a Protestant?'

'Yes, my lord, I think so,' muttered How.

'My lord asks you,' put in Jeffreys quickly, 'are you a Protestant?'

'I was – I was never bred up in the Protestant religion.'

The invaluable Miles Prance helped again. 'He is a Catholic, my lord; he was the queen's carpenter.'

'Nay, now you spoil all,' sneered Justice Dolben. 'You must do penance for this. What! Deny your church?'

This repetition of, 'What religion are you of, what religion are you of, what religion are you of?' was beginning to turn Hill's brain. He could hear nothing else. He must make them see what he meant. He found himself almost screaming:

'What time was it on Saturday morning I was with you?'

'About nine o'clock', responded How.

'And how long did he stay?' asked Scroggs.

'From nine to two.'

'Are you sure 'twas nine, now?'

How looked down under the glare of the Lord Chief Justice. 'No man can swear punctually to an hour,' he said. He added viciously, under his breath, 'As you said yourself, about Prance.'

'What think you of ten?' suggested Scroggs, with the air of one making a fair business-proposition.

'It was thereabouts.'

'If I am rightly informed,' spoke up Jeffreys, who had been carrying on a whispered talk with the Clerks of the Crown below the bench, 'Mr. How is outlawed for recusancy.'

'Is he so? Pray let us know that!'

'My lord,' said one of the clerks, 'I have made out several writs against him, for several years together, and could never get any of them returned.'

'He tells you,' insisted Hill with a last appeal, 'that I was with him from nine o'clock on Saturday morning until two in the afternoon.'

'Yes. But that is just as true as that he is Protestant, and how true *that* is you know.'

It was a good thrust, which caused the jury to snigger. Though Hill called three more witnesses, their testimony carried little weight as an alibi for the night. Another witness had been summoned – a certain Mr. Ravenscroft, in whose brother's employ Hill had previously worked, and who had given great assistance to Mrs. Hill in preparing the defence – but Ravenscroft was not at the moment in court. As a last attempt, when the impatient court called on Green now to present his evidence, the aggressive Mrs. Hill fought her way forward and offered a paper containing reflections on the indictment. Scroggs would not allow it to be read, and ordered Green to speak up: 'In the meantime, what can you say for yourself, Mr. Green?'

Green, poked and roused out of his apathy, got up voice enough to call for his landlord, James Warrier, and the landlord's wife, Avis Warrier. James Warrier – called first – was probably the very worst witness, for a well-meaning dodderer, who could have been summoned. He rambled up and down to such an extent that he almost succeeded in confusing Scroggs. Mr. Warrier began with a direct statement: 'I will say that the 12th of October Green was at my house, half an hour after seven, and he was not out of my house until after ten.' Asked how he remembered the date so particularly, he said he had 'recollected his memory'. By what? By his work: and at each repetition it was always, 'By my work, and everything exactly,' with monotonous cheerfulness. 'When did you begin to recollect yourself?' 'A pretty while ago.' 'But pray when you came to recollect yourself, how did you come to do it?' 'By my work.'

'My lord,' interrupted Captain Richardson, 'since the arraignment of these three prisoners, I went to them to know what witnesses they had. Green told me of his landlord and landlady. I then asked Mr. and Mrs. Warrier if they could say anything as to this particular day – and they said they could not do Green any good at all.'

'I did not then call it to memory,' said Warrier.

'Well, WHEN did you call it to memory?'

'I did say,' repeated Warrier, with foggy obstinacy, 'I could not do it then presently, as I have done since, in five or six days.'

Scroggs blinked at him. 'How could you recollect it then?'

'By the time he came into my house, which was a week before,' rambled the witness, with complete incomprehensibility, but with the frank air of one who had the whole business reasoned out clearly in his own mind: 'and also by the work that was done.'

Scroggs appealed to the ceiling. 'God damn it, what could the work do as to this? Can you tell me by that, any thing that is done at any time? Where were you on the 9th of November last?'

'Truly, I can't tell.'

'Well, how came you then to recollect what you did on the 12th of October, when you did not know where you were on the 9th of November?'

'I can tell by a great many tokens. He was but fourteen or fifteen days in our house. . . . Sir, I remember other days besides that. But I say,' concluded the witness with dogged triumph, 'I never knew the man out after nine o'clock in my life.'

Scroggs looked at Green. 'Have you anybody else?' he inquired, with remarkable restraint after his bellow. 'As for this man, I can't tell what to make on't.'

'Here is the man's wife to give evidence,' said Green.

'First,' the Lord Chief Justice implored, 'consider what you say.' Mrs. Avis Warrier had done so. She bounced forward with great determination. She was a small woman with a large voice: she had the love of meticulous detail, of worming into the smallest circumstance and coming out with it as flat as she would smack her hand on a table, which her husband conspicuously lacked. Mrs. Warrier stationed herself without any shyness, took a good view of bench and bar, and began vigorously.

'To tell you the truth, I thought the man was so clear of this accusation that I never troubled my head with it. But when Captain Richardson came to my house, I told him that Mr. Green was never in our house by daytime, except – being cushion-layer in the chapel – he used to come in half an hour after eleven. And many times he would desire me (because we were Protestants) to put in a little flesh meat with ours. Sometimes he would sit down and eat his meat in the kitchen, and his wife with him; and his wife would say to him, " 'Tis a troublesome time" – meaning the Plot – "pray see that you come home early."

'I did not at all remember the day of the month (October 12th) at first, nor the action. But my husband and I have since remembered. We were desired by Mr. and Mrs. Green once to eat a fowl with them; and my husband did *command* me the Sunday after to invite them to dinner with us. So I went in the morning very early, I think, and bought a dozen of pigeons, and put them into a pie: and we had a loin of pork roasted as well. And when Mr. Green was gone to the chapel on *Saturday* in the afternoon, his wife came to me and said, "My husband is not well, and when he comes home he will ask for something of broth;" and so away she went to market to buy something to make broth of.

'While she was at market her husband came home, and asked where his wife was. "Why, Mr. Green," said I, "she is gone to market." "What an old fool!" said he, "is this, to go out so late on such a night as this is! But," said he again, "I will go to the coffee-house and drink a dish of coffee, and pray tell my wife so."

'In the meantime,' flew on the inexorable witness, looking sternly at Scroggs and nodding with great vigorousness at each point: 'in the meantime she returned, and by the time she had been in a while, Mr. Green came in. And Mr. Green being there, my husband came in and called to me, "Prithee, sweetheart, what hast thou got for my supper?" "Prithee," said I, "sweetheart." ' – Mrs. Warrier quoted archly – ' "thou art always calling for thy vittles when thou comest in." Then Mr. Green goes to the stairs and calls to his wife, and bids her bring down some vittles. And she brings down the bread and cheese, and he stayed there till it was nine o'clock; and then saith Mr. Green to his wife, "Let us go upstairs, for there is a fire." '

Scroggs interposed at last. 'What day was this?'

'Why, it was the Saturday fortnight after Michaelmas Day.'

'Why might it not be that day three weeks?'

'It was the day Sir Edmund Godfrey was missing!'

'When did you begin to recollect what day it was that they said he was missing?'

'On Friday morning, that was October 18th,' said Mrs. Warrier emphatically, 'our milkman came and told us that one Mr. Godfrey was found murdered. Now, I know a gentleman of the Exchange of that name, and I thought it might be he. But about the Saturday night before, we went up with Mr. Green to his chamber, and we sat there till the tatoo beat.'

'All the thing is,' roared Scroggs, 'how do you know it was this Saturday?'

'It was the Saturday fortnight after Michaelmas Day.'

Justice Dolben, who had been making a calculation on his fingers, leaned forward suavely. 'Are you *sure* it was the Saturday fortnight after Michaelmas Day?'

'Yes; we did look upon the Almanac, and reckon it so.'

'Then,' said the other coolly, 'that was the 19th of October.'

'Why,' cries Scroggs, 'you told him you could do him no good, and indeed you do not!'

She was hauled away, and, though the Warriers' maid testified that Green came in every night before nine o'clock,

Green's only witnesses were down without much difficulty. At this point Mr. Ravenscroft, the witness whom Hill had called previously, appeared in court; and Hill asked permission to let him testify. Hill's fury at this repeated questioning of, 'What religion are you of, what religion are you of?' caused him to mutter something which Ravenscroft evidently understood. Ravenscroft nodded. He stepped forward briskly, a determined and rather pompous man of no little intelligence. He wore a good black suit, fine lace at his throat, and an oiled periwig.

'Mr. Ravenscroft, what can you say?'

'What I can say, my lord, is this. This Lawrence Hill — I have known him thirteen or fourteen years, and he served my elder brother for so long, very faithfully. Afterwards he lived with Dr. Godwin towards the latter end of the last two years, and he married my mother's maid.'

The old question came out. 'What religion are you of?'

'My father and mother were Protestants.'

'But you are a Papist, are you not?'

'I have not said I am a Papist, yet.'

Justice Dolben tumbled headlong into the trap. 'In the meantime, I say you are one!'

'Do you so?' said Ravenscroft, lifting his head and eyeing him. 'Then pray go to Southwark and see.'

Mr. Attorney-General coughed warningly. 'My lord, I think he hath taken the oath of allegiance and supremacy.'

'Well, sir, go on with your story.'

Ravenscroft explained that a little before Christmas he had heard about the arrest of Prance as being concerned in the death of Godfrey. 'My house was in the Savoy,' he went on, 'and my father's house is in Holborn. I used often to go and see my father, and, coming home again, I went to see the maid — now Mrs. Hill — at her new house in Stanhope Street. She had not been long there, and she was standing at the door of the house. I asked her what news. Says she: "There has been a man here telling us Prance has discovered several of the murderers of Sir Edmund Godfrey; and they talk up and down strangely of it, and ask me whether my husband is acquainted with him." I said, "Is he?'' She answered me, "Very well; they have been often together," and she told me the people did mutter and talk of her husband. "But," said I, "what says your husband to it?" Says she, "He defies Prance and all his works." So I went away, and came again the next morning, and found Hill was arrested the night before. All that I say is, that it was good evidence of his innocence: he had notice of it in advance, but he did not run away.

'My lord, I have one thing more to say. Upon the occasion of these things, this woman hath been often with me,' he nodded towards Hill's wife, 'and hath desired to know of me what defence she should make. I saw that Hill's wife and Berry's wife were all simple people, without defence for themselves, and they did desire that I would examine and see some of the witnesses, and see how it was. She had got me some papers, and I conferred them together: there are witnesses that will attest the copy.'

Mr. Attorney-General's sour eye raked him up and down. 'What is all this to the purpose?' he growled. 'Only this gentleman hath a mind to show he can speak Latin.'

Ravenscroft returned his look with interest. 'I thank God I can speak Latin as well as any man in the court.'

'Well, all this is nothing,' said Scroggs, reasonably enough. '*Berry*, what have you to say?'

In exactly three minutes there was a mutter in court, the case had altered, and the defence was on its feet again. Berry called Corporal William Collet, and Troopers Nicholas Trollop, Nicholas Wright, and Gabriel Hasket. The latter three had been sentinels at Somerset House, and swore that no sedan-chair had gone out of the gate during the entire night of October 16th. The corporal's testimony was clear and detailed. He explained that he had placed the sentinels that night: Trollop guarded the gate from seven until ten, Wright from ten until one, Hasket from one until four.

'And where did you place them?' demanded Scroggs.

'To the Strand-ward.'

'That was the gate they carried him out by,' said Justice Wild in a warning tone.

'Do you hear?' said Scroggs in the same warning tone. 'Do you hear? Where did you place the sentinels? Within the gate?'

'Yes, within the wicket.'

Trooper Wright spoke up. 'There was no sedan came out in my time!' and Trollop agreed with him: 'Nor in mine. There was one came *in* in my time, while I stood there, but none went out.'

'Was it an empty sedan that went in?' asked Scroggs quickly.

'I suppose it was,' said Trollop, 'but we had no order to keep any out.'

'But you might know whether it was an empty sedan or no, by the going of it through the wicket,' insisted Justice Wild.

'There is an empty sedan that stands there every night,' said the corporal.

'If any sedan had gone out, you would not have stopped it, would you?'

'No, my lord, we had no order to stop any.'

'How can you then be positive that no one did go out?'

Trollop was vehement. 'None did go out again in my time!'

'Come, come,' said Justice Dolben, growing wrathful, 'could not the porter open the gate as well as you?'

'Yes, my lord, he could,' said Corporal Collet; 'but I should have seen him then. He did not open it in my time.'

The court was in a buzz, for these soldiers refused to be shaken: their testimony might break down the whole case against all three prisoners. Green was openly praying, Hill stared hard at them, and Berry had a sort of wild cheerfulness. The soldiers remained looking defiantly round while the judges conferred together. Then Justice Wild, fixing a stern glance on the witnesses, attacked in what seemed the most plausible and promising manner.

'Let me ask you but one question! Did not you go to drink or tipple all that time?'

Trollop's voice was raised. 'No, nor walk a pike's length off the place of sentry!'

'Has not Berry an ale-house hard by?' asked Wild shrewdly.

'Yes, but I did not drink one drop.'

'How can you remember so particularly, so long ago?'

'Why, I was twice before the Committee.'

'For,' put in Corporal Collet, giving the prosecution's case its most damaging blow, 'for we were all examined before Prance was arrested.'

This was worse and worse. The judges next pitched into Gabriel Hasket, the third sentry, who swore to the same thing. Questions were flung at him in the hope that he would stumble or contradict someone.

'What day of the month was it?'

'The sixteenth,' said Hasket promptly.

'What day of the week?'

'Wednesday.'

'Did you see Berry then?'

'No, I did not.'

'He was gone before you came,' said Scroggs; 'I was fast enough a-bed at that time,' declared Berry. At the end of it the judges were compelled to let the witnesses go without a scar. Scroggs called out to Berry, inquiring whether he had any more witnesses. Berry called the maid at his house, Elizabeth Minshaw – and the prosecution received another violent blow.

Elizabeth Minshaw testified that on Wednesday night, October 16th (which she remembered because it was the day the queen left Somerset House for Whitehall) Berry had returned home at dusk from playing a game of bowls. After that he had not gone out of the house all night. He went to bed at twelve, the same time that the maid did; but she knew he could not have gone out afterwards, because in order to go to bed he had to pass through her room.

The scale-pans wavered, and an excitable Mrs. Hill attacked Prance.

'I desire Mr. Prance may swear why he did deny all this?'

'Stand up, Mr. Prance,' said Scroggs. 'That gentlewoman does desire to know what induced you to deny what you had said.'

'My lord, it was because of my trade,' Prance responded sadly; 'and for fear of losing my employment from the queen, and the Catholics: which was the most of my business: and because I had not my pardon.'

'I desire,' cried Mrs. Hill, 'he may swear whether he was not tortured?'

Instead of being scandalised, as they had a right to be, their Lordships hastened to rebut this. 'Answer her! Were you tortured?'

'No, my lord. Captain Richardson hath used me as civilly as any man in England. All the time that I have been there, I have wanted for nothing.'

'There are several about the court that heard him cry out,' said Mrs. Hill. 'And he knows all these things to be false, as God is true; and you will see it declared hereafter, when it is too late!'

'Do you think he would swear three men out of their lives for nothing?'

'The sentinels,' protested Berry, 'the sentinels that were at the gate all night let nothing out.'

'Why, you could open the gate yourself,' retorted Scroggs, with a knowing smile at the jury. 'Well, well,' he added, as Berry broke out again, 'the jury have heard all, and will consider it. Is there no more?'

Mrs. Hill, who had been conferring with Ravenscroft, played the last card. 'Here is another witness, my lord: Mr. Chiffinch.'

Then up rose William Chiffinch, Page of the Backstairs to his Majesty, private agent and representative of the king. Though he must be treated with outer civility by the bench, they did not trouble too much to conceal their hostility. Chiffinch stood large and hook-nosed, his hands on his hips, and gave a completely full and completely truthful account of Prance's denial before the king. On his part he did not trouble to conceal his own views of the matter; and, though he could not mention Charles's name, the inference as to the king's opinion was clear. There was a silence, broken by Scroggs's saying that Mr. Prance never denied he had spoken thus, but the statement was forced from him by fear.

Thus the evidence for the defence was ended, and angry counsel for the prosecution rose in full panoply to address the jury. Sir William Jones said with sour persuasiveness that he would not dwell on the evidence at length, as he had intended: the evidence for the crown had been so much stronger than he expected, and the evidence for the defence so weak, that it would be a waste of time. But nevertheless he pointed out the convincing agreement of Bedloe and Prance, and launched into a tirade against Papists, concluding: 'I remember in the Book of Judges, "The people said there was no such deed done, nor seen, from the day that the children of Israel came out of Egypt": and I may say that there was never such a barbarous murder committed in England since the people of England were freed from the Pope's tyranny. And as 'tis said there, so I say now – "Consider of it, take advice, and speak your minds." '

Solicitor-General Sir Francis Winnington followed him, with a very sober, very persuasive, and very good speech vindicating Prance from the charge of denying his first accusation. But it was left for Scroggs to make out the strongest case in his summing-up to the jury, which he did with great ability.

The point of Scroggs's speech in praise of Prance was: 'There is not any one thing that is not backed up in some particular circumstance or other. And it is no argument against Prance,' he went on, 'no argument against Mr. Prance in the world that he should not be believed because he was a party to the murder, or because he afterwards denied what he first said. First, because you can have nobody to discover such a fact except one who was privy to it: so that we can have no evidence but what arises from a party to the crime. And, in the next place, his denial after he had confessed it to *me*, does not sound as an act of falsehood, but of fear. It is not a good argument to say that he is not to be believed because he denied what he once said; for he tells you he had not his pardon – he was in great consternation – the horror of the act itself, and the loss of his trade and livelihood – was enough to do it. But how short was his denial, and how quick was his recantation!'

S

Scroggs praised the evidence of Bedloe, noting the points on which it tallied with that of Prance, and refusing to believe the story could have been anything but truth. 'Upon that matter, you have two witnesses in almost everything.' As for the evidence put forward by the prisoners, all that was contemptible, 'All their evidence is slight, and answers itself, or else is not possible to be true,' with the exception of one point. This point was the evidence of the sentinels. But it could be put forward for the intelligent consideration of the jury whether the sentinels might not easily have been mistaken: the darkness of the night, making it easy for Berry to open the gate: or else the sentinels might merely have forgotten the circumstance. 'Now how far that single testimony of Nicholas Wright the sentinel will weigh . . . I leave with you, which may be mistaken either by reason of the darkness of the night, or those other particulars I have observed to you.'

His peroration was very long, and he had worked himself into a great state of eloquence towards its end. All this,

'I leave to your consideration: having remembered as well as I could the proofs against them, and all that is considerable for them. Add to this the condition that we are in at this time, and the eagerness of the pursuit that these priests make to gain the kingdom. For my own part, I must put it into my litany, *That God would deliver me from the delusions of Popery, and the tyranny of the Pope*: for it is a yoke which we, who have known freedom, cannot endure, and a burden which none but that beast who was made for burden will bear. So I leave it to your consideration upon the whole matter, whether the evidence of the fact does not satisfy your consciences that these men are guilty. And I know you will do like honest men on both sides.'

The jury retired, and were not long out.

'Gentlemen,' intoned the Clerk of the Crown, 'are you all agreed of your verdict?'

'Yes.'

'Who shall say for you?'

'Our foreman.'

'Robert Green, hold up thy hand. Look upon the prisoner; how say you, is Robert Green guilty of the felony and murder whereof he stands indicted, or not guilty?'

'Guilty.'

'Henry Berry, hold up thy hand. Look upon the prisoner; how say you, is Henry Berry guilty of the felony and murder whereof he stands indicted, or not guilty?'

'Guilty.'

'Lawrence Hill, hold up thy hand. Look upon the prisoner; how say you, is Lawrence Hill guilty of the felony and murder whereof he stands indicted, or not guilty?'

'Guilty.'

With each one the question concerning goods, chattels, lands, or tenements had been asked, and the Clerk of the Crown concluded: 'Hearken to your verdict as the court hath recorded it. You say that Robert Green is guilty of the felony and murder whereof he stands indicted. You say that Henry Berry is guilty of the felony and murder whereof he stands indicted. You say that Lawrence Hill is guilty of the felony and murder whereof he stands indicted; and that neither they, nor any of them, had any goods or chattels, lands or tenements, at the time of the felony committed, or at any time since, to your knowledge. And so say you all.'

'Yes.'

'Gentlemen,' cries out Lord Chief Justice Scroggs, 'you have found the same verdict that I would have found if I had been one with you; and if it were the last word I were to speak in this world, I should have pronounced them guilty.'

At which words the whole assembly gave a great shout of applause.

'Will your lordship please to give judgment this evening?' asked the Attorney-General, well satisfied.

'My lord, I am ready,' said Justice Wild.

'No, brother,' said Scroggs; 'I am to sit at *nisi prius* this afternoon, and 'tis time we broke up the court.'

'Captain Richardson,' said the Clerk of the Crown, 'you shall have a rule to bring the prisoners up to-morrow, for sentence.'

The court broke up. As the dazed prisoners were hauled

away through the crowd, the tipstaff of the court set upon them and pulled off their outer clothes, saying that the clothes were his fee.

．　　　．　　　．　　　．　　　．　　　．　　　．　　　．

There was one mercy. Since they had not been convicted on a charge of treason, the sentence would be one of hanging only, without the adornments of drawing and quartering. On the following day, Tuesday, February 11th, they were brought up to receive sentence from Mr. Justice Wild. Sir George Jeffreys entered a protest against the tipstaff's having stripped off the prisoners' clothes, and the tipstaff was admonished. 'This seems a very barbarous thing, to take their clothes off their backs,' observed Mr. Justice Wild. 'It doth so, brother, and they must be restored,' agreed Mr. Justice Dolben.

When they were asked if they had anything to say why judgment should not be passed, the prisoners gave no reply except that they were innocent. Mr. Justice Wild then treated them to a lengthy and powerful religious homily on the subject of the crime of murder. He that sheds man's blood, said Mr. Justice Wild, by man shall his blood be shed; for in the image of God created He him. This murder of a magistrate, merely because he was so zealous in prosecuting Papists, must be the most impudent and barbarous crime ever done in a civilised nation: inspired by the devil and blessed by the Jesuits: and above all Mr. Justice Wild exhorted them against the sins of cruelty and injustice.

'I have now done what I intended to say to you,' he concluded, after a final appeal to trust in their Redeemer; 'and what I said, I spoke to deliver my own soul, and upon no other account. I now pass the judgment which the law hath apointed to pass upon such malefactors, and that is this:

'*That you go from hence to the place from whence you came, and from thence to the place of execution, where you shall be severally hanged by the neck until you are dead, and may God have mercy upon your souls.*'

Hill spoke with his head bowed, after that pause. 'I

humbly beg one favour, that I may have the privilege to see my wife and children, and my brother, before I die.'

'Ay, God forbid else,' agreed Scroggs.

'Any day, I hope, my lord?'

'Captain Richardson, let them have the liberty of seeing their friends, but do it with care and caution.'

'And I will say this more to you,' added Justice Wild: 'If you would have any religious Protestant divines come to you, they shall be sent you, but none of your priests.'

'I desire only my relations.'

'You shall have them, and we offer you the others?'

It was the tongue-tied Green who spoke out now most fully and strongly. 'I have no relations that are Catholics, but two, and they are not priests.' Suddenly he found the bench of judges swimming round him, and their voices sounding far off, for his eyes brimmed with tears. He lifted his hand as high as the manacles would let it go. 'GOD SAVE THE KING! And I desire all good people to pray for us.'

Justitia facta est.

VIII

'UNDER THEIR OWN VINE AND FIG-TREE'

The Passing of the Plot

'Give them but rope enough, and they will hang themselves.'
                                            KING CHARLES THE SECOND.

'Le Roi de la Grande Bretagne a une conduite si cachée et si difficile
à pénétrer que le plus habiles y sont trompés.'
                                    BARRILLON, to Louis the Fourteenth.

I

Oxford, March 17th, 1681.

EVERY road into the old grey-spired city was a-drum
with hoof-beats as the great Whig lords rode under the
gates amid armed escorts, and the Londoners poured in for
the meeting of Charles the Second's fifth and last parliament. The Whig contingent wore in their hats badges of
lacquered tin, inscribed, 'No Popery, No Slavery'. At the
gates red-ribboned Tory supporters ran to meet them,
shaking clubs, staves, and swords. 'Make ready! Stand to
it! Knock 'em down! Knock 'em down!' Already the
town was filled with pamphleteers, song-writers, lampoon-
men, and caricaturists. Caricatures were passed from hand
to hand. One showed the Duke of York (called MacNinny)
as half devil and half Jesuit, the latter half setting fire to
London with a lighted brand. Another depicted half a
dozen huntsmen, booted and spurred, sitting on the Church
of England and riding it like an old hack to Rome. Still
another pictured old Roger l'Estrange – the great Tory
pamphlet-writer and king's journalist – as a dog with a
broom tied to his neck and a fiddle to his tail, running away
from the whip while the two Universities in square caps
cried, 'This is our Towser.' Already there had been disturbances. Down to Oxford strode that striking figure

Mr. Stephen Colledge, 'the Protestant joiner'.   Mr. Colledge appeared in town wearing a helmet and a coat of mail,
carrying a pistol and a carbine and a stock of Whig ribbons,
screaming, 'No Popery!'   Then up rose an indignant Tory
and punched Mr. Colledge in the nose, with sanguinary
effects. 'I have lost the first blood in the cause,' cries Mr.
Colledge, striking a great attitude, 'but it will not be long
before more is lost.'   Three days before, the king himself
had ridden into Oxford amid his Life Guards. It promised
to be the last great and bitter session of parliament, at
which the Whig grandees believed they could make the
king yield at last. But, although they did not know it,
Charles had his enemies – at last – exactly where he wanted
them.

Those two years, March 1679, to March 1681, found the
king still dexterously avoiding each dexterous trap they
set for him. A dozen times they thought they had him,
and on each occasion he was not there when the deadfall
snapped.

Early in March, 1679 (shortly after the execution of
Green, Berry, and Hill for the murder of Sir Edmund
Godfrey), he met the new parliament which had just been
elected. It had a powerful Whig majority, and Charles set
out quietly on a plan to deal with it. He persuaded the
Duke of York to go abroad to Brussels for a short time:
'You may easily believe that it is not without a great deal of
pain I write you this,' he told York, 'being more touched
with the constant friendship you have had for me than with
anything else in the world': but he said firmly that he expected York to obey him. At the same time, since Shaftesbury was now openly declaring that the Duke of Monmouth
was a legitimate son, Charles issued an official declaration
that he had never been married to any woman except
Queen Catherine. Thus on March 6th he met his new parliament in a spirit of almost gentle persuasiveness and
candour.

'I meet you here with the most earnest desire that man
can have to unite the minds of all my subjects,' he told them
disarmingly. 'And I resolve it shall be your faults if the

success be not suitably to my desires. I have done many things already in order to that end – as, the exclusion of the Popish lords from their seats in parliament, the execution of several men, both upon the score of the Plot and of the murder of Sir Edmund Berry Godfrey. And it is apparent that I have not been idle in prosecuting the discovery of both.

'I have disbanded as much of the army as I could get money to do; and I am ready to disband the rest, as soon as you shall reimburse me what they have cost me, and will enable me to pay off the remainder. And, above all, I have commanded my brother to absent himself from me, because I would not leave the most malicious man room to say I had not removed all causes which could be pretended to influence me towards Popish counsels. Besides that end of union which I aim at,' he warned, 'I propose, by this last great step I have made, to discern whether Protestant religion and the peace of the kingdom be as truly aimed at by others, as they are really intended by me.'

His whole object in summoning the parliament had been to get money, of which he was in great need, and so far no exception could be taken to his remarks. But they wished without delay to show all men exactly what they thought concerning the Popish plot. A resolution was passed re-affirming belief in the plot, just as later they passed a bill against Popery so long and all-inclusive that it took the Speaker an hour to read it. Oates and Bedloe were summoned before them for thanks. Bedloe was awarded the £500 reward for discovering the murderers of Godfrey, and Oates presented a curious expense-account amounting to £678 10s. 6d. – it contained such items as, 'For books which the Jesuits had of me, £40', 'For money owed to me by the Jesuits, £80', 'For my council, £20', – and the expense-account was duly paid by the Commons. For Oates and Bedloe were busy accusing Danby of the horrible crime of discrediting and tampering with their evidence, and parliament proceeded with the impeachment. On March 22nd Charles saved his Lord Treasurer by letting him resign from office and granting him a free pardon. 'I will give it him ten times over,' he told them, 'for I will secure him in his person and fortune, which is no more than I commonly do to my servants when they quit my service – as the Duke of Buckingham and my Lord Shaftesbury well know.'

This thrust Shaftesbury could not answer, though the Commons were busy voting a Bill of Attainder against Danby on the grounds that the king's pardon was illegal. Shaftesbury had already made his position on the kingship clear in debate: 'I think we are all agreed that in this kingdom there are no creatures of the king's power; there are none but creatures of the divine power, and the power of the king does not extend any further than the laws determine.' On March 25th he made a tremendous speech on the evils of the government in Scotland, which was little less than an incitement to rebellion there. He painted an affecting picture of the sad state of Scotland: 'We have a little sister, and she hath no breasts.' On the same night news-couriers galloped north with forty copies of the speech. In Green Ribbon coffee-houses it was believed – with reason – that the Covenanters, when they received assurance that they were backed by such a powerful party in England, would be up in arms.

Again Charles moved shrewdly. In April he announced that he was dissolving his Privy Council, and forming a new one in accordance with a suggestion of Sir William Temple. To demonstrate that he had no wish to surround himself with evil counsellors or secret cabals, to show his zeal for good government, this new council should be composed of only thirty members – *and its chief members should be leading Green Ribbon men.* In fact, my Lord Shaftesbury himself should be President of the Council.

This was that ancient English practice known as grasping the nettle. By putting them directly at his side, by closing his hand upon them, he put them into a position where he could oversee whatever mischief they tried to do; and it was probable, he thought, that they might come to trouble among themselves. That was precisely what happened, but at the moment Lord Shaftesbury, peering suspiciously, accepted. Halifax, Essex, Holles, and Russell

were the chief Green Ribbon men who became members.[1]
It gave rise to Charles's celebrated whisper, 'God's fish, they
have put a set of men about me, but they shall know
nothing! – keep this to yourself.' The new Secretary of
State was that thin, languid, and drawling[2] young elegant,
the Earl of Sunderland, who was (somewhat) libellously supposed to have a face like a calf, and whose manner in draw-
ing-rooms was much admired.

No sooner had the nation ceased to huzza at this republican move, which convinced some that the embryo Whig
party had won, than the Commons brought in a bill to exclude the Duke of York from the throne.

Long had Charles awaited this, the direct act to put up
a bill and vote upon it. The Commons began by making
an address to the effect that the Duke of York's succession
to the throne was the most outstanding encouragement to
the present damnable Popish plot. Charles's reply was a
polite refusal to alter the succession. Matters thereupon
grew so inflamed in the Commons that one wild member
suggested impeaching York on a charge of high treason.
On May 11th a voice came up out of the past and the grave
when Richard Hampden – son of the Buckinghamshire
squire who, nearly forty years gone, had raised a county
against King Charles the First – proposed the Exclusion Bill.

---

[1] The full roster of the new Privy Council was: Prince Rupert; the Archbishop of Canterbury; the Earl of Nottingham, Lord Chancellor; the Earl
of Shaftesbury, Lord President of the council; the Earl of Anglesey, Lord
Privy Seal; the Duke of Albemarle; the Duke of Monmouth, Master of
the Horse; the Duke of Newcastle; the Duke of Lauderdale, Secretary
of State for Scotland; the Duke of Ormonde; the Marquess of Winchester;
the Marquess of Worcester; the Earl of Arlington; the Earl of Salisbury;
the Earl of Bridgwater; the Earl of Sunderland, Secretary of State (in
place of Sir Joseph Williamson); the Earl of Essex; the Earl of Bath; the
Viscount Faulconburg; the Viscount Halifax; the Bishop of London; John
Lord Roberts; Denzil Lord Holles; William Lord Russell; William Lord
Cavendish; Henry Coventry, the other Secretary of State; Sir Francis
North; Sir Henry Capel; Sir John Earnley, Chancellor of the Exchequer;
Sir Thomas Chicheley; Sir William Temple; Edward Seymour, Esq.;
Henry Powle, Esq.
[2] This fashionable drawl, the substitution of 'aa' for 'o' and 'e', can
be illustrated by a speech out of Vanbrugh's play, *The Relapse, Or, Virtue
in Danger*: – 'Nat that I pretend to be a beau, but a man must endeavour
to look wholesome, lest he makes so nauseous a figure in the side-box,
the ladies should be compelled to turn their eyes upon the play. Naw,
if I find it a good day, I resalve to take a tarn in the park,' etc.

Four days later they heard the reading of it: 'Be it hereby enacted that James, Duke of York, Albany, and Ulster (having departed openly from the Church of England, and having publicly professed and owned the Popish religion, which hath notoriously given birth and life to the most damnable and hellish plot, by the gracious Providence of God lately brought to light) shall be excluded, and is hereby excluded and disabled,' from the throne. On its second reading it was triumphantly passed with a majority of seventy-nine votes.

It remained for this bill to go to the Lords, and there was little doubt that the Whigs had power enough to pass it there. This had been a momentous session, for the Habeas Corpus Act was passed; an address had been made to remove the Duke of Lauderdale as minister for Scotland, in order to help incite a Scottish rebellion; and an inquiry was being made into the system of secret-service money. But, before the Exclusion Bill could go to the Lords, the king prorogued parliament. A few weeks later he dissolved it.

The angry members had barely ridden away from Westminster before our lords of the Green Ribbon heard, with glee, news of tumult in the north. The Scottish Presbyterians were up in arms. Archbishop Sharp had been dragged out of his coach and hacked to death near St. Andrews, and a great field conventicle was held within ten miles of Glasgow, where old pulpit-pounders rhymed Lord and Sword. A body of royal guards rode out to disperse it; there was sharp firing, and the guards left thirty dead men when they fled. Singing the psalms of old, the Covenanters marched on to Glasgow. By that time their numbers had swelled to eight thousand, so that the Earl of Linlithgow's horse, foot, and dragoons retreated before them. The Covenant was declared again in the west of Scotland, and the rebels demanded a free parliament.

Troops must be sent from London to quell this outbreak. When Charles attempted to dispatch them, Shaftesbury very nearly succeeded in preventing him. Pamphlets and speeches urged the court against making preparations for war, the Presbyterian leaders interceded in England, and

Shaftesbury argued that English troops could not legally be sent to serve in Scotland. Charles parried this with the neat suggestion that the troops should be commanded by the Duke of Monmouth. 'Come, think of the glory and prestige there is to be got for him!' Shaftesbury withdrew his objection, but arranged to have put into Monmouth's instructions an order which would empower him to 'deal' with the rebels. That is, Monmouth should be permitted to come to terms with them on an amicable understanding: this rebellion would be so gently pardoned that it would offer Covenanters a direct incitement to start another one. Charles was aware of the trick, and at the last moment – just as Monmouth was preparing to start – he revoked that part of the order, substituting for it instructions to fall upon the rebels and exterminate them without argument.

While Monmouth rode north, on a white horse and with his laced hat raised to cheering crowds, there was published in London a terrific pamphlet which threatened to brew rebellion in England. It was called, 'An Appeal from the Country to the City'; it was composed at the Green Ribbon Club; and it recalls the most luxuriant days of war-time propaganda. Protestants were urged to picture their wives and daughters being ravished before their eyes by long-toothed Papists, the brains of their children smashed out against the wall, and the Babylonish Beast stalking amid the flames of London. The Duke of Monmouth was called upon, as a patriot and saviour, to seize the crown at once.[1]

The eloquence of this pamphlet was supported by a noise of gunfire from the north. On June 22nd Monmouth met the Covenanters at Bothwell Bridge over the Clyde. The Covenanters – having received private assurance that Monmouth would treat with them – expected no clash of pikes

---

[1] With the following ingenious argument: 'He (Monmouth) will stand by you; and therefore you ought to stand by him. And remember the old rule is, He who hath the worst title ever makes the best king; as being constrained by a gracious government to supply what he wants in title: that instead of God and my right, his motto may be, God and my people.... A king with a bad title makes a better king than he that hath a good one; for he shall be obliged to comply with and humour the people for want of a title.' – From 'An Appeal from the Country to the City,' read at the trial of Benjamin Harris, February 1, 1680.

at all. When he replied that he had no such commission, and threw out an advance line to take the bridge, they stood looking on like men out of their wits. Down went their arms at the first charge; the carrying of the bridge became a butchery which Monmouth stopped as soon as he could. He was never cruel, and he said he could not kill men in cold blood. It enhanced his reputation in England, where the excitement of the Popish plot had now reached its height.

On June 13th Thomas Whitebread and John Fenwick – the Jesuits who had been up for trial before, with Ireland, Pickering, and Grove, but who had been sent back to prison because there was not enough evidence against them – were again brought into the dock at the Sessions House. With them now were three more Jesuits, William Harcourt, John Gavan, and Anthony Turner. The witnesses for the prosecution were Oates, Bedloe (who now remembered much that he had forgotten before), Prance, and that galloping new knight of the post, Stephen Dugdale. The evidence was what Scroggs called 'long and perplexed'. The Jesuits called sixteen witnesses to show that Oates had been at St. Omers during April and May 1678, the time he had alleged he was present at that famous consult in the White Horse Tavern; and Oates retaliated with seven witnesses to prove he had been in London. On this occasion the lying was so complicated that its classic purity grew somewhat obscured, and Scroggs's summing-up was a trifle more mild than usual. But he declared himself entirely satisfied with the evidence of Stephen Dugdale, who explained how on Saturday night, October 12th, Harcourt wrote a letter to Staffordshire announcing that Sir Edmund Godfrey had been satisfactorily murdered. All five prisoners were condemned to the usual consequences of high treason.

The next day Richard Langhorn, a lawyer whose practice lay chiefly among Catholics and Quakers, was convicted of having treasonable dealings with the Pope. A feature of the defence was the fact that Langhorn called as a witness the proprietress of the White Horse Tavern. So much had been heard of this tavern, and so little known of it, that to view its landlady must have been like seeing Father Christmas or Pope Joan. Oates had sworn that fifty Jesuits had met at the White Horse Tavern for their consult, eighteen or twenty in a room. The proprietress asserted that there was not a room in her tavern which would hold more than a dozen people.

'Is this Dr. Oates, my lord?' she asked, looking at Titus.

'Yes, that he is,' replied Scroggs.

'I never saw him in my house in my life.'

'Was there nobody ever in your tavern but who you knew?' asked Scroggs. 'What! Can you tell all the people that were ever in your tavern?'

'The most of my company were people that I knew.'

After some wrangling as to how fifty Jesuits might have been fitted into the house, rather like a fox-and-geese problem in a puzzle-book: 'Good woman,' said Scroggs, 'is your house a little house?'

' 'Tis a small inconsiderable house. There is not a room in it that will hold above a dozen. I never remember so great a company was in my house at one time, except once, in all my seven years: and that was a Jury of the Parish, and they could not be together, but were divided into three rooms.'

Whereupon there instantly arose in the court three men, alleged strangers. The first swore that the biggest room at the 'White Horse' could easily contain sixteen people. The second swore there were two rooms that could contain twenty-five or thirty, and the third agreed with him. A fourth gentleman then arose and said this room could contain fifty. Thus the size of the biggest room at the 'White Horse' was swelling to inordinate proportions, and it crushed Richard Langhorn. But he had already been crushed by William Bedloe. Bedloe – beginning his testimony with a loud complaint to the Lord Chief Justice that there was a Catholic lady taking notes in the spectators' gallery – professed to have seen Langhorn writing treasonable matter in his study at the Temple. Langhorn was convicted and executed.

A month later the miracle occurred. A month later there

was an incident which could not have startled the Green Ribboners more if Sir Edmund Godfrey had walked alive into the 'King's Head'. On July 18th – at the trial of Sir George Wakeman, the queen's physician, for attempting to poison the king at the instigation of the queen – the Popish plot received its first great check.

And that check was administered by Sir William Scroggs.

II

Half the fate of the whole plot depended on this trial, for it was the beginning of the Whigs' attempt to prove treason against the queen. The evidence seemed as strong against Wakeman (and the three Benedictine monks, William Marshal, William Rumley, and James Corker, who were tried with him) as against the previous victims. The witnesses were equally confident. But suddenly, and in the middle of the trial, Lord Chief Justice Scroggs executed a complete *volte-face*.

It was in the heat of midsummer, and the trial droned like the flies in the cramped and greasy Sessions House, buzzing drowsily towards an inevitable conviction and towards the flies that would presently swarm round Wakeman's carcass on Tyburn Hill. The evidence went dead against the prisoners. Oates swore to his old story of hearing, through a half-open door in Somerset House, Sir George Wakeman and the queen planning Charles's murder. Bedloe testified along similar lines: he said that he had heard Sir George Wakeman say to Father Harcourt, concerning the poisoning, 'I find more encouragement from my good lady and mistress than from any of you all.' Oates had even seen a receipt from Wakeman, in his own handwriting, acknowledging £5,000 as a third part of his fee for committing the murder. It went on in the approved fashion until Wakeman called Sir Philip Lloyd in his defence.

'I desire to know of Sir Philip Lloyd,' said Wakeman, 'what Mr. Oates said of me before his Majesty and the council, the last day of September. Sir, you were there present.'

'I will, my lord, as well as I can, recollect and tell you

(as near as I can) what Mr. Oates did then accuse him of,'
replied Sir Philip Lloyd. 'It was upon the one and thirtieth
day of September. Mr. Oates did then say he had seen a
letter from Mr. Whitebread to Mr. Fenwick at St.
Omers, in which letter he wrote that Sir George Wakeman had
undertaken the poisoning of the king, and was to have
£15,000 for it – of which £5,000 had been paid him by the
hands of Coleman. Sir George Wakeman utterly denied
all, and did indeed carry himself as if he were not concerned
in the accusation; but he did tell the king and council that
he hoped he should have reparation and satisfaction for the
injury done his honour. His carriage was not well liked
by the king and council; and, it being a matter of such consequence as this was, they were willing to know further of it.
And, because they thought this evidence of Mr. Oates was
not proof enough to give them occasion to commit Sir
George – it being only out of the letter of a third person –
thereupon they called Mr. Oates in again. My Lord Chancellor desired Mr. Oates to tell him if he knew nothing personally of Sir George Wakeman, because they desired
sufficient proof – and Mr. Oates, when he did come in again,
and was asked the question, did lift up his hands – for I must
tell the truth, let it be what it will! – and said, *"No, God
forbid I should say anything against Sir George Wakeman,
for I know nothing more against him."* And I refer myself
to the whole council, whether it was not so.'

After a terrible pause, when there was not a creak or
movement in the court, the whole bench sat up. And in
the midst of that pause two voices cried out.

One was Oates's: 'I remember not one word of all this!'

One was Wakeman's: 'My lord, this is a Protestant witness too.'

'My lord,' said Oates in great bluster, 'give me leave to
make an answer. When I did report this letter, the council
did ask me whether or no Sir George was in any ways concerned with this letter. I replied, I had it by report that
Sir George had received £5,000 of this money. My lord,
the council did not press me to my knowledge. I will not
be positive; but if the council did not press me, and I did

make that answer, I do appeal to the whole board whether or no I was in a condition to make any answer at all, when by reason of my being hurried up and down, and sitting up, I was scarce *compos mentis*.'

Then Scroggs turned on him. 'What! Must we be amused with I know not what, for being up but two nights? You were not able to give an answer when they called you to give a positive charge; and now you tell us a story so remote! What! Was Mr. Oates just *so* spent that he could not say, "I have seen a letter under Sir George Wakeman's own hand?"'

Whereupon Glorious Titus made the blunder of sneering at the king and council. 'To speak the truth, they were such a council as would commit nobody.'

'You have taken a great confidence, I know not by what authority,' roared Scroggs, 'to say anything of anybody! . . . Gentlemen, we hear that the council sent for Oates again, and asked him, "Do you know anything of your own knowledge?" IF he had come in then and said, "Yes, I have seen a letter subscribed under his own hand," would they not have committed Sir George Wakeman then? Surely they would. And the council's not committing him is an argument that they had not sufficient evidence, and Oates did omit at that time to charge him with this letter.'

Even after a long trial, Scroggs came out clearly with his opinion in the summing up to the jury: 'I tell you plainly, I do not think a man could be so weak and weary but that he could have said, "I saw a letter under his hand." It was as short as he could make an answer, and 'tis strange that he should go and make proclamation that he knew nothing. And so I pray you weigh it well. Let us not be so amazed and frightened with the noise of plots as to take away any man's life without reasonable evidence.'

The court sat thunderstruck. When Bedloe put in a complaint that his evidence was not rightly summed up, Scroggs looked at him with such contempt that Bedloe moved back. 'I know not by what authority this man speaks,' said the Lord Chief Justice, and the stentorian voice of the Clerk of the Crown took it up: 'Make way for the

T

290 THE MURDER OF SIR EDMUND GODFREY

jury, there! – who keeps the jury?' Everybody in the room was puzzling over this complete reversal of Scroggs's opinions, while the Lord Chief Justice swaggered off the bench to take a mutton-chop upstairs, and they were still puzzling when the jury returned an hour later.

'George Wakeman, hold up thy hand. Look upon the prisoner; how say you, is he guilty of the high treason whereof he stands indicted, or not guilty?'

'Not guilty.'

'Down on your knees,' cries Captain Richardson to the prisoner, in the dazed silence that followed; 'down on your knees!'

'God bless the king and this honourable bench,' said Sir George Wakeman.

Not guilty. In five minutes the report was going down the Old Bailey, through every coffee-house, and gathering speed as it went. Not guilty. The prosecution against the queen had broken down; Oates had been called a liar; Oates had suffered defeat. Nobody knew why Scroggs had done this thing. Nobody knows to this day. Roger North had one explanation of it,[1] but it cannot possibly be true.

The most probable explanation seems to be that Scroggs, who always went violently in one direction or the other, was sick to the teeth of Titus Oates. Once before, at Coleman's trial, he had burst out against Oates over precisely the same point as in this one: Oates's failure to say more of the prisoner when the first denunciation was made at the council-board, and Oates's shuffling whines about bad eye-

---

[1] 'It fell out that when the Earl of Shaftesbury had sat some short time in the council,' Charles's new-model council, 'and seemed to rule the roost, yet Scroggs had some qualms in his politic conscience; and, coming from Windsor in L. C. J. North's coach, he took the opportunity and desired his Lordship to tell him seriously if my Lord Shaftesbury had really so great power with the king as he was thought to have. His Lordship answered quick, "No, my lord, no more than your footman hath with you." Upon that the other hung his head and, considering the matter, said nothing for a good while. . . . After that time he turned as fierce against Oates and his plot as ever before he had ranted for it,' Roger North, *Life of Lord Guilford*. This cannot be credited. If there was one person in the world whose influence had no weight with Charles, it was Shaftesbury. Scroggs could not help knowing what everyone else knew: that they were the two worst enemies England could show. Nor could Scroggs for a moment have believed that in prosecuting the plot he was pleasing the king.

sight and bad health. For eight months Scroggs had been exposed to all this. After the trial of Richard Langhorn he had learned from a legal crony that, by Bedloe's mere description of Langhorn's rooms in the Temple – where Bedloe said he had seen Langhorn writing treason – Captain Bedloe was a liar. It may also be true that Scroggs, knowing the temper of the king, would have nothing to do with an attempt to fling mud at the queen. It may even be possible that Scroggs (like a few others beginning to shake themselves out of their hypnosis) had begun to wonder uncomfortably whether he had not been making (in the literal sense of the term) a bloody fool of himself over the Popish plot.

There were signs of a returning sanity, although the mob under Green Ribbon proddings would not acknowledge it. By most Whigs the acquittal of Wakeman was regarded with an emotion very much like horror. What! Impeach the sacred evidence of Dr. Oates: besmirch that deliverer in open court? It was argued that if Oates and Bedloe were not to be believed, and the queen were not a traitor, then their whole party was done for. All the blame fell on Scroggs. It was announced that he had been bribed with a barrel full of gold. The jury had been bribed. When he went on circuit during the autumn assizes, the mob threw a half-hanged dog into his coach, and Oates and Bedloe later brought legal proceedings against him for daring to maltreat their tales. But at last it showed that there had come to be a growing variety of opinion. And in August there was cause for consternation of another kind.

For in August the king lay dying at Windsor.

After a long game of tennis in the heat, he had taken cold by walking in the evening mists at the riverside; a fever developed, and he lay crying in delirium. By the beginning of the last week in August the doctors had given up hope of saving him. The Duke of York was secretly sent for – not four men knew of it – and James hurried back from Brussels. With a curious shock people looked at each other and faced the thought, 'What if he should die?' Though the possibility had often been discussed as an

almost humorous abstract proposition, still they could
not credit it when they saw Death come in at the door and
pluck back the bed curtains. It could not happen; it would
leave too great a void. The old gamecock, lean and stringy:
Old Rowley, who smiled and jested with you in the Park,
and was for ever alive: the best-beloved man in the kingdom: it was not possible for this man to be put down under
the earth at noonday, when all those flowers were out.
Among other things, it would mean civil war.

Thus during that balanced time it occurred to men that
they had better draw closer to him; that they might do well
to trust his judgment, if death spared it to them; and that
the schemes of the Green Ribboners *might* be a trifle violent.
And, as the king had hoped from the beginning, there was
already trouble among the republican leaders in his new
Privy Council. Lord Halifax definitely refused to support
Monmouth as heir to the throne, and he was falling away
from Shaftesbury. Halifax favoured banishment of the
Duke of York, and at most a proposal to invite over William
of Orange to govern. But Monmouth, never so popular
as after his heroic conduct during the slaughter of Bothwell
Bridge, was turning the heads and hearts of good Protestants: and most of the Green Ribbon leaders had selected
him as king if the old gamecock should die.

Charles did not die. The old gamecock was too stringy.
By September 2nd, when James arrived at Windsor, Charles
was sitting up in a chair in the best of spirits, eating mutton
and arguing with the doctors. But the temper of the nation
had been a little influenced by his illness: though he sent
James back to Brussels, he gave him permission to return
and await the issue of matters in Scotland. Monmouth also
he determined to send away, for the young man's swagger
was beginning to be dangerous. With both bones of dis-
content out of England, and nobody to come muddling
into the midst of his plans, Charles knew that his chances
were day by day becoming more equal. Despite Shaftesbury's protests, Monmouth was packed off to Holland.

My Lord Shaftesbury had to take quick action of some
kind. On October 7th the new parliament met – and

Charles instantly prorogued it. He was almost penniless, but he did not dare risk parliament yet. But Shaftesbury's counter-attack was not long in coming. It was an 'exposure': the exposure of a so-called Popish scheme to fasten the plot on the Presbyterians. A certain Mr. Thomas Daingerfield made a great show of finding a bundle of letters concealed in a meal-tub, a cry went up that the damnable Papists had been conspiring again, and within a week the whole inflamed town was precisely where it had been before: mad with terror over the Popish plot.

Whereupon Shaftesbury, while the bogy of the 'horrid' Meal-Tub Plot was abroad, followed it up with one of the most brilliant public spectacles which ever antedated Messrs. Barnum and Bailey. On the night of November 17th, the anniversary of the accession of Queen Elizabeth, was held the first of the genuinely elaborate Pope-burning processions. A glare of links illumined it, all windows were bright with Protestant candles along the way, and two hundred thousand spectators packed the streets to see it go by. In front walked six whistlers to clear the way, making an eerie din. Next walked a bellman clanging his bell and bawling, 'Remember Justice Godfrey!' Behind them, on a white horse, hung a limp body which represented Sir Edmund Godfrey; gouts of blood were on his wrists, his shirt, and his white gloves, a cravat was knotted round his neck, and a man representing Lawrence Hill sat behind him to hold him up. Just after them came a Jesuit distributing pardons to all those who would murder Protestants. Next, in a truly impressive line, strode six Jesuits with bloody daggers upraised. A consort of wind music set up a hellish screeching just behind them, and the music was followed by four Popish bishops in purple and lawn sleeves. Then came the Pope's chief physician, with Jesuits' powder in one hand and a urinal in the other. Finally, in triumph and magnificence, rode the *pièce de résistance* among all these effigies: the Pope himself. The Pope sat robed and crowned on his throne in a wagon drawn by horses decked in red ribbons. Silk banners, painted in designs of bloody daggers for murdering heretical kings, waved before him;

294 THE MURDER OF SIR EDMUND GODFREY

and crouched just behind him, whispering in his ear – red-clothed, horned, and whiskered like a Frenchman – was his sharp-tailed counsellor, the devil.

Altogether it was a spectacle to be proud of, and it drove the town half mad again. Godfrey's effigy was laid down at the doors of Somerset House, and the Pope was burnt on a vast pyre at the foot of Queen Elizabeth's statue.

Titus himself had been adding fuel by editing two great pamphlets, 'The Pope's Warehouse, Or, The Merchandise of the Whore of Rome,' and, 'The Witch of Endor, Or, The Witchcrafts of the Roman Jezebel,' dedicated to Lord Shaftesbury. Titus had paid a visit to Oxford without, unfortunately, being awarded a degree of Doctor of Divinity there, although Shaftesbury declared he should have been made a bishop. Ten days after the great Pope-burning procession, the Green leader prepared a new and dramatic raree-show. Without Charles's knowledge, Monmouth had been secretly summoned to come back from Holland.

Shaftesbury, who had been dismissed from the new Privy Council, now had no need of subtlety. Few at White-hall knew what was happening when, at midnight on November 27th, a clashing of bells through the city was followed by a crackle and flare when bonfires took light, and the voices of watchmen grew more distinct as they approached Whitehall bellowing Monmouth's name. He appeared like a spectral visitant to those who were roused out of sleep and crowding to the windows: straight-shouldered on a white horse, wearing the oiled periwig, the buff-coat and jackboots of the conqueror, his feathered hat raised and his handsome face smiling at all those night-capped heads with their candles held high. He was the Protestant champion. He was King Monmouth. His arms now bore the lions of England and the lilies of France without the bend sinister of illegitimacy. The clatter he made through those streets grew, in the next few days, to rapture. Even Nell Gwyn entertained him at supper. When his angry father refused him entrance to Whitehall, he took refuge in the city.

If the Green Ribbon leaders could compel the king to

convoke parliament, they now felt that the Exclusion Bill would be passed and Monmouth's succession assured. But, as the year 1680 was ushered in, Charles still refused. His new Privy Council had come to pieces. Shaftesbury was dismissed; Halifax and Essex had gone into retirement: and in January, when Charles announced his intention of bringing home the Duke of York from Scotland, then Russell, Cavendish, Capel, and Powle asked leave to resign. Charles said he assented with all his heart. His chief ministers were now 'the three Chits' – young Sunderland of the calf's head, young 'Lory' Hyde (son of Clarendon), and the discreet Sidney Godolphin – whose callowness was much burlesqued.

Still Charles prorogued parliament. He was in genuinely desperate need of money, so much so that Buckingham openly expressed a many-oathed wonder as to how the devil he could get along at all. The court was shut up like a theatre, and as desolate. Matters were so bad that someone even proposed the shocking expedient of reducing Dr. Oates's pension. Since all these informers were paid out of the royal Treasury, there was nothing for the salaries of honest servants. But Charles would not give way. For again he had opened negotiations with Louis the Fourteenth, very ingeniously letting Louis make the advances and putting the favour on his own side. The king of France had begun to perceive, with some uneasiness, that this constant bribing and supporting of the Green Ribbon opposition was going too far. It was a very good move to keep Charles from opposing France by setting his own parliament about his ears: but there would be exceedingly sour results if – on Louis's money – the Catholic Duke of York should be deposed, the Protestant Monmouth declared successor, and a republican government turn to attack France. Or suppose (which was worse) that the Protestant William of Orange, Louis's worst enemy, were to succeed to the English crown?

Already Barrillon had been authorised to offer Charles a subsidy of £200,000 for three years. Charles affected to have no great interest in it: only once did he break out,

'For God's sake, you must help me!' Very deliberately, to increase his price, he arranged a treaty of alliance with Spain – thus allying himself dead against Louis in the old fight for the Spanish Netherlands. There was much talk of an alliance to be made with Holland as well. Barrillon, smiting his forehead, said that he could not understand the king of England; but Charles was in no hurry. As for the Green Ribbon leaders, 'Give them but rope enough. . . .'

They were taking rope enough. In his effort towards forcing Charles to convoke parliament, Shaftesbury had now no recourse except the new device of Petitioning. Petitions showered on Whitehall. Petitions turned up in the gallery, the Park, on the dinner-table, even on the bed-curtains. Counter-petitions from the Tories urged the king not to convoke parliament. Frantic political opinion divided itself into Petitioners, Birminghams, and Exclusionists on one side; Anti-Birminghams, Abhorrers, and Tantivies on the other. In the midst of the petitioning, Shaftesbury had come secretly to Whitehall – offering Charles all the money he wanted from parliament, and the Exclusion Bill to be shelved, if he would only divorce Catherine and marry a Protestant wife. Charles refused, but he saw that Ambassador Barrillon heard of the proposal: Barrillon was in agony, and Charles's price went up in the eyes of the French king, as he had intended, while he waited for English public opinion to swing behind him.

For, during that riotous summer of 1680, the great Plot had begun to languish a little. It was beginning to languish because it had now grown so complicated that nobody on earth knew what was going on. The knights of the post were making too many discoveries; they had commenced to plant papers on each other, find spoons in each other's sleeves, crawl in and out of loop-holes with such rapidity that the business began to resemble farce-comedy. They were not now making the Pope evilly plot murder in his secret cabinet: they were making him turn hand-springs at Charing Cross and squirt water through his front teeth. 'I cannot tell you what to-day's plot is,' wrote one puzzled observer; ' 'tis something to do with yesterday's plot, but I have not heard about yesterday's plot yet.' It now became permissible to examine the evidence, and a series of acquittals ensued in the courts. In May, when again the king was dangerously ill, the Middlesex grand jury ignored an indictment for treason against the Catholic Countess of Powis. The Earl of Castlemaine was tried for high treason and acquitted. Shaftesbury had already tried the effect of a great Irish plot; and, though the London mob did not laugh, there was some mirth in the council. On June 26th the Green Ribbon leader, supported by five members of the House of Lords, nine members of the House of Commons, and Titus Oates, indicted the Duke of York and the Duchess of Portsmouth as Popish recusants; but Scroggs discharged the jury before they could find a true bill. 'Does the king walk fast?' said Shaftesbury; 'I'll walk him leisurely out of his dominions!' In July Oates's pension was reduced from £12 to £2 a week; he and Tonge had begun to squabble over who had invented the plot.

But Shaftesbury's support of Monmouth – especially with that tale of the 'black box' which contained proofs of Monmouth's legitimacy – still kept him in a position to do anything he liked. He had gained one great success in electing his own Sheriffs for the City of London, so that henceforth juries could be packed and give verdicts according to Green Ribbon orders. A Whig majority in parliament, a shouting Whig mob in London, would give him victory if only parliament could be called together. And, in the autumn of 1680, it was learned that at long last parliament would meet on October 21st.

Charles was about to test his strength. It was the most dangerous thing he had done yet: parliament would straightway bring up the Exclusion Bill, the Exclusion Bill would straightway pass the Commons, and the odds were about seven to five that it would pass the Lords as well. But Charles had his eye on Ambassador Barrillon. He meant to announce to parliament his strong anti-French intentions in his alliance with Spain and projected alliance with Holland, thus compelling Barrillon to give him secret terms

from Louis so that he could dispense with his parliament
altogether. It was possible that parliament itself, in the
slow turn of sympathy towards him, would not be so an-
tagonistic as before. In any case he must take the risk, or
show to the world the comic spectacle of a king of England
quite flatly unable to buy a joint of mutton for dinner.
He must not turn into a caricature, or he was done for.

After all his patience during the evil days, he very nearly
miscalculated. That session of parliament began with a
whoop which presently made Lord Chancellor Nottingham go home feigning illness. All the wrath of a full year's
prorogation went into it. Mr. Thomas Daingerfield, one
of the leading knights of the post, was brought before the
Commons to give revelations against Papists. Then there
was a solemn interlude: one of the great informers had
died during the summer: and his dying deposition was
read. It comes with a shock, but towards the end of
August Captain William Bedloe had died at Bristol. On
his death-bed Bedloe had affirmed to Sir Francis North,
Lord Chief Justice of the Common Pleas, that every word
he had uttered about the plot had been completely true.
Then he moved on to dubious glory, having 'broken his
gall' by violent riding, and he was buried with pomp and
tears in the mayor's chapel at Bristol. His funeral sermon
was preached from the text, 'So then every one of us shall
give an account of himself before God.'

There is no need to quote the dreary panegyrics or even
drearier lampoons that were written about his going. He
lied and he died; but on his death-bed he affirmed that all
his statements had been true, and the Commons could not
doubt his oath. On October 28th his statement was read
before them, and two members were ousted from the meeting for discrediting the Plot. Parliament fell upon the
Anti-Petitioners with cries of treason. Then came the
Exclusion Bill. So truculent had the session become that
in the whole court there was not one unterrified person
except Charles: both his Secretary of State, Sunderland, and
the tearful Duchess of Portsmouth begged him not to oppose
the Commons, or he would find himself besieged by a mob

in Whitehall. While Charles sat at supper among a group of gloomy-browed retainers, Sir John Reresby told him of the threats against Anti-Petitioners. 'Do not trouble yourself,' said Charles; 'I will stick by you, and my old friends; for if I do not I shall have nobody to stick by me.'

Yet many feared he would not, 'for,' commented Sir John, 'the want of money was so pressing, and the offers of the parliament-men so fair if he would relinquish his brother, that nobody seemed secure which way he would bend.' On November 4th the Exclusion Bill had its first reading in the Commons. One friend of the Duke of York flung defiance at the Green Ribbon: 'There has been talk in the world of another successor than the duke, in a black box. But if Pandora's box must be opened, I would rather have it in my time, not in my children's, that I may draw my sword to defend the right heir.'

Swords were half-way drawn on the floor of the Commons. The Whig followers promised civil war. Round Westminster the mob had gathered, ready to march on Whitehall when the bill should be passed; and City trainbands stood under arms to do the will of parliament. On November 11th the bill was passed by the Commons. Four days later, with Lord William Russell triumphantly bearing it aloft, it was carried to the House of Lords for debate, with a great body of Commons following, and the Lord Mayor and alderman to lend support.

It was nearly five o'clock in the afternoon. The winter twilight had begun to close in; candles were lighted under the great gilt roof of the Lords; and uneasy peers prepared for trouble when that tumult came along the corridors. The king stood in his usual place by the fireside, silent, but very cool and watchful. The fight was joined when Shaftesbury, in a brilliant and fiery speech, called for nothing less than the exclusion of a traitor. Essex followed him with a speech no less able. Then up rose Lord Halifax, the most remarkable and persuasive speaker in either House; he looked benignly at them, and nearly everyone there believed that his wit would be directed also against the Duke of York.

'I must disagree *in toto*,' said Halifax unexpectedly, 'with everything the noble lords have said.'

Startled members looked at Charles, and saw that he was smiling. Halifax was leading the defence. For almost seven hours the House of Lords saw a debate such as it had never heard before. Halifax was constantly on his feet, like a swordsman; he met every attack of Shaftesbury and Essex, turned it off with an epigram, and appealed to the Lords at the end of it. Charles, staring, would not leave the place during that wild time. Food was brought to him in an adjoining room. He heard Monmouth speak – a good speech, Barrillon thought it – not attacking the Duke of York, but piously urging that exclusion must be voted in order to save the king's life. Charles said one word: 'Judas.' The Lord Chancellor was absent, sending word that he was ill. Buckingham was absent. In the midst of the session, Sunderland lost his nerve and bolted to the Green Ribbon side. Tempers went up to a mighty pitch: sixteen times the invincible Halifax spoke against almost certain defeat – and it was clear that he had begun to win over the doubtful. As blades came out on the opposition bench, king's men hurried to Halifax's side and surrounded him with a ring of swords. By eleven o'clock they were voting. Among the king's party, Sunderland, Anglesey, Suffolk, and Manchester voted in favour of the bill. A dense crowd in the lobby outside the doors could hear the mutter and roar. Then, at twenty minutes past eleven, the doors were knocked open; they knew the verdict when a Tory voice, in ecstasy, cried, 'Beaten, by God! – beaten!' The Exclusion Bill had been defeated by thirty-three votes.

III

To describe the Commons' state of mind after this defeat would be arduous: they were in such a state of rage that they had outdone superlatives. It may be summed up with mildness by saying that they passed resolutions against everything they could think of. They asked for the removal of Halifax. They threatened to print Coleman's letters.

They read articles of impeachment against the Treasurer of the Navy. They wanted to impeach Scroggs and North. They swore never to give the king another penny of supplies until the Duke of York was excluded.

The Lords – although they had not been willing to exclude James altogether – wished, like Halifax himself, to truss him up in such fashion that he would be incapable of active kingship. Several alternatives were suggested, among them Shaftesbury's favourite device of having Charles divorce the queen, marry a Protestant, and beget a Protestant heir. There was one highly naïve argument, in the presence of the king, at which the pros and cons of Charles's ability to produce children (at his present age) were discussed in some detail.

'Can any one doubt,' cried my Lord Shaftesbury in a great rage, rising and pointing at Charles as the latter stood rocking amiably in his usual place by the chimney-piece, 'can any one doubt, if he looks at the king's face, as to his being capable of producing children? Why, he is only fifty. I know people, upwards of sixty, who are still capable of it.'

'Ay, but,' said my Lord Clarendon, 'Lory' Hyde's elder brother, 'but I know the queen to be like other women. I know she hath been pregnant, and once she had a child larger than a rabbit.'

'I do not feel altogether pleased,' says Charles, amid a roar of mirth, 'at my Lord Clarendon's knowing so much about my wife's concerns.'

It was left for the Bishop of Rochester to deliver a final very weighty summing up. 'If a man,' declared his Lordship, 'hath bought a mare for breeding, and the vendor should give him a mule instead, then he would not be obliged to pay the purchase-price.'

But these elegant conceits did not amuse Shaftesbury, who, though he had a pretty wit himself, was now beyond mirth. That defeat of the Exclusion Bill marks a turn in his life: old and shrivelled, 'fretting the pigmy body to decay', he had come to a point of obsession where it might be advanced as a tenable theory that he was never quite sane afterwards. He had gone mad on one subject. He

declared that he would have Charles the Second's head as
he had helped to have Charles the First's head in the old
days. His face was wasted to the bone, and his hair clear
white under the weirdly youthful-looking flaxen periwig.
But there were many of the grandees who felt almost as
strongly as he did. They must have a victim – a final victim
for the dying Popish Plot – and they fastened on the Catholic
Lord Stafford, whose trial had already been voted, and who
had been selected because he was the oldest and feeblest of
the Popish lords in the Tower.

Lord Stafford was seventy. He was of no particular value
or importance, except as a man may be valued to himself:
he was thought to be of little courage, and would have difficulty in raising his voice high enough to be heard. Against
him paraded a strong list of witnesses, led by Oates and
Dugdale, and on November 30th, 1680, they brought him to
trial for high treason before the Lord High Steward (the
Earl of Nottingham) in full-dress grandeur at Westminster
Hall. 'Crazy and old,' Roger North thought him; and
Burnet's opinion was: 'He was on ill terms with his
nephew's family, not gracious with the king, and of small
consideration with the duke; so that his fall may be ascribed
not so much to his guilt as to his want of friends to support
him.' Yet he defended himself with startling resolution and
complete courage. In its own way, as Reresby thought, this
was a test case for the whole plot: it was now to be determined whether there were more people who believed in it,
or more people who thought it very damnable nonsense.

And there were very many who still believed in it, particularly among the lords. Thus Mr. Attorney-General, Sir
William Jones, had seldom prosecuted a prisoner with such
savagery or guile. The king had a box for this gala trial
before the Lords; so had the queen and the Duchess of
Portsmouth. They heard Oates swear that Lord Stafford
had a patent to be paymaster-general of the Popish army
which should come to cut Protestant throats. They heard
Dugdale swear that Lord Stafford had offered him £500 to
kill the king. They heard a new witness named Turber-
ville swear that in Paris, during the year 1675, the same offer

had been made to him. They heard – throughout a seven days' wrangle – the witnesses tell palpable lies, contradict themselves flatly, get caught in lies by the defence's witnesses: and, finally, they were treated to such inspired shuffling as this:

Lord Stafford: This witness is called 'Dr.' Oates: I beseech your lordships to ask him whether he were a doctor made at the universities here, or abroad?

Oates: My lords, if your lordships please, any matter that is before your lordships I will answer to; but I hope your lordships will not call me to account for all the actions of my life. Whatever evidence is before your lordships, I will justify.

Lord Stafford: He is called a doctor, and I would know whether he did never declare upon his oath that he took the degree at Salamanca?

Oates: My lords, I am not ashamed of anything I have said or done. I own what is entered as my oath before your lordships, and am ready to answer it; but I am not at all bound to say what does not at all concern this business.

Lord Stafford: My lords, it is entered on your books that he swore before the council he was at Madrid, and knew Don John of Austria – I would know of him whether he swore this?

Lord High Steward: Have you sworn anything of Don John of Austria?

Oates: My lords, I refer myself to the council-book.

Lord Stafford: I beseech your lordships, may I have that book?

Lord High Steward: I believe it is in the narrative. If Mr. Oates will not acknowledge it, we must stay till the journal is brought.

Oates: My lords, if your lordships please, I will repeat as well as I can what was said at the council-table. . . . But, my lords, I always thought the council-book was no record upon any man.

But Mr. Attorney-General said the book could not be brought in as evidence, even if it could be found, and the managers of the trial would not find it. And again:

Lord Stafford: He says he feigned to be a Papist when he was not, and that they showed him presently all my letters. Did he keep any one of my letters?

Lord High Steward: Have you any one of my lord's letters by you?

Oates: My lords, I could not keep any letters sent to the fathers. I had a sight of them; but none of them to my particular use.

Lord Stafford: Does he know my handwriting? Did he ever see it in his life?

Oates: Yes. I do know his hand. I believe I have a letter of my lord's by me, but not about me – it is of no concern – I am sure I have one of my Lord Arundell's.

Lord Stafford: But he says he has a letter of mine! Let him show one of my letters.

Oates: He writes a mixed hand. I think it is but an indifferent one.

Lord Stafford: So many commissions, and so many letters, as are spoken of – and not one to be found or produced!

But, after seven days of this, assisted for the prosecution by Stafford's rambling manner, the result was an apparent triumph for the Green Ribbon Club. By a vote of the lords, he was condemned to death on a majority verdict. Thirty-one peers voted him innocent, fifty-five voted him guilty.[1] It was a very respectable minority vote: though it may be doubted whether this was any particular consolation to a very infirm and bewildered old man who had just been sentenced to hanging, drawing, and quartering.

Again the king refused a pardon. Charles, very pale after hearing a verdict in which he had hoped for an acquittal, was firmly going to let the poor devil die: in that death he saw at last the death of the Popish plot. The Whigs had got their verdict, but it was the fool's stroke

---

[1] All his own relations, of his name and family, condemned him except his nephew, the Earl of Arundell, son of the Duke of Norfolk. Among others who voted him guilty were the Lord High Steward, Nottingham, the Earl of Anglesey, the Earl of Sunderland, and (of course) Shaftesbury, Buckingham, Essex, Wharton, and Grey. A hundred years later, Lord Chief Justice Kenyon was quite right in pronouncing this trial a legal murder; but it is true that at the time a number of completely honest and honourable men still believed in the Popish Plot.

which at length would put the whole support of the nation behind the king. For two black years he had held his own against every trick they could use, and he did not mean to let half a dozen innocent men keep him from the victory he would shortly have. The most he would do was to change the sentence to one of beheading; but even here the Opposition was not satisfied. William Russell clamoured in the Commons for the full penalty with all its details, and Charles had his way only after a sneer from the Sheriffs of London. Lord Stafford was executed on Tower Hill, and he died like a Roman.

The Opposition, though a little disquieted, now triumphantly thought that they must force the king to yield. 'After sitting so long with no effect,' Charles had suggested suavely, 'what would you do for me if I should yield?' By a vote of the Commons it was answered that they would put him into a condition to defend the much-menaced Tangiers, would pay off all his debts, would put the fleet into good condition and make him able to assist his allies – provided he would exclude the Duke of York, pass an Act for more frequent meetings of parliament, and change such of his ministers as they should nominate. Some thought jubilantly that he would comply, although Halifax doubted it: 'That is like offering a man money to cut off his own nose, which nobody would do for an even greater sum than that.' There was one thing they did not know:

On the same day they were making their proposals, the French ambassador came in secrecy to Charles. And Charles had won what he schemed for; Barrillon was authorised to give him good heavy subsidies from France.

Now he could relax a little, though outsiders wondered at his cheerfulness when the dangers seemed no less thick than they had ever been. On Christmas Eve, 1680, when the court was still as desolate as a shut-up playhouse, he went to his great bedroom attended by only four followers. They heard the bells ringing in the Noel-time, and one depressed courtier noted: 'He seemed extremely free from trouble or care, though at a time when one would have thought he was under a great deal; for everybody guessed that he must either dismiss the parliament in a few days, or give himself up to what they desired.' But he lounged in a chair before the fire, taking two hours to undress, and in a reflective mood. He gave a long dissertation on the subject of those who pretended to be more holy and devout than others, and said they were generally the greatest knaves: giving a few examples, with a chuckle, from which it may be presumed that one great Green name was not missing. At half-past one he went to bed at last, and relaxed his ageing bones as though into a warm bath.

During the next two weeks, while wagers were being laid as to whether he would or would not yield, he planned his course. This parliament should be dissolved, and another summoned: the elections would determine how far popular sentiment had come over to his favour. Three months or so should be given for heads to cool still further, and then parliament should be summoned – at Oxford, where Shaftesbury could not rouse the mob or begin a miniature civil war with City trainbands. And there the country should see, as though in silhouette, the fantasy and violence of Green Ribbon counsels. If the Commons grew too violent, and were not prepared to retreat an inch, he could dissolve them and manage his affairs on money from France; but it would turn all opinion in his favour. Parliament was summoned for March 21st, 1681, at Oxford; and, said Halifax, 'If the king would be advised, it is in his power to make all his opponents tremble.'

The opponents did not think so. They were in a great state of temper at the parliament's being called at Oxford. After so many incredible setbacks in the past few months, which seemed to them almost contrary to the will of God, they were rushing ahead and making the blunder of asking for a final decision, a last stroke. Charles made no objection: he was going to make them tremble: the more wrathful they grew before the world, the better for his purpose. Shaftesbury, Monmouth, and Essex presented a great petition declaring that parliament must not be held at Oxford: with so many crawling Papists, even in the king's Guard, all members of parliament would go in danger of their lives unless the meeting were held at Westminster as usual. 'Do you think so, my lord?' Charles said to Essex; 'I don't,' and he bade them good day.

Though the elections favoured the Whigs, after a prop-aganda-campaign concerning rape and massacre by Papists, there was a noticeable gain on the Tory side. Shaftesbury complained that he was having trouble with the damned city to keep it from falling away. He had sworn to have the heads of those who had counselled dissolving the last parliament, and he meant to keep his oath. Also, he was a lonely man. His only real friend, Mr. Locke the philosopher, was in Somerset: to him some time ago my lord had written, 'I recommend you to the protection of the Bishop of Bath and Wells, whose strong beer is the only spiritual thing any Somerset gentleman knows.' His young crony, the very wild and very drunken Earl of Pembroke, was in jail again. My lord Pembroke could not keep out of trouble, though he generally confined his escapades to breaking the heads of such unimportant people that he did not suffer for it. Returning from a drinking-bout at Turnham Green, Pembroke had got into an argument with a watchman and stabbed him; and Shaftesbury had been angry for some months. But all his energies were concentrated on the coming meeting of parliament, and of again forcing through the Exclusion Bill.

On March 14th Charles settled his financial agreement with Barrillon. Only Lory Hyde and the Duke of York were acquainted with it. Charles's promises were small: he undertook to extricate himself from the very flimsy Spanish alliance of the previous year. In return Louis was to preserve the peace of Europe, waging no war on the Low countries, and was to pay Charles 2,000,000 crowns for the first year, 500,000 crowns for each of the succeeding years. It was done. With a coiled whip in his hand Charles set out for loyal Oxford, bulwark of Tories. Lord Oxford's regiment was posted along the road in case of trouble; in the streets, as the king's coach rattled through amid the Life Guards, there was a mighty shout of, 'Let the king live, and

the devil hang the Roundheads!'   All things led to one
fusion-point:

Oxford, March 17th, 1681.

Every road into the old grey-spired city was a-drum with
hoof-beats as the great Whig lords rode under the gates amid
armed escorts, and the Londoners poured in for the meeting
of Charles the Second's fifth and last parliament.   The
Whig contingent wore in their hats badges of lacquered tin,
inscribed with, 'No Popery, No Slavery'.   At the gates red-
ribboned Tory supporters ran to meet them, shaking clubs,
staves, and swords.   'Make ready!   Stand to it!   Knock 'em
down!   Knock 'em down!'   Already the town was filled with
pamphleteers, song-writers, lampoon-men, and caricaturists.
Caricatures were passed from hand to hand.   One showed
the Duke of York (called MacNinny) as half devil and half
Jesuit, the latter half setting fire to London with a lighted
brand.   Another depicted half a dozen huntsmen, booted
and spurred, sitting on the Church of England and riding it
like an old hack to Rome.   Still another pictured old Roger
L'Estrange – the great Tory pamphlet-writer and king's
journalist – as a dog with a broom tied to his neck and a
fiddle to his tail, running away from the whip while the
two Universities in square caps cried, 'This is our Towser.'

Already there had been disturbances.   Down to Oxford
strode that striking figure Mr. Stephen Colledge, 'the Protestant joiner'.   Mr. Colledge appeared in town wearing a
helmet and a coat of mail, carrying a pistol and carbine and
a stock of Whig ribbons, screaming, 'No Popery!'   Then up
rose an indignant Tory and punched Mr. Colledge in the
nose, with sanguinary effects.   'I have lost first blood in the
cause,' cries Mr. Colledge, striking a great attitude, 'but it
will not be long before more is lost.'   Three days before,
the king had come into Oxford amid his Life Guards.   It
promised to be the last great and bitter session of parliament,
at which the Whig grandees believed they could make the
king yield at last.   But, although they did not know it,
Charles had his enemies – at last – exactly where he wanted
them.

All the colleges were put at the disposal of the parliament.

The Geometry School was to be used for the meeting of the Lords, Convocation House for the meeting of the Commons. A hospitable University set out into the streets tables laden with liquor, and flat-capped gentlemen compelled passers-by to drink the health of the king on their knees. But, when he made his opening speech to the session on March 20th, the king had designed a very moderate and very persuasive address which he meant the popular mind to contrast with the uproar which must follow.

'My lords and gentlemen,' he said. 'The unwarrantable proceedings of the last House of Commons were the occasion of my parting with the last parliament. For I, who will never use arbitrary government myself, am resolved not to suffer it in others. I am unwilling to mention particulars, because I am desirous to forget faults. But whosoever shall calmly consider what offers I have formerly made, and what assurances I renewed to the last parliament – and shall then reflect upon the strange, unsuitable returns made to such propositions – perhaps may wonder more that I had patience so long.'

He went on with calmness and great firmness, saying that he was ready to remove all fears of a Popish successor, ready to meet any man half-way in order to preserve peace and liberty, but: 'What I have formerly and so often declared touching the succession, I cannot depart from.' He wished them to be convinced that neither their liberties nor their properties could subsist long when the rights and prerogatives of the crown were invaded, or the honour of the government brought into disrepute.

'I conclude with this one advice to you: that the rules and measures of all your votes may be the known and established laws of the land – which neither can nor ought to be departed from, nor changed, but by act of parliament. And I may the more reasonably require that you make the laws of the land your rule, because I am resolved they shall be mine.'

He got the response he had expected. It took them several days, impeded by a wild quarrel between Lords and Commons over the impeachment of a rogue named

Fitzharris, before the Exclusion Bill came to be debated. Charles sardonically watched the old arm-flinging begin again. On March 24th, before members had taken their seats and proceedings opened in the Lords, Shaftesbury approached him. Several of the peers overheard that conversation.

'Come,' said Shaftesbury, 'if you are restrained *only* by law and justice, rely on us and leave us to act. We will make laws which will give legality to the measure.'

A few people heard Charles flare out at last. 'My lord, let there be no delusion. I will not yield, and I will not be bullied. Do you understand that? Men usually grow more timid as they grow older. It is the opposite with me. For what remains of my life I am determined that nothing shall be said against my name. I have law and reason on my side, and good men will be with me. There is the church,' he pointed to the bishops, 'which will support me. My lord, we will not be divided.'

Then the oratory began to thunder. Most of the Commons thought that Charles's attitude was sham, or he would have summoned no parliament at all; they had him trapped, and they were jubilant. Monday, March 28th, was fixed for the first voting of the Exclusion Bill. On the evening before, Charles held a closed conference with his council whose purport nobody outside suspected. On Monday morning he sauntered to the Geometry School, and behind him was carried a sedan-chair – with drawn curtains – in which incurious idlers supposed some peer rode to the meeting. All possible suggestions and expedients had now been offered to the Commons, to show to the world how urgently the king desired to please them: the banishment of the Duke of York, a regency for Mary of Orange: but they had refused them all. On that Monday morning, while a speech was being made about Magna Charta, the Black Rod tapped at the Commons' door. They were summoned to the presence of the king. And they were still more jubilant, for they knew this must mean that he had yielded after all.

Crowding into the Lords, they stopped in stupefaction to see the king sitting in his robes of state – which had come in the closed sedan-chair. There was a dead silence after the babble, and Charles spoke.

'My lords and gentlemen. *That all the world may see to what a point we are come* – that we are not like to have a good end – when divisions at the beginning are such: therefore, my Lord Chancellor, do as I have commanded you.'

The Lord Chancellor rose up. 'It is his Majesty's royal pleasure and will that this parliament be dissolved,' intoned Nottingham; 'and this parliament is dissolved.'

Send a fast, curving ball down the skittle-alley: catch the head pin a little to the right: and you will hear the crash as every pin flies wide. He had caught them just thus. A dissolution was the last thing they had prepared for. They could make no protest. Not only had he turned their whole holy zeal into burlesque, but he made a burlesque of their whole position. They were not now in London, with a mob to support them and the City trainbands to lend a weight of dignity to civil war. They were in Oxford, amid angry loyalists; if they refused to disperse, and insisted on further proceedings, the king's Guard would come in and pull them out by the ears, like schoolboys, as a jest for every coffee-house. Though Shaftesbury tried to make them stay, within an hour they were running for it. The crush in which they struggled to get out of town was like the rout of an army. Charles had not only dissolved parliament; he had dissolved bombast and civil war. He was free to take his revenge, and, as he had promised himself by Catherine's bedside, God in heaven! but it should be a terrible reckoning. The thing was no less true for being a platitude: he had given them all the rope they wished – yard upon yard of the smoothest hemp – and they had hanged themselves.

In the attiring-room, taking off his cumbersome robes of state while the din of coaches fled away in every direction, Charles put his hand on Bruce's shoulder.

'It is better to have one king,' he said, 'than five hundred.'

.   .   .   .

Thus, over twisted roads, the Popish plot came to an end – and it left behind only one great riddle. That riddle was its soul and its centre; upon that riddle depended some of the mightiest issues of the seventeenth century; without that riddle no plot could ever have been proved. That Oates and Tonge and Bedloe were liars needs no demonstration. Sweep your hand through the whole tissue of nonsense, and you perceive that the nightmare of the Popish plot was nothing but a nightmare from beginning to end. Yet there remains the riddle, the one bloodstain, the one concrete fact. Upon it depends the whole judgment of those tortured years.

Who killed Sir Edmund Godfrey?

AN ENDING FOR CONNOISSEURS IN MURDER

The Solution

TWELVE theories have been propounded before this club. Eleven of those theories must be examined, and proved (so far as is possible) to be false, before we can say with any degree of confidence that the twelfth hypothesis is the correct one. Therefore let us examine all the evidence, and see what it amounts to. The reasons for each have already been stated: now for the counter-reasons.

I

That Sir Edmund Godfrey committed suicide, by falling on his own sword.

This theory, although elaborate and ingenious, is the easiest of all to disprove. By two incontrovertible pieces of physical evidence we see that it could not have happened: (*a*) the neck was broken, (*b*) there were *two* wounds. All the ingenuity of *post-mortem hypostasis* to produce apparent bruises, and the blocking of the wound by the sword so that there was no blood, and a tight collar causing the ring round the neck – all these things completely omit the fact of the neck being broken. That the neck was broken cannot be denied: two surgeons gave testimony to that effect at the trial. There is no suggestion that Godfrey, pitching forward into the ditch, could in any fashion whatever accidentally have broken his neck to add to all the other injuries: his head did not even touch the ground, but rested upon his arm. Finally, remember those two wounds. One went as far as a rib: then the sword was drawn out, and thrust in again. Now, this shallow wound must necessarily have been the first wound made. If Godfrey had first tried to stab himself – and then, failing that, had fallen forward on the sword – then there must first have been a great evacuation of blood from the shallow wound. His clothes would have been drenched with it, and the ditch as well. But there was no blood on his clothes, and no flow of blood whatever from the first wound. Therefore both wounds were made on a dead body, and the first theory must be discarded.

II

That Sir Edmund Godfrey committed suicide, by hanging himself, and that afterwards – to prevent his estate being forfeited to the Crown – his two brothers, Michael and Benjamin Godfrey, arranged other trappings to suggest murder.

Now let us revert to the testimony of Dr. Zachariah Skillard at the trial, which went thus:

Mr. Attorney-General: But are you sure that his neck had been broken?

Skillard: Yes, I am sure.

Mr. Attorney-General: Because some have been of the opinion that he hanged himself, and that his relations, to save his estate, ran him through. I would desire to ask the surgeon what he thinks of it?

Skillard: There was more done to his neck than *ordinary suffocation or hanging.*

One point must be indicated here. In the seventeenth century, and for a long time afterwards, hanging by means of breaking the neck – a drop on a rope, which shall break the neck for an instantaneous death, as we know it now – was unknown.[1] Hanging meant suffocation only. The victim stood in a cart with the taut rope round his neck, the cart was drawn away, and he was left dangling until he died: the hangman, if he were well paid, pulling the victim's legs downwards so as to tighten the rope and choke him more quickly. This was true of public executions, and explains the surgeon's words at the trial. But it is far more true of suicides by hanging. Suicides by hanging had the resolu-

[1] *Cf.* William Andrew's *Bygone Punishments*, 1-37.

tion to choke themselves, as Sir Thomas Clifford did in
1672, and as suicides by hanging have done in any age.

Not only would it never have occurred to Sir Edmund
Godfrey to do this in 1678, but the physical evidence proves
that he could not have done so. We must take it as certain
that he was strangled with his own cravat or neckband: the
marks on the neck were exactly those which it would have
produced, the cravat was carefully removed from the neck,
and the collar buttoned up so as to hide its absence. Now,
the linen band or cravat of the seventeenth century was not
as long as an ordinary modern necktie. Let us suppose that
you are going to hang yourself, from a hook in the wall or
the limb of a tree, with your own necktie. One end goes
round the support, the other end round your neck: how
much space remains between them? Say, roughly, eighteen
inches, and in the literal sense give it plenty of rope. In
other words, your neck is almost against the support from
which you mean to hang. Is there, then, any position into
which you can twist yourself – any gyration of any sort –
that would conceivably *break your neck*?

With the neckband of the seventeenth century, Godfrey's
head must have been almost directly against the support
from which he hung. In this fashion he could have killed
himself only if he had resolutely remained in that position
(like a man in a strait-jacket) until he strangled. To break
the neck requires a very powerful drop and jar – six full
feet are required by law, and even then it is sometimes
bungled. It is not conceivable that Sir Edmund Godfrey
managed it with a drop of six inches. Dr. Skillard the surgeon answered that very question in court nearly two hundred and sixty years ago, to the satisfaction of all who heard
him.

Again, if we put forward the theory of suicide by hanging,
what becomes of the black bruises on his stomach? So far
the answer has been that it might have been caused by *post-
mortem hypostasis*, the gravitation of blood to the lowest
part of the body. And in the very definition of the term
we perceive that it must be discarded. Godfrey's breast was
not the lowest part of his body. He was lying head down-

wards in a ditch, tilted like a man going headfirst down a slide. If there had been any suggillation, there would have been no mass of black marks on his breast, for the blood would all have gravitated to the neck and head.

Therefore we cannot accept the second theory either. It must be established that the man was strangled, and at the end of it his neck was broken by a murderer; that this murderer had beaten or stamped upon his breast. Having decided that this crime was murder, our examination leaves us with one question which we must presently answer: Why was Godfrey the victim of such an inordinately savage and brutal attack as this?

III

That Sir Edmund Godfrey was murdered by his two brothers, Michael and Benjamin.

This explanation rests solely on the belief that it was the two brothers who, on the Saturday the magistrate disappeared, started the report that he had been trapped and murdered before it could even have been known he would not return in the usual way.

That the two brothers did originate this rumour may be considered as probable. But, far from being suspicious, their conduct is so entirely natural that it would have been odd if they had said anything else. Anyone who has had some small experience with the ways of families will, heartily and perhaps profanely, endorse this view. For what happened? The brothers knew – what all London knew – that Sir Edmund was supposed to be in terrible danger from the Catholics. They were wrong; but who was to know that? On the morning of Saturday, October 12th, they went to the house of Mr. Welden, where Mr. Welden told them of their brother's behaviour the night before. He told them of Sir Edmund's great agitation after the vestry-meeting at St. Martin's-in-the-Field; of his wild conduct, his careful settling-up of all debts like a man going out to fight a duel, his flat statement, 'Shortly you will hear of the death of somebody,' his acknowledgment that he walked in danger; and, finally, his uncertainty as to whether he could accept a dinner-engagement for the next day. When Michael and Benjamin Godfrey were told this, what would they naturally say? What would *you* say, under the circumstances? The most obvious cry in the world would be: 'The Papists have caught him and murdered him!'

Aside from this, the clear and natural thing to say, there is no evidence of any kind against the brothers. Quite to the contrary, they are shown to be the most innocent of all. For if they had murdered him in order to get his estate, the last thing in the world they would have done would have been to murder him in a way that looked like suicide: or his estate would have gone to the Crown. But if, on the other hand, they had murdered him for a private reason – if they cared nothing about the estate – then why were they so frantically anxious to prove it was not suicide? It is very seldom that a murderer works hard and long to show that his crime is murder: it is very seldom that he is not content to show, even with eagerness, that the victim killed himself. This third hypothesis must very quickly be set aside.

IV

That Sir Edmund Godfrey was murdered by Jesuit priests, because of a dangerous secret which had indiscreetly been communicated to him by Edward Coleman.

Since there has been a trial for the murder, since a number of new actors have been introduced subsequent to the time this theory was first propounded in our 'Interlude', it is now possible to outline this hypothesis more fully. The hypothesis is this:

Coleman was associated with Godfrey, and let slip to him the 'dangerous secret' that the Jesuit consult of April 24th, 1678, was held in the home of the Duke of York at St. James's Palace. The Jesuits were afraid Godfrey would reveal it, and determined to silence him. Those chosen to murder him were really *Le Faire, Walsh, and Pritchard* – the identical Jesuits mentioned by Bedloe – *and Prance was*

really associated with them in the murder after all. Bedloe
knew just enough about it to denounce them for the reward
of £500. Then Bedloe, who honestly had seen Prance by
the body of Godfrey, denounced him as well. Prance (a
highly astute Jesuit agent) was determined at all costs to
protect Le Faire, Walsh, and Pritchard, the real murderers.
Whereupon he accused three innocent men, Green, Berry,
and Hill, letting the others get away. That, in bald
outline, is the case which has been brilliantly treated elsewhere.

But, first of all, how on earth was Prance protecting Le
Faire, Walsh, and Pritchard by accusing Green, Berry, and
Hill? The first three had already been denounced by
Bedloe; for eight weeks the law had been searching for
them; and, if they could have been found, they would have
been sentenced to death along with the others. At the trial
Bedloe accused them of having planned the death of Godfrey, and they were still in it as deeply as they had ever
been. Prance had thrown no dust in the eyes of the law.
All he did was to kill three men for nothing, for he never
once entered a denial that Le Faire, Walsh, and Pritchard
were concerned in the murder.

Second, if Godfrey was so deep a sympathiser with Coleman that he had already risked his neck to warn Coleman
and the Duke of York, he was not likely to step completely
out of character by informing on them merely because a
consult of priests had met at one place rather than another.
To the contrary, he would not have dared do so, or he would
have convicted himself of misprision of treason. 'How did
you learn that there was to be a consult at St. James's
Palace?' they ask him. Godfrey could not reasonably reply,
'Coleman and I have been intriguing some time in the
Catholic interest; he told me in confidence, after I had
betrayed my duties as a magistrate by warning him to destroy his papers.'

Third, by Godfrey's own words to Thomas Wynnel, this
'dangerous secret' with which he was entrusted could not
have led him to fear violence from the Catholics. On the
contrary, Godfrey said: 'The (Catholic) lords are as inno-

cent as you or I. Coleman will die, but not the lords.
Oates is sworn and is perjured.' Later he said: 'There is a
design against the Duke of York, and this will come to a dispute among them. You may live to see an end on't, but
I shall not. This much I tell you: I am master of a
dangerous secret, and it will be fatal to me.' The key word
is *them*. A dispute among what group of people? Not the
Catholics, who of all people had no design against the Duke
of York. If Godfrey's 'dangerous secret' came from anyone,
it came from Protestants.

All this case is built up on two suppositions: (*a*) that Godfrey, for no reason at all, would betray the friends whom he
had already risked his life to defend, and (*b*) that there was
communicated to him by Coleman a secret so dangerous
that the Jesuits would murder him rather than risk his telling it to anyone. Therefore it all comes down to the question: How dangerous *was* this knowledge that on April 24th
a Jesuit consult had been held at St. James's Palace? And
it has been discovered that the deep secret was no secret at
all. In the year 1680 there was published in London a
pamphlet which openly described the meeting on April
24th.[1] In other words, at precisely the time when the Duke
of York was being most violently attacked, at precisely the
time when – if this theory be correct – his ruin would have
followed the exposure of the secret, the secret was exposed.
And nothing happened; it was not even used against him.
Indeed, such knowledge would have surprised nobody. It
was a very mild piece of information compared to some of
the charges which were made against him.

It is not likely that the Jesuits would have murdered a
magistrate for possessing such an open and even dull secret
as this, any more than it is likely they would have murdered, out of all London, the one magistrate who was
friendly to them. We must put this hypothesis aside, even
though one question still remains unsettled. If Godfrey
really possessed a dangerous secret – and if it was not this
one, but some Protestant secret – what was it?

[1] *A Vindication of the English Catholics.*   See Rev. J. Gerard, *The Popish
Plot and its newest Historian,* 7.

V

That Sir Edmund Godfrey was murdered at the instigation of the Earl of Danby.

This theory, though ingenious, is not only supported by no evidence whatever, but in itself it is a contradiction in terms. Let us suppose that Danby (crying up the plot to keep the Commons from attacking him) assisted Oates, invented lies for Oates, became involved with Oates; that Godfrey discovered this, threatened to expose it, and was therefore murdered by order of the Lord Treasurer.

That Danby cried up the plot there can be no doubt. But this is precisely the flaw in the whole case. So far from being in any danger if it became known that he had abetted Oates, he was actually impeached – and very nearly went to the block – on a charge of *stifling* the plot and discrediting the evidence of Titus Ambrosius. So far from being a menace to him if it became known that he had aided Oates, even that he had told a few whacking lies in Oates's favour, it would have been his salvation. Reduce the matter to plain terms, and see what secret Godfrey could have known about Danby. As early as the arrest of Coleman, it was being charged that Danby had tried to stifle the plot. Suppose, then, that Godfrey had gone to the Attorney-General with some such information as this: 'My Lord Treasurer concocted half of this plot himself, giving assistance to Oates, and he is a traitor.' The Attorney-General would have answered: 'You must not speak so about the Lord Treasurer. If what you say is true, it proves that he is a great patriot, greater than we thought; and that he is helping Dr. Oates to unmask this hellish plot against the king.' Far from wishing to kill Godfrey for any attack of that sort, Danby would have had reason to fall on his neck in an embrace of rapture.

What then remains of any possible motive for Danby to kill Godfrey? We have seen that the other charge, of stifling the plot, is manifest nonsense. Danby himself disposed of it in his speech before the House of Lords, December 23rd, 1678: 'I had the fortune to be particularly instrumental in seizing Mr. Coleman's papers, without which care there had not one of them appeared.' It was Godfrey himself who had concealed the plot. From whichever side we look at the conduct of the Lord Treasurer, we must see that the case against a good servant and a good man is too flimsy for a moment's consideration.

VI

That Sir Edmund Godfrey was murdered by Titus Oates.
Titus Ambrosius is the right villain, but the wrong murderer. He is the right voice, but the wrong hand. However we spin him (like one of the commemorative coins or medals with his own head stamped on it), he gives out a false clink on the counter. Though it is true that the murder of Sir Edmund Godfrey made his fortune and created him the saviour of the nation, he is still the wrong type of man. It rests on a matter of his courage and temperament. It is said that he had the physical courage to endure pain with fortitude, as instanced by the terrible floggings he received after his trial in 1685. But that is altogether a different thing: he knew it was coming to him, he could not escape it, it involved no stand-up-personal-contest with someone else, and his peculiar psychological bent could sustain him in his strong love of the martyr's role. What he lacked was the courage to stand up physically against physical opposition – steel, fists, firearms – in a personal contest.

Consider his history. At St. Omers he had a pan broken over his head, and was beaten round the playground by a much smaller boy, because he had not the courage to strike back. He owned that he could not fire a pistol or touch a sword. When he went out with the soldiers to arrest Jesuits, he hid behind a buttress when there was danger of swordplay. He is always hiding behind somebody's skirts. At the trial of Lord Stafford in 1680 he whined desperately to the judges that the Lieutenant of the Tower, whom he had called a rascal, threatened to break his head. It is significant that the one time in his life when he was known to raise his hand in wrath, and beat someone with a cane, the person he attacked was a woman.

This is the most that can be done by way of refutation, for there is no real evidence to combat. All is, 'Titus might have done this,' which does not go far in the way of proof and is contradicted by his peculiar temperament. On the contrary, if we are to go by what he might have done, it may be argued that – if he had really committed the murder – he would have made much more spectacular work of it. He would have made his murder as sensational as his evidence. At best the verdict on Titus must be 'Not proven', and we must look elsewhere for a murderer.

VII

That Sir Edmund Godfrey hanged himself, and that Titus Oates, who had been shadowing him for purposes of blackmail, came on his body and arranged a 'murder' to give credit to the plot.

Though affording a plausible case, and fitting in much better with Titus's genius, it falls to the ground because of the physical evidence which demonstrates (2) that Godfrey could not possibly have broken his neck by hanging himself with his neckband.

VIII

That Sir Edmund Godfrey was murdered by the friends of Edward Coleman.

It is entirely possible that Godfrey may have been taking bribes of Coleman, and that he was being blackmailed because of it. But here the theory becomes difficult. In fact, the distinguished writer who suggests it does not advance it as a concrete theory, but merely as a general suggestion in which direction the truth *may* lie. As a suggestion, therefore, it cannot be grappled with. What friends of Coleman? What was Godfrey to be asked to do? (see p. 169). Granting that this case must be left out of court because it has not been fully advanced, still the motivation appears somewhat doubtful.   Again reduce it to plain terms.   Any friends or associates of Coleman could not have complained of Godfrey's conduct: in what we know of what he did do, he did even more than might have been expected of him. He warned Coleman; he sent a copy of Oates's depositions to the Duke of York; he did not investigate the case or report to the government, although he thought himself in danger of hanging; in short, either as man or as magistrate, no Jesuit agent could have done more in Coleman's cause.   He could not have 'betrayed' Coleman in any way, since Coleman had already been denounced by Oates.   He could not have helped the Jesuits any further, because it was out of his province.

But this line of thought brings us to one question, which must be answered if we are ever to get a reasonable solution, and this question is perhaps the most puzzling and contradictory feature of the whole case.   The question comes of these two anomalous facts, (a) that Godfrey was the victim of a savage attack, almost the attack of a maniac or a drunken sadist; and (b) that he was coolly kept in captivity for two days, without food, while the whole town was looking for him.   If the maniac merely wanted to kill him, why was he kept in captivity?   If the cool-headed captor wanted him in duress for some deliberate purpose, why – at the end of it – was he murdered in such mad and clumsy fashion as having his neck broken?

It may be said that, whether the murderer was a furious man with a grudge or a cool man with a purpose, the intent was the same: torture.   The man with the grudge locked him up somewhere, beat him and kept him without food, and at the end of it brutally murdered him.   The man with the purpose, in order to make him confess something, kept him in duress and tortured him until – extracting nothing – it was determined to kill him.   But he could not have been physically tortured: if he were physically tortured, certainly it was the queerest kind of torture ever applied to a human being.   The only place his body bore a single mark of beating, aside from the strangling that killed him, was *on the chest*.   His face had no mark of any sort.   No arm or leg was broken, bruised, or wrenched. No mark appeared anywhere else on the body. With all possible methods of third-degree and refined cruelty open to a torturer, we cannot conceive that any man who wished to torture another man would stand there pounding him on the chest and doing nothing else. He would be attempting to cause pain by attacking the one part of the body where pain would be least felt!

Furthermore, this beating on the chest could not have been a continuous beating, carried on over a few days. We can easily perceive that no torturer would confine his activities merely to beating the breast; and we can see just as easily that, if this had been done for some time, there would have been damage to the inner organs of the body which the surgeons would have discovered after death. No such damage was done. The bruises on the chest, then, were the result of a quick and violent attack when Godfrey was set upon.

And here is the discrepancy. He is knocked down, kicked and beaten furiously, and put into captivity. Then, apparently, the murderer goes away and leaves him there – doing nothing for two days. At the end of this time the murderer returns, and (for some reason) flying into the original rage with which he attacked the magistrate, he sets upon him again to break his neck. How is this curious conduct to be explained?

IX

That Sir Edmund Godfrey was murdered by Christopher Kirkby.

The case for Kirkby's guilt is not strong, though it does serve to illustrate one of the points that may lead us towards a solution. The case against him is based entirely on the assumption that Kirkby thought Godfrey a traitor because the magistrate had warned Coleman and the Duke of York: therefore the fanatical Kirkby killed him. But what is the basis for the assumption that Kirkby knew this at all? The all-seeing Oates did not know it; the government did not know it, or Godfrey would have been arrested for misprision of treason, like Coleman; how, then, did Kirkby know it? Even granting that he did know it, would any man have *murdered* Godfrey because of this, when it would have been so much simpler merely to have denounced him to the authorities? Kirkby, his own conduct shows, was a mild and even timid sort of man. If he knew this about Godfrey, he could have seen Godfrey punished – and terribly punished – without the slightest risk to himself, merely by a word to Oates. Oates would have taken care of it with great satisfaction. Kirkby had not previously been behind-hand with making any denunciations, for he had introduced the Popish plot to the king. To point out Godfrey as a fellow-conspirator of Jesuits, to prove the magistrate's guilt, would serve him just as well in what he most hoped to do: convince the king that some plot was brewing.

The fact of his having a suit of clothes like Oates goes for nothing, since it would be of value only if somebody had caught a glimpse of a murderer in such a suit; and there is no evidence to show that anyone did. Equally valueless is the suggestion about the method of the murder, and the reason why Godfrey was kept in captivity without food. We cannot picture so weird a scene: the timid Kirkby setting on a tall, powerful man like Godfrey, battering him round, imprisoning him in a house – and then mildly sitting down to watch Godfrey drink poison so that the victim may die without fuss. It is another contradiction in terms, and one which makes us discard this theory altogether.

The one valuable point in it may be applied to any other private person just as well as Kirkby. That is the point of the mysterious letter, so disturbing to Godfrey and to the members of his household, which arrived on the night before he died. Let it be repeated: it is not conceivable that a minister of state, with Godfrey's death in mind, would write a letter making either a threat or an appointment; he would not be such a fool, considering that the letter might not be destroyed. Nor is it conceivable that hired bravoes would indulge in any such formality; they would wait for their quarry in a dark lane, and seize him: the more unexpectedly,. the better. But it is precisely the course that would be pursued by a private person (and an incautious, fanatical private person) laying a trap. Who, then, wrote that letter?

x

That Sir Edmund Godfrey was murdered at the instiga-tion of the Earl of Shaftesbury.

This deserves to be considered carefully. But, after exam-ining all the evidence, we must acquit Shaftesbury as well – because the crime was not worthy of him. It was too clumsily carried out.

We must not say that a crime was brilliantly managed, and had a brilliant brain behind it, merely because the real truth has never come to light. The identity of Jack the Ripper, for example, has never been discovered; but nobody would maintain that his crimes were managed by a great intellect. If a man ever courted discovery, and only escaped capture by blind luck, it was the Scourge of Whitechapel; and the very slap-dash madness of the murders was the assassin's best safeguard against being caught.

Similarly, we cannot praise Godfrey's murder for the ingenuity of its sham suicide, and say that the thrusting of a sword through the dead body was a subtle trick intended to throw suspicion on wily Jesuits. For one thing must be acknowledged as certain. However Godfrey died, the Catholics were bound to be accused in any case. If he had died peaceably in his bed, of fever or the stone, it would be fixed in the public mind that Catholics had poisoned him. If, in full sight of fifty witnesses, he had slipped on a cobble-stone in the street and broken his neck, it would be believed that the cobblestone was a contrivance of subtle Jesuits. Imagine what taking-off you like, from the sublime to the comic, still the Jesuits would have had the managing of it.

Suppose Shaftesbury had managed the murder. Now, if he really contrived the disposal of the body, then he botched every glowing opportunity. He acted with a moderation, not to say a tameness, which never characterised his be-haviour in any other matter. Is this the man who never does things by halves? Is this the man who arranged that

sensational funeral, who arranged that sensational Pope-
burning, who managed that campaign of propaganda which
outruns modern thrillers for blood and thunder?   What
has he done, by this theory?   On the day Godfrey disap-
pears, Shaftesbury has set moving his whole whispering
organisation, his vast club of tongues, to breathe terrible
rumours concerning the murder of the magistrate by Papists
– with what result?

   With the result that, when the body is found, Shaftesbury
has left not one ghost or shred of manufactured evidence to
show that the magistrate *was* murdered by Papists.   Quite
to the contrary, the coroner's jury almost returned a verdict
of suicide.   Gentlemen, it won't do.   'Quick!' shouts the
pale alarmist; 'oh, friends, come quickly and see the Pope
murdering Justice Godfrey!'   We enter agog, and fearfully.
Yes, but where's the Pope?   Where's the evidence to demonstrate that the Pope was ever here, and that (as the showman
assures us) we don't see him because he has just slipped out
through the back door of the tent?   No rosary left behind?
No scrap of sinister writing?   No gleam from that wagging
mitre?   No bloody dagger with *pax vobiscum* engraved on
it?   My Lord Shaftesbury has given us some noble spectacles in his time.   It is incredible that, on the one occasion
when it was most vital to him to do his best, he failed to
provide any show at all.

   He has even bungled the effect of putting the body in the
right place.   Why has he chosen Primrose Hill – a waste-
ground three miles out of town, certainly not pointing in
the direction of the Papists – when there are a hundred
better places which would irrefutably involve the people he
wanted most to involve?   There is Somerset House, the residence of the queen.   There is St. James's Palace, the residence of the Duke of York, and all the premises round it.
There are the premises round the houses of any leading
Catholics in all London, any of the Jesuits who now repose
in Newgate, any of the people on whom my Lord Shaftesbury was working and praying against with every nerve.
To find the body in any of these places would be to prove
at one stroke what he most wanted to prove.   But no: he

dumps the body down at Primrose Hill – the place to which Godfrey has asked the way on Saturday morning. Shaftesbury must have known that he would not strengthen his case merely by proving a reasonable doubt against it.

It is useless to speak of 'subtlety'. That sort of subtlety is an invention of modern detective-story writers, merely to befool a jaded reader. It would be useless in real life; it was useless in the seventeenth century; it was particularly useless to Shaftesbury, who never in his life worked along those lines. He gave them Thrill, like the Pope-burning processions. What he wanted was flat, staring, plain evidence; what he wanted, like the Fat Boy, was to make their flesh creep. And in his treatment of witnesses, his attempts to get them to swear to one thing or another, he showed it. His wild runnings-about after some clue, his threats to Smug the Blacksmith or Whip the Coachman, showed that he was as puzzled as anyone else. If he had really 'planted' that body on Primrose Hill, he would swiftly have had the body found, he would swiftly have manipulated his evidence: he would, in short, have attained his object of crushing the Duke of York in a fortnight. He did not do it.

Examine also the circumstances of the actual capture and murder of Godfrey:

If Shaftesbury was behind this, we must assume that Godfrey was snared – probably by several people – kept without food, tortured to make him tell something or swear something, and finally murdered. Now, reasons have already been given why it is not altogether convincing to believe that torture was applied. But the great objection lies in whether or not Shaftesbury would have dared to do such a thing – to a man like Godfrey, of all people.

We can judge what a man is likely to do only by what we know he has done. What do we know of Shaftesbury's conduct so far in the case? Did he ever do anything like that, even to the humblest and poorest witness who could never have struck back at him afterwards? He caught the coachman, Francis Corral, and threatened to roll him down a hill in a barrel of nails. Did he do it, or anything like it?

No; he merely sent Corral to Newgate, applying no torture, and let him go later. He made similar threats to the two men who had found the body – and never touched them. He caught Mrs. Judith Pamphlin, and threatened to have her torn to pieces. Did he do it, or apply any force at all? No: he let her go. If there is anything Shaftesbury did throughout the whole course of the case, he kept strictly within the letter of the law. These threats were bluff and bluster. He sent the prisoners to Newgate, he carefully refrained from doing anything to them with his own agents. He acted in this fashion – although to force a confession from any of them, to make them swear according to his orders, was what he most wanted in the world.

If he thought it too risky to apply force to a humble coachman, a blacksmith, and a baker, what must he have thought of applying it to the most famous magistrate in London?

Indeed, it is difficult to see what Shaftesbury could hope to gain by keeping Godfrey in captivity. The only two possible reasons are (a) that he was pressing Godfrey to go out and swear something against the Catholics; or (b) that he was trying to find out the depth of Godfrey's relations with Coleman and the Jesuits. The first reason is dubious. Any captor would be aware that Godfrey might promise to swear anything; but that, the moment pressure was removed, he would walk out of there and tell the whole truth to the authorities – after which, God help the whole Green Ribbon Club. The second reason would be vital and powerful, since Coleman might have betrayed to Godfrey the secret of Coleman's bribes to the Green Ribbon men, and Godfrey therefore constituted an active menace to Shaftesbury: the second reason would be vital and powerful, if it were not for one fact. *The Green Ribbon men did not learn anything of Coleman's relations with Godfrey until the first week in November, more than a fortnight after the murder.* So far as they knew at the time Godfrey was entrapped, he was an ordinary upright justice. True, Godfrey was inclined to discredit Oates's depositions: but that is all the more reason why they could not be so foolish as to think they could get him to swear the reverse, even if they dared to apply to one of the most prominent men in London a pressure they would not exercise on a baker or a blacksmith.

In summing up, then: Shaftesbury did not instigate this murder because in every set of circumstances he must have acted as he had never acted in real life. He steps completely out of character. On the one point where he was always careful and cautious, he acted like a maniac. He would not have a finger laid on Francis Corral, but he would have Sir Edmund Godfrey's neck wrung like a fowl's. On the one point where he was always flamboyant to the point of mania (the arranging of terrifying spectacles, the planting of evidence, the supporting of accusations), he acted rather as though he were trying to conceal the crime than trying to reveal it. He was trying to prove the murder against Catholics – but he left not one shred of evidence against them, even in the place where the body was found.

This leads us to two questions: Why was the crime so clumsily carried out? Why was the body placed on Primrose Hill? They await consideration.

XI

That Sir Edmund Godfrey was murdered by the three men who came to be accused by the government, and who were tried for it on February 10th, 1679.

This need not detain us long. We have listened to the complete evidence at the trial, and it needs no argument here to demonstrate that Green, Berry, and Hill were innocent – as, in fact, Prance later confessed. But it brings us to another of the questions which have been asked at the end of each solution.

Godfrey was a well-known and conspicuous figure: 'a man,' writes one of his contemporaries, 'so remarkable in person and garb that, described at Wapping, he would not be mistaken at Westminster.' Furthermore, 'his daily custom was to go about alone, creeping at all hours in lanes and alleys, as his fancy *or occasions* led him.' His gold hatband, his tall stooped figure, his hooked nose and black garb, were as familiar in the streets as a caricature. This outstanding figure was missing for five days, and all London was looking for him. For at least – at very least – two days, he was kept alive without food in someone's house. Whose house? Where could he have been kept?

Somerset House was, of course, chosen for political reasons in the trial of Green, Berry, and Hill. We know the prisoner could not have been kept there, but it is important that we find a direction in which to look. So we come at last to

XII

That Sir Edmund Godfrey was murdered for a private reason, by a private person who was not suspected at the time.

Here we are apparently left in vagueness, for nothing is suggested. Before we can look for actual evidence of this, we must have a contention to support: we must have a candidate. We start only with the suggestion that some private person – alone and unaided – murdered Godfrey. We do this, on slender first grounds, because of the letter.

That letter has kept bobbing up throughout the case, and we cannot over-estimate its importance. Godfrey's household did not over-estimate its importance: they considered it the key to the case. Godfrey did not over-estimate it: for just after he had received it on Friday evening, he flew into all that wild behaviour at Welden's house. It has been indicated that a minister of state would not have written a letter of the sort we infer this to be, because the minister would not be such a fool; a hired bravo would not have written it, because his whole success would lie in the unexpectedness with which he struck from a dark lane. Neither sort would send a threat or a challenge. No group of men would send a threat or a challenge. It is the conduct of an angry and incautious private person acting alone, without the advice of a wiser head. Granting for the moment that this is merely a cloudy hypothesis, let us see where it leads. On the physical facts which have been presented, let us build up a picture of the murderer – and then see whether there is any proof for it.

At the conclusions of certain of the theories here outlined, certain inferences drawn from the evidence have been presented in the form of questions. Those questions can now be rearranged and restated in groups, with any further questions which arise of themselves, to give us assistance in looking for the murderer. Once we answer them, we shall have at least a picture of him, and we shall know in what direction to look for evidence.

A

1. Why was Godfrey the victim of such a savage attack?
2. Why was the crime so clumsily carried out?
3. Why was the body placed on Primrose Hill?

It is the third of these questions which gives us a starting-point. On Saturday, October 12th, Godfrey went out of his house and inquired the way to Primrose Hill. He walked there; he came back to town—and in town he disappeared. He did not kill himself on Primrose Hill, as we know: he was killed somewhere three miles away, and his body carried there. Why? How and why did the murderer come to choose the very place to which Godfrey walked on Saturday morning? It cannot be coincidence. And the clear answer is: The murderer wished it to be thought that Godfrey had really committed suicide on Primrose Hill.

The report that he had asked the way there – with the intention of suicide, everyone feared – was freely bruited about when Godfrey's disappearance was publicly announced at a funeral on Tuesday. This gave the murderer his cue. And thus we come immediately to the second question: Why was the crime so clumsily carried out? The circumstances fit in with the clumsy contrivance of taking the body to Primrose Hill. The neckband with which he had been strangled was cut away, and the collar buttoned up in the forlorn, foolish hope that nobody would pay great attention to such a thing. The sword was run through him in the hope that it would be thought a suicide.

Thus the crime becomes no 'subtle' trick, but the act of a wild and not over-bright person acting in fright or fury after the murder has been committed. It fits in with the hypothesis that a man who would write a threat or a challenge in a letter would be this sort of man. And it fits in with the first question in the group, Why was Godfrey the victim of such a savage attack? We may do well to look for someone of muddled and almost maniacal head, who set on him in that mad fashion. At this point (still granting that this is pure hypothesis), we are justified in assuming that such an attack was the result of a personal grudge or hatred. Again, we may safely say that this person must have been a large and powerful man. Godfrey, though old, was still resolute and powerful himself; he did not fear anyone who came fairly at him.

Now, what manner of man can we look for – rich man, poor man, beggar man, thief? Godfrey had dealings, in his magisterial duties, with all of them. In the groups of questions the next may supply a hint as to this.

B

1. What is the significance of the wax-stains on his clothes?
2. What is the significance of the polished shoes?
3. Where could the murderer have kept him in captivity?

It has been established that wax candles were used only by priests or by noblemen and people of quality. As a starting-point, to see where this leads, let it be supposed that the murderer might have been a nobleman, and that the wax candles were used in his house.

What about the polished shoes? It might have been an ingenious trick, by which the murderer gave a fresh gloss and polish to the dead man's shoes just before throwing him into the ditch, in order to prove that he could not have

walked to Primrose Hill and thus destroying the effect of
the sham suicide as it was meant to be destroyed. If this
is the case, it puts our present theory out of court: we are
assuming that the murder was done by a muddle-headed
assassin who wanted the death to be supposed a suicide.
But examine it again. Now, if the murderer polished the
dead man's shoes, it must have been done in the house where
Godfrey was kept, both before and after he was murdered.
The polishing must have been done before the body was
bundled into a coach and taken to Primrose Hill; we cannot believe that the murderer would gallantly carry brushes
and blacking along with him, and stand on a dark night
fumbling with the shoes on Primrose Hill.

There is testimony that for that entire week the weather
had been bad, and it was continually raining. We must
furthermore be certain that the body was carried to Primrose Hill by night, since the place was too exposed for even
the most foolish murderer to have taken a tolerably large
and cumbersome corpse across such fields by day. In the
ordinary course of events, then – if the body had been taken
to Primrose Hill and flung down somewhere – in a very few
hours the state of the weather would have got both Godfrey's
shoes and his clothes so soaked and sodden that nobody on
earth would have been able to tell whether the shoes had
ever been polished in their history. It might even be several days before he was found: and the rain went on. If you
meditated taking a body out into the open fields in stormy
weather, would you think that a brilliant polish on the
shoes would last long enough to let shrewd detectives
notice it?

By the sheerest accident, the magistrate's body was flung
into the one ditch so covered with brambles and bushes that
neither his shoes nor his clothes were wet. If we assume
that the murderer chose that ditch deliberately, so that the
rain would not splash up the polish, we must assume that
on a dark night: carrying the body of a tall old man: roam-
ing loose on several acres of bad ground, the murderer
searched until he found a suitable ditch into which he could
be certain no drop of rain would fall. This is making too

much of too little.   This is the subtlety of the modern detective-story (not the seventeenth-century) carried to a point
where it cannot be believed even of a murderer in a book.
If a criminal indulged in any such elaborate hocus-pocus,
in order to prove that this death was not suicide and throw
suspicion on the Catholics, he would have left some other
clue which really would throw suspicion on them.

No: the most natural course of events is that Godfrey's
shoes were polished just before he was entrapped into the
murderer's house.   He would not walk in them or get them
soiled when he lay in captivity, nor would he take much
pedestrian exercise after he was dead.   On Saturday morning he had taken a walk in the fields round Primrose Hill,
where he had got his shoes into a clogged and miry state,
and, after he returned to town, he got them polished just
before his 'appointment' with the murderer.   This is
entirely reasonable, but there is still another cause to suspect it.   Why, in addition to ordinary fastidiousness, should
he get his shoes polished?   Well, remember that – just
before he went out of his own house on Saturday morning –
he started to put on his best coat.   After hesitating, he
changed his mind and said his ordinary coat would serve
the day well enough.   But why did he want his best coat?
For the same reason that he did not want his shoes clogged
to the tops with mud: because he was going to a nobleman's
house.

Candles, coat, and shoes conspire in favour of this suggestion.   Let us look on to the third question: Where could
the murderer have kept him in captivity?   There is certainly a direction in which to look, the only clue we have
after Godfrey's disappearance.   He was reported to have
been traced by another magistrate to a place in St. Giles's,
very close to a mansion in – Leicester Fields.   Leicester
Fields contains a number of noblemen's houses, and it is
curious how Leicester Fields recurs in scraps of evidence.
For there is another reference to it by the testimony of someone else as well.   On the afternoon of Thursday, October
17th, a few hours before the body was found, Mr. Adam
Angus was accosted in a bookshop near St. Paul's by a

mysterious young man – never identified – who said: 'Have
you heard the news? Sir Edmund Godfrey has been found
in Leicester Fields, near the Dead Wall, with his own sword
run through him.'[1]

This statement, of course, was incorrect about the place,
but uncannily accurate about two details: the sword, and
the fact that it was Godfrey's *own* sword. The latter is
important. When you report the murder of someone, it is
customary to assume that it is somebody else's sword which
has been used. If this is a coincidence, it is surprising
enough; but what if that man knew something of the real
murder? What if it had been originally intended to throw
the body near the Dead Wall in Leicester Fields; but that
the intention was altered? The man, not actually a party
to the murder, knows that much and cannot refrain from
creating a sensation with what he believes to be the truth.

In any case, if there is anywhere in this business a certain
nobleman (1) with a strong personal grudge against Godfrey, (2) of savage and muddle-headed disposition, to make
the most of any wrath, (3) of powerful physical build, (4) living in Leicester Square, (5) addicted to assaults of just this
description, then we should at least have a man under strong
suspicion.

There is such a person.

Mention has been made before of the murder of one
Nathaniel Cony, in a tavern in the Haymarket, on February 4th, 1678. The circumstances were these. Nathaniel
Cony, a man of good family and apparently a gambler with
false dice, was returning from the City late in the evening
of Sunday, February 3rd, with a friend of his named Henry
Goring. Both were very drunk. With the elaborate
courtesy of the thoroughly boozy, Cony insisted on accom-
panying Goring to the latter's lodgings; but on the way, he
said, they must stop and take a last bottle at Long's Tavern.
They had to knock heavily in order to gain admittance, for
the hour was late. When they got inside, Goring was so
drunk that he could not stand up. While they were taking
the last bottle, the door of an adjoining room opened, and

[1] Testimony of Adam Angus, *L'Estrange*, III. 88.

a particularly drunken young nobleman – who had been
tippling there with three of his rollicking acquaintances –
poked his head out. The peer was acquainted with Cony,
and invited him to join them. Had he a friend there?
Well, bring the friend along. Cony and Goring joined the
other four, and more bottles were produced. Whereupon
Goring, growing quarrelsome, became involved in a hot
dispute with the nobleman. 'My name is better than yours,'
Goring tells his Lordship, and, 'I am a better gentleman
than you': whereupon my Lord throws a glass of wine in
his face, and draws his sword. My lord's friends intervened,
and thrust a protesting Goring out of the room without his
hat, sword, or periwig. Just as he was being thrust out,
Nathaniel Cony entered what seems to have been a com-
paratively mild protest, 'Sir, why do you put my friend out
of the room?'

At this point, for no discernible reason, my Lord flew into
one of those maniacal rages which he had shown before, and
was to show afterwards. He flung on Cony. He knocked
Cony to the floor, either with a clip across the ear or a mere
swing of his hand – witnesses were not sure which – and
proceeded to *stamp on his breast*. One witness admitted
that he lifted his foot 'to a pretty height' in order to do it.
Afterwards Cony was laid unconscious across some chairs,
and my Lord staggered out without apparently thinking any
more of the matter.

Of the injuries he received that night, Cony died on
February 10th, 1678. Three jurors who viewed the body at
the coroner's inquest gave evidence at the trial of the nobleman for murder. Thus:

Attorney-General: Did you see the body of Mr. Cony
after he was dead?

William Brown: Yes, my lord, I was one of the coroner's
inquest, which after view of the body went into another
house. But some of us, seeing the body swelled at that
rate as it was, and being unsatisfied of the cause, went
back again to look upon it, and there I saw upon his right
breast a great black bruise; and I looked upon the caul,

which was all wasted away; and on the left side again a
great black spot, and in the bottom of his belly a quantity
of very ill-looked blood.

Attorney-General: When was this you saw it?   What
day?   How long after his death?

William Brown: The day after he died.

The witness added that he was 'black and blue in divers
places'.   And again:

Attorney-General: Richard Wheeler, pray tell my lord
what you know.

Richard Wheeler: My lord, I was summoned upon the
jury by the coroner, and according to my duty I made
such an inspection as I could into the body.   I did observe
upon his right breast a very black and very great bruise,
and on the left side of his belly a very black and very great
bruise, which was indeed of another-guise colour than
that of settled blood, for I have of my own knowledge had
a sad experience of that kind.

Thomas Roberts also swore to this.   The evidence was
clear enough, and the nobleman who had kicked Cony to
death in this fashion was brought to trial before the House
of Lords.

*The man who caused this nobleman to be indicted for
murder was Sir Edmund Berry Godfrey.*

*And the nobleman was Shaftesbury's friend – the young
Earl of Pembroke.*

.   .   .   .

Philip Herbert, Earl of Pembroke and Montgomery –
who has figured before in this chronicle – was 'a madman
when he was sober and a homicidal lunatic when he was
not', one of the few evil products of an illustrious and
honourable name.   He was only twenty-five when he murdered Cony, and he died, of furious drinking, at thirty.   He
became seventh earl at the death of his elder brother in
1674; he married Henriette de Kéroualle, sister of the
Duchess of Portsmouth; and he was so notorious that nobody would sit near him in a tavern.   One of the most signi-

ficant things at his trial for the murder of Cony was the statement of Cony's brother, who attended the dying man from February 4th onwards. He testified: 'One day when Dr. Conquest came out of his (Nathaniel Cony's) chamber, he seemed to be in a huff, and said he was only kept there to do the drudgery; and when I asked him what he thought of my brother, he answered me short, *I cannot tell whether it be a Pembroke-kick or no.*'

Therefore it may be taken as probable that the 'Pembroke attack' was not unknown as a style of onslaught, and the 'Pembroke-kick' no unfamiliar thing. It is certain that his customary behaviour was familiar. On February 5, 1678 – just one day after his attack on Cony – a certain Mr. Philip Ricaut sent a petition to the House of Lords. And the petition was that he might be protected from Pembroke. The petition ran:[1]

'That he (Philip Ricaut) being to visit a friend last Saturday in the evening, whilst he was at the door taking his leave, the Earl of Pembroke coming by, came up to the door, and with his fist, without any provocation, struck the said Philip Ricaut such a blow upon the eye as almost knocked it out; and then fell upon him with such violence that he almost stifled him with the violence of his grip in the dirt,' – here we appear to have a little strangling – 'and likewise his Lordship drew his sword,' – sword-drawing is next in order – 'and was in danger of killing him, had he not slipped into the house, and the door been shut upon him. The said Ricaut humbly begs that this House will be an asylum to him and give him leave to proceed against the Earl of Pembroke as the law shall direct.'

Altogether, 1678 was a bad year for Pembroke. In January he was imprisoned in the Tower for using 'blasphemous words', and was released on a petition to the House of Lords. On Saturday, February 2nd (as soon as he got out of jail) there occurred this attack on Ricaut. On the night of Sunday, February 3rd, he attacked Cony and stamped on his chest. We may be justified in assuming that the two events came in a continuation of the same furious spree, and that

[1] *House of Lords' Journals*, XIII, Feb. 5, 1678.

he probably had no recollection of what he had been doing: for he spoke no word in his own defence at the trial, did not offer to explain or describe what happened at the tavern, and did not question any of the witnesses for the prosecution.

Now, in 1678, to indict a peer of the realm for murder required no little degree of courage. Peers of the realm were too powerful and influential. The indictment was made by a Middlesex jury of gentlemen headed by Sir Edmund Godfrey. The head of a group like this had duties that were not merely nominal, like those of a present jury: Godfrey, in his capacity as magistrate, acted as both prosecutor and detective. His was the responsibility. He was the prosecutor who brought Pembroke to trial. The blame, if blame existed, lay on his head. Whether Godfrey thought he had anything to fear may be deduced from the sequel.

By reason of this indictment, Pembroke was brought to trial before the House of Lords on Thursday, April 4th, 1678. How exactly Cony's injuries were like those of Sir Edmund Godfrey may be indicated from the defence Pembroke's witnesses made. The defence maintained that Cony died a natural death, of excessive drinking, and that there were no bruises at all. 'As to the matter of the (black) blood,' said a Mr. Raven, apparently a physicion, 'that was not an extraordinary thing, for it is known to physicians that in all natural deaths, there must be extravastated blood in the lower belly.' In short, the defence maintained what many people maintained later concerning the death of Sir Edmund Godfrey.

Pembroke was found guilty – not of murder, but of manslaughter. Whereupon he instantly pleaded his right of Benefit of Clergy, and he walked out of court a free man. The Lord High Steward granted him that pardon as his right, but he added these significant words:

'But your Lordship must give me leave to tell you that no man can have the benefit of that statute but once; and so I would have your Lordship take notice of it, as a caution to you for the future.'

What did Godfrey think of this acquittal, when he had

brought about the indictment? We know what he did. In that same month of April, just after Pembroke was discharged, Godfrey left the country. He stayed out of England until late in the summer, travelling on the Continent. In other words – though he was not a rich man, and not accustomed to do such things – he left his business and took a four months' holiday.[1] He had no partner in his business. In fact, a business man who did that nowadays would be likely to invite some comment, not to say investigation.

In other words, we have two murders in the same year, with injuries to the chest which are precisely the same, although stamping on the breast is not a common form of attack: and we have both of them committed on a man who had in some fashion offended the Earl of Pembroke. If this is a coincidence, it is a very long one. How else do the conditions we have outlined fit this particular candidate?

He was of the muddle-headed sort; he was also tall and very powerful. A lampooning pamphlet, published to commemorate another of his escapades in 1680, is called, 'Great News from Saxony, Or, A New and Strange Relation of a Mighty Giant Koorbmep.' (Read 'Koorbmep' backwards; it is always spelled thus in the House of Lords Journals.) Above all, he lived in Leicester Fields. The Calendar of State Papers, Domestic, for February 26, 1680, contains the entry: 'Mrs. Hunt, that long has been suspected to keep a bawdy-house near the Earl of Pembroke's house in Leicester Fields, was the same day at Hicks' Hall convicted of being a bawd, and will shortly receive her punishment.' It is not stated whether the complaint was lodged by Pembroke himself, though this may be accounted as very doubtful: but we may remember the persistent rumour, going round at the time of Godfrey's disappearance, that the magistrate had been seen in a bawdy-house. This, however, is not important and probably means nothing. What *is* important is that in Shaftesbury's MSS. there is a report from another magistrate that the last time Godfrey was seen

---

[1] Tuke, *Memoirs*, 52-3, states that this was for the benefit of his health. It would appear only too true. (Quoted in Pollock, 89.)

alive he was seen in the neighbourhood of a house in St. Giles's,[1] *close to Pembroke's house in Leicester Fields.*

Finally, would Pembroke have been apt to write a note, asking Godfrey to meet him somewhere on the Saturday? Does it fit in with what we know of his conduct? It not only fits in, but it can be demonstrated that he was in that habit of doing just such a thing, and that he did it in November 1678. He sent word to Lord Dorset, with whom he was having a squabble, asking Dorset to meet him for a friendly bottle under amicable circumstances. In the House of Lords' Journals for November 27th, 1678, appears the following account of what happened then:

'The Earl of Dorset gave the House an account that on Wednesday last, late at night, the Earl of Pembroke sent one Mr. Lloyd, who told him that the Earl of Pembroke desired him to speak with him at Mr. Locket's house. The Earl of Dorset asked whether the Earl of Pembroke was sober, and was answered yes. And when his lordship came, he found the Earl of Pembroke in a low room, who told him that he had done him an injury; therefore he would fight him.' Fight? says Dorset. When? Where? *Now*, says Pembroke – and went for him. His assault was so violent that both the messenger and a footman had to intervene, and disarm him.

Before the House of Lords, Pembroke replied to the charge that he 'remembered no such thing'. It is quite possible that he told the truth, as we have before suspected; and that he had no recollection of it afterwards. But here is still another curious parallel to the Godfrey case. It is as though every fact of Godfrey's murder had been acted out, at another time, to give an indication of the murderer's character and habits. If these things are *still* coincidences, if chance can still work out these permutations and combinations, we have reached a point of the supernatural.

---

[1] 'Once more, there is an extract from a letter by Hariot, Godfrey's colleague on Pembroke's Grand Jury, amongst the Shaftesbury papers. The letter was addressed to Charles Cheyne, M.P. for Great Marlow, and states that Hempson (another colleague) had given him information of a man who followed Godfrey on the day he was missing, and "housed him in St. Giles's". . . . Why is the rest of that letter missing!' – J. G. Muddiman, *The Mystery of Sir E. B. Godfrey, National Review*, September, 1924.

Under these circumstances, an attempt must be made now to reconstruct what happened,[1] to see if it will fit in with the further facts of the case, and answer the group of questions which remain unanswered. These questions are:

C

1. What was the 'dangerous secret'?
2. Why was Godfrey kept for two days without food?
3. How can we explain the contradictory points that the murderer has first set on him and beaten him savagely; then gone away and left him for two days, and finally, coming back again, set on him for the second time and broken his neck?

The points of the dangerous secret, and of the justice's

---

[1] One version of what happened – assuming Pembroke to have been the murderer – has been set forth by Mr. Muddiman. This suggestion is that in the disposal of the body Pembroke was assisted by a butcher of St. Giles's named Edward Linnet, who carried the body to Primrose Hill in his cart. It is believed that Linnet himself later 'found' the body in the company of Bromwell and Walters, but that Shaftesbury conveniently forbore to question him, and left him out of it altogether. Afterwards there was a conspiracy of silence on the part of the court and the authorities, although they knew quite well who had committed the murder; and that the Duchess of Portsmouth used her influence to get his pardon when he later got into trouble over an affair at Turnham Green. Finally, when Sir Roger L'Estrange (in the reign of James the Second) came to write of the case, he tried hard to prove that the death was suicide in order to keep Pembroke's secret, and never included mention of the circumstances that Linnet 'found' the body, that the wheel-marks in the lane were those of a cart rather than a coach, that traces of hay were found there, or any evidence which would at all point towards the real murderer.

Though this is vouched for by an account written by William Griffith, Secretary to Henry Coventry, it is difficult for one person at least to believe. It is difficult to believe that the whole church was singing in this fashion. It is difficult to believe that the whole army went out of step in order to match the pace of one tipsy corporal. Pembroke was a Protestant Whig. He would hardly have been shielded by a whole battalion of Catholic Tories, especially the Tories who were so harassed with accusations that to prove a Protestant Whig guilty of the murder would have been to burst the whole sham of the Popish plot.

It is especially difficult to believe that the furious Tory L'Estrange – writing in the reign of James the Second – would have suppressed such evidence, or that he could have done so if he wished. The most vital testimony in the case cannot have disappeared so completely, so that nobody else ever heard of it. It does not seem to have been mentioned anywhere else. In short, L'Estrange could not have falsified *all* the records, when so many were alive to speak differently. Nor does it seem plausible that James the Second (of all people) would have gone to such extreme lengths to protect the memory of one of Shaftesbury's anti-Catholic friends and henchmen.

being kept for two days without food as though to get information from him, would seem at first glance not to fit in at all with the hypothesis of a murderer who killed furiously for private vengeance. They would seem rather to belong to the hypothesis of political guilt on Green Ribbon men's part. Yet it is just possible that these ostensible contradictions form really the key which will unlock the whole mystery.

On Friday evening, October 11th, Godfrey receives a letter from Pembroke: that is our theory. This letter contains either (a) a threat or challenge, or (b) an invitation making an appointment. The probabilities are strongly in favour of the latter. Pembroke may have determined to have his revenge (if only to the extent of a beating within an inch of the magistrate's life); but he would not forget those ominous words of the Lord High Steward at his trial: 'No man can have the benefit of that statute,' pardon by Benefit of Clergy, 'but once; and so I would have your Lordship take notice of it, as a caution to you for the future.' More probably, then, the letter was couched in terms of an invitation: 'Come and crack a bottle and forget old scores,' or 'I have something of the most vital importance to communicate to you as a justice of the peace.' The latter of these two suppositions again is much the more probable; it would be precisely the bait to fetch Godfrey.

Whereupon we come to the objection to this. We ask: Whether it was a challenge to an appointment that Godfrey received, or a shrewdly worded invitation to entrap him, *why did the damned fool go?* If it was a threat, and he must support his conscience by going, why not take along a couple of constables? Not even the most conscientious justice of the peace would ever outside Bedlam be fool enough to go alone: he would probably not go at all. If he received a honeyed invitation, he would never have been dupe enough to walk into the obvious trap of a notorious killer who had a grudge against him. In either case, why did he go?

Which is the point of the whole case. If Godfrey had been in the position of an ordinary justice of the peace –

concerned with Pembroke alone, and Pembroke's personal vengeance – having nothing else on his mind but that – he would never have thought of keeping such appointment. But Godfrey was not in that position.   Quite to the contrary, he was the most worried man in England.   He feared he was going to be hanged for suppressing evidence of Oates's plot, for being found out as Coleman's associate, for every branch of fear that sprang from these.   He was in possession of a dangerous political secret.   Never mind for the moment what that secret was, since it did not concern Pembroke: but he had the secret, and it was dangerous to him.

At this point he receives a letter from Pembroke asking him to come somewhere for a meeting.   *As Pembroke,* the man is too dangerous a playmate for a quiet chat.   But this is the Earl of Pembroke, a close follower of Shaftesbury, a close follower of the man who is taking up the Plot, a close follower of the man who is most dangerous to the magistrate who sympathises with Coleman!   Is Shaftesbury's hand to be seen in this letter?   Godfrey must wonder that to the point of torture.   And if (as seems overwhelmingly probable) the dangerous secret was a statement from Coleman of the fact that the Green Ribbon leaders had been taking bribes from France, then Godfrey's perplexity may be understood.   Is this letter an invitation from the Green Ribbon leader: a threat, an offer of a bribe, something that will get Godfrey out of this mess or get him deeper into it? In any case, he must set his worries at rest by knowing the best or the worst.   He must go to that appointment and find out his fate.

He is worried on every score.   For he is afraid (which is true) that this is a trap of Pembroke's; but he must know. So far as we have any knowledge, Shaftesbury did not at this date know Godfrey was associated with Coleman; he did not learn it until the first week in November.   But how was Godfrey to be aware of that, when he received an invitation?

If we accept this explanation of the letter, it explains every one of the contradictory facts.   It explains Godfrey's tortured cry when he received the letter, 'I don't know what to make of it!' It explains his conduct among his friends at Welden's house that night. Although he uttered dark prophecies and predicted death to himself, he still would not drop any hint of where he was going or why he was going: he dared not. 'Will you come to dinner to-morrow?' 'I cannot tell yet,' says Godfrey grimly: for he knew that the invitation might be a device of Pembroke, or it might be an offer to have business-dealings with Shaftesbury. He has got to risk it.

On the following morning he rises early, and calls for his best coat. But he takes it off again, and wears his ordinary one. The doubt in his mind has kept him up all night, restless and terrorised. He dare not even take a constable along with him to a meeting such as this. There is always the worst fear of all: that both Shaftesbury and Pembroke may have designs against him, that he may be trapped either way. There is a potential murderer on each side of him. But he is drawn by the most powerful of human lures – he must know what is happening, one way or the other. One expedient remains to him. At the last minute, he may flee out of the country, as he did before. And hence the very large (the too large, for ordinary purposes) sum of money he puts into his pockets.

Yet, after going to Primrose Hill to walk and wrestle with his problems, he keeps the appointment. . . .

Here we must get into surmise for which there is no chapter and verse whatever, not even an indication. But he vists Pembroke, he is conveyed by secret means into Pembroke's house, perhaps into a cellar or some other secret place. We have never yet met Pembroke when he was not drunk; and at least it is extremly probable that he was drunk for his meeting with the justice. Pembroke has acted on his own grudge; Shaftesbury knows nothing of this. Whereupon, after wild talk, Pembroke sets on the magistrate. He does not kill him. He beats him insensible, as he beat Cony. Then – in the course of another of those sprees, exactly like the long one of the previous winter, in which he attacked Ricaut and Cony on successive days – he does what he did before: staggers away from the place. He locks up the unconscious magistrate in a cellar in his own house, with a couple of waxlights burning beside him, and goes out to continue a happy and uproarious brawl.

This is Saturday. There is a very terrible awakening on Monday evening or Tuesday morning, when he comes to his senses again. In his cellar, locked up where nobody can get at him, is the magistrate for whom all London is looking. If that magistrate gets out now, there is genuine trouble in store for his Lordship. Matters are not sweetened by a talk with the weak and bruised justice, who is now at a point of fury and collapse from his two days without food. Pembroke might still avert trouble for himself; after all, he is a peer of the realm and wields mighty influences. But he does the foolish thing. He flies into another of his tempers, and lays hold of the magistrate's neckband. . . .

When it is all over, he attempts to think what must be done. In a genuine ague of terror now (and possibly with the assistance of one of his retainers), he determines to arrange a 'suicide' – the body to be flung out by the Dead Wall[1] in Leicester Fields, with the magistrate's own sword run through it. But that is too close to home, and a better notion is conceived when the news is spread abroad (on Tuesday) that Godfrey inquired the way to Primrose Hill on the previous Saturday. Here is a miraculous help, for talk of suicide is in the air. The body is conveyed to Primrose Hill, probably on Wednesday night. But the whole scheme is managed in the clumsy fashion we have observed,

---

[1] I have tried without success to discover definitely where this 'Dead Wall' was. Charles Lethbridge Kingsford's *Early History of Piccadilly, Soho, Leicester Square, and their Neighbourhood*, makes no mention of it – under that name at least – although it was evidently well known at the time. Mr. Charles W. F. Goss, of the London and Middlesex Archaeological Society, conjectures by references in Kingsford (53-59) that it may have been the high brick wall to the north, enclosing the Military Yard, shown in Faithorne's plan of 1658. Mr. Goss, to whom I am much indebted, adds: 'This wall of the Military Yard may have been in existence as late as Godfrey's time.' There is, of course, no certainty. But if this were really the wall, it would be the most reasonable choice for anyone living in Leicester Fields, since it faced the new and unfinished neighbourhood of Soho. Godfrey's body could be deposited there without great danger of observation to those who carried it, yet at the same time it would be sure to be discovered within a short time.

THE MURDER OF SIR EDMUND GODFREY

and one of the great riddles of history is propounded by a
half-stupefied young man who only wishes to get rid of a
cumbersome corpse.

That Philip Herbert, Earl of Pembroke, murdered Sir
Edmund Godfrey may be the solution of the riddle. We
cannot say it is: we do not know, and we shall never know.
Certainly we are never likely to learn the full details. Then,
too, there will always be questions. Did Shaftesbury know
about it? Did Shaftesbury set him on? The most probable
supposition is that Shaftesbury knew nothing of it at the
time of the murder; but that he learned of it afterwards,
after the disposal of the body, when it was too late to arrange
any great spectacle according to the Green Ribbon leader's
taste; and thus he prevented any inquiry into Pembroke's
slap-dash methods. But the end, as the end of all things,
must still be a riddle. And there is one writer at least, if
he were ever by any inconceivable chance carried to a state
of beatitude t'other side the Styx, there is one writer at
least whose first question of Charon would be –

AFTERWORD
by Douglas G. Greene

Did Philip Herbert, seventh Earl of Pembroke murder Justice Godfrey?

During the half century since the publication of *The Murder of Sir Edmund Godfrey*, some of Carr's conclusions based on the physical evidence have had to be modified. In a 1952 BBC radio broadcast, Professor C. Keith Simpson, a pathologist, analyzed the original post mortem report (unseen by Carr) and determined that Godfrey had been dead for at least five days before the body was discovered, and therefore that there was no period of captivity. In addition, Simpson pointed out that the post mortem showed no evidence that Godfrey had been starved. This conclusion is confirmed in notes made during the post mortem, recently discovered by Stephen Knight and reproduced in his *The Killing of Justice Godfrey* (1984). Moreover, according to Simpson, seventeenth-century assertions that Godfrey's neck was broken do not hold up to modern analysis. This is an important, perhaps a crucial, observation, for Carr's main argument against suicide and in favor of murder was the broken neck (pp. 314–315).

Are we, then, back to the suicide theory? Did Godfrey hang himself? Both King Charles and his brother James believed that Godfrey died by his own hand, and the seventeenth-century journalist Roger L'Estrange was quite certain of the fact. Their opinion cannot easily be dismissed, for they knew the actors in the drama and were in a position to evaluate character and opportunity. On this hypothesis, the events go in the manner of Carr's theory II (pp. 154–159), with a few minor modifications. Of a melancholy disposition and faced with possible charges of treason for having informed Coleman of Oates's information, Godfrey committed suicide. His brothers somehow came across the body, and fearful of losing his estate to the crown, kept it hidden for five days. After they heard the rumors that he had been murdered, or perhaps after they started the rumors themselves, they arranged the body to make it look like murder. When they went before the Privy Council, they were at pains to claim that Sir Edmund's death could not be suicide; it was, they said, clearly a Papist murder. The comments of Sir Robert Southwell, Clerk of the Council, make it plain that Godfrey's brothers were interested in saving the estate. In short, their statements were at the least self-serving and possibly suspicious in their eagerness to foster the idea of murder.

But despite finding that Godfrey's neck was not broken, Professor Simpson still believes that Godfrey was murdered. The bruises on the body, he argues, could not have been from hypostasis but from a beating. Moreover, the location of the marks on the neck was inconsistent with

Godfrey's having died from hanging; they were low on the neck, but hanging leaves marks near the jaw. Godfrey, Simpson concludes, was strangled by a cord or cloth, probably the missing cravat. In summary, although there have been new interpretations of the physical evidence, Carr's contention that Godfrey was murdered remains valid.

Except for the possibility of suicide, there has been little additional discussion of the various theories that Carr outlined in his "Interlude for Connoisseurs in Murder." It should be pointed out, however, that K. H. D. Haley (*The First Earl of Shaftesbury*, 1968) dismisses claims that Shaftesbury may have instigated the murder because "the Earl, being in Dorset at the time, can hardly have been directly involved." No evidence has ever been found against Shaftesbury anyway, and as Carr demonstrates the murder was completely out of character. But the matter is worth mentioning because Carr's method of telling the story—combining conversations from various times and placing them in connection with the events of the Popish Plot—can be misleading, especially when he has the king and others talking with Shaftesbury in London when in fact the earl was far away.

In a recent book on the crisis begun by Godfrey's death, *The Popish Plot* (1972), John Kenyon makes a new suggestion. Although he admits that "no one would call it a contribution towards solving the murder," his idea is provocative and reminds us that we too often make the mistake of assuming that an event which had important results must have had an important cause or at least involved important people. Kenyon suggests that an unknown footpad may have had a grievance against Godfrey, probably for the same reason suggested as a motive for the Earl of Pembroke: Godfrey in his position of magistrate had acted against him. This criminal, unconnected with any of the political events, beat Godfrey, and then, realizing that he had been recognized, strangled him. The sword thrust was "a clumsy attempt at mystification." Godfrey, Kenyon continues, was not robbed because the footpad did not want the authorities to look for an ordinary thief. Perhaps with his family's help, he kept the body hidden for four to five days until he could obtain a cart to transport it to Primrose Hill.

Kenyon's theory leaves much unanswered. It doesn't explain any of Godfrey's actions or statements before his disappearance, and its explanation of the sword thrust is unconvincing. How was it supposed to mystify anybody? Kenyon does not answer the question, but we might suggest that the murderer stabbed Godfrey to suggest that the magistrate had commited suicide by falling on his own sword. That explanation, however, seems too clever by half, especially if the crime was committed by an uneducated footpad. Nor does it seem likely that a professional criminal would have ignored the opportunity of robbing the body of its valuables. The body was not robbed because, as contemporaries knew, the murderer was someone who did not need the money. That fact and the wax drippings are strong indications that Godfrey was killed by someone connected with the upper classes.

Now at last we come to an evaluation of the Muddiman-Carr theory pinning the murder on the Earl of Pembroke. Several objections have been offered:

1) Kenyon says that "it does not explain how he was kept, where or why, from October 12th, when he disappeared, until the 17th, when he was found on Primrose Hill, clearly having just been dumped there. It would have been very difficult for Pembroke to hide him at his house in Leicester Fields without his servants knowing or suspecting something." It's possible, he continues, that Pembroke concealed the body elsewhere, "but all this implies a degree of planning inconsistent with his manic temperament." In short, "there seems no reason to keep the body for four or five days." The answer to this last point seems obvious. Pembroke's homicidal attacks occurred when he was drunk, and as Carr points out he then forgot what he had done. If he killed Godfrey, he might then have wandered off or collapsed unconscious and not recalled anything about the murder until he came across the body wherever he had left it. Since we know nothing of Pembroke's domestic arrangements, we cannot say whether the body was kept at his Leicester Fields house or whether his servants would have known of it, but, whatever the case, it seems extremely unlikely that they would have informed on their master.

2) Kenyon also comments that "no contemporary seems to have made the connection which Muddiman makes between him and Godfrey, though some of course may have suspected it." This objection holds water only if Pembroke's motive was political — whether he acted alone or as part of a conspiracy — but if we assume that Pembroke killed Godfrey in a drunken rage and that his memory was at best hazy on the events; and if we further assume that only he was involved with the crime, with possibly the help of a servant or two to hide and dispose of the body, it seems improbable that contemporaries would have known of Pembroke's involvement.

3) K. H. D. Haley remarks that "the trouble about this ingenious theory [of Pembroke's guilt] is that there is no evidence that Pembroke was in London at this time." And here we might again point out that Carr's method of reconstructing events is misleading since it definitely places Pembroke in London. In any case Haley answers his own point in a footnote: "he did not attend the House of Lords until 5 Dec. He was at no time a regular attender, and may or may not have been in London."

4) Carr's solution does not explain all of Godfrey's statements before his death. Why, for example, did he predict that he would become the

first "martyr" to the Popish Plot? There is no indication that his worries were associated with Pembroke, and much to indicate that they were connected with political events. "Have you not heard that I am to be hanged?" he asked.

In *The Killing of Justice Godfrey*, Stephen Knight devised a theory that attempts to explain everything. Whether it explains everything convincingly, we shall now examine. Knight agrees with Carr and Muddiman that Pembroke was the culprit, but he unnecessarily denigrates their contributions. Muddiman's article, he says, "was so slapdash and. . . so full of errors that most of his 'evidence' against the giant [Pembroke] is useless." Although many of his arguments resemble Carr's, Knight doesn't even mention that Carr also named Pembroke, with far more evidence than Muddiman presented. "In his introduction," Knight claims, "Carr said that the book was hardly a serious addition to the history of the case," and as evidence for this extraordinary assertion he cites Carr's statement (p. 15) that "to write good history is the noblest work of man, and cannot be managed here; the intent is only to amuse with a detective story built on facts." Knight seems to have misunderstood what Carr was saying. He was not writing history in the sense of analyzing the age: "we enter not as doctors, but as visitors and even as revellers." What Carr meant is obvious in the sentence immediately preceding the one that Knight quoted: "This record does not presume to be history, except insofar as it tries to be true." Carr presented a solution which, as he said, tries "to meet with the full requirements of the historian."

Before examining the Godfrey case, Knight had investigated the Jack the Ripper killings (*Jack the Ripper, The Final Solution*, 1976) and, instead of attributing the murders to a lone psychopath, he claimed that the murderers were part of an elaborate Masonic conspiracy to protect Victoria's grandson, the Duke of Clarence. Behind the murder of Sir Edmund Godfrey, Knight also found a conspiracy. Knight's most important contribution is his discovery of a paper written by a government informant in 1677 which listed Godfrey as a member of a radical republican movement headed by Sir Robert Peyton, a member of Shaftesbury's Green Ribbon Club. Knight believes that Peyton's "gang," consisted of the "very honorable friends" mentioned in Israel Tonge's diary. Tonge, it will be recalled, is described by Carr as a "buzzy fanatic" (p. 42) who was the first believer in Oates's revelations. According to his diary, Tonge's "very honorable friends" suggested Sir Edmund Godfrey as the magistrate to whom Oates could swear to the truth of his accusations. Godfrey heard Oates's deposition, but he was a friend of Edward Coleman, and, moreover, may have felt it dangerous to support the Green Ribbon Club. He therefore informed Coleman of the charges against him. For the next several weeks, Godfrey worried about the possible results of his action. Would the government arrest him as member of a republican movement? Would his Green Ribbon associates, who were Tonge's "very honorable friends," kill him as a traitor to their cause, someone who knew too much to be left alive? The mysterious letter Godfrey received before his disappearance was, Knight believes, from the Green Ribbon Club, summoning him to an accounting. The Club had already decided to kill him and assigned the deed to Shaftesbury's associate, the Earl of Pembroke. A sword was thrust through Godfrey's body in order to direct attention away from the well-known "Pembroke kick." Godfrey's body was hidden for five days so that rumors could be spread that he had been killed by Papists. Knight adds a considerable amount of detail to this outline, including involvement by others, but his case stands or falls on the above pattern and its major points must be analyzed:

1) *Godfrey's association with Sir Robert Peyton's "gang."* Historians have learned to be suspicious of the claims of informants, who were generally willing to swear to almost anything, and the paper listing Godfrey as an associate of radical republicans is unhelpfully vague. Moreover, if this connection actually existed, it seems likely that a contemporary would have mentioned it in a pamphlet or broadsheet during the Popish Plot. At the least, Roger L'Estrange, the king's journalist, should have known of the connection, and discussed it in his *Brief History of the Times* (1687–1688), the first detailed investigation into the Godfrey case. But except for the paper, written a year before the revelation of the Popish Plot, no one said anything. In short, although it is not impossible that Godfrey had radical connections, the case must be listed as unproven until confirmatory evidence is discovered.

2) *The identification of Tonge's "most honorable friends" with Peyton and the Green Ribbon Club.* A manuscript copy of Israel Tonge's journal is preserved in the Public Record Office in London, but a transcription is printed in a book I edited in 1977, *Diaries of the Popish Plot*. Tonge probably did not write the diary immediately after the events that it describes; it gives every indication of having been written two years later, in 1680. The surviving copy was prepared for publication probably by Tonge's son, Simpson. The manuscript, however, fell into the government's hands before it could be printed. Tonge's purpose in writing the journal was to magnify his own role in the discovery of the plot, and thus he emphasized that he had brought Oates and Godfrey together, and he stressed the word "honorable" to refer to his friends in order to indicate that he had acquaintances in high places. Even if they existed, we have no idea who they were. The journal never names them or indicates their associations with Shaftesbury, Peyton, the Green

Ribbon Club or anyone else besides Tonge.

3) *The Green Ribbon Club's choice of Pembroke as the killer.* It is at this point that Knight's case about a conspiracy collapses. No one in his right mind would have assigned a political killing – and entrusted his own safety – to an unpredictable alcoholic like Pembroke. If Pembroke had said anything in his cups, the entire scheme would have collapsed and the gates of the City of London would have been decorated by the severed heads of the Green Ribbon leaders.

After three hundred years of debate and speculation, can we say that the Godfrey mystery is solved? No, not with absolute certainty; but where the probability lies is obvious: it seems to me clear that Carr (as well as Muddiman and Knight) is correct in naming the Earl of Pembroke as the murderer. His homicidal history makes him a major suspect, and the "Pembroke kick" is a strong indication of his guilt. Carr is also correct that the motive was personal, for if political conspirators had a normal sense of self-preservation they would never have brought anyone as unreliable as Pembroke into their scheme. But what about Godfrey's melancholia and his statements made to various people before he disappeared? These statements were not recorded until after he was killed, and some of the remarks, including his prediction that he would be a "martyr," have such a religious flavor that it seems probable that the witnesses invented them, or at least reworded them, after everyone was certain that the Papists were guilty. Nonetheless, there is no denying that Godfrey felt himself under threat and that his comments indicate that the danger had something to do with politics.

– Douglas G. Greene
Norfolk, Virginia
September, 1988

Perhaps the Godfrey case has remained a mystery all these years because two unrelated series of events came together. Since 1678, investigators have assumed that Godfrey's fears for his life must have been connected with his murder. But were they? We don't need to accept Knight's theory about the "honorable friends" and the Green Ribbon Club to acknowledge that Godfrey had good reason to be worried. He had revealed Oates's accusations to Edward Coleman. Might the government charge him with treason if Coleman were to escape? Was he afraid that Oates or Tonge, whom almost everyone considered unbalanced, would kill him if his connections with Coleman were discovered? We can agree that neither Oates nor Tonge was likely to attack anyone physically, but Godfrey had no way of knowing that. It is unfair in a detective novel to explain things by pure coincidence, but in life coincidences happen all the time, and it seems likely that Pembroke's murder of Godfrey had nothing to do with the magistrate's earlier worries. It is of course possible that once the deed was done, the Green Ribbon Club spread the rumors that Catholics were responsible. Certainly Shaftesbury and his friends took full advantage of the situation.

Douglas G. Greene

BIBLIOGRAPHY AND NOTES

Ailesbury, Thomas Bruce, Earl of: *Memoirs.* (1890)
Airy, Osmund: *Charles II.* (See note B.)
Bedloe, William: *Narrative and Impartial Discovery of the Horrid Popish Plot,* 1679.
Belloc, Hilaire: *James the Second.*
Bellot, Hugh H.L.: *The Temple.*
Besant, Walter: *Westminster.*
Birkenhead, Lord: *Famous Trials.*
                Fourteen English Judges.
Bryant, Arthur: *King Charles II.*
                The Letters, Speeches and Declarations of Charles II.
                The England of Charles II.
                Samuel Pepys: The Man in the Making.
                Samuel Pepys: The Years of Peril.
Burnet, Gilbert: *History of My Own Time.* (6 vols., 1833; vols. 1, 2.)
Calendar of State Papers, Domestic, 1678 (ed. H. Blackburn Daniell).
Care, Henry: *The History of the Damnable Popish Plot, in its various Branches and Progress,* etc. 1680.
Christie, W.D.: *Life of Anthony Ashley Cooper, Earl of Shaftesbury.* (2 vols., 1871.)
Clarendon, Edward Hyde, Earl of: *Life.* (3 vols.)
Clark, G. N.: *The Later Stuarts,* 1660-1714.
Clarke, J.S.: *Life of King James the Second.* (2 vols., 1816.)
Crew, Albert: *The Old Bailey.*
Cunningham, Peter: *The Story of Nell Gwyn and the Sayings of Charles II.* (ed. H. B. Wheatley, 1892.)
Dalrymple, Sir John: *Memoirs of Great Britain and Ireland.* (2 vols., 1771, 1773.)
Danby, Thomas Osborne, Earl of: *Impartial State of the Case of the Earl of Danby,* 1679.
Dictionary of National Biography.
Dryden, John: *Poems.* (ed. W. D. Christie, 1878.)
Echard, Laurence: *History of England.* (1720 ed.)
Evelyn, John: *Diary.* (2 vols., ed. William Bray.)
Foxcroft, Miss H. C.: *Life and Letters of Halifax.*
Gerard, Rev. J.: *The Popish Plot and its Newest Historian.*
Hall, Sir John: *The Murder of Sir Edmund Berry Godfrey* in *Four Famous Mysteries.*
Hamilton, Anthony: *Memoirs of Count Grammont.* (2 vols.)
Holdsworth, W. S.: *History of English Law.* (vol. 9.)

Hooper, W. Eden: *History of Newgate and the Old Bailey.*
Hume, David: *History of England.* (Students' abridgement.)
Irving, H. B.: *Life of Judge Jeffreys.*
Journals of the House of Commons.
Journals of the House of Lords.
Kingsford, Charles Lethbridge: *Early History of Piccadilly, Soho, Leicester Square, and their Neighbourhood.*
Kirkby, Christopher: *A Compleat and True Narrative of the Manner of the Discovery,* etc., 1679.
Lang, Andrew: *The Mystery of Sir Edmund Berry Godfrey in The Valet's Tragedy.*
L'Estrange, Sir Roger: *A Brief History of the Times,* 1687, 1688.
Lingard, John: *History of England.* (13 vols., 1839–vol. 12.)
Lucas, Theophilus: *Lives of the Gamesters,* in *Games and Gamesters of the Restoration,* introduction, Cyril Hughes Hartmann.
Luttrell, Narcissus: *Brief Historical Relation of State Affairs,* (vol. 1.)
Macaulay, Lord: *History of England.* (1849 ed., vol. 1).
    Essays. (1885 ed.) Sir William Temple, Leigh Hunt.
Marks, Alfred: *Who Killed Sir Edmund Berry Godfrey?*
Masefield, John and Constance: *Lyrists of the Restoration, from Sir Edward Sherbourne to William Congreve.*
Molloy, J. Fitzgerald: *Royalty Restored.* (2 vols.)
Muddiman, J. G.: *The King's Journalist.*
    The Mystery of Sir E. B. Godfrey, 'National Review, September,' 1924.
North, Roger: *Examen,* 1740.
    Life of Lord Guilford. (1816 ed.)
Oates, Titus: *True Narrative of the Horrid Plot,* etc., 1679, also reproduced in H.L.J., without extra flourishes.
Ogg, David: *England in the Reign of Charles II.* (2 vols., especially vol. 2.)
Parliamentary History. (ed. Cobbett.)
Parry, Sir Edward: III-VII in *The Bloody Assize.*
Pearce, Robert R.: *A Guide to the Inns of Court and Chancery,* with Notices of their Ancient Discipline, Rules, Orders, and Customs, Readings, Moots, Masques, Revels, and Entertainments, etc. (1855)
Pepys, Samuel: *Diary.* (ed. Lord Braybrooke.)
Phillipps, Samuel March. A study of the *State Trials,* prior to the Revolution of 1688. (1826)
Pinto, V. De Sola: *Sir Charles Sedley.*
Pollock, John: *The Popish Plot.*
Prance, Miles: *True Narrative and Discovery of Several Very Remarkable Passages relating,* etc., 1679.
Ranke, Leopold von. *History of England.* (6 vols., translation, 1875, vols., 3-4.)

BIBLIOGRAPHY AND NOTES

Reresby, Sir John: *Memoirs*. (ed. James J. Cartwright, 1875.)
Seccombe, Thomas: *Titus Oates* in *Twelve Bad Men*.
Shadwell, Thomas: *Plays*. (Mermaid series, ed. George Saints-
bury.)
State Trials. Cobbett, vol. 6-7. Also a little-known folio edition,
A Complete Collection of State Trials and Proceedings
upon Impeachments for High Treason and Other Crimes
and Misdemeanours from the Reign of King Henry the
Fourth to the End of the Reign of Queen Anne; printed
for Timothy Goodwin, John Walthoe, Benj. Tooke, John
Darby, Jacob Tonson, and John Walthoe, jun.–4 vols., 1719.
Stephen, Sir James: *History of Criminal Law*, vol. 1.
Smith, John: *Narrative of the Horrid Popish Plot*.
Strickland, Agnes: *Lives of the Queens of England*, vol. 4.
Sydney, William Connor: *Social Life in England during the XVIIth
Century*.
Teonge, Rev. Henry: *Diary*.
Thompson, C. J. S.: *Poison Romances and Poison Mysteries*.
Timbs, John: *Curiosities of London*.
Traill, H. D.: *Shaftesbury*.
Treby, Sir George: *A Collection of Letters*, which contains some
of Coleman's more explosive letters, 1681.
Ward, Ned. *London Spy*. (Gossip and social pictures of much
later date than the time of this record, but still containing
authentic Carolean 'local colour'.)
Wood, Anthony: *Life and Times*.
Wycherley, William: *Plays*. (Mermaid series, ed. W. C. Ward.)

A.

In a book where so much attention is devoted to details of
place, background, and furniture, I might add that the exterior
and interior details of Whitehall Palace come from a survey
(1930) at the Guildhall Library; from the Fisher and Unwin
plan; from a model of old Whitehall at the Royal United Service Museum; from contemporary prints; from the diaries of
Pepys and Evelyn, and the memoirs of Ailesbury; from Timbs
and Besant. Timbs describes the old Houses of Parliament.
The descriptions of Newgate are from Hooper and Crew; legal
details, institutions, customs, etc., come from North, Pearce and
Bellot. There is a description of Primrose Hill in the trial of
Thompson, Pain and Farwell in 1682, and also in Timbs.

B.

Aside from the full descriptions of them in contemporary
accounts, the appearances of the various characters are taken
wherever possible from portraits or prints. Those in the National

Portrait Gallery and at Hampton Court are well known; there is a good picture of James in his younger days at the Nottingham Museum, though I don't care particularly for that of Charles in the same gallery. Some fine examples of portraits and furniture are to be seen at Kenilworth Castle. Airy's *Charles II* contains some good reproductions; and there is a highly sinister-looking print of Shaftesbury in the first volume of Christie's *Life*. With minor characters of the book there has been more difficulty, though Oates's appearance, of course, is famous. Kirkby is described as looking and dressing like Oates because he was once mistaken for Titus. The description of Tonge comes from Wood and Burnet; Bedloe from a contemporary print. Captain Charles Atkins is merely given the costume of a seafaring man; little details like the handling of the pipe are in Samuel Atkins's account. For Prance there is almost no evidence except for the fact that, since he had a fair periwig made for himself, his own hair must have been fair. There are hints as to the descriptions of Green, Berry and Hill in L'Estrange. We have Green's small stature, reddish periwig, and crucifix; Hill's presumable height and beard from the way they speak of him; but Berry (I acknowledge) is made stout for no other reason than that he kept an alehouse. The appearance of witnesses at the trial has been deduced from their speech – not much to go on, but a hint – and from the way the judges treated them. As for the legal gentlemen, their portraits are to be found at Guildhall.